IGNITING
THE BALANCE BRINGER

THE BALANCE BRINGER CHRONICLES
BOOK FOUR

USA TODAY BESTSELLING AUTHOR
DEBRA KRISTI

Ghost Girl
publishing

❀ Created with Vellum

Also By Debra Kristi:

IGNITING
THE BALANCE BRINGER

THE BALANCE BRINGER CHRONICLES
BOOK FOUR

USA TODAY BESTSELLING AUTHOR
DEBRA KRISTI

For Christy
And every reader who loves a great fantasy escape.

"The mind is not a vessel to be filled but a fire to be kindled."

Plutarch

Loreitta Village

Painted Stones

Gaea's
TEMPLE RUINS

◇ Ivey City

HUSHMAN'S MEADOW

LISTLESS R

Norde Sorlonte
Homestead ▪

Old Cottage ▪

Ancient T
RUINS

GRA
GO

N

NARFOLK
BAY

HIDDENKEL

ANCIENT ELVEN QUEEN'S DOMINION

FORREST OF the WHISPERING LEAVES

AMP OF TING LIGHTS

PALINOT WOODLANDS

AUGUR CLIFFSIDE DOMICILE

ae King's tral Castle

linot ◇

• Guardoone Point

• Maitias Garrison

• Royal Fae Castle Estate

Queen's Crossing

Marsoun Mansion

FIRES OF GUARDOONE

• Tower South

• Time Keep at Season's Cape

ONE

Lying in an unreachable sleep realm, Jaden has become the beloved, snatched away by a beguiling devil. And I, like the Maiden Moon, will never stop searching for him.

Only, my search won't be limited to once a season, as in the story Jaden shared with me about the Maiden Moon, the Ondine, and the man trapped in a fate between them. No, I will search every day until I successfully pull him back to me.

The jealous Ondine stole the man away and dragged him to the ocean floor, and since the Maiden Moon continues to search for him, he has likely never been found, or released by the sea.

That. Will not. Be our story.

Although Jaden does not stir, nor send me thoughts through our connection, his emotions continue to tingle along my receptors. Occasionally, I get an image. Like a screenshot taken from one of his dreams.

If he is dreaming and his feelings are detectible, then every chance exists that his restoration and return is merely a matter of time. The question is, how much time?

Black gunk seeps from his many orifices—eyes, ears, nose, mouth, around the edges of his fingernails. Every bit of the muck—remnants of the darkness he syphoned from me. For me.

Before I relieved Zarah of the job, she had been diligent about cleaning away the infection with a soft rag and warm water. His hands now hang over the edge of the bed, buckets positioned on the floor directly below. Stuff oozes from under his fingernails, dropping the distance, not to a splash but to a small plop onto the ground.

The amount of seepage has mildly decreased since yesterday, giving me an ounce of hope... even as his lack of color, his edge-of-death appearance, clenches at my heart.

The drainage is a good thing. If he were clean and pretty, we'd have no need for concern. Concern that the darkness was staying with him. But it appears to all be coming right back out, just as Madame Marrouske had suggested it would.

Thank Gaea and the Maiden Moon.

I share the space on his bed, curving my body against his, and rest my arm gently across his chest, careful not to disrupt the infection drip, or disturb the multitude of stones positioned across his chest and abdomen. Both drip and stones, no doubt, integral elements to his healing.

Zarah's parting instructions to me; we're to wear gloves, clear any leaking residue, and talk to him.

Using a cloth, I dab at the dark sludge oozing from the edge of his eye, his ear.

"I need you to come back to me," I whisper and trace a gloved finger across his forehead in a gentle arc. I would prefer to ditch the glove, but as long as any hint of the infection remains, I can't chance skin-to-skin contact.

If he is the deep slumber, then I hope to be the caffeine that stirs him into consciousness.

Jaden has been in a comatose state since my balance binding. Since he took the darkness unto himself, freeing me from the affliction. I slept for over a day afterwards. The binding returned to me my sisters, my many Balance Bringer incarnations, but lost me my Tracer. I pray that loss is only temporary. An extremely short stint.

My gloved finger gently drags along the side of his face, over his shoulder, and down the length of his ribs, where I press my palm flat against his bare skin. This was not the way I envisioned time alone together, soaking in the shirtless form of him. His beautifully chiseled muscles now gleaming with a thin layer of sweat brought on by bodily distress.

Circumstances can be so cruel.

I breathe in the scent of him, only his usual aroma of cedar is tainted with something vile, something rotten. The infectious darkness. Not a memory of him I want to carry forward. My stomach twists into a knot, and my hand curls into a fist.

"You fight, Jaden! You hear me? Fight and come back to me." I shove lightly into his side. "We need you. *I* need you." He shows no sign of having heard me. No flinch, nothing.

But an image flares bright in my mind. A moving memory of us at a young age, playing a game scratched into a patch of dirt beneath the shade of a tree. I'm laughing…and winning. And then I'm Deona and he's Jove. We're at the watering hole near the family homestead, splashing up a good time with my sisters and Sol.

The door creaks open, and the healer Airmed enters the room. "I am ready to attend to him if you are amiable."

The peek into Jaden's dreams vanishes.

"Of course." I slip off the bed and step aside, granting her easy access to Jaden. "How is Clef?" Jaden's clan mate had been unconscious when he was carried into Madame Marrouske's sanctuary. He was sleeping when I checked in on him yesterday, and I haven't yet had the opportunity to visit him today. He'd been significantly injured in a fight with the enemy—Dreya's forces.

"He is coming along nicely." Airmed dunks a cloth in a pail of clean water, rings out the excess, and dabs at Jaden's lips.

I raise my chin, indicating Jaden. "Any prognosis on his condition? How long do you think he may remain this way?" I bite my lip, preventing further comments or questions from spilling forth. I'd prefer to keep my insecurities tucked safely away.

I may remember most, if not all, of what I am, but no Balance Bringer incarnation prior to this…to me…has dealt with an infected soul in this manner.

Except maybe Deona, with Jove's friend Sol, and that didn't end in a way I'd like to see play out with Jaden.

Airmed's lips pull into a tight line, and she runs a scrutinizing gaze over Jaden. Over the residue seeping from his fingernails. "There is not much I can tell you. This is new territory for me."

I nod and swallow hard.

Understandable. But he will *be all right,* I remind myself. He is my tracer, and no other outcome is acceptable.

We are bound forever through time. I chose him. *Me.* Not the fates or destiny.

Deona made the choice when she healed Jove using the magic-infused hairs gifted to her from the unicorns. She made the choice before Meira, Aunt Meira, or Madame Marrouske as she is now known, decided to magically bind Deona and Jove ceremonially with the dagger.

I rest my hand over his sheet-covered leg, to the spot I recall Jove being injured those many lifetimes ago. The same place Jaden was injured by Dohlan with the dagger.

An unlikely coincidence. Closing my eyes, I try to reach Jaden's consciousness through the connection. Probe for a reason Dohlan would cut him in the same place.

The unicorn magic has to be the reason.

But how would Dohlan know, not only about the magic used but, *where* it was used.

And why attack Jaden in that same spot? The magic was used on Jove, not Jaden.

Had Jove's magically cured injury somehow translated through the various incarnations to Jaden's body, here and now?

I probe deeper, trying to find anything beyond the current static hum Jaden has become. The connection to his dream is gone. I get nothing...until. Garr. Garrthmal. With his hooves and horns.

I yank my hand away and ogle Jaden.

Why would I get hints of Garr when touching Jaden? Garr had put a serious whammy on Jaden when we stayed at the village set high in the trees. Did something linger?

The door pops open once more. This time, Jaden's brother, Azure, peeks his head in.

If it weren't for Azure's brilliant blue eyes, he'd be the spitting image of Jaden. Twins with different colored eyes. Jaden with his green and Azure with blue. The two colors dominate in Jove's eyes—normally green, but blue when in transition from glimpsing forward.

The sight of Azure thrusts my head and heart into a tangle of emotions. I could be staring at Jaden. Only, he's not Jaden. He lacks Jaden's tender, insightful soul. *And* he practically tried to kill me, with his attempt to extract the infectious darkness from me at the most inconvenient time *ever*...while running from Dreya's goon squad.

"Sorry to interrupt," he says. "The matron requests our presence." His gaze sweeps from me to the healer, then drops and lingers on his brother.

The matron, meaning Madame Marrouske. "Our?" I ask. "As in everyone?" Although, not actively avoiding Azure and Ruby, I haven't made an attempt to seek them out. Not since my Balance Bringer binding. I'm not exactly Ruby's favorite person. Nor she mine. And Azure...with what happened between us and all that has befallen Jaden, I haven't been able to bring myself to face him.

Of Jaden's fellow clan members, Jaden and Clef are injured, Al and the clan mother are missing, and Shadow is spending time at the far end of the compound with some of his kind. Azure doesn't have to say the words. I see the truth in his eyes. He...and likely Ruby...fault me for the current status of their clan. Broken and scattered.

Azure's face tightens. "Just you and me."

So, this has to do with Jaden then. The summoning of the two individuals closest to him. "Go ahead," I say with a slight nod. "I'll be along shortly."

He disappears, pulling the door to an almost close, leaving the slightest sliver of space.

With a sigh rising and falling in my chest, I turn back to Jaden and rest my hands upon his ankles, hidden beneath the thin sheet covering his lower body.

"I have to go," I say to him. "But this in no way gives you permission to slack off in the healing department. You hear me?"

I pause as if giving him the opportunity to respond, even though I don't believe he will.

"I expect you to look ten to a thousand times better when I return." And when you're awake, we can work together to figure out why I perceive hints of Garr along the location of the cut on your leg. Hopefully, identify the connection.

"I do not think—"

I cut Airmed's words off mid-sentence with a sharp, flat palm to the air. Some of the Fae are far too serious in their interpretation of the things I say, and I don't want to hear my request is an impossibility.

I wish to place a soft kiss on his temple, but I can't, so I opt for a mild smile. I then remove my gloves, set them aside, and leave the room. Head for Madame Marrouske's chamber.

I am barely a foot into the hallway when a tight grip clasps around my wrist, yanking my attention to the dark-haired, angry-eyed vixen standing beside me. Ruby.

"I would avoid her for a while if I were you," Zarah had warned.

Too late now.

Ruby's gaze narrows. "I was wondering when I would see you around here. You've been rather scarce lately." There's a growl in her voice and a razor-sharp leer at her mouth. I attempt to extract my arm from her hold, but her grip intensifies. "Feeling guilty?" she asks. "You should, you know. You did that." She tilts her head toward Jaden in the room beyond.

She's not wrong. If it weren't for me, he wouldn't be in his current state. But I can't change what has already been done. He made the call when I was too weak or too enabled to stop him. What has happened to him is the result of his choices, not mine.

My back straightens and I stand a tad taller, embrace a gallon or more of confidence. "Blame me if you want. But Jaden is a big boy and makes his own decisions. That right there…" I stretch a straight-arm point to Jaden. "Is the result of his decisions. No one else's but his."

With a hiss, she lurches forward, within a breath of my cheek. "You shall never again find comfort in his embrace." Her words are a shiver across my soul. "And if he doesn't recover, you'll wish you died in that damned beast-infested forest." She shoves me back and walks away.

"By the way, you look uglier than usual," she calls over her shoulder. "Must be those donkey ears."

My skin is a landscape of goosebumps and I stare after her, until she turns the corner and disappears from view. Only once she is gone do I check my ears. They seem normal enough, so I shift my attention to my arm, and rub the skin at my wrist.

The place where she held me is red, slightly warm, and tender. The slight remnants of her crimson tattoos linger on my skin, slowly fading as if sinking into the depths of my blood beneath.

TWO

I f Jaden doesn't recover, I'm fairly certain any emotional abuse I inflict upon myself will be far worse than whatever Ruby can come up with.

"*But it was his choice,*" Crystia's words whisper at my ear.

She no longer lingers around me but now holds a place inside of me...with many other versions of her, and of me, and of Kaia...since the binding. Although, Kaia's been ultra quiet, Crystia's thoughts and words warm me, if only a smidgeon.

I slip a piece of worn paper from my pocket. The letter Jaden left for me right before the binding. I've read it a thousand times. Now, I shall read it once more, a thousand and one.

The wax seal is not only broken, but gone, and the paper wrinkled with endless folding and unfolding. As I do so now, setting my gaze upon his eloquent writing. Beautiful, elongated curves and arcs. An art form long since forgotten by the education system of my upbringing.

My handwriting looks like dung next to his. The readability of my fast and furious scribble is a miracle.

I devour his words once more, needing the solid reminder that he knew what would come of his choice and he decided to follow through regardless.

Dearest Ana,

If you are reading this, then I have been successful in my task, and you are cleansed—healed as promised. Worry not for me as you are, and always have been, the key.

My system is strong, and I have taken every precaution in preparing for this moment. But my purge may take time, and you must not allow me to slow you down. You must continue on your path. Promise me that.

Many are depending on you, and I know the burden that thrusts upon you, but try not to let that dim your spirit. Think about Crystia, the sister who grew up at your side, and how she would feel for the people of this land and their plight. She had a natural connection with those around her, which means, somewhere in that guarded heart of yours, you do as well.

Maybe it is time you get out there and get to know some of those people. Get a feel for them, so that you can develop a better understanding for what it is you are supposed to be fighting for. Then and only then, will your heart be truly vested in the fight. A necessity for what you must accomplish.

I believe that is all you really need. Everything else is already inside of you. You must merely acknowledge who you are, what you feel, and what you can do.

I have watched you grow from a wee thing into the amazing woman you are today. I know you, and know you have the strength of mind and body to accomplish anything you set your focus upon.

Tap into that core source, use it, and above all, believe in yourself.

Forever yours,

Jaden

The truth is right before me, in his own handwriting. He knew. Knew what he was doing. Knew what results to expect. Knew and did it anyway.

My breath rises strong in my chest, and my shoulders square. Jaden made a difficult choice out of strength, so that I could follow through with my own fortitude. I won't let him down.

Refolding the note and slipping it back into my pocket, I make my way along a window-spotted, curved hallway, to Madame Marrouske's chamber.

The house is really a tree house…since Madame Marrouske's sanctuary is built into the base of the largest tree I've ever laid eyes upon. She called it the tree of life. According to her, no one carved out or built into the tree, but rather, the tree morphed and created the various spaces to accommodate her and the others.

Raundel, the statuesque white stag elf, stands beside the closed door to Marrouske's chamber. I've had little interaction with him since the predawn of my arrival when he led us into the sanctuary, then helped me in the Lagoon of Lucidity. My first impression of him had been tainted with my own exhaustion and infection.

As he stands now, he looks like a Michael Angelo sculpture with his perfect form, white hair and skin. He steps in front of the door and crosses his arms, his smooth lips held in a firm unyielding expression and his eyes filled with wisdom of countless millenniums.

"You are to wait here." He holds his chin high.

A crooked frown pulls to my lips, and I fold my fists into the hollows of my armpits. Hold my foot still against the desire to tap, tap, tap. "But I was told to come *now*."

"So you were." His gaze lowers to meet mine. "She requested a few minutes alone with the blue-eyed one. She will be with you momentarily."

The clench of my teeth tightens. What could she possibly want to talk to Azure about…alone?

Standing in Raundel's silent presence causes the skin at the back of my neck to itch. Yet, I don't scratch, not wanting to appear anxious or uncomfortable. Instead, my attention darts from the floor to the door, the curved walls, and settles upon the old stone tablet hanging above the entrance to Madame Marrouske's chamber.

Carved into the tablet is a simplistic drawing of an eye. Within the center of the eye, a triangle...or possibly a pyramid...each tip melding with the outer ring of the represented pupil. Various incarnations of myself hold memories of Madame Marrouske explaining the design.

"The eye represents the inner eye. In this case, your tracer." Jaden. *"Having the ability to see future events, as they will take place. I,"* Madame Marrouske. *"Work on a higher consciousness with my own inner eye, granting me a knowing or feeling pertaining to various people, places, or events.*

"I sometimes catch a glimmer of a thing here or there, and I'll know how those, too, will play out. And the triangle within the eye represents the line of the Balance Bringer. You and your sisters, one soul divided by three. A point for each sister, a continuous, unbroken thread, coming together to work as one."

The carving symbolizes all of us, Mystic, Balance Bringer, and Tracer, united as essential parts of the working solution.

Three petite elves enter from a side corridor, each carrying a small bowl. Their arrival pulls my attention away from the ancient art. I recognize the lead elf as the one who helped me get through the gate to the Palinot Woodlands.

We have yet to be formally introduced, but she looks like she could be distant kin to Raundel. Or even Jaden's fellow clan member Al, for that matter.

The oversized, dry and cracked double doors to Madame Marrouske's chamber swing open, and Lobrka steps into the outer foyer.

"Deona," he says with a wicked grin and a quirk of one eyebrow.

He moves aside and motions for me to enter, tipping his long, pointy ears like spears in my direction. They appear especially dangerous today. More so than Raundel's tall elven tips. Lobrka is the fall of night to Raundel's dawn of a new day. One elf of the light and one of the dark.

"Just call me Ana," I say, swaggering past him into the chamber beyond. "Deona is taking a backseat this time around."

He chuckles. From the sound at my back, I suspect Raundel joins him in the small delight. They can laugh all they want, and Deona can make suggestions and advise at the back of my brain until she's blue in the face, but I am not handing over control of my life because some ancient elves did a spell that resulted in me. The many versions of me.

Madame Marrouske's chamber is cluttered with stacks of books and papers, bowls and jars of who-knows-what, crystals, large and small, and a plethora of scrying, ritual, and offering bowls made of stone and shell and metal.

Tall, ornate shelves crammed full of interesting goodies line the farthest spaces. The walls and floor are a glossy petri-fied wood. And plenty of light brightens the space, despite the room being windowless. Pure white light emanates through cracks running high in the outer walls.

The three petite elves sweep into the room and set their delivery on a half-round table pressed to the side. A large, flat oval stone sits atop the table like a mirror, except it shows no reflection. Only hints of shapes. Without a word, the elves turn and leave. Behind me, the double doors thud closed.

My gaze sweeps over every visible space, absorbing every hint of Madame Marrouske's past and the person she now is. I may have known her lifetime after lifetime, but that still leaves a ton of time unaccounted for. The Deona in me wants to trust her explicitly. But me, Ana me, is playing things safe, the way Ry taught me.

"I haven't seen you since the whole Balance Bringer memory download," I say, continuing to scrutinize the items packing her space. "I've been up and moving among the land of the living for close to two days now. I would have thought you would have wanted to catch up. You know…" I swing my gaze to her. "On goals, missions, old memories."

I make no attempt to hide the sarcasm in my voice…after all, I just crossed worlds to meet this woman and she left me waiting. But then, I also used my downtime, my recovery time, endowed with my increased knowledge from my other incarnations, to work with my brother, Ry, planning our return to the city—to help the people and find our mom.

Madame Marrouske and Azure are on either side of a larger table occupying the center space of the room. She smirks at me and stands, her grey hair falling down her back in large, loose ringlets, crocheted with fine streaks of white.

"Come." She circles the table and beckons me to the three bowls deposited by the elves.

My gaze shifts to Azure. He's shown no response to my entrance, and sits with his back to me, his gaze lowered to the floor and his hands clenching and unclenching in his lap. His demeanor is not that of a man having received any news of the positive.

My chest squeezes. Did she tell him something unpleasant about Jaden? I need to know. "What's with him?" I ask nonchalantly.

She tosses him a dismissive wave. "Nothing some reflection and a little time together won't sort out."

"A little *what?*" I jerk. Time with whom? I'm the only other one in the room, but surely she doesn't mean me…given our relation, our history.

She doesn't verbally respond, but instead, meets me in front of the table holding the glossy black stone and three bowls. She folds my hands between her own and peers into my eyes as if searching for an answer to a question not yet asked.

"I've been hearing whispers," she says, her gaze shifting to the table and then back to me.

"What kind of whispers?" My brow and shoulders tense.

She shakes my hands in hers ever slightly. "Are you aware

that your elemental ability is less of a mastery, and more of a partnership?"

I hadn't given the relationship much thought. I'm guessing now, maybe I should have. My lips press together, my lower lip puckering.

"You're saying that I don't outright control them, but that they choose to work with me, hearing my requests and granting them?"

A mild smile graces her lips, and she motions to the three bowls sitting on the table. One filled with water, one with dirt and leaves, and the other with small chips of wood. Three elements because air is all around us and cannot be delivered on a platter...or bowl.

"Water, earth, and..." I stare at the third bowl. "I take it the wood chips are meant to represent fire."

Across the room, Azure rises to his feet and turns to face us. "Jaden said you had only displayed talent for the three; water, earth, and air." There's an air of incredulity in his delivery. Possibly surprise at my mention of an element for which I've shown no talent.

"Maybe so," I retort, heat rising up my neck and across my cheeks. "But I'm not an idiot. I know what the fourth element is."

"Show me," Madame Marrouske says, ignoring the exchange between me and Azure. I flinch, my nose wrinkling. "Show me that you can still command the elements," she says. "Stir the water, earth, and air. Kindle the fire."

"But I've never done anything with fire." Few of the Balance Bringer incarnations have. Deona did once or twice. Another scorched the land so that it could bloom anew. Another yet resulted in a horrid inferno. Fire is a beast not willingly controlled.

She tilts her head toward the bowls. "Give it a try anyway."

With a hard swallow in my throat and a frown on my lips,

I turn my attention to the gathered elements on the table. My brow pinches with the intense focus. I ask, then plead and beg, the water to swirl, the air to whip, the earth to move. I stare at the bowls for what could be an eternity…or merely minutes.

The water remains flat as glass. No smoke, much less fire, ignites from the wood chips. And the earth, only a tiny puff of a dust cloud rises.

An SUV-sized boulder drops into my gut. "What does this mean?"

"Fear not, my child." Madame Marrouske places a consoling hand upon my shoulder. "The elements have not abandoned you. There is merely some mending and atoning to be done." She turns her gaze to Azure. "In many areas."

Emotion ripples over Azure's features. Irritation. Resignation. The site of him shoves confusion upon me.

Madame Marrouske steps away from me and returns to her position on the far side of the center table. "For the time being, Azure will take Jaden's place and work with you on mending your elemental connection."

I gasp, my mouth popping wide. "I can't. I can't work with him." I fling a distasteful jab toward Azure. He's not Jaden. "He's not my Tracer."

Azure merely closes his eyes, giving no support to my argument.

"You are wrong on that account," Madame Marrouske counters. "Jaden and Azure are of the same soul. But you already knew that, didn't you?" Her eyes spark with the clear depth of her knowledge.

With a sigh, I bow my head. *I did know.* An incantation learned from Edna, Meira or Madame Marrouske's counterpart. A stick and a magical split. A mistake made a lifetime ago. A mistake we are all now paying for.

"You will begin tomorrow."

Azure's gaze meets mine, his eyes filled with a matching dose of frustration.

THREE

I didn't travel all this way to return to basic training. And if I require training, then I prefer to work with Jaden. If not Jaden, then my brother, Ry. I do not want to spend any more time than necessary with Azure.

My insides are fuming, incinerating my words, and turning my thoughts to vapor. I spin on the balls of my feet and march from the room, thrusting the double doors open with more force than required. Madame Marrouske makes no effort to stop or follow me.

"Where's my brother?" I say to no one in particular as I storm through the outer hall. "I need to talk to him *now*."

"Sir Ryland and his mate left several minutes ago."

I jerk to a stop and swirl on Raundel. He is the only one standing outside of Madame Marrouske's chamber. "He what? Where did they go?" My words stammer, riddled with disbelief.

The tightness of his face softens, as if attempting to lighten the blow of the coming information.

"Ana" Azure approaches, and without sparing him a

glance, I wave him into silence. Motion for him to go away. He halts but doesn't leave.

Raundel's chest rises, and with the intake of breath, his entire body becomes an even more immovable mass than previous impressions would imply. "Your brother met with our lady this morning. It was decided that he would make a visit to the city of Palinot."

"Without me?" My voice spikes.

"You have things to do that require your presence here, and I do not expect his lordship to be away for long."

His lordship. I shake my head. "But he's my brother, and last we knew, the city was dangerous, under attack. I need to be with him, to protect him." My insides are churning, my muscles twitching.

Raundel's eyebrows arch. "And how would you protect him?" His gaze shifts to Azure who stands to the side, listening and waiting. Clearly, Raundel is aware of the arrangement Madame Marrouske made. He knows my elemental control is currently lacking and in need of work.

My hands fist and jaw clenches. "When did they leave?" *Why? Why would he take Zarah into a potentially dangerous situation?*

"Ten. Twenty minutes ago."

I pivot and run. Run the curve of the hall, to the grand foyer, and out the main entrance.

I don't care that I left Azure without addressing whatever thought or question he had. I don't care if I am going against Madame Marrouske's wishes, or that I may appear childish to Raundel. I need to be with Ry when he finds our mom.

I run through the landscape with reckless abandonment, bolting through gate after gate, heading toward the path of intertwined banyan tree roots.

The energy around me changes with every step closer to the edge of the fortified sanctuary. The atmosphere shifts from the soft flow of air, to the resistance of water, and finally to the thickness of jelly. And yet, I press forward, the route ahead blurring.

I think I see them—Ry and Zarah—making their way through the tunnel of trees, but they're so far away, they're nothing more than tiny figures moving amongst the bark.

The world around me thickens to packed mud, and the earth drops into silence, but with a push and a drag, I force my leg, my body forward, past the last surrounding wall and gate. Sound and mobility explode around me. I am free of the barrier.

Tiny bell chimes sing in the air above as if in celebration of my arrival...or notifying others of my departure. Then, exotic, intoxicating, spices waft heavily at my nose.

Odd, for the woodlands. Probably something I should investigate, but I have more pressing matters on my agenda.

I stare after Ry and Zarah, only I discern no hint of them anywhere in the terrain ahead.

I bite the edge of my lower lip and allow the emptiness to fill my chest. Sense the heavily spiced aroma growing closer, stronger.

Moving as if on autopilot, I turn in the direction of the scent. I already know what I'll find. I feel it internally, or more appropriately, feel him. His closeness.

Dohlan.

Is he just lurking outside the sanctuary perimeter like a creepy stalker? That's not unsettling.

My gaze flickers from tree to tree, searching for him. I may currently be at odds with my elemental gifts, but immortal warrior blood still courses through my veins. I concentrate on expanding my hearing and listen for any sound I can attribute to him.

The sweet chiming bells burst into high-pitched rings; the sound emanating from the other side of the wall, from somewhere within the sanctuary—the tearman—clarifying my earlier wonder.

Definitely a warning system.

The sound rattles my bones, my senses. I shut it out, hibernating my higher sense and returning my hearing to that of a normal person.

Dohlan steps into view. "I suspected you would come sooner or later, and I had to know."

"That I survived?" Dreya's attack, the exit from the city, the Balance Bringer binding. I blink wide, and a rush of warmth fills my chest. Never have I felt the pull to him more strongly. It's practically magnetic.

"*You know why*," Crystia whispers in my ear.

I swallow hard. *I believe I do.* This is my first time being physically near Dohlan since the binding. Since merging with Kaia…in some shape or form. Her feelings are no doubt affecting me even more so than before…in spite of my lifetimes connection with Jaden, going all the way back to Jove.

"She loved you," I whisper. "Deeper than any root system and with more intensity than the surface of the sun."

Pain flickers across his eyes, and his response is evident even without words. He loved her just as fiercely. Equally, if not more.

He closes his eyes and smells the air between us, as if he can smell Kaia somewhere within me.

"Hey!" A voice calls from the woodlands at our side, pulling my attention. White mist weaves through the trees, materializes into bodily form several feet away. Al, the white ghost, Augur clan member.

I survey the tree line at her back. Nothing but vegetation. Still, if she has returned, then maybe…

I turn back to Dohlan, but he is gone, taking with him his intoxicating spicy scent.

"Who was that?" Al asks, clearing the trees and walking straight up to me. All her weapons are sheathed, and she carries a limp bag on her shoulder. I wave Dohlan's disappearance away as if it's nothing.

"I'm so happy to see you." I throw my arms around her and hug her to me. She stiffens but does not pull away. Neither does she hug me back, so I step away allowing her space. "Is Mo with you?" Mo and Jaden's clan mother, Opal, went missing at the same time.

She shakes her head. "They are together and safe. Are your people with you?"

I hadn't allowed myself to think about it before now, not with Jaden in a healing sleep and Mo missing, but… "No." Not with Ry and Zarah on route for Palinot City. "Yours are, though."

Her eyebrow arches. "Well. That is good news."

"Deona. Step away." I recognize Raundel's firm tone without sparing him a glance.

He moves through the gateway, weapon at the ready. Lobrka and Klarda at his back.

Al sweeps an appraising gaze over the approaching group and takes several steps back, raising her hands in a show of armistice. "Two elves and a hobgoblin. That's an unexpected surprise."

"Surprises are generally unexpected," Raundel quips, leading the group of three into a protective line between me and Al.

"True." She nods, and reaches for her shoulder bag, shifting the flap to reach inside.

Raundel, Lobrka, and Klarda all stiffen and extend their weapons an inch forward. Al slows her movements and extracts a wax sealed letter.

"I am here to deliver a message. I was told to deliver it directly." She holds the letter up in front of her, giving each of them a clear view that the seal has not been tampered with. "Do you have a Meira Morxisys here?"

Raundel's gaze tightens. Intensifies. "No one has used that name in a great many years. Likely, longer than your existence." He scrutinizes Al.

"I only know what I was told," she replies. "No more, no less."

He grunts. Shifts a leery gaze to Lobrka. "See that Deona is taken safely inside. Kladra and I shall deal with the newcomer."

"It's Ana, not Deona," I remind. "And please don't hurt her. She's an important member of Jaden's clan."

"She travels with your Tracer?" Raundel tilts into the question, his curiosity clearly peaked.

"Used to," Al corrects. "He's been away from the fold for a while now, running around with this one." She lifts her chin toward me.

Her tone pinches a nerve, and I don't know if I should be irritated or not. Regardless, I choose to ignore what feels like a slap to my relationship with Jaden. Instead, I allow Lobrka to lead me away, back to the sanctuary of the tree. Raundel, Klarda, and Al follow several feet behind in grumpy silence.

A moment or two into our return walk, a soft voice flutters in my ear. "Thank you." It's all she says, barely audible to my internal system, but I know the voice is that of Kaia.

Regardless of her reservations involving the binding…the fear of losing herself…she is thankful enough for my words to Dohlan to finally speak to me after days of silence. My heart warms with gratitude for having been able to give her that tiny bit of solace.

"You're welcome," I whisper back.

Lobrka glances sideways at me. Down at me, actually, because of his inhuman height. "You are different this time around. I haven't decided if I prefer you better this way or not."

Um… "Thanks?" My lifetime memories involving Lobrka don't go back nearly as far as those with Raundel. If those memories are correct, he has always had a wicked side.

He barks, then drops into a low growl. "It was foolish of

you to run all the way out here like you did. I don't think any of the other versions of you would have done that."

I keep my eyes forward on the uneven terrain. "Did any of the others have a brother?" I should actually know the answer to that question. I search within myself…my many selves.

"None that brought one along," he replies.

"Well, there you go." I grant him a delicious smirk. "People do crazy things for family."

"Neither has one had a mother who tried to shield them from their truth, their destiny," he adds.

The smirk slips from my lips, and I fold my arms across my chest. "That's the thing about family. It's a chaotic package of good, bad, delightful, and ugly. We don't get to chose one or some of those aspects. It's an all or nothing kind of deal."

Lobrka falls silent leaving no indication on whether he agrees or disagrees with my statement. I possess no memories in my multi-self of him sharing any information about his family. The return walk is long without the company of small talk…or the chatter of the surrounding nature. I didn't realize how much I appreciated that facet of my gifts.

Between the last surrounding wall and the massive tree sanctuary, Jaden's clan member, Shadow, is tending to Belmiso, the black unicorn disguised as a horse that helped us along our journey. Shadow rubs down the horse's sides and gives him special nibbles.

I haven't had a ton of interaction with Shadow, but this kinder, gentler version is refreshing. I've only seen him in the face of adversity. Attempting to keep me safe during the attack on Palinot or racing through the woodlands to reach this place.

Belmiso turns and bobs his head in my direction. *I see you*, he seems to say. *See what you are and what you are made of.*

Shadow raises his gaze and startles, then breaks into a run our direction. "Al! You're all right. Thank the god and goddess."

Lobrka grabs the front of Shadows shirt, yanking him to a stop before he can get any closer to Al, or the point of Raundel's weapon. "She will see our lady first. You may not talk to her before then."

"Why?" He balks. "She's not a threat." His beseeching gaze shifts to me as if searching for support. I simply shake my head, signaling him to drop it.

"It's all right," Al calls from behind me. "I am okay, and mother is fine. I merely must attend to a small matter first."

Shadow backs away from Lobrka, his mouth open and head shaking. He doesn't tear his gaze from Al. "I shall get Azure. He will get this settled." With a single glance my direction, he turns and races up the grass-and root-riddled slope to the front entrance. Disappears inside.

We make the rest of the trek in complete silence. Al is ushered into Madame Marrouske's chamber, and I wait in the outer hallway. Raundel, Lobrka, and Klarda stand like pillars against the door, preventing anyone from coming or going.

As if I would try to get past them.

A week ago, I may have tried, but today...today I'm feeling a little less inclined.

I wait and wait. Lean against the wall, slide my butt to the ground, and wait some more.

Shadow appears with Azure and Ruby in tow, and avoiding Ruby's gaze, I talk to them only long enough to confirm Al is inside and I don't know anything more. They chatter softly among themselves after that, leaving me to stew in my own thoughts. Thoughts that are making me all kinds of itchy.

Why did Al come here alone? What is in the letter? Where is Mo? Is Mo all right? Al *said* Mo was all right, but I don't know Al well enough to know if she would lie to me or not. So, in this situation, seeing is believing.

Klarda is summoned into the room, dropping the Augur clan chatter into utter nothing. Their fidgety behavior signals their agitation. A couple minutes later, Klarda escorts Al from the chamber, and the Augur clan immediately clusters around her.

"Back off," Klarda snaps, thrusting her arm out, commanding space. "You can meet with her in the gathering hall in ten minutes. Now go."

She flicks her arm, motioning their departure. The clan members back off but do not leave. Klarda directs Al down the hall, pausing momentarily at my side.

"One minute," she says, not as a request but as a command.

Al nods at Klarda and turns to me, stepping close, and dropping her voice. "Jaden?"

I swallow hard, and suck back my lips, shake my head. Al's eyes tighten. "They tell me he is going to be fine," I say, needing to hear the words, not only for her but for myself. "He just needs time."

"Okay." She starts to step back, but I grab her hands and pull her close. This time closer.

"What was in the message?" It may be none of my business, but I tend to think otherwise. Plus, I want to know.

Al's shoulders lift in a slight shrug. "All I know is that Mother requested a meeting elsewhere. It is set for tomorrow, when the moon is at its highest."

"Why not just come here? Is she unable to travel? Did something happen to her the other day when we were traveling through the woods?" Al shrugs again, then follows up with a shake of her head. "Where is the meeting to take place? Where is Mo?"

"Where is Jaden?" she counters, her shoulders tightening.

I huff and reign back the desire to rattle the answers off her lips. "Down the hall. I'm sure Klarda will show you." I glance past Al to the large, muscular woman impatiently waiting. "That's assuming you aren't under arrest."

Al scoffs at the suggestion. With an eyeroll, her shoulders

droop. "Mother and Mo are staying at a small cottage along the shore. It did not look like anyone had been there in ages, but Mother was adamant we shelter there."

I flinch back and release my hold of Al. My gaze instinctively sweeps to Raundel. He continues to block the entrance to Madame Marrouske, his sharp eye trained on the three other members of Jaden's clan.

Deona had first met Raundel at a cottage on the shore. It is the only cottage nearby known to any of my past selves.

"Long enough." Klarda grabs Al's arm and pulls her into a walk down the corridor. I should thank Al for the information, but I don't. I merely watch them walk away, followed by the other clan members at a relatively safe distance.

Ruby's complaints follow them down the path. "Why did you let her talk to Ana and not us?"

If Klarda responds, I don't hear it. Instead, I glance back at Raundel. He meets my stare, his intense glare daring me to speak what's on my mind.

I wonder if he knows the clan mother is staying in his old home?

And that tomorrow at midnight, she'll be meeting with Madame Marrouske. Or Meira, as that is to whom the letter was addressed. Who is Opal to my mystic?

I don't know, but I'm going to find out.

My lips pull into a taunting grin. His gaze narrows, silently asking to hear my thoughts. He can't and I'm not sharing. I turn and walk away. Head for Jaden's room. I have things to tell *him*, discuss with *him*.

And then tomorrow…tomorrow I will be at that meeting.

My thoughts are all a jumble, counting the minutes and devising a plan to get me out of the sanctuary and to the midnight meeting. The only way I can possibly get outside of the tearman protections is to slip through with Madame Marrouske and whatever entourage accompanies her.

I tell Jaden as much during my visit. I spill all the details about Al and the letter she delivered. I update him about Ry

and Zarah's departure, Clef's continued healing, the arrangement Madame Marrouske has made for me and Azure, and
Ruby's threat to me.

The small hope that he might react to the menacing
vixen's promise vanish when his eyelids don't even flutter. If
anything were to pull him from his sleep-healing, it would be
the idea of me sneaking out late at night, alone, with Dohlan
waiting in the woodlands. But even that information garnishes
nothing. I even speculate out loud about seeing Garr when I
last touched his leg. Nothing works.

I chose not to bring up any discussion of Dohlan. I know
the guy is a sour subject where Jaden is concerned, even if he
is relatively well controlled in the face of his so-called enemy.

By the time I crawl into bed at day's end, my mind is so
burdened with thoughts that I toss and turn, unable to find
peace in sleep for hours. When I finally do find slumber, I'm
awakened too early by a shove at my shoulder.

I moan and push the hand away, my thoughts returning to
the last thing I was considering before I fell asleep. Today, I'll
need to find Shadow and somehow convince him to help me
get past the sanctuary barrier.

"Come on. Get up." The hand shoves at my shoulder.

Again, I bat the hand away, then blink and try to focus.
Jaden, healthy, handsome, and strong is staring down at me.

He huffs a funny snort laugh. I blink, allowing reality to
settle into place.

Not Jaden, but Azure. I groan. Need more sleep.

Then jolt, eyes wide. "What are you doing in my room?"

FOUR

What kind of person lets themselves into the bedroom of another without knocking? Especially *while* that person is sleeping?

"You overslept," Azure says by way of explanation. "And you and I have an agenda we must keep to."

I rub my eyes and sit up, wipe the edge of my mouth. "An agenda?" My voice is still gravely with hours of disuse.

"Yes. Get dressed and meet me out front." He opens the door and steps into the hall, leans back into the room. "By the way, you were drooling like a big 'ol dog." He pulls the door closed, cutting him off from my sight.

"Jerk," I whisper to the wall but slip out of bed without any further delay. I wash up, get dressed, grab a snack to eat on the run, and meet Azure out front. Together we make our way to a nearby stream.

I keep my eyes forward and avoid conversation. He makes no attempt to look thrilled with the arrangement either.

"I don't understand why Madame Marrouske thinks you can help me," I finally say when the stream comes into view.

Azure clears his throat. "I understand." I turn a sharp

gaze on him. He doesn't look back. "She told me, you know."
I push my chin forward and widen my eyes, silently seeking
further explanation. "About me and Jaden, being one."

My mouth pops open and I avert my gaze. What a
burden, to be weighted with such information. I know what it
feels like, and I wish she hadn't told him. I see no reason for
him to know. He should have been allowed to live his life
without ever having to shoulder such knowledge.

"If Jaden and I were to…I do not know…like you and
your sisters…"

Oh Gaea. No. I wave my hands, signaling him to stop talking. Stop the thought completely. "Don't go there," I say.
"Don't do that to yourself."

"But now that I know, I cannot stop myself." He sighs.
"And Ruby would slit my throat if she knew."

A little harsh, but yeah, vicious she can be.

"Anyway, the point I was trying to make is that I understand," he continues. "That if Jaden and I are two pieces of
one soul, and your connection to that soul goes back eons
upon eons, then there is a chance I can somehow help, if only
a tiny bit, while he heals."

I'm too slow to stop the frown from pressing at the edges
of my lips. I have felt nothing Tracer like from him since
we met.

"Please, do not be like that," he says, glancing at my
expression of doubt. "That mystic witch of yours is incredibly
old and wise. If she sees a possibility, I believe we should pay
heed. You are not the only one in need of work. I think this
assignment is for both our betterments. Of course, for any of
this to work, we will need to trust one another."

I want to be trusting. He is Jaden's brother, after all. I
consider the way he sought Jaden privately to clue him in on
my infection of darkness. Not involving the rest of the clan in
that situation was commendable.

But then he attacked me in the woodlands. Held me down

and inflicted a physical pain only surpassed by the Balance Bringer binding. That action was nowhere near cool in my book.

Yeah, sure, I was infected. But seriously, dude. Timing.

We step over thick ground roots, half-buried boulders, and between high-rising trees. Stopping at the edge of the stream.

"Now what?" I say, steering the conversation away from things I'd rather not say.

Azure lowers himself to one of the nearby rocks. "Come. Sit." He motions for me to join him. I grimace, move with hesitation. "Ana?" He prompts. "Are you all right?"

"Yeah. Sure." I shrug. Take a tentative seat on a nearby rock. "I'm. Fine." I draw the words out slowly, still unable to fully trust his intentions.

"Why do you do that?"

I look at him with a blank expression plastered on my face. As far as I am aware, I haven't done anything.

"You refuse to lend me your trust, even the tiniest bit." His expression is one of solid frustration. The look is similar to one Ry sometimes gets when I refuse to do things his way.

"Can you really blame me? You did try to kill me. Remember?" I know he remembers. And I have plenty of witnesses, since it happened in front of *everyone*.

The pain. It will be forever unforgettable.

"When are you going to believe I was not trying to kill you. My intention was only ever to heal. For your sake and Jaden's." He sounds like a man who has run the same argument a thousand times.

My lips pull into a firm line, and I don't respond.

"Fine. I can see this discussion is going nowhere." His eyes turn cold and flat, and his face becomes devoid of all emotion.

Readjusting my position on the cold, hard stone, I pull my knees tight into my chest. I claimed a position at the edge of the lagoon so that I might dip my fingers into her soothing drink and play with the vigorous water spirits. Should they choose to show. And respond.

I don't know what we are waiting for. I'm fairly certain we didn't come to this spot to sit in silence for the rest of the day. But at present, I'm quite fine with the situation.

Bending forward, I drop my hand, and my fingers glance off the surface. I feel nothing. No welcome, no energizing warmth. Just the usual cold, wet water. My stomach constricts as I raise my fingers to eye level and study the way the water runs off them.

"Still fine?" Azure asks.

"Yes." My answer is slow and uncertain. Despite Madame Marrouske's explanation of my elemental disconnect, I am looking for an explanation as to why I don't feel anything. Anything at all.

He sighs. "So, you came to us broken this time around. What a lot of good that will do us." His sarcasm is undeniable.

"I'm not broken." A few months ago, I would have been floored at the idea of having the ability to control the elements. Now, I can't accept the idea of being unable to do the things I'm supposed to…of being broken.

My hand drops back to the water, and I search within its reflection for an answer to my plight. Seeking any sign that might give me hope. What I spy is a soft-featured, feminine face gazing back at me. Each feature, the curve of the nose, lips, or wisps of hair, molded from the water itself.

From past experiences, I know her to be smart and beautiful. But she's only ever presented herself as bright, sparkling orbs beneath the water's surface. Peering at her now, I envision her as the Ondine mentioned in the tale Jaden told me. The nasty water spirit that stole the Maiden Moon's beloved from her.

As if responding to my thought, her face distorts, and she zips away quick as a jet stream.

"Did you see that?" I ask of Azure, pointing after the retreating water spirit.

"See what?" He sounds mildly annoyed. Looks it too.

"*That.*" Leaning closer to the water, I point with vigor, as if a stronger point will help him see her.

My feet slip, almost as if they've been yanked out from underneath me. I slide toward the water, my hands scrambling for purchase.

It's no use. I'm going in.

I tense, preparing for the inevitable cold slosh. The stone slides beneath my shoes, and I note the jagged rock protruding from the hidden bluff beneath the surface. I squeeze my eyes closed, slide and topple.

Water slaps up around my legs, droplets smacking me in the face and arms.

But soaking wet…

I don't hit the water.

Azure scoops me up in his arms, saving me from what was sure to be a nasty collection of cuts and bruises.

I open my eyes with a gasp.

"You see," he says. "I am not going to hurt you." He carries me out of the stream and sets me firmly on the dry ground. "You should be more careful. You could have been injured."

"Would you have really cared?" I should have simply thanked him, but it's too late now.

"I do not hate you. I just want more for Jaden."

"And you think I'm not good enough?" His words cut deep, but I refuse to let the pain show. I hold my expression calm and open.

"That is not it," he says and pauses.

I wait, allowing my silence to prompt a continuation of his explanation. All of nature around us is equally quiet, as if everything waits on his next words.

He rubs the back of his neck. "Ever since this thing

between you two developed, his whole life has changed. Never again will a normal life be possible for him. But normal, or as possibly close to normal, is what I would like him to have."

He turns his full blue-eyed gaze on me. "How is he ever going to have love and a family when he has this thing with you?"

I want to tell Azure that I will be Jaden's family and forever love, but I hold my tongue and simply stare at him.

His eyes are set heavy with sadness. "Your connection will push any other woman away. It is unfair to him."

Azure's words cut deep and leave my heart to bleed. The last thing I want to do is ruin Jaden's life. This version of him may not have chosen this situation, but neither did I. I didn't choose any of this. And yet...

I would choose Jaden again and again, Ruby be damned. "What about me? I could love your brother." I *do* love your brother. "I can be all those things for him, love and family and purpose."

Azure walks away from me shaking his head. He takes a seat on an old fallen tree trunk. "History has proven it will never work."

My skin warms. I hate the fact that everyone seems to know more than me on every topic of my ever-important history. "What do you mean?"

Lifting his face, we lock eyes. His expression is placid, somber, serious. "I am sorry, Anala. No Balance Bringer has lived far beyond childbirth. The life expectancy of what you are is not a long one."

Okay. So, that sucks. But it would explain why all the various incarnations of me appeared rather young during the binding.

"*Others only decide your destiny if you allow it to be so,*" Deona whispers within me.

A deep breath combs through my system, and my body relaxes into a steady calm.

I can't change what happened to the others who came

before me. Nor can I change what others say about the Balance Bringer line. All I can do is use what time I have, be it long or short, to live the moments to their fullest and make a difference in this world…and hopefully in the worlds beyond.

Who wants to live forever anyway?

"I am so sorry." He reaches a hand for mine. A touching gesture that I don't move to match. "I did not mean to upset you. But I felt it was important you knew."

I bite my lower lip and nod. Decide to change the subject. "What are we doing here, anyway?" I glance around us at the trees, rocks, stream. I doubt we came here for this. Whatever this is that we've been doing.

Grass and bushes rustle at our back. Twisting in my seat, I spy the young elf who opened the gate to the woodlands moving toward us, carrying a large basket of linens.

I really should get her name.

"Here we are," she says, setting it on the ground between me and Azure. "Our lady said you would know what to do." Azure nods.

Two short men approach at the elf's back, each one carrying a basket as well. Baskets that dwarf them by comparison. Despite the cumbersome load, they navigate to their intended destination with expert skill and without the slightest hint of distress. A testament to their strength…. among other things.

"Hello there," I say to the two little men as they march past me with their baskets brimming with materials.

"No talking me!" The closest one snaps.

I startle and stiffen, and Azure laughs.

"So full of warm fuzzies." Crystia chimes in my left ear.

"I'm sorry." The young elf slaps her hands on her hips and stares after them. "Gnomes *can* be civil at times. At others, not so much."

Gnomes.

Maybe I should be making a list of all the amazing species I have met since coming to Hiddenkel. Mere fantasy where I grew up. Reality here.

The gnomes set down their baskets and march back toward the house, flashing an odd look in my direction as they pass. With a painful, uncommitted smile on my face, I wave goodbye. They look away and keep walking.

The young elf sighs. "Again, I am so sorry. They are cranky about being forced to carry the baskets down here." She laughs awkwardly. "We have not been formally introduced. I am Gitta." She bows to me.

"Oh!" I wave my hand. "You don't need to do that. The bowing, I mean."

"You are royalty, are you not?" she questions. "Daughter of Marduk the Fae King?"

I guess I am, I think with a loose grimace. Although, Madame Marrouske, Raundel, Lobrka, and Klarda haven't given me any royal treatment. "While I'm here, just think of me as Ana. Nothing more than that."

"But you are the Balance Bringer." Her eyes widen and body stiffens, as if my request falls into the realm of unthinkable.

"Again. Just Ana." I smile with what I hope is a soothing message.

She shivers, a smile wavering at the edge of her lips. She blinks and turns her attention to Azure.

"You *do* remember what this is for?" She points to the basket, her eyes widening with the question. He responds with a nod. "Then I shall take my leave. Good luck." She glances my direction.

"Thank you," Azure says. "You have been most helpful."

She starts to leave but then pauses and turns back. "I almost forgot. There is a woman looking for you. She was rather vocal, but I neglected to tell her where to find you." Her lips pull into a puckered line. "I thought you should know."

Azure's chest heaves with a large sigh. "Thank you, Gitta."

The vocal woman is without a doubt Ruby. I can only imagine how she would react should she find me and Azure here together, and alone. I shiver. "We're keeping this a secret from Ruby, right?"

"From everyone," he replies. "It is best that no one knows you are broken."

"I am *not* broken." My hands ball into tight fists, and a firestorm crashes in my chest.

"The old woman, your mystic, begs to differ. She is the one who sent this down for you." He motions to the baskets in a sweeping move of the hand. I blink with confusion. "She said some part of you should remember, and that this process will serve as a solution. Only, it will not happen overnight. Understand?"

"Oh, yes. Laundry in the stream. I rather enjoyed that chore." Deona, Fianna, and Estala begin to softly chatter at the back of my thoughts, reminiscing about their use of the elements in the cleaning process. Deona worked with the water to spin and wash the garments, Estala plucked them free with tree limbs, and Fianna sent a warm wind to quickly dry.

I doubt I'll be doing any of that today. Nevertheless, I bite my lip and nod that I understand what is expected of me.

This is to be a process. A possibly slow and painful one, but a necessary one. This disconnect isn't like a broken gadget in need of fixing. No...

What I am now suffering is the emotional distance experienced after a fight between friends. Best friends. And it is my responsibility to bridge that gap and make amends. Restore the relationship.

The sooner I accept the truth and the role I played in getting us here, the better chances I have at repairing the Balance Bringer in me.

"Good girl." Azure needles.

Rolling my eyes, I look away. *Condescending bastard.*

Azure jumps to his feet. "It may not have been of your doing, but the fact of the matter is, you went dark. The land, the air, the water spirits, they recognize that fact, and they do not appear to be happy with it. Or with you, for that matter."

I stretch my neck and sit straighter. "But it was either Raundel or Lobrka who suggested the dark infection could somehow help me in the fight that is to come."

Azure starts to pace and scrutinizes me like I'm his failing student. "Maybe a strategic approach I have trouble seeing?" He stops and narrows a tight stare upon me. "If that is what you believe, then you must find a way to convince the elementals that your dark experience was somehow beneficial to the overall goal."

And how do I do that?

"A simple sorry will not suffice. You will need to atone for the times you misused their gift. You will start by doing laundry."

Great.

"*It will be fine*," Deona chimes.

I glance over the baskets left for us, the mound of material rising from each. "Three loads. If we work as a team, we could probably get this all done in an hour." My estimate is a hopeful one, yet I finish the sentence with the hint of a question.

"I did not say *we* would be doing laundry." He smirks. "I said you. *You* are going to do laundry in the stream. This is something you need to work on with the water elementals. I suggest you take a more open-minded approach, so that the spirits do not pick up on any hostility you are projecting toward the task and take your emotions as an insult. That would only serve to make matters worse."

He lifts one of the baskets and shoves into my arms. It weighs heavily in my grasp, but I accept the burden of responsibility without argument.

This is my mess…mostly…to fix. "Fine. What do I need to do?"

"Wash the laundry," he repeats.

"I only wash laundry?" It seems a bit too simple and easy, but maybe that's the best place to start. Increase the efforts from there.

"And always, always *be respectful of the surrounding nature,"* Deona whispers.

Deep in the well of my many incarnations, Deona and the others are sharing with me the knowledge of how to do the laundry without a washing machine. Setting the basket on a rock protruding into the stream, I remove my boots, roll up my pants, and wade into the water.

Start washing. And washing. And washing.

All the while, keeping my mind open and my attitude positive. Occasionally, I reach out to the water spirits and get no reply, so I keep on with the repetitive chore, taking care to be respectful of all the natural elements surrounding me.

Azure settles into a restful position with his back against a tree, an endless stare in his eyes and a contemplative expression upon his face.

I hang a cloth over a branch to dry and grab the next item from the closest basket. "If my task is to make amends with the elements, and we both have issues that require work, what is it you are here for?"

He shrugs. "I am not certain. Could be a number of things. Maybe, discerning my area of need is part of the process for me."

"Maybe what you should be looking at," I say. "Is your need to push your will on others."

Like when you pushed the darkness extraction attempt on me while we were in the midst of running for our lives. I aim to soften my smirk with a light shrug. He frowns, nonetheless.

"Or," he counters. "I am actually here in case you anger the water spirit, and she tries to drown you."

"Very funny." I give him a snotty expression and turn back to my work. I balk at his comment, but what he said about the elemental could very well be true. "Sorry," I whisper to the water, and continue washing.

Piece after piece after piece.

My feet are cold, my body aches, and I want for a long nap by the time we return to the main house. Once inside the grand entry, Azure bids me adieu and heads off down the hall, likely to locate Ruby. And I head back out, across the compound in search of Shadow.

I find him tending to a small garden with a few others who look to be of the same or similar species.

He appears happy enough, but something in my gut tells me that the others of his kind are keeping a close eye on him. I can't help but wonder if all the members of Jaden's clan are being closely observed, and if so, what is at the root of the distrust, and who is keeping tabs on Ruby or Azure.

Shadow waves at my approach. "Hello Ana. This place is pretty nice, is it not?"

I kneel at his side, between the rows of blooming vegetables. "You don't find it a little bit *boring*?" I capitalize on the word he used to describe life with the Augur clan when he followed me into the battle zone in Palinot City.

His expression drops flat, and he blinks. A moment later, a wicked grin begins to pull across his lips. "What are you up to?" His tone is taunting, a tease lighting his gaze.

I glance around to verify no one else is nearby, then I lean in close. Drop my voice. "I could use your help." His eyes brighten at the unspoken prospect of working outside of the rules and guidelines. "Tonight."

"I knew there was a reason I liked you." His eyes sparkle and eyebrows perk. "What, when, and where?"

FIVE

Madame Marrouske leaves the sanctuary with her two most trusted confidantes at her side, Raundel and Lobrka. Klarda has the task of keeping an eye on Al at all times. Al, apparently, has yet to earn the Madame's trust. And Gitta is left in charge of the sanctuary during the mystic's absence.

Shadow and I hide in the darkness of his own making, absorbing all the information, as we follow the three through the sanctuary halls, out the door, and across the landscape to the woodlands below. He is magnificent at living up to his name and no one notices us as we move in Madame Marrouske's wake.

He grabs at my wrist, prompting me to hold back in our follow. "I hide us in the shadows," he says at a barely audible volume. "So, they cannot see us, but they can still hear us and smell us."

He sniffs me. "And you smell rather distinct."

I gasp, my nose wrinkling, then turn my nose toward my armpit.

His smile brims of laughter. "It isn't a bad smell. On the

contrary, it is a magical blend of the elements. Lavender, sea water, a fresh breeze, all rolled into one wrapped with a fine layer of power."

Unsure how his remark makes me feel, my nose wrinkles. With an ultra-light chuckle, he shakes my shoulder and then hugs me to his side.

"Anyway. Those three..." He continues and swings a finger back and forth indicating the group we're tailing. "Have extraordinary senses. We need to be stealthy to the point we are practically nonexistent."

I nod my head to let him know I understand, even as fear creeps into my chest that my breathing may be too loud. Once or twice, I swear Raundel and Lobrka peer over their shoulders, searching.

We continue to the last magical barrier undetected. And when Madame Marrouske lowers the protections, Shadow and I chance moving closer so that we can cross the threshold before the magic is set back into place.

Hidden amongst the trees outside of the sanctuary, I tug Shadow behind an extra thick banyan tree air root. "You should turn back now, before all the safeguards are back in place. We don't want to risk setting off the alarms."

My heart is thumping in overdrive at the prospect of going forward alone, but that is what I must do. This is my risk to take, not his.

"I want to go," he says, delivery firm and unwavering. "This is the most excitement I have had in days."

Since our trek here, no doubt.

I press my palms to the side of his head and rest my forehead against his. "Thank you," I say at a whisper. "You're a great friend. But I must insist you return. I need you to cover for me should anyone start looking."

"No. No." He shakes his head. "I must go with you to keep you safe. Jaden would never forgive me if I allowed something to happen to you."

At the mention of Jaden, I sigh and glance away. Shadow grabs my wrists and tugs, pulling my attention back to him, our gazes connecting and refusing to relent. For moments on end, we stare at each other and say nothing.

We're wasting time. His way back into the sanctuary will soon close.

I smirk. "Do you really think I need protecting?"

His face pinches. He doesn't know I am suffering a major disconnect from my magic, and he doesn't need to know. I still make a more than decent warrior without all the otherworldly power. I learned how to fight long before I learned how to manage the elements.

"You don't need to worry about me," I add. "Jaden cured me of the infection. I am golden. Clean. And in fine form." Physically…mostly.

"I still think…"

"Do I need to pull rank on you?" I glance to the gap in the magical barrier. We're running out of time. It's bound to close any minute, and he needs to be on the other side when it does. "I am the princess, after all." I cast him a firm glare.

He grunts, a pure grumpy reaction to my leverage. "I will cover for you if need be. But if you get hurt, or do not return, I shall send every elven warrior in this place after you."

A laugh bubbles in my chest, and I can't stop the smile that jumps to my lips. "Understood." I lay my hand on his shoulder and wink. "Now hurry."

With an air of reluctance, he turns away and vanishes into darkness. Heavy shadows race across the ground, crossing through the magical gap with hardly a second to spare. The protections snap back into place with a shimmer. He materializes, waving at me from inside the sanctuary perimeter.

Satisfied he is safely back inside and will keep silent regarding my nighttime foray, I make haste tracking Madame Marrouske, Raundel, and Lobrka to the cottage at the shore. The moon is not yet at its apex, but we have much ground to cover. I am baffled that they didn't leave earlier.

Although, I'm not baffled for long. The surrounding air roots shift and form tunnel after tunnel that appear to cut distances significantly. Like portals or wormholes. Much like the rock tunnel Jaden, Ry, Mo, and I used on the mountainside to escape Dohlan and Dreya's mutated army.

Leaving Mo's people and fleeing through the trees—that memory feels like a lifetime ago. All of Hiddenkel was so new to me then. Even now, the many things I see and experience never cease to amaze.

I glance down at the crystals twined to my wristbands, then clutch the one hanging at my neck. Mine, Crystia's, and Kaia's.

"Keep me safe," I whisper to them, then follow my mystic and elven warriors through the space-shortening tunnels at a safe distance, making sure never to lose sight of the towering elf warriors and the shrouded mystic they follow.

When we reach the end of the tree line, with the cottage sitting on a tiny bluff above the shore in sight, I hang back and watch from a distance, as the others approach the designated meeting place.

"What's it feel like to return home?" I whisper to Raundel.

He can't hear me. He's too far away, his back to me. But a part of me wishes I could see his expression. Deona's memories of him and this place are solid and bright, as if they were my own. In many ways, I guess they are.

Madame Marrouske climbs the steps to the front stoop and knocks on the door. It opens and all three enter the cottage. Logic tells me they won't all *stay* inside. Not if Opal wishes for a private meeting. I race across the open land, away from their prying eyes while the opportunity is present.

It serves to my advantage that no one has lived in the small house for some time. The surrounding landscape is unkept and overgrown. I slide to the side of the house, and slip behind a thicket of shrubbery, hidden and situating myself beneath the window. It's propped a smidgeon open, likely to help air out the dusty smell of years of disuse and neglect.

According to Deona's memories, a table—an ideal meeting place—should be positioned on the opposite side of the wall.

Greetings and introductions are coming to a close by the time I settle into place. "And the girl in the other room?" Madame Marrouske says. "Why does she sleep?"

The girl. Is she talking about Mo? What has Opal done to her? I clench the lapel of my jacket with an intensity that bleeds the color from my knuckles. Before this meeting is done, I will devise a way to get Mo to safety.

"We shall discuss the girl shortly." The voice belongs to Opal, but something about the tone rings with familiarity to me, a different version of me. And I do not recall that familiarity belonging to the Clan Mother.

I scratch my temple and try to remember where I know the voice from.

"For now, it is safer that she sleep," Opal adds. "Lobrka, it's been nice meeting you. Raundel."

At the clear dismissal, the room on the other side of the wall falls silent for a moment.

"Wait outside," Madame Marrouske says.

One of the elves grunts, but their footfalls exit the cottage and descend the front steps, where they move into the yard beyond. From my vantage point, they are partially visible through the cluster of leaves.

"You watch the front; I'll take the rear." The delivery of Raundel's order skirts a growl.

Lobrka places a hand on the hilt of his sword and nods. Raundel pivots and walks my direction. My heart squeezes to a stop, and my breath catches in my throat. My hands press to my lips, as if to remind myself not to speak.

He strides past my hiding place without a hint of hesitation and takes up a station at the back corner of the cottage. His head is angled to the side as if listening to the whisps of conversation drifting through the open window. Or possibly, listening for me.

Maybe my presence hasn't gone undetected after all.

I bite my lip and send a loud wish to lady green, the earthen elemental. *I'm so sorry. Please forgive me and hide me from the detection of these superpowered beings.*

Lady green does not respond.

But something else does. My own inner courage.

Because fear has left me so hyper focused on the two elven warriors, I am missing the conversation I came to hear. Fear is the enemy. The destroyer of potential and accomplishment.

I close my eyes, block out the thoughts of Raundel and Lobrka, and set my full attention on the Clan Mother and Madame Marrouske.

"You have been busy since last we met, sister," Madame Marrouske says.

Holy Gaea and raging gods.

Realization slams into me like an out-of-control troll. Heavy as a mountain.

Jaden's clan mother, Opal, is the elf Deona knew as Edea. That is why her voice rang with familiarity. Like Madame Marrouske, Meira, she, too, has taken on a new identity.

But why? Why the need for a name change in a world where so many live impossibly long lives? Such as my mother and brother.

I now listen with the ears of Deona, Fianna, Estala, and myself. Each version of me, deeply invested in what words are next spoken.

"I have, yes," Edea replies. "While you've been hiding inside the tree like a good little woodland elf, I have been traveling everywhere and learning everything."

Meira, Madame Marrouske, cracks a cackle. "In the manner of a proper dusk elf, I take it." Edea, Opal's response is unspoken, so I am left to guess as to her answer. "The years and travel have not been kind to you."

Indeed. Now that I am looking for the resemblance, it is extremely slight. Meira has aged...a lot...but I can still see the bones of the woman I once called Aunt. The new name does nothing to hide who she is at her core. But Edea...Opal...

"This last century, yes. But I have learned much over the millenniums," she says. "How about you, Meira. Are you current with the state of our girl? Of the boy you bound to her?"

Silence drops over their conversation like a thick winter blanket. I find myself holding my breath and counting the seconds and minutes. My imagination jumps into overdrive, trying to picture what is taking place between my age-old aunts.

"Why did you not come to me at the tree?" Meira's voice is soft, almost consoling.

"You know why." A crack in Edea's voice is evident in her delivery. "Glynnii. That's why."

"*Because of what happened to my mother,*" Deona whispers. Deona's mom, Glynnii, died at the tree's site, and the tree of life absorbed her. Not just physically, but in all ways, assuming the persona that once had belonged to Glynnii, an elf of the light, the sun.

Deona's memories of the tree of life flood me and my throat closes. The tree that absorbed her mother, our mother, now serves as a sanctuary, a home base for aunt Meira... Madame Marrouske. All the facts are a tangled web of emotions.

"So you chose to meet here, at the foot of our girls' graves?"

At Madame Marrouske's question, more memories flood into my consciousness. My head automatically turns in the direction of the hill, at the top of which Deona buried her sisters, Estala and Fianna, overlooking both the water and Raundel's cottage. My heart cracks.

I can see the similarities now, between Crystia and Estala, Kaia and Fianna. Both are slightly different, but yet, the same.

"I was overdue for a visit." I'm unsure if it is agitation or remorse that I detect in Edea's tone. "The girl is now safe at the tree?"

"She is." Meira's voice is yet again soft.

"She almost fell into Dreya's clutches."

"Dreya is not a concern in the larger picture. The goal to which we strive," Meira replies.

"But she might be," Edea, Opal counters. "She is family to this one, and the woman is driven by madness. The very darkness we had trapped within Sol." Meira sucks back an audible breath.

"*Poor, poor Sol,*" Deona muses. Sol and Jove had been friends and fellow travelers. If it hadn't been for Sol, Deona and Jove would never have met. Sol befell a horrible fate at the hand of multiple mistakes.

I clench my chest.

"There are many more considerations this time around," Edea adds. "Dreya, Garr…" Meira whispers his name. "Our unbalanced Balance Bringer, a splintered Tracer…"

"I am working to repair the Balance Bringer and Tracer," Madame Marrouske says with an air of arrogance.

I am more than just the Balance Bringer. I have a name.

"And how will you fix them?" Edea, now Opal, counters.

"I have a plan."

Opal hums to Meira's response. "When will you admit this entire experiment is a failure?"

Me? An experiment?

Opal continues. "The issues expand far beyond our girl and that boy. The worlds she created, when she tore ours apart, they too are falling into ruin. The one you plucked her out of might as well be on its way to a hell dimension, for its darkness and lack of respect for the elements or each other. So much hatred dwells there.

"And speaking of a hell dimension, the pocket world, filled with residue energy, split in two. Two *more* worlds, hosting dangerous life. One, turned to an unholy sanctuary for dark magical beings and the other *born* of hellfire. I hear the inhabitants call it Helvíti and they revere one they call the god of death."

Deona recalls creating the division of world, but...

How many worlds did I create?

Madame Marrouske inhales deep. "Things will straighten themselves out once she balances the scales, again." Her words ring with confidence, but a slight hint of concern is nevertheless evident.

"Will they?" Edea, Opal says. "Even the Mother's Core, the Eden of worlds, and homeland to our people, is being affected. Oh..." A scrape and scuff signals movement. "And the girl in there, she came from the nethers. Can you tell me how that is possible?" A beat of silence. "The nether has only ever been a one-way trip."

"*Except for me*," Deona whispers. "*I know the way in and back out.*"

I search her thoughts for anyone else who might know a way to traverse the veil between Hiddenkel and the nethers. I find none. Deona's father lived out the end of his years in the nethers, never able to return. For him, Deona created a passage through which she could visit.

A passage hidden in Kaia's cottage. My chest squeezes, snagging my breath. *In the back room, beyond a tunnel of darkness.*

My mystic clucks her tongue. "I suppose you have a plan to fix everything?" Sarcasm seeps into her delivery.

"Maybe," Opal quips.

"Do these children you have collected have anything to do with this plan of yours?"

Edea and Meira may likely be as old as dirt, but calling us children? *Come on.*

"They may have. Although, plans can change, as they sometimes do. I sense my time running short and therefore must make a few adjustments."

Meira scoffs at Edea's comment.

Edea continues. "At least *I* have provided a support group within her age group to whom she may be able to relate. Not just a bunch of ancients stuck-in-their-ways."

Meira grunts.

Edea is clearly referring to Raundel, Lobrka, and Klarda.

The scuff of a chair moving strikes sharp in my eardrum, and I wince. "Walk with me," Edea says. "Let us visit our sweet, sleeping girls."

The sounds of the women's exit moves through the small cottage and out the front door.

"We are going to take a short walk to the top of that hill," Madame Marrouske says to Lobrka and points to the location where Estala and Fianna were buried many lifetimes ago.

Raundel strides to the front steps. "It is good to pay respect to loved ones lost." He offers his hand to Madame Marrouske and helps her off the path onto the uneven terrain. "Lobrka shall accompany you."

"You do not wish to come?" she asks, surprise in her tone.

"I shall stay behind, keep watch over the sleeping one, and maintain security."

"Very well." She pats his arm and, together with Edea and Lobrka, makes way for the hill and the graves at the peak above. The climb is steep and their walk slow.

Wrapping my arms around my legs, I pull myself into as tight of a ball as I can and watch them make the trek, while remembering the day of the burial with painful accuracy.

Footfalls and noises mark Raundel's movement into and around the interior of the cottage. The window above my head closes. I can't even imagine the nostalgia he must be experiencing. That is, if elves experience such emotion.

I guess I have some elven in me...if I were to trace my lineage back far enough.

If only Raundel would join the others at the gravesites, then I could get to Mo. Move her to safety. I peer upward to the sky, but from where I am hidden against the side of the cottage, the moon is not visible. I can't judge how much time has passed. How much time I may have before someone... most likely Azure...notices I'm missing.

I still have time, yet. The world remains covered in the darkness of night.

Something tight and ungiving grabs my arm and yanks me upward. I gasp.

Raundel's face is inches from mine, his fangy canines bared, and a growl in his throat.

Crap. Crap. Crap.

"I may have chosen not to make the others aware of your presence, but that does not in any way translate into me forgiving you for this trespass." His eyes spark with unmatched fury. "You are to get yourself back to the sanctuary immediately."

I will not allow his age, and height, and muscle, and clear predator tendency to intimidate me. I straighten my back and stand tall, with chin high. "I can't go. Not yet. I came for Mo. Plus...I need you guys to open the tree tunnels in order for me to get back."

A guttural growl rips through his chest, and his eyes turn obsidian black. "I will take care of the girl."

"Her name is Mo," I say.

He ignores me. "You wait at the edge of the tree line and follow us back when we leave." He glances over my attire. All dark earth tones. "I assume you can handle the return trip with as much stealth as you used getting here?"

"Of course." I balk that he might insinuate anything other.

"Then go." He spins me around and shoves me toward the trees. I stumble to a stop and turn around, open my mouth. "I will handle the girl. Now go." The order is sharp and finite.

Deciding his plan is probably the best one under the circumstances, I head to the tree line as quickly and quietly as possible. There, I hunker down and wait.

Wait while the aunts visit with my sisters from a different lifetime. Wait while they walk down the hill and then step back into the house. Wait while they say their goodbyes at the front of the cottage. And wait while Madame Marrouske and Lobrka make their way my direction, to the path that will lead them back to the sanctuary.

Where is Raundel? What about Mo?

Madame Marrouske and Lobrka are several feet from the tree line when Opal...Edea... appears on the front stoop. She's clearly talking to someone inside the cottage. Raundel, I decide.

A moment later, he steps out into the night air, Mo in his arms. He descends the steps and crosses the terrain to catch up with the others, while Opal returns to the cottage interior, smoke soon emanating from the chimney.

Raundel passes close enough for me to catch a glimpse of Mo's sleeping face. She appears peaceful, unharmed.

My heart eases. Mo is with us once more.

I have so much to tell her, starting with the loss of Dohlan's ring. She has always been keenly interested in that tiny gold band. And despite my failure to lose it when I actually wanted to...it always managed to find a magical way to come back to me...it is now gone. Lost somewhere in the labyrinth of the woodlands, likely having fallen out of my pocket during one of the battles.

No doubt, she'll want to hear that story. I crack a smile

and turn to follow Madame Marrouske, Lobrka, Raundel, and Mo back to the sanctuary.

Stop short.

Dohlan stands two feet away blocking my path. An arrogant grin pulling at his lips.

"She told me I could find you here."

SIX

Dohlan's grip on my arm is ungiving. It presses against the edge of my wristband, shoving it deep into my skin.

He tugs and twists me into a walk at his side, his arm wrapped firmly around my waist, guiding me. "I like the new look. It's sexy."

My nose wrinkles. I want to ask him what new look he is talking about, but I won't allow him to distract me so easily from the real question needing to be asked. "Who knew I'd be out here?"

I struggle to keep pace but give no fight. "Opal? Is she the one? Who is she to you?"

He dips his head, pressing his nose to my crown, and sniffs my hair. "The more appropriate question is, who is she to you?"

"I know exactly who she is to me." I stop hard and yank free of his hold. "What I want to understand is who she is *to you.*"

He closes his eyes and drops his head back, taking a deep breath in the process. "Listen, Ana." He returns his gaze to mine. "There are too many people pulling my strings. You are one of them." I startle. "When they are all pulling in different directions, and I am tearing at the seams, it is only a matter of time before I snap. Break apart, leaving something no one wants to deal with."

Everything about him is more open, more vulnerable than I've ever witnessed, and it takes me back. Fills me with surprise and grief.

I stare at him and try not to let the pity I feel show. This is the man Kaia loves, or loved, and right now, when I look at him, all I can see is a beaten and wounded guard dog still trying desperately to please its master. Or, according to him, his many masters.

"Who besides Dreya has their claws in you?" I ask.

He chuckles softly, but it lacks conviction. "You, Kaia, Dreya."

He wraps his arm around my shoulders and guides me forward once more, as if we are simply two friends headed out for a walk beneath the stars. But his grip is firm, making it clear which direction I am to go. "Let us go together to meet with the first woman to ever hold rule over me."

We cross the clearing, with wide strides, making our way toward the cottage.

"Why do you not struggle? Fight to get away?" His questions almost sound like pleas, as if he wants me to run, but at this point, I have no intentions of missing this face to face—now that I remember who Opal truly is.

"Because we're all curious where this is leading," I reply. Dohlan stops dead, his body going rigid. He glances at me sideways with one eyebrow arched. "Well…" I tilt my head. "Mostly, it's me, Kaia, and Crystia who are curious."

"So, it is done, then?" He shifts to face me. "You and your sisters, you are all in there together?" He swirls a point to me.

"Seems that way." I nod.

He drops his head. Tension riddles his brow, his eyes.

"Can I talk to Kaia?" The question is soft-spoken, as if he was almost afraid to ask. Even now, with the clear vulnerability he is showing, I have a hard time picturing Dohlan afraid of anything.

"Yes." Kaia's response is loud, ringing through my soul.

"Maybe later," I say, not wanting to chance a loss of control when we are about to cross horns with my aunt from a thousand lifetimes ago.

In a conversation between Kaia and Dohlan, I'd likely only be translating for my sister. But since we haven't yet attempted such communication, I'm not taking chances at a time like this.

He appears to accept my response, although with clear disappointment, and we cover the rest of the distance in silence.

Opal is waiting for us when we enter the cottage. Her eyes as white and unseeing as before. Except, I get the impression she saw a lot more than one would expect. Possibly even more than a person with clear sight.

I study her features, searching for aunt Edea in the woman standing before me. I settle on a few similarities in the nose and cheek bones, the shape of the chin and stretch of the neck.

"I am so glad you could join us, Anala," she says, swinging a welcoming arm wide.

The interior of the cottage isn't much different than Deona's recollection. Small, sparsely decorated. Extremely dusty.

A few items are set on the mantel, among them I notice the knife Dohlan had claimed from the street, the night I escaped the lunatic car thief who called himself the Task Master.

At the time, I had wondered what he had done with the weapon. No doubt, it was my blood and not the knife that had been desired. I had assumed it had something to do with

Dreya. But with all that has since happened, I had forgotten about the blade, the blood, and Dohlan's theft.

Of course, if the knife is now here, then it was likely Edea, and not Dreya, who wanted that organic trace of me.

The fire in the hearth sparks, burns exceedingly hot. And something flashes in the flicker of the flame, drawing my gaze.

A dagger, ceremonial in style, is propped with the blade in the flame.

I take a step back, bump into the wall of Dohlan. His hand clamp over my upper arms, but rather than hold me firm, he rubs up and down and up and down, as if to sooth.

"I'm sorry I didn't recognize you the first time we met, Aunt Edea," I say.

"I shan't hold that against you. I am much changed since you last saw me." She motions me forward "Come. Let me have a better look at you."

I frown. Don't move. "I heard a lot of what was said."

"As expected."

I jolt. Not the response I was anticipating. With a minor tilt of my head, I gaze into Dohlan's eyes. His expression reveals nothing, but he drops his hands, removing his soothing touch.

"I'll tell you what I didn't expect," I say. "Whatever this thing is you have over Dohlan. Which is what exactly?"

Humor rocks through her chest in sharp laughter. "Every good boy is obedient to their mother."

My head flinches back, and my heart suddenly feels heavier. So heavy, it's pulling me through the ground. "Like the clan? Was he part of an earlier group?"

She shakes her head. "Not a child by choice, but a child by birth. He has inherited that which is in my blood and what dwelled within his father. He is impossibly strong willed, and, well…" Her gaze shifts past me to the man standing at my back. "Well suited for the darker version of yourself." Kaia. "I saw to that palliative pairing personally."

My mouth drops open. "Are you saying he was engineered for Kaia?"

Holy Gaea and god. My heart cleaves in half for Dohlan.

"Engineered?" She shrugs her chin into her shoulder. "This is not a word of our world. But he was...is...what helps balance the one tipping the scales. Blood calls to blood, my sweet."

"How could you do that to your own son?" My muscles are tight, trembling, and I can't believe the woman talking is or was once my aunt Edea.

Dohlan's hands drop onto my shoulders. "It is all right, Ana."

I spin to face him. "All right? Nothing about this is all right. She toyed with your life. Treated you like a puppet."

In some ways, with what she is doing to Dohlan, Edea isn't much different than Dreya. Both puppeteers. Dreya of many, Edea of one. The one Kaia fell in love with.

His gaze softens. For my concern? My irritation? Maybe. He doesn't appear to be bothered by Edea's manipulation of him and his life. His love.

Kaia's energy within the well of my many mes has dulled, and I don't know what to make of the change. Although, I suspect she is reeling in the newly discovered reality.

I swing back to Edea. "I heard your declaration of impending death. Did you want me here so that you could clear your conscience?"

"Not at all." A mild smile flirts across her lips. "I may be guilty of many mistakes in my lifetime, but my son is not one of them." Her hand clutches the nearest chair, guides her a step forward. "What I would like from you, is for you to free my son from Dreya's control. She has polluted his magic. Twisted him into something...unsavory."

Unsavory? As in the dream succubus Ry said Dohlan to be.

Edea's request gives me pause, and within the inner well of my many incarnations, Kaia gasps.

I glance back at Dohlan. His features built for sin, a face, a smile, that could melt the sun. All a lure for Kaia, Kaia's darkness, but it also snagged Dreya.

Something inside of my chest tugs. Kerthumps. "And you, with all your millenniums of experience, wisdom, and magic, can't manage that task?"

"Dreya and I have a small history. She has made it increasingly difficult for me to get close and my time to try is running thin."

"Because of your impending death?" I ask. I sound harsh and part of me is instantly guilty. This woman and I have history. Some of it beautiful, warm family history. But altering Dohlan to serve a purpose… I don't know that I can forgive that. *Ever.*

"*Please help him.*" Kaia's whisper is soft. So soft. And I ignore it.

"The way I see it…" Edea, now Opal says. "If anyone can get close to Dreya, it would be you. She has a special interest in you, because of who you are."

Both Balance Bringer and family. Two things she apparently hates. "I've noticed." And how I wish it weren't true. "But in my current state, I wouldn't hold a candle's chance in a blizzard against that mad woman."

"Then what do you say to us getting you on the road to full recovery starting tonight?" Her brow lifts.

"Madam Marrouske…" I stop myself. "I mean, Meira is already working on that."

She snorts. "So I have heard, but she does not know all the things that I do. She is merely a woodland elf."

An ancient woodland elf with countless years of experience.

"So?" I say with a sharp tongue.

"I am a dusk elf. The most knowledgeable of all the clans." Pride exudes in her statement. "Our passion is to seek new and growing knowledge in all areas of life. We can see things in the patterns that are invisible to others."

Dohlan sighs and the rise of his chest presses at my back. "She created the oils that helped you through your transition more quickly and easily."

The oils he rubbed all over me that left me withering in death for what felt like days. When he kept me, like a captive, in the bed he used to share with Kaia. Not exactly a ringing endorsement.

My lips quirk.

But my earthen gift did bloom exceptionally fast afterwards. And I didn't even realize I was transitioning into air until I was in the midst of change.

And now they are all gone.

I want them back.

Dohlan squeezes my shoulders, almost as if he senses what I am thinking or feeling and is sending a comforting gesture.

My gaze flickers to the knife on the mantel. The one Dohlan took the night I tossed myself out the back window of Ry's car, in order to escape the Task Master.

Dohlan follows my gaze, his lips tugging into a firm line. "Neither she, nor I, am responsible for the wounds inflicted upon you that night. We merely borrowed your blood."

"Borrowed?" I highly doubt they intend to give it back to me. "You licked the knife. I saw you."

The taut line of his lips lifts into a small smile, one of remembrance. "You tasted much like Kaia."

Gross. I grimace.

Edea weaves her fingers together. "The sample was useful in helping me better understand your current state, and upcoming needs," she says before I can vocalize my inner thoughts and questions. "It served to solidify my thoughts regarding your unbalanced nature and your sister's unhealthy portion of darkness."

She waves her hand as if to silence a question I had yet to

form. "Do not misunderstand. Darkness in the mix is a must, but it must be balanced, and after what you did during your last life…you remember, do you not?"

*The splitting of the stick. The words spoken…*to help that version of Jove, to fight what I now suspect was Garr's influence. *The mistakes made.* The consequences, my unbalanced state between my sisters, and Jove's soul splintering, resulting in both Jaden and Azure. I nod that I remember. Painfully remember.

"You must find a way to assimilate the darkness and balance the scales," she continues. "That will start here, should you choose to move forward."

"How can I trust you after what he…" My gaze shifts to Dohlan. "…did to Jaden? Cutting him across the leg." Dohlan huffs a laugh, does not respond, but lifts his chin and turns his gaze away.

It is Edea who speaks. "Did not the cut force you and Meira to take a long, serious look at your Tracer?"

Maybe. That and the affects upon him from clearing me of the dark infection.

Her unseeing eyes twinkle with a knowing grin. "Now you can properly address the deeply rooted source of your Tracer's problem, rather than pressing another bandage to the issue."

"What do you know about Jaden's issue?" I ask.

Her lips pull into a lopsided smile. "You already know what I know."

Garr. The name whispers in my head. *What did he do to Jove?*

"So what say you?" Edea presses. "Shall we begin? Shove your elemental connection into a quick start? Nudge those yet to awaken?"

"Can I think about it?" I ask, not wanting to commit on a whim to Gaea-knows-what. And to an aunt who has chosen to go down a questionable path in her quest for balance.

"For a moment," she replies. "We have only tonight. The time is nearing when I will no longer be able to help you."

Because she's dying…or thinks she is. My chest tightens.

As if sensing my unspoken thought, Edea continues. "Big magic has consequences. Sometimes, hard to handle blow backs. And I have performed my fair share over the years."

And you're asking me to allow you to perform more…on me.

Within me, Deona pushes me forward. *"She may have made mistakes,"* she says regarding Edea. *"But I know her heart and intentions were pure. She will always fight for our best version."* Meaning not only sisters and Balance Bringer, but worlds, as well.

"Okay…" The word reluctantly slipping from my tongue, I shift my weight and shove aside any anxiety or discomfort attempting to scratch at my resolve. "Let's say I agree to whatever it is you think you can do for me. What do we need to make it happen?"

The edges of Opal's white eyes crinkle. "We already have everything we need right here. Are you prepared and willing to give whatever is necessary to regain balance?"

"Whatever it takes." The words no sooner slip from my lips than a spike of fear splices into my gut. "Wait," I say and take a moment to collect myself. "What exactly do you mean by whatever is necessary?"

She shrugs a slight lift of the shoulders. "We are dealing with the elementals and gods as ancient as time. There is no saying what they may require, but there are bound to be sacrifices."

Her neck pulls taut. "All things of true worth require some sort of sacrifice." She pauses for a moment, allowing her words to sink in. "So, what say you? Shall we get started?"

I don't like the not knowing. Too many things exist in my life that I don't care to lose. But if I do nothing and find myself unable to restore balance, won't I lose them anyway, and possibly more?

I swallow hard and glance over my shoulder to Dohlan. He nods once, his gaze blazing with intense focus.

I press my lips together, steel my nerves, pray nothing bad comes of my decision, and then step forward. "Let's get it done. Restore me to full Balance Bringer mode."

WHEN I AGREED to do things Edea's way, to mend the Balance Bringer side of myself, I didn't expect that I would end up laid out on Raundel's old kitchen table, like a maiden sacrifice in some forbidden ritual.

And yet, that's where I am. My jacket discarded, and my sleeves and pant legs torn to expose skin. My shirt is also adjusted to reveal my midriff and upper chest.

Dohlan bends down close to my ear. "Are you sure about this?" I sense hesitation, a fracture of concern.

What's the worse that could happen? *I could die.* And then I would eventually reincarnate to do this all over again.

"Yes," I say, with enough confidence to spark pride in my chest. "I've got this."

Blessed Gaea, I hope that is true.

"Apologies for the straps," Edea says. "But you would not want to hurt yourself with the thrashing."

The thrashing, a reaction to whatever magic she is about to bestow upon me.

Dohlan secures my wrists and ankles, tying them to the table. He stares at me, a flicker in his eyes I can't quite discern. "Are you sure about this?" he asks again, this time of his mother.

"Of course." She waves the question away. "It will hurt, but it must be done, and she will survive plenty fine." She pulls the heated blade from the fire. Etchings in an ancient language glow in hellfire red and gold. "The quickest way."

Inferring the quickest way to healing what I have broken

will not be pleasant. She waits for my reply. Making sure I am truly on board with what we are about to do.

"Let's just get it over with," I reply.

She motions to Dohlan, and he offers me a stick to bite down on.

"Do I really need that?" My gaze flickers from the offered bit to his wavering expression.

"It is recommended." He presses it forward in a silent request. I open my mouth, and he gently sets the stick between my teeth. I bite down ever slightly. Just enough to hold the piece in place.

Opal, once Edea, stands over me, with glowing blade in hand. "There is no saying how much sacrifice the elements will require, but it will start with blood...and tears. Pain to atone for the pain caused, and *your* pain to help guide your future understanding for any pain inflicted upon the other.

"The spill of blood to reconcile the enormous losses, to earth and air and water. To life and health and the goodness of all kind. To the path of the righteous, and the unbalanced shift from love and light to benevolence and dark."

I nod, steel my nerves, and bite down on the bit in my mouth.

"What I now do," she says, not to me but to the air above, tilting her head back to gaze at the roof of the tiny shack of a cottage. "I do for the good of all worlds and all kind." She raises her arms high and wide. "Empower me, all mighty elemental gods and goddesses. Guide my hand and words. Lead us in our redemption."

A gentle wind sweeps through the room along the floor, circling around Opal, and rising.

She drops her gaze to mine. "Ready?"

"By the power of Gaea and god..." *I sure hope so.*

The blade lowers to my exposed skin, the tip blazing with a sweltering heat, I expect it to melt straight through to the bone. Four slashes across my belly, one for each element, each of them an injection straight to my gut. A drowning by earth and water, a beating, thorough tossing by wind, and consumption by fire.

Fire, fire, *fire*!

My clench upon the bit in my mouth intensifies, pressing grooves into the hard wood and staying my scream.

Living, dancing flames burst to life along the edge of the blade.

"These are the fires of your soul," Opal says, twisting the blade in the air between us. The flame flickers in shades of blue, orange, and yellow. "The fire of the soul never goes out, merely transforms. It is more ancient than our worlds." She turns the blade back on me, slicing a thin line along my arm. "We now invite this ancient soul fire to purify the instrument within which it dwells. Purify it, both body and soul."

I want to clarify that *I am* the instrument, but my words are bottled by the bit in my mouth, the clenching of my teeth against the pain, and the screaming...the unrelenting screaming in my head.

She moves around my body, creating cut after cut, the blade slicing through my skin as if the gashes already existed and were merely waiting for someone to nudge them open. Like tugging on a zipper.

Despite the fire in the hearth and the fire dancing across the blade, my body is cold. Dropping deeper and deeper into a pit of ice. With the blood that seeps from my many wounds, so does the warmth of me. The warmth of my body, my life.

"The elements," Opal mumbles, likely to Dohlan.

He sets a stone bowl filled with dirt on the table beside my hip, into which Opal pours a small bottle of water. She exhales a breath onto the two combined elements and then mixes the contents of the bowl, using the burning blade dripping with my blood.

Earth, water, air, and fire, coming together so that I might fix a broken Balance Bringer inside of me.

She begins to sing while she mixes. And the more she sings and mixes, and the more I stare at her from my place strapped on the table, the more the vision of her in my sight changes. She is younger, wilder, other.

The rhythmic pattern of her song lulls and soothes. It's hypnotic, and I find myself seeking a mental escape and drifting away from the torture of the ritual.

My eyes blink, blink, blink, fighting for the control to remain in the moment. Conscious and aware of everything taking place.

I am brave. I can handle the pain, I remind myself. *I can handle anything Opal or the elements thrust at me.*

She moves to the hearth, bowl in hand, placing her back to me. Her verse and song bounce off the stone walls surrounding the fireplace, echoing through the whole of the cottage. And the flames in the hearth explode with a sudden, quick and gone, blast.

Opal or Edea are gone when the woman spins back to me. Something or someone new inhabits her, gazes out at me from her white eyes turned molten gold.

At the sight of the change, Dohlan lurches forward, his expression wide and overflowing with worry. But with the lift of her hand in his direction, he is thrust backward across the cottage and dropped into a seat against the farthest wall.

His wild gaze darts back and forth between his mother and me. "Mother?" His voice is etched in pleading and concern. His body struggles but appears unable to lift from the chair.

The lyrical chant resonating from her lips, in the air around us, doesn't skip a beat for his beseeching, and he is left to sit and watch, trapped in place by magic unseen.

The possessed Edea scoops a palmful of the ingredients out of the bowl and slathers it over the cut on my left arm.

"Forthwith to the arms for strength," she says and smears more on my other arm, my other cut. Red lightning flashes through my bloodstream, behind my eyes. My upper body shakes.

She repeats the process, smearing the elemental mixture and chanting, moving from my legs to a thin slice along my hairline and finally, a long, fine cut down my chest, from my collar bone to my breasts.

"Straight away, bring speed to the legs.

"Clear to the mind, send thoughts straight and true.

"Direct to the heart, overflow with thy grace and goodness."

A soft breeze plays at my torn clothing, my hair, swirling around me with ever increasing intensity. A mini whirlwind, morphing into a windstorm that expands to encompass the entire room.

But the indoor storm doesn't phase the melodic chant slipping from Opal's lips.

Her white hair blows around her crown in every direction. Her molten gold eyes, no longer looking human…or elven, glow with wild magic.

Her hands, thick with the elemental mixture, slap down on the four cuts across my midriff. Pain explodes in every blood vessel, cracking my bones and frying my internal electrical system. The air rushes out of the room and I scream.

Scream like never before.

Everything is spinning and crashing, heating and freezing. Rattling to cinders. I have become the nucleus of magical chaos…the eye of a dimensional breaching storm.

The thrashing begins.

My arms and legs slamming against the constraints for freedom. Testing the strength of the bonds holding me in place. My body is burning and crumbling from the inside out.

"Close your eyes, Ana." Dohlan's words carry through the storm. His tenor a call to calm.

I turn my head and stare at him, my eyes wide and holding no shield against the panic. He remains pushed up against the wall. The distance across the room might as well be seven football fields.

"Focus not on the outer world, but the transformation taking place within," he says.

I gulp, nod, obey. Close my eyes.

Everything is heavy, weighted, like a blanket of thick chain has been laid over me. The life within me feels as if it is withering away, leaving me a spent and empty shell.

The transformation has me drained, tired, hollowed.

Opal, once Edea, now someone or something else, rubs a hand across my belly, pushing the elemental combination deep into the scores across my body.

"Love and wonder, understanding and compassion,

"Reason and control, trust and courage, hope and affection.

"May all these things be bestowed upon our daughter, chosen by the utmost high.

"Bringer of Balance, let the amends begin, the price be paid, and the healing ensue."

The whipping wind circles the request into my thoughts. Her words take shape in my mind, scrolling letters across the empty chasm of my consciousness.

Slow, deliberate molten fire burns at my flesh. Searing my tissue, my muscles, my soul. Every millimeter of my body vibrates and tingles, externally and internally. At my ears, a thrumming. A low beating drum.

Invisible tentacles, roots maybe, wrap around my inner self and pull me down. Down and down, away from my physical self. My grip on the here and now slips.

A sweet, soft lullaby lures me deeper.

Someone calls my name. Someone begging me to come back, open my eyes.

But it is too late.

I am leaving, following the lullaby.

SEVEN

With a whap, whap, whap, a butterfly lands on my knee and stills its colorful wings.

Remember, whispers through my essence.

I am surrounded by pure, unadulterated darkness. Slowly falling away from everything and everyone. And yet, I still recall the butterfly…on more than one occasion. Currently, it is the only hint of light and color in the void that now surrounds me.

And so the caterpillar bloomed into the butterfly, spread its wings, and flew over the world.

Content to be disconnected from the physical pain inflicted upon my body, my mind is empty, creating no response to the disembodied message.

You are the caterpillar. Time to bloom and spread your wings.

Tiny white dots pop into position over me, cutting into the darkness. A night sky. I land softly in a bed of grass, within a circle of trees reaching for the moon above. Two horses, one white and one black, nudge their noses against me, their long spindly horns glistening in the moonlight.

A different perspective from one of Deona's memories. She is among the trees, meeting the unicorns for the first time.

Remember, whispers through me once more.

The unicorns? Their gift to Deona?

A gift intended for you, the one to bring balance.

Yet Deona used the gift to heal Jove.

With the endowing, your mate was chosen.

Yes. Jove, now Jaden.

Like the caterpillar to the butterfly. You, too, must break free of your cocoon. Bloom.

Is this still about my broken connection with the elements?

My mind races, searching for the answer.

The horses and trees vanish, leaving me alone, lying in the grass, beneath an endless night.

"Take her." Opal's voice booms over my little world.

Is this a dream? Some sort of psychotic break? A drug induced hallucination?

Her voice...that of Edea...slips close to my ear, nothing more than a whisper. "The old you was shredded open to allow the new you to step through."

Something shoves beneath me, jolting my body. An army of nails slams into my skin, both from within and without. I scream...internally.

The only thing to escape my lips is a moan. I am rising, rising, rising back to a state of consciousness. A place swarming and blazing with pain.

"Hold on, I have you." Dohlan's voice is near. So incredibly near. Yet, when I open my eyes, I can hardly make out the surrounding scene for my vision is clouded with a swimming film of blood. "This will get better," he adds.

He doesn't say as much, but I sense the word *hope* was dropped from his delivery. He hopes it will get better. I will get better.

I'm in his arms, and we are moving through the trees, not

nearly as fast as I know he's capable of traveling. He has slowed his speed for me because of every yelp and howl that escapes my lips with the jarring movement, skirting trees, climbing or jumping over roots, thick and high as retaining walls.

The pain is a bleeding hemorrhage in my chest, at the back of my skull. I embrace the empty and pass out, again.

Slip into a new dream...an ancestral dream walk, calling me with the familiarity of my mom.

THE SCENT of my mom is strong, pulling me from the empty void of nothingness, into a memory played out many years ago. In a time before me.

I miss my mom. Wanted to go with Ry to find her. But at least, for now, I can have this moment, living a day...an event...in my mom's shoes.

Mom and one other are in a large, stone-walled room, decorated in many fine pieces. Thick rugs, rich woods, decanters filled with colorful liquids.

I, as Mom, approach the Fae king from the rear, weapon in hand.

"Nerine." His voice is flat, showing no emotion. But the mere fact that he knew I was here has halted me dead in my tracks.

The king, my father, but not yet. Not even a love interest for Mom.

I know this because, in this dream walk, I'm living the memory from her perspective.

My mom, Nerine, stands three feet behind the king, blade held ready to plunge deep into the thick of his neck.

He turns to face me, my mom, a book held open in his hands, and his eyes bright with sadness. "Is this really how you want things to play out? You fought for me once. Has your sorrow now turned you so far against me?"

Mom keeps her lips sealed, allowing the silence to build between them.

And then, disconcerted by my—her—actions, Mom lowers both her head and weapon. Stares down at her hands.

He sighs. "I thought a kinship was building between us. I know you have been distant, it's understandable, but I thought...I felt...something nonetheless. Was I so wrong?"

I stare at him, unable to force the words from my throat. It matters not if I have feelings for him. I am immortal warrior clan, he is not, and so nothing may ever come of such things. Not to mention...king.

Him and his war.

It is because of the ridiculous war that my Usoff is gone. Usoff. Father to my son Ryland, and the warrior with whom I belong.

And yet...

New emotions have been stirring for some time now, and they refuse to stay buried.

My lips start to move, but my voice does not come. Something in King Marduk's expression, his stature, freezes me. Keeps me from putting more distance between us.

We are different in race, something that should never take place amongst the warrior clan. We keep our bloodlines pure for the betterment of our inherited battlement memories, which are shared with our ongoing bloodline. Still, that difference doesn't stop me from wanting to step closer.

I should give no thoughts to another outside of Usoff. *Oh, the guilt it churns.*

He slams the book he holds shut, turns away, and navigates across the room, returning the reading material to its proper place on the shelf.

"I have been following a lead from the morning of the battle," he says as he walks to the window and the view of the kingdom beyond. "It would appear a young chronicler and her mother were present."

He speaks of Zarah. Ry had mentioned something about Zarah being there at his dad's death.

"Unplanned, but yes, it is true." I affirm. "They recorded Usoff's passing that afternoon."

He turns and looks at me, his gaze scrutinizing my everything, expression, stance, rate of breath. My skin comes alive with itches. *Maybe I shouldn't have mentioned the death.*

"Well." He returns his gaze to the window. "It would seem that the young chronicler saw something out of the ordinary. Something that has put her life in danger." His back rises and falls with a larger than normal sigh. "I suspect something nefarious took place on the battlefield that day, and Usoff may have been a casualty."

Shock knocks me—my mom—sideways, and I forget my immortal warrior training, allowing emotions to enter the conversation.

"What are you saying, Marduk?" For the first time since we met, I drop his royal title and call him by his name. I spoke without thinking and I'm immediately horrified.

"My apologies, my king!" I bow deep. Deeper than I have ever before bowed. I close my eyes and clench my teeth, expecting a hammer hard flash across the cheek when I straighten.

I will take my punishment without argument.

"Rise," he says. I do, standing shoulders squared, back firm.

He is close, ready to strike, hand rising. But no hard crack brandishes my jowl. Instead, the warmth of his heavy, thick palm cups my cheek and soothes the curve of my face.

His unexpected reaction to my clear, and punishment-worthy misstep, draws my gaze directly to his own.

A sad smile gently curves the edges of his lips. "I suspect more was at work than just your average battle, and I believe Usoff fell victim to whatever evil was at hand. I promise you, my dear Nerine; I will not stop until I get to the bottom of it and bring the events of the day to light."

Standing closer than he ever has before, his warm breath rolls in waves off Mom's skin. His words ring sincere within the depths of his gaze.

I, as mom, want nothing more than to believe every word he speaks. And now...as he gazes with such intensity at me...I realize I want more.

Forgive my heart's betrayal, Usoff, but it has been long, and I feel it is moving on without my permission.

"Nerine," Marduk's voice is low and inviting. "Usoff has been gone several years now." *Three.* Slowly, gently, he pushes his hand through her hair.

"I know." My response, my mom's, is leading. *Am I truly prepared to go against what I've been taught my entire life? What if...*

What if a union between the two of us would be the one? The pairing to bring forth the next Balance Bringer.

I, Mom, shake my head. It is foolish to believe I might be the one chosen.

Marduk's sweet scent fills my mom's senses. The aroma of giant oak and banyan— something rare and precious in this realm. I hadn't noticed that about him before, a unique scent, the scent of the mystic's fortress. That must mean something. But what? A clear mystery to be solved.

A nerve pinches in my back, and I am instantly aware of my body outside of the parental dream walk.

REMEMBER, whispers in the back of my head.

My eyes flutter partially open to a multitude of colored lines cascading all around me. Through everything, the rocks, trees, animals...Dohlan. We're still deep in the woodlands, and he holds me firmly in his arms.

"You're awake," he says, noting the crack of my eyelids.

"It will only be a moment, and you will be inside the safety of the sanctuary."

I was unconscious for the entire trip back. *Did it work? Did the ritual work?* I'm too weak to test my connection to anything, magical or otherwise.

Dohlan lifts his chin indicating something up ahead. "I can see him coming now."

Him? Who is coming?

Has Ry returned? Jaden awakened? Maybe Shadow hung back and is waiting for me by the gate.

I turn my head against the pain of a thousand and ten tendons attempting to keep my neck straight and unmoving. The snarl reaches my ears before I have him in my sights.

Raundel.

My heart quickens a beat. *Or Raundel.*

My stomach turns to stone.

He stomps our direction. Even with the colored lines disrupting my vision, his fury is clear to see. He covered for me, then gave me only one order. An order I failed to follow.

The protective barrier between us starts to shimmer, opening a gap through which he may pass.

Dohlan lowers his head and bestows a soft kiss on my forehead. "Rebirth takes time. Try not to let impatience get the better of you," he says. "I am sorry it must be this way."

What way? I blink twice, rapidly, my stone stomach turning to flutters.

With a gentle hand, he lays me on the ground, then turns and disappears between the trees, before Raundel can reach us.

"Come back here, coward," Raundel yells after Dohlan.

Even though it is not yet sunrise, and we are in the shaded woodlands, the earth at my back is as warm as rocks in the blazing sun. The heat soothes my aching muscles and irritates my prickly skin.

Raundel's angry and discontented growls mark his approach.

I stare after Dohlan's retreat, breathing in and out and in and out, attempting to calm the rage of lingering pain clouding my body. And preparing myself to face Raundel.

"I asked only one thing of you." He kneels beside me, and I know I can no longer avoid the inevitable confrontation. I turn and meet his gaze. The hard anger and irritation lining his face, mutates into concern. "What has he done to you?"

"Not him," I say and attempt to push my upper body onto my elbows. I succeed, with a wince and a withheld bark of discomfort. "It was Edea. She said it would help me…"

My words fall away, and I leave the sentence unfinished. I don't know how much Madame Marrouske, Meira, has shared with him, and if he doesn't already know about my disconnect, I'm not so sure I want him to know.

A throaty grunt vibrates in his throat. "She is much changed."

I nod, an attempt at a smirk on my lips.

"Can you walk?"

"Don't know," I answer honestly. "But I'll try."

With his offered arm as support, I pull to my feet. My legs shake beneath me and give out. The places of my incisions scream in protest. Although they no longer bleed, fresh scabs mark the lines.

Raundel catches me and just as quickly sweeps me into his arms, marches us back within the sanctuary's protection barrier.

"You should have never followed us to the cottage." His comment is full of irritation. At me. At himself. At the situation.

"What's done is done," I lament and stare out at the surrounding terrain. The never-ending web of roots running from the mammoth tree of life. "Mo?" I witnessed him walk out of the cottage with her. I assume she's now safe, but I prefer confirmation.

"Your friend is well and good."

I nod, content that at least one confirmed good thing came out of the night's caper, and he falls silent for several steps.

He tilts his face to mine. "Did it work?" I turn my questioning gaze to him, unsure what it is he's asking. "This thing Edea did to you, did it work?"

"Hope so. Time will tell."

A grumpy sigh settles in his chest. "Did she need to inflict so many injuries upon your body?"

"They will heal." I'm a fast healer. My disconnect from the elementals shouldn't have any effect on that little superpower. I heal fast because I am both immortal warrior and Fae. Two quick healing races.

"Yes, but..." His face tightens. "I shall take you directly to the healer."

My chest squeezes at the thought. "Please don't," I say. "Can we just go straight to my room and give all this..." I glance down at my body, scabbed and dressed in torn clothing. "...a chance to do its magic? Let it help heal me." And give me a chance to sleep because I am oh so tired.

His attention snaps from the path to me. "How is this meant to help heal you? By what I see, this method is not logical."

"Just give it a chance, and please don't tell Meira. Not yet anyway."

At my request, his gaze returns forward, a muscle in his right cheek twitching.

Contemplating and considering? Or merely irritated? I'm not sure. Raundel and I have a limited history. He has spent far more years with Meira, between my various incarnation visits.

"I remember you, you know," I say, attempting to appeal to his sentimental side…if he has one. He is pure elf, something none of my incarnations have ever been. "The way you helped us when we first ended up on your shore." My lips tug to the side. "I still recall the story of your journey that landed you in that little cottage. You helped Deona then, and you have helped many variations of her since then." *Please help this one, me.*

His gaze flickers to me for a mere moment, then back to the tree ahead. "To skip the healer may not be wise. The markings to your body…the smell of whatever she did…it is unusual." From the lift of his nose and the show of his canines, I gather the smell is unpleasant. "I do not know if Edea can still be trusted. I do not know if she ever could."

"Please," I plead. "Give it a day or two, and if I do not improve by then, I'll willingly go to the healer."

"By then it may be too late." His jaw tenses.

Maybe. Maybe not. "Please?" I attempt a seriously pathetic puppy-dog plead. He rolls his eyes but does not answer.

We approach the sanctuary within the tree. The habitants likely still sleeping for all is quiet.

He takes us in, not through the front entrance but another door, avoiding many of the most used spaces. The hallways he carries me through are dim and empty. As is my room when he shoves the door open with his foot.

He lays me on the bed, removes my shoes, and pulls back the sheets. "Your clothing should be burned. They are ruined and reek of whatever magic she used." He yanks a nightshirt from the drawer and tosses it at me. "I shall retrieve a healing salve."

"Leave it," I say. "No salve." Nothing that might interfere with the magic performed.

"Deona." His response is pure argument. I narrow my gaze. How many times must I tell him? "Ana," he corrects.

"Let it be, Raundel." I kick my legs back and forth over the side of the bed. "See. Already showing better mobility."

He doesn't look convinced. Instead, he drops his hands on his hips and glares at me. As if he expects the stare down to change my mind somehow.

Colored lines continue to race through everything around me, but softer than before. I definitely won't mention that new development, for then he would surely insist on the healer, or Madame Marrouske.

"So…" I pull the nightshirt into my lap and wad it in my hands. "Are you going to give me some privacy to change? Or should I disrobe right here in front of you?"

He growls and stomps from the room.

My shoulders droop, my back hunching. Whether or not he will keep my secret, Gaea only knows. I cross my fingers and raise them at my side, give them a solid jerk, as if the action will tether Raundel to my will.

I glance down at my torn and bloody clothing. I could use a bath, but I don't want to wash anything away that Edea smeared into my skin…just in case it's still working its mojo. With slow, awkward motions dictated by my body's discomfort, I tug my belt free and begin to unbutton my shirt.

The dark lines across the room shift and Shadow steps into view. "What happened to you?" His expression is five shades past concerned.

Clutching my shirt closed, I spin to face him. "What are you doing here?" As in here, in my room, without my permission. First Azure, now Shadow. What is it about the Augur Clan's men?

He balks, his head jerking back. "I feel responsible. It was me who got you outside of the sanctuary. I needed to make sure you returned unharmed." He drops an appraising gaze over me. "Which it would appear you have not." His head tilts toward the door at his back. "Plus, you got caught."

"Don't worry about any of that." I button my top and

twist on the bed to better face him, lifting my left leg onto the bed's surface and bending it back in on itself.

"Again," he says. "What happened to you?"

"Nothing I can't weather," I say matter-of-factly.

His nose crinkles. "I am unfamiliar with that expression."

With a weak eyeroll, I shake my head, then pull my socks free. "It means I'll be fine, and you don't need to worry about me. All I need is a few hours of sleep." Or more.

He scowls. "I did not get the impression Raundel agrees with that sentiment."

I wave off the implication. "Raundel worries too much."

"Does he?" Shadow lowers his gaze. "You reek of magic. Immense and Ancient."

A frown is quick to tug at my mouth. It makes sense that whatever Edea did, it would be old like she is. And big, because...why not?

Dragging back a deep breath and releasing it slowly, I allow the action to sooth me. As much as possible, that is.

"The magic is Balance Bringer related," I say. "You don't need to worry about it."

His eyes narrow. "Like the magic used on Jaden was...is... Balance Bringer related? Look how well he is fairing?"

He'll be fine. He's going to be fine. Fine fine fine.

Shadow takes a seat beside me on the bed, his hand dropping over mine. "I just worry about you, Ana. We all do. You are family now." Because of my ties to Jaden. My ties of which they are unaware of to their mother, Opal—Edea.

"Thank you." I flip my hand, matching us palm to palm, wrapping my fingers around his hand and squeeze. "You're concern means a lot to me."

His gaze warms, and a gentle smile spreads across his lips.

Bumping my shoulder against his, I nudge him away from me. "Now go," I say. "I'm tired and need to change."

He huffs, but doesn't argue, standing and stepping away from the bed. "Well," he says, with an air of irritation. "You should know that while you were gone, Azure was looking for you. Ruby too." He grimaces, no doubt imagining the reasons Ruby might want to find me.

"Of course, they were." I frown. "Did they say what they wanted?"

"No. They were each looking for you, separately." Another grimace. Another supporting comment that Ruby's intentions aren't likely pretty.

Great. I can't even imagine what Ruby wants. Maybe she found out about me and Azure working together, and she wants to yell at me some more.

"I gave them both the same story. Said I had last seen you visiting Clef." I nod. "But as it turns out, Clef is now out of the forced sleep, and is awake and talking. He has no memory of your visit."

Because I didn't. Still, I smile. "Clef's awake? Is he feeling better?"

"Yes." He heaves a heavy breath, and I spot both relief and joy in the action. "I may have suggested to him that you had visited while he was still dozing. I am not sure he accepted my explanation, but there it is."

"Thank you, Shadow." I reach for his hand and fold it between both of mine. "I really asked too much of you, but I am so very glad you helped me."

"Then everything we did was worth it?" His face widens, his gaze seeking.

"I hope so," I reply. "We should know soon enough."

His head nods and nods, his lips pulling gently to the side.

"Now, if you don't mind. I'm still messy and tired and would like to get some sleep."

His lips pucker, and he glances over me once more. "I understand." He turns for the door but peers back before stepping out. "After you have rested, I expect you to explain this to me." His finger circles in the air between us, indicating my physical state.

I simply smile, not wanting to commit.

When I am finally alone, I set my now dirty and blood-splattered crystal wristbands and pendant on the nightstand and dress for bed. Curl up with my pillow. My body quickly secures slumber, but peace…no.

I find myself standing in an overly opulent room covered in a thin layer of ice. Furniture and fixtures dripping with ice crystals.

A pint-sized Dreya spins toward me. "Get out!"

EIGHT

An ice encrusted castle. Once home to my father. My family. Aunt Dreya, too. A place now likely filled with the horrors of her. A place Dohlan told me to never go.

The walls bang and bang and bang.

"Get out," young Dreya yells again.

Bang, bang, crash.

And then ice. So much ice. Covering the walls and floors of the opulent home.

A door slams. Heard, not seen. And a horse appears beside me, nuzzles into the curve of my neck. He's large and powerful with shimmering hair of black and a swirling opal horn. Belmiso.

"Remember"

Behind him, the white unicorn, Velsa, moves into view. *"Time to bloom, spread your wings and fly."*

Bang, bang. Clomp, clomp, clomp.

The imagery of two different experiences is overlapping, bleeding together. The frozen castle and a visit from two unicorns.

Only the dreams, the visions, are interrupted. Ruby is shaking me and yelling. "You stay away from him, or I will curse you against all men, not just Jaden." My eyes are heavy, unable to stay open for her rant. But then, they don't need to. Someone is pulling her away, and I'm slipping back into grisly walks, down long, wintery-encased hallways.

Who am I to stay away from? Azure? What does she mean, cursed against Jaden?

Thoughts of Ruby and her accusations slip into a back recess, where they will be addressed later. Yet, as I continue to move through my glacial nightmare, the red marks where she grabbed me in the hall the other day twist and glow against my skin. Ice, Ruby, a nudge from a horse…a unicorn.

And Deona, grabbing my shoulders. *"Do you think your father is trapped within the ice of the castle?"*

What? No. I shake my head. "I witnessed his death on the battlefield."

"Are you sure?"

Please don't put doubts in my head over this. Please don't.

"I lost my father to the nethers. I at least found a way to visit him. If there is even a spark of a chance for yours…"

"I saw him die." My tone is splintered with finality and pain.

She bows her head. "Very well." She stares at the ground between our feet for an endless number of minutes and then fades into the ice-induced fog of the dream.

Velsa, the white unicorn, bursts through the cloud of fog, trotting down the glazed-over castle interior. She comes to a halt a foot and a half away. Stares at me with unwavering intent.

"You are a light," she says. *"But remember, for a light to shine at its brightest, the dark must be at its side. Without the dark, the light does not exist."*

I don't understand. I press my palms to the sides of her muzzle, gaze pleading for an explanation.

"*Light and dark in balance, Balance Bringer. Do not fear it. Embrace it. Own it. And then shine above it.*"

Edea's words return to the forefront of my mind. "*You must find a way to assimilate the darkness and balance the scales.*"

When I eventually swim out of sleep, I pull myself upward knowing several things: I must decipher the messages from the unicorns and visit the castle. But why must I go to the castle, my father and Dreya's home, I cannot yet say.

I only hope, by some strange miracle, a shred of credence exists within Deona's speculation about my dad. Maybe, just maybe, he isn't really dead.

Can Fae survive being frozen in ice for countless years?

Also, Ruby implied she cursed me. So, I need to find out if she really did and in what way.

With a yawn and a stretch, I slowly pry my eyes open a sliver. Blink against the burn at the back of my eyeballs. I think I would rather still be sleeping, but I have personal needs to which I must attend.

"Good. You're finally awake." Gitta leaps from the chair at my right. "Raundel asked to be informed as soon as you awoke."

I rub my eyes and then push to my elbows. "Have I been asleep long?"

"I'm not sure," she says. "Twenty, thirty hours, I think."

I blink wide, a tiny gasp escaping my throat. "Seriously?" I pull back the sheets and slowly swing my legs over the side. My sleeping shirt slides up my leg, exposing the cuts Edea sliced into me. They are fully healed, leaving only a hairline scar.

Gitta shrugs. "There was a bit of excitement around here. You missed it since you were sleeping, but you seemed to have brought with you a curious change from the daily norm."

"Like what?" I comb my fingers through my hair in a weak attempt to tame my unruly bedhead.

She smirks at my attempt. "Since Raundel has been eager to talk to you, I am sure he will tell you all about it."

With a frown pulling across my lips, I slip from the bed, the floor cold and hard against my feet.

Gitta eyes me wearily. "I heard you were not in the best of shape. Are you sure you are ready for that?" She waves her hand to reference my intention of getting out of bed.

My cuts are healed, and I slept as long as a hibernating bear. "I'm good. Plus, I kind of don't have a choice." Not fully awake, and with legs of rubber, I make my way across the room slowly.

"Then you won't mind if I step away for a minute?" she asks, grabbing the door and holding it open for me.

"You're not really needed here. I'll be fine," I say and consider her comment regarding Raundel. "And also, you don't *need* to tell anyone." Like the large, overbearing white stag elf.

"Good try." She rolls her eyes, waves me off, and heads down the hallway. No doubt, to inform the mighties of the sanctuary that the rule breaker is now awake.

At least I'll get a few free minutes while I tend to my needs before the interrogation begins. I head straight to the washroom. When I am done, Raundel is in the outer hallway, waiting on me. He's leaning against the wall with ankles crossed and arms folded, a ready-to-peel-back-my-skin look in his eyes.

The streaming ribbons of colors I experienced when Dohlan brought me back the other morning are still visible in everything. They blend in a cohesive manner, adding a new depth to all the elements around me. What I now spy coursing through Raundel suggests age, wisdom, strength, and significant levels of annoyance.

I'm really not ready for whatever it is he is bringing my way.

"She finally rises." His voice is bitter.

"Do we need to do this now?" I ask. "Or can it wait for a bit?" I'm hungry and I want to check on Jaden, especially after recalling Ruby's threat about a curse.

Raundel pushes forward to a straight-backed stand. "And why should I allow you any more time than I already have?"

"Duh." I pivot and head in the direction of Jaden's room. Raundel follows. "Because I'm a living being with needs." I glance over my shoulder to him and note no reaction in his features. "I've been sleeping during all that time you supposedly have allowed me," I say. "Now that I am awake, before you bury me with questions and reprimands, I have an empty belly to fill, and a still healing Tracer to check in on." Plus Mo. I need to make sure she's all right after all she went through.

It suddenly occurs to me that I don't actually know if Jaden is still in his healing sleep. But since he wasn't waiting at my bedside, I'm going to guess yes.

"He *is* still sleeping, right?" I toss Raundel a questioning gaze.

"He slumbers, yes."

"And Mo?" I haven't seen her since Raundel carried her out of the cottage the other night.

"She is well. Although, I suspect she would favor a visit from you." A hint of warmth touches his delivery.

"I'll visit soon." *I hope.* "And what of my brother, is he back yet?"

"No."

I jerk to a stop and spin on him. "What do you mean he's not yet back?"

"He has not returned to the tearman."

"I got that part." My fist clenches, and my body goes rigid with tension. "But it's been days. Like, days upon days. Shouldn't he have returned by now?" My mind begins to race with endless, unthinkable scenarios. "What if something happened?"

Raundel's chest rises and falls, his brow-arched gaze

peering deep into my eyes. "Lord Ryland is fine. Our assets have informed us that the majority of the military forces have moved out, leaving behind roughly two battalions to safeguard the city."

They left? I balk. "And my mom? Brother?"

"Your mother is the commanding officer," he says. "It is my understanding, she left with the departing troops."

My heart flops. Cracks and crumbles. She was so close... and I didn't get to see her. Hug her and tell her how sorry I am for everything that has happened.

My lips part, preparing to ask about my brother and Zarah, but Raundel cuts me off.

"The young chronicler has been moving through the streets of Palinot, paying many visits to collect the varied views of witnessed history." His brow lifts. "Lord Ryland has remained at her side."

Ry didn't go with Mom but stayed with Zarah, so... "They'll likely be back soon then?"

"Possibly. I cannot say."

I frown at his answer, but accept it nonetheless, and turn back on my mission to find Jaden's room. We're close and within a few steps, I am pushing my way through the door, into his space.

He's laid out on the bed as he was the last time I saw him, only this time, no evidence of any dark bleeding infection is evident. Jaden is clean of the black gunk.

Thank Gaea.

He's beautiful and peaceful and...off.

I stare at him, moving deeper into the room. Raundel starts to follow me in, but I spin around and press him back into the hallway.

"It's all right if you wait out here," I say to his grunted complaint, then close the door between us and turn back to Jaden.

The familiar colors dominated by shades of green swim

over and through his resting body, but a few threads of grey and brown are present. They are so incredibly dark, they boarder on black. I shift closer and study the weave of colored energy shifting through his biological network.

The darkened strains could be a fragment of the infection left behind, but...

I lean near and scrutinize the energy.

I don't think they are. I think what I am seeing is something different, yet to be explained. Dark and warm, I want to slip my hand through the shadowy colors of his verve.

I bite my lip and contemplate the idea that what I'm looking at might somehow be related to Ruby's curse. Only, she said she cursed me against Jaden. Not the other way around.

If that is the case, would the traces of such a curse be visible in him? Or only in me? And if I were able to see the curse upon him, would I find it oddly appealing...as I do now?

I glance down at my arm and the faint red marking twisting around my wrist. Threads of red energy radiate and shift in a pattern around the magical imprint.

Red, like Ruby's love connection gift. And red for her enacted curse. "What did you do?" I whisper, as if Ruby could hear me and would give me an honest answer.

"I don't know what's going on here," I say to Jaden, not expecting any type of response. "But we'll figure it out." I drop my hand to his exposed arm and graze my fingers along his skin. "You will be healthy and strong once more. I promise."

The words have barely passed my lips when a shock akin to a bed of eels electrifies my fingers and races up my arm, straight to my chest.

I yelp, yank back my hand.

The release is a brief reprieve. Jaden's hand jolts upward, his fingers locking around my wrist, halting my escape. His eyes have not opened, and his casual breathing remains unchanged. It is as if his limb has reacted in a sort of autopilot state.

The tips of his fingers morph to black and send wave after wave of voltaic-powered pain through my body. It's a sadistic twist on the beautiful thrum of electricity that Jaden and I share though our Balance Bringer and Tracer connection.

This, I decide, must be Ruby's curse. The impossibility of touch without utter agony. Subversive and brilliant.

The thundering hooves of a herd of unicorns crash in my chest.

My pounding heart is spiked with terror over the inability to touch Jaden…and…blackened fingers. *What does that mean?*

Each second Jaden and I are connected is another stab of excruciating voltage jolting through my entire system. I yell and pull against Jaden's hold. He doesn't easily release, so I put a heavy backward thrust into my attempt.

My arm rips free of imprisonment, the motion sending me crashing backwards across the room.

At my holler, Raundel explodes into the room, just in time to catch me before I slam into the wall.

Jaden's hand has returned to its original resting place upon the bed, his fingers looking normal, without a trace of dark shading.

"What happened?" Raundel asks, righting me and glancing over me for damage.

"Jaden." I jab a point in his direction. "I can't touch him without getting electrocuted. Ruby cursed us."

His eyebrow arcs, and he shifts a curious peer over my sleeping Tracer, then returns his attention to me. "This is a new predicament in the saga of the Balance Bringer." He almost sounds entertained by my pain.

"Ruby is problematic," he continues. "She and her friends were escorted from the tearman yesterday."

My mouth pops open. "She's gone?" I shake my head. He nods.

"She was provoking trouble."

And she was escorted from the safety of the sanctuary... along with her friends. "Which friends?" I ask. "Will Edea be upset once she finds out?"

He smirks, a minute laugh in the gesture. "Edea's emotions are not of my concern. As for those who left, Shadow was invited to go for his participation in helping you follow us to the cottage the other night."

Oh, my dear Gaea. What have I done? Poor Shadow.

"And the little injured one..." he says about Clef. "When he heard that Shadow and Ruby were being asked to leave, he decided to make the exit with them."

I press my folded fingers to my lip, holding back the worry bubbling inside of me regarding the plight of Jaden's fellow clan members. "Azure? Alabaster?"

He nods at a slight tilt. "For now, they have remained with us here."

So, Ruby and Azure have been split apart. Her hate for me has likely now exploded into full blown revulsion. At least Shadow and Clef are with her to soften the blow. "Is he, Clef, well enough to travel?"

"He shall be fine." Raundel's neck straightens, giving him instant height. "He left something for you. Klarda has it."

I blink wide. "What is it?"

"You'll need to ask Klarda." His gaze shifts to Jaden's sleeping form. "And we shall ask our lady about this new issue the ruby one has bestowed upon you." He presses a light hand to my arm. "Come. Let us go."

I toss Jaden one last fleeting glance and allow Raundel to lead me out of the room and down the hall. If Meira wants to talk to me, that's fine. I have plenty I'd like to talk to her about, too.

"Does Meira know?" I'm guessing she knows I followed them to the cottage.

Shadow's forced departure a likely consequence for having helped me. But does she know I listened in on much of her conversation with Edea. That is the question implied, yet not fully articulated.

He heaves a deep breath. "When we are in ear shot of others, you shall refer to her as Madame Marrouske. That is what everyone here knows her as."

He guides me around a corner making it clear to me he's taking us directly to her chamber. "But to answer your question," he continues. "Yes. When you continued to sleep past a day, and through the things happening around you, mere excuses regarding your unconscious state were no longer sufficient."

I grab his arm and tug him to a stop. He glares down at my hold as if it has crossed the line of offensive. I don't particularly care. Instead, I tug him down a side corridor. One that leads toward the kitchen. "Let me grab some sustenance to go."

He responds with a gesture of indifference, so I lead him on a detour through the kitchen where I grab a chunk of bread, a couple slices of cheese, and a fruit that looks like a pear but tastes like a cross between an apple and an orange. I work on filling the void in my stomach while we continue our path to Madame Marrouske's chamber.

"So...what kind of things?" I say, shepherding us back into conversation. He shoots me a questioning glance. "What kind of things did I sleep through? Gitta hinted that there might be a worthy story in the happenings." I take a bite of the bread. It's fresh and warm and makes my nose instantly happy.

"Gitta is young and has not yet seen much in the way of adventure." He peers at the trail of crumbs I'm leaving in our wake and frowns. "She was in the room when Ruby barged in and started shaking you and yelling. Apparently, the girl was not pleased with the arrangement our lady made for you and the blue-eyed sibling to work together."

As I gathered.

"Gitta took great joy in extracting Ruby, not only from your room, but from the entire wing of the sanctuary."

Wow. Go Gitta. Bet that pissed Ruby off to no end.

"You are already abreast with what happened after that," he continues as we follow the stretched curve of the hallway running along the outer wall of the tree sanctuary. "Shadow and Ruby met with our lady, Lobrka, and me, and were asked to leave."

I'm sure that wasn't uncomfortable at all. I purse my lips. *Shadow's exile is one hundred percent my fault.*

"But…" A heavy sigh rolls through him. "I suspect the *happening* Gitta found the most exciting, would be when that black horse of yours…" *Belmiso.* "Charged into the tearman, crashing his way through the rooms and corridors, until he found you."

"Belmiso was in my room?" My eyes widen. A horse running through these hallways. "What a sight that must have been."

Humor touches the edge of his lips, appears as a gleam in his eye, if only for a nanosecond. "He was at that. The beast was most determined to find you."

I wonder if his intrusion had anything to do with my dream of the unicorns. "And once he found me? What did he do?" I ask.

"Ridiculous beast." Raundel shakes his head. "He nibbled at you. Licked you like you were a ball of sugar." He shrugs his head into his shoulder. "And was content to leave after that."

With a frown pressed to my lips, I contemplate what Belmiso's actions could possibly mean. The messages from the dream replay through my thoughts: Remember, become the butterfly, so that I may spread my wings, and embrace the relationship between the light and the dark.

How does Belmiso nibbling and licking at me have anything to do with any of those?

We arrive at the double doors leading to Madame Marrouske's chamber, but rather than knocking or heading inside, Raundel leads me down a hallway to the left. One I have yet to investigate.

I ogle her chamber door as we move past without even a slight pause.

He slows as we approach an opening on our right. A door sitting slightly ajar. "You may find it interesting to know that several more horses showed up at the front gate. They appear to be friends of your black beast."

My heart pounds an extra beat, and the smile grows wide across my lips. The rest of the herd made it. I press my hand to my chest.

"One of them joined the black one in the raid upon your room." Velsa. I saw her in the dream. "They are all currently grazing in the back portion of the protected outer regions," he adds, bringing us to a full stop in the hallway beside the slightly ajar door.

"Were there three or four?" I ask. "In addition to Belmiso, the black beast," I add.

"Ah." He lifts his chin. "Four showed up, so there is now a total of five."

All of Velsa's herd, plus Zarah's horse Nox. I close my eyes and sigh.

"We are here." Raundel pushes the door open wide and motions for me to enter.

The room beyond is a library, stacked wide and high with endless volumes of stories and knowledge. The end of the space is not visible, the rows of shelving disappearing into the depths of the tree, both wide and high. A few spiral staircases lead up to higher levels, housing more shelves and more books. And several tables are scattered throughout the open aisles, one of which is laden with a multitude of volumes.

Illumination drops from the ceiling in something that looks like membrane balls hung with spider webbing. And a few of the exposed grain lines of the tree's growth lines glow in a warm white light.

My Aunt Meira, Madame Marrouske or our lady to everyone here, sits at a table some fifteen to twenty feet away. She drops a book to the surface, letting the cover slam shut with a thump.

She turns her wise and hard glare upon me. "Start talking." She points to the open seat next to her own. "Explain to me why you thought Edea's idea was worth chancing your life."

NINE

In long, quick strides, I cross the room to her location.

No point in playing it remorseful or coy. I did what I did, and I will not be ashamed. Hopefully, all that I've done and endured will not be in vain. I have yet to find out. Yet to test my elemental connections.

Raundel takes a seat at the table nearest the door and studies the sidewall, pretending not to hear or care about my conversation with Meira.

I drop into a seat across from her, rather than at her side, so that I may lean into the table while staring her straight in the eye. Which I do, with my fingers weaved together, elbows propped on the hard surface.

"What do you have to say for yourself?" she prompts, pushing all the books to the side, clearing the space between us.

I had actually been giving the situation a lot of thought, in between the various questions and answers Raundel and I volleyed back and forth during our approaching walk. With a heavy sigh, I push my weight into the back of the chair.

"The way I see it," I say. "My soul is plenty old, and there is a ton of available information in here…" I tap the side of my head. "Just waiting to be accessed and utilized. After all, I remember it all, as if I have lived it. And, in a manner of speaking, I have. You may be old and experienced, but in many ways, so am I. So, when it comes to matters involving me and my destiny…" I use air quotes. "I don't rightly appreciate you and Aunt Edea keeping secrets."

Meira's gaze narrows, and the edges of her eyes crinkle. "So, this is what we get when you have been exposed to the ways of the outerworld?"

My eyebrows arch, but I don't respond.

Her shoulders droop. "I suppose you are correct. At this point, there is no reason you should not be involved and informed. Now that you are bound and remember your many selves and sister-selves."

I grin, feeling the win touch my eyes and cheeks.

"But you still have the elemental gifts to address," she adds.

"Yes, well." I nod, wishing I'd had the opportunity to test my elemental connection since awakening. Actually…

I glance around our surroundings. The tree we are currently inside. The air all around us. And somewhere I know there's water.

The Lagoon of Lucidity. The Tears of Clarity. Wells, pools, streams, and more.

"What are you doing?" she asks.

"Checking something." I splay my hand at my side, palm up, and whisper to nature and the wind. Neither responds.

"Daughter." The title emanates from all around me. *"All things in due time."*

The warm glow of grainlines in the room brightens, and the white hidden designs on my skin come to life. They are a painting of ancient words and meanings, long lost and forgotten. For a moment, the walls and my body are shining bright, and then the light is gone. The room once again normal.

I startle and swing my gaze around the interior of the long, tall library. "What was that?"

"The light? I can only guess. The voice..." Meira's eyes turn mellow, weigh with sadness. "Glynnii, Deona's mother. Or, actually, the tree of life. As it absorbed Glynnii's essence."

I recall Deona's memory of learning the truth from the tree, many lifetimes ago. What I don't remember is the tree talking to any version of me between Deona and now. "She's been quiet all these millenniums. Why now?"

"Who is to say." Meira chuckles lightly. "Maybe she, too, senses the changes coming." Her gaze intensifies. "The changes in you, and what you are. What you've done."

I huff. "Maybe all that I have done, all that I am, is what's needed. The old ways clearly weren't working. I mean..." I throw my arms wide. "All these lifetimes settling balance, or attempting to do so, and look where this world is...no better."

"Worlds," Meira corrects, to which I nod.

Worlds which I, as Deona, created during a young girl's fit. "My point is, it's probably time for a new approach."

She frowns. "And you know this because of your many remembered lifetimes?"

"Partially." I shrug a shoulder. "But also, because I'm paying attention to all the messages that keep getting thrown at me." I jolt to a stand and lean over the table. "And let me tell you, some of those messages are a mess to figure out."

I release a breath, letting my shoulders droop with the action.

"I want to do right by you..." I motion to her. "By the worlds, by everything and everyone in those worlds. I just think, this time I'm going to rely on my gut a little more than on your direction." Meira's frown deepens. "Let's face it, auntie, you haven't actually been getting it done. And so, when this major disconnect happened in me, and Aunt Edea suggested she might be able to help me mend the issue faster than a hundred laundry lessons, I figured why not."

"You thought you could cheat the process? Skip the work and get the reward?" she asks.

"That's not it at all," I rebuke and settle back in my seat. "I didn't skip the process. I changed it. And trust me, I gave heavily of myself in order to atone."

"And did it work?" Her question is the same one Raundel had.

Not yet. My lips pucker. *But hopefully soon. Rebirth takes time,* Dohlan had said. He told me to rein in my impatience. But for the sake of everyone and everything, I pray the process doesn't take too long.

"It'll happen," I reply. "I recently received several messages from the energies. They're preparing me." I'm not so sure I'm speaking the truth, but I hold my head high, keep my back straight, and exude confidence all the same.

"I hope you are right." She folds her hands together.

I am. "I heard most of what you and Edea talked about the other night. I know you both have doubts. About me. About what I currently am."

Her lips pull to the side. "Then you know the many lengths she has gone to in order to force conditions to fit her vision."

"I know." Some if not all. "But there are still many things I need to understand."

"Such as?" She tilts her head.

My hands flip palms up, and my chin lifts. "Where do I begin?" The list starts forming in my mind, and I check off the items as I vocalize them.

I ask about Jaden, and whatever it is that is happening to him. I mention Ruby's curse, the electric shock, Jaden's darkening fingers, and the change in his energy makeup. Which brings me to seeing energy running through everything around me.

To this, Meira cocks an eyebrow.

I ask her why a young Balance Bringer named Izza is

trapped in a world where none of the other versions of myself remember her. I want to know why that young girl is haunted by Garr.

I want to understand what happened to him, that changed him from the friend Deona once had to the thing he is today. And why I got hints of him when I touched the wound on Jaden's leg.

I ask about her plan to rectify all the previous mistakes made, by her and Edea, me and Jaden.

Meira has no definitive answer to any of my questions and concerns. All she can give me is an "I am working on it" or "It is being looked into." Neither of those responses settle well with me.

We sit across the table staring at one another, exasperated.

"This has been terribly enlightening," I say, my words steeped in sarcasm.

"What was it Glynnii said to you?" she muses about the message from the tree of life. "All things in due time." She smiles, appearing unphased by the failure to answer any of my questions. "We shall discover all that we must know, together."

I hold back a cynical laugh. "The unicorns told me it was time for me to bloom," I say. "To spread my wings and fly."

At this, Meira appears taken back. "I. I did not realize the unicorns had any contact with you beyond that night." She's referring to the night two unicorns, one white and one black, visited Deona. The Ying and Yang of Hiddenkel's fantastical world.

"They have, and they do."

I glance toward Raundel. His legs are stretched out, and his head is bowed. But somewhere beyond him, beyond the outer walls of this massive tree, Velsa the unicorn and her herd of four graze nearby.

I return my attention to Meira. "Even now, they have been with me. They helped me get to you, for example." I narrow my gaze and study her expression. "Curious that you had no knowledge of their involvement."

"A unicorn hasn't been sighted since that night," she says, her eyes giving away the thoughts and calculations taking place in her head.

"I imagine they haven't." Because unicorns use magic to look like regular horses…to most.

"It is said…" Her tone is soft. "That unicorns inspire action, rather than getting actively involved."

The muses of the fantastical world. Maybe so, but I won't turn down a single ounce of inspiration.

The room falls into silence, and neither of us speaks for a minute or three. Across the large space, Raundel coughs, the tiny spark pushing me forward with my thoughts.

"What do you think the plan should be?" I ask, leaning deeply into the table's surface. "Because I'll tell you a thing or two about my agenda."

"I'm listening," she says, her gaze patient.

"I am going to mend my elemental connection, even if I must grovel to do so. Then I am going to balance Dreya right out of current history. Wipe her infection on the worlds clean away. And I believe a visit to my family's old home…" The frozen castle. "Is the place to start that particular part of the plan."

She shakes her head firmly. "Neither Dreya nor the castle are your mission. You need to set them outside of your concern."

"How can you say that?" I jump to my feet, my right shoulder jerking back. Out of the corner of my eye, I catch Raundel's gaze shift our direction. "She destroyed my dad, my sister, and has enslaved countless beings across all of Hiddenkel. Not to mention, covering the land with sticky black infection. How can she not be a priority?"

"She is merely an agent, not the source to be addressed," Meira replies. "You need to stay focused on the proper path, finish what you must for the task of balance, and then all things will fall into place."

I huff with a frown and stare her down.

"Put more work into fixing your elemental connections," she continues. "Listen to what they have to say, *then* determine if your desired path is the proper one or not."

My frown deepens.

Lifetime after lifetime I have listened to her, followed her without question, and I can't help but feel like no progress has been made. Am I wrong? Or is she simply too stubborn and trapped in her ways, like Edea stated?

Deciding this conversation is no longer serving either of us, I move around the side of the table and head for the door. But she quickly rises to her feet and snags my arm, pulling my gaze.

"You must learn to embrace patience," she says. "Going after Dreya is a foolish move and could end up getting people you care about hurt...or worse."

Or worse. In other words, dead.

Her eyes and posture soften. Extending her age-spotted, fragile hand, she tenderly fluffs my hair like my mother used to do.

"As an instrument of a higher purpose, you will always walk a fine line, from which it will be easy to slip, get lost, and overly entranced in the wrong things. It is your job to rise above petty emotions such as revenge. Same goes for the glory of accomplishment. All that you do should be about, and for, the people and elements you serve—they who benefit from your deeds. Not so much the deeds themselves. That is why you exist...to bring balance, not to ride off on a wild crusade fueled by emotions."

Her words stick in my gut like tar.

"*She's talking about pride,*" Crystia whispers in my ear, telling me something I already know. Still, it's good to hear her voice.

It's the first I've heard from either sister, or any incarnation, since Edea's ritual.

With lips pressed tight together, I drop my head and heave a breath. "I'll continue to work at fixing my elemental connections. I'll think on the rest, and we shall see."

I walk from the room with my head held high.

"I am here to protect and guide," she calls after me. "It has always been my honor. Utilize my power and knowledge."

I leave the library and head to destinations unknown. No one follows.

My INTENTION WAS to check my anger and potential sulking beside the library door and go check in with Mo to see how she is doing. To hear her, no doubt wild, story. Instead, my movements take me right back to Jaden, pulled to him by an internal feeling, new and unfamiliar to me.

When I arrive, Azure is in the room. A depressing sight, he sits in a chair at Jaden's bedside, with his head hanging low, and a death grip upon his brother's hand.

"Oh, I'm sorry." I turn to leave. "I'll come back later."

Azure's gaze snaps to mine. Exhaustion plays heavily at his features. "It's fine," he replies and stretches his arms wide. In the flurry of the motion, something about Jaden catches my attention. Rapid eye movement behind his lids. But when I focus on his face, nothing appears to have changed.

"I am in need of a break anyway." Azure stands. "Want to spell me?" I give him a silent nod and we switch places, him making his way toward the door.

"I heard about the members of your clan," I say, not wanting to bring attention to Ruby specifically. "Are you okay?"

He turns back. "I've been separated from them before. Many times, for long periods. I'll be fine." He sighs and sweeps his gaze back at his brother...my sleeping Tracer. "In that respect."

His words give me pause, and I scrutinize the way he stares at Jaden.

"But not in others?" I push. "This situation has been hard on me. I can't imagine how it must be for you."

His eyes cloud with something I can't pinpoint. The sight reminds me of a weaker version of Jaden's expression when he is clouded with future visions. "Things have been changing and the longer I am here, the less I feel like I know myself."

"What do you mean?"

"I feel Jaden, in here..." He two-finger points to his head. "And in here." He drops a flat palm over his heart. "And when I peer in the mirror, there are times when I am unsure who it is I am looking at."

Azure feels Jaden, just as Jaden can, or did, feel me. Is this a two-parts-of-the-same-soul sort of deal? I study the energy lines coursing through his body and pick up on several signatures similar to Jaden's. *I wonder.*

He shakes his head, letting his gaze drop to my feet. "Sometimes, I think he is trying to tell me something."

I gasp. "You can communicate with him? Like mind to mind?"

Crystia and Kaia whisper messages in my mind, but they are now on the other side of the veil, parts of my separated soul now returned to me. Jaden is not dead...but he is part of a shared soul with Azure, so maybe...

His face tightens. "I am not sure. If so, not well. I am fumbling around in my attempts."

I bite my lip, an idea blooming to life. "Do you think you could pull me in so that I can see, feel, hear, whatever it is you do when you are in one of those connected states with him?" My gaze bounces to Jaden, then back to Azure.

"Possibly." He rakes his hand through the hair at his crown. "I guess I could try."

I brighten. Straighten, a tiny hopeful smile curling my lips.

"Later, though," he adds. "I need to wash up, eat, rest, and reenergize, before I make any further attempts with Jaden."

I let him know I understand, and he takes his leave. I, on the other hand, settle into the one chair placed in the room and watch Jaden breathe. I can't touch him, not without physical pain...to me, at least...so I make myself comfortable and rest my arm against the edge of the bed, three inches of space between his body and my arm.

I confess all my thoughts regarding my visit with Madame Marrouske, my aunt Meira from another life. "I wish you could talk to me," I say. "Help me figure out what to do."

The weight of my choices, the expectations set upon me, begin to press upon my desire to move. The desire to keep my eyes open.

I shouldn't be tired, I tell myself. I just slept over a day's worth of time.

And still, my limbs are laden.

Closing my eyes, I begin to sing for Jaden...and to keep me awake. In a melodic voice, I sing a Celtic lullaby I don't recall ever learning. Something from a previous me, I assume.

"...who is it swinging you to and fro...

"I am thinking it is an Angel fair,

"The Angel that looks on the gulf from the lowest stair..."

My fingers stretch, start to reach to touch him. Then realization kicks me in the gut, and I pull back. Keep singing, hoping somehow my words will reach him and wake him up.

"It is he whose faintest thought is a world afar.

"It is he whose wish is a seven-mooned leaping star.

"It is he, sweet Jaden, to whom you and I and all things flow."

My voice gets smaller and smaller until it is no more. I lay my forehead upon my resting arm and hum. Hum and wish. Wish and hum.

"Please, Gaea," I whisper to the bedsheets. "Bring me... bring us answers. Bring us results."

I close my eyes and empty the thoughts from my head, hoping Gaea will fill the void with her wisdom. But after endless minutes of waiting, maybe twenty, and with no wonderous inspiration taking shape, I dive into the thick volumes of my many lives, searching through lifetime after lifetime for advice.

Do I follow Meira once more? Or do I finally walk my own path?

I become absorbed in discussions between me, Crystia, a few words from Kaia, Deona, Estala, Fianna, and so many more. The passing of time becomes little less than an afterthought. A tiny part of me is only vaguely aware when Azure steps back into the room.

My eyes are still closed, my thoughts focused elsewhere, but other senses—warrior or animalistic—track his every shift and twitch as he moves through the room. Coming to stand beside me, he slips his fingers into the relaxed curve of Jaden's hand.

"I am back, brother," he says softly, as if thinking I am asleep, and he is trying not to wake me. "Has Ana managed to evoke any change in you?"

He places his palm upon my shoulder, an ultra-light touch, and yet a dampened jolt rocks my system.

My head snaps up and the room around me is hazy. Azure looks down at me with a weary smile, but he, too, is fuzzy. If I weren't sitting down, I think the ground would slip out from under me. Sights and sounds are distorted, and my equilibrium is off kilter, as if I have stepped into yet another dream.

Maybe I have.

Or...

Maybe Azure has somehow pulled me into a mindscape, in hopes of connecting with Jaden.

Only Jaden still rests peacefully on the bed, and...

And...

My upper body straightens, leans away, and my eyes grow ever wider.

Two dark spindle-like horns protrude from the sides of Jaden's forehead. They're like short, dark, unicorn horns, only with two, instead of one. And each possessing a slight curve in their backward thrust. They are unlike Garrthmal's horns, but slightly reminiscent.

I blink twice and the vision before me does not change.

I whisper Jaden's name.

His eyes pop open, and his head turns to me, his gaze filled with a swirl of smoke and shadow. He flick's Azure's hand away and reaches for me, his fingers dipped in shades of iron. His lips move, mouthing my name, but no sound comes out.

With a lift and a twist, he stands and steps away from the bed...the sheets slipping to the floor, exposing every perfect inch of him. Sculpted lines and chorded muscles. His leg appears healed, his skin tone is healthy...and utterly other.

Only his hands, eyes, and newly grown horns are a noted change. I push my chair back and stand, no clue as to what I should do. Jaden fills the space before me, my Tracer, and yet I don't understand what it is I am looking at.

How is he...why is he so changed?

"Anala." He steps toward me and I back away, knocking into the chair. He pushes forward again and again, until I am trapped against the wall. "Do not run from me. You are all that I need, and I am all that you want. It is because of you, because of us, that I am what I am."

Grabbing my wrists, he pins me, dips his face to the curve of my neck, and grazes his teeth against the exposed skin in the curve of my neck and shoulders.

A shiver, coupled with warmth and desire, races over me. "Jaden?" My voice sounding far too mousy, but I'm at a loss for what to do. Is he still Jaden? Is Jaden trapped inside? If either are true, I don't want to hurt him. "Please."

His body stiffens and he shifts back a step, his face a torn expression of confusion and anguish. "Ana?" His eyes clear and the horns sink into his skin, leaving my Jaden before me.

In a blink, he no longer stands, but is laid out on the bed beneath the sheet, and I am sitting in the chair, near his side. The scene, our placements…it's as if someone flipped a switch and reset the room…or the moment.

Azure lifts his hand from my shoulder and steps away. "I am sorry I didn't warn you."

I spin hard in the seat and stare at Azure. Unleash my anger. "What the heck was that?"

"I have no idea." He shakes his head. "That is what I have been trying to figure out."

TEN

I'm not sure what it was I experienced, but whatever it was, it couldn't have been real.

Jaden looking and acting like a dark prince of...of...I don't know what?

I shake my head, and shivers jolt through every piece of me. And yet, I can't stop staring at him, appearing ever so peaceful and beautiful in his sleep, while something sultry, alluring dwells beneath the surface.

Not that he wasn't already those things.

Only, what I just witnessed magnified the pull of him in a wicked, twisted, I-hate-to-admit-I-kind-of-want-it sort of way.

With his hand at my elbow, Azure herds me from the room, and we decide to keep the experience, Jaden's condition, just between us...at least, until we figure out what's real and what's not, and what it all means.

My hand wraps around the door handle, and I pause, reluctant to leave. All I can think about is the power of him, how it enveloped me, and...

I try not to entertain the memory, try not to look, but I

glance back at him and recall the way he stood before me, bare and breathtaking.

Azure is close on my heels, yanking the door open in my hesitation. "You appear to be feeling better," he says, likely as eager as I am to direct our thoughts elsewhere. "I expect this means we'll be paired for chore duty again tomorrow."

Immediate mood killer. I return my attention to him, to our exit.

"Put more work into fixing your elemental connections." Meira's words ring in my ears, and I roll my eyes.

"Unless, of course," he continues. "You've fixed your *issue.*"

Nope. "We'll likely be working." *Giving us more alone time to contemplate this new Jaden situation.* I step free of the room and walk straight into Mo.

She startles and jumps back. I, too, jolt. But the second my surprise thaws, I throw my arms around her and hug tight. Try to bury my guilt for not having visited her immediately after my meeting with Meira, deep within the embrace.

"Well," she chokes out the word. "Unexpected, but I do enjoy this welcome."

"We were all so worried about you." I step back and take in the sight of her. She has cleaned up and put herself together. Any signs of her ordeal with Edea, gone.

"Not everyone." She shoots Azure a nasty look.

"Ignore him," I say, waving him away.

He seems to relish the opportunity to escape and does so promptly, leaving a quick reminder about tomorrow's chore session in his wake. I know it isn't really the chores he is thinking about, but Jaden.

I watch his departure and then wrap my arm around Mo. "We have so much to catch up on."

I hold no answers on how to help or understand Jaden, and so I need Mo to distract me.

"I say we do." Her eyes widen. "How about we start with the ears. When did that happen?"

My head flinches back. "What are you talking about?"

"Have you not looked in a mirror recently?" She blinks twice. "You have cute, petite ear points."

I have what? Elven ears? I run my finger along the edge of my ears and, sure enough, my ears are nowhere as long and pointy as Raundel's or Lobrka's, but they are definitely pointer than they were a week ago. "How in the…"

I blink. Blink.

"You are full of surprises." An amused smile graces her lips.

Why hasn't anyone said anything about my ears before now?

No sooner does the question form in my head than I am remembering Ruby saying I had donkey ears, and Dohlan calling my new look sexy. The shape of my ears has likely been changing since the binding.

How had I not noticed? If Ry was here, he would have made me aware. Same with Jaden or Zarah.

I release a sigh. I miss my team. *My* family.

The girl I was in high school is dissolving into something new. Hair and eye color changed. The appearance of disappearing skin markings. And now this…pointy Fae or elven ears. I'm Ana, and Deona, and bits of all the others in between.

I search the memories of my past selves for something similar and discover my changes are to be expected.

What else can I look forward to?

A barrier slams into place, blocking me from the memories of my many others.

"*It is best not to know one's future,*" Deona says, softly in my head.

Right. Like what may come of Jaden's condition. I glance at the door to his room. Of course, this situation with Jaden is new territory, so I doubt any existing past-life memories would help his current case.

I wrap my hand around Mo's and tug her away from Jaden's room, wanting to seek a distraction from the transformation I am undergoing and whatever strangeness is happening to Jaden. But Mo slips from my hold and pushes at the door to Jaden's room, then peeks inside.

"He's sleeping?" she looks back at me.

"Lately, that's all he does." I tilt my head, suggesting we take our conversation elsewhere.

We move to the dining hall and chat over warm mugs of broth. At her request, I go first, filling her in on *most* everything that happened since we got separated. She heard bits and pieces, witnessed the exodus of Ruby and Shadow, but I am able to fill in a lot of the missing fragments.

"Unfortunately, my story is rather short," she replies. "One minute, I am guarding the old clan mother, at the back of the group, and the next, she has magicked me and is dragging me away from everyone, hiding us in the trees." She shakes her head. "I should have been better prepared. I just thought...old lady, what is she going to do to me? Plus, I believed we were on the same side." She blinks wide. "Lesson learned."

I nod. "The old lady's got mad magic." Mo frowns at my descriptions, likely unfamiliar with slang usage.

"The old woman did say one curious thing to me," she adds.

I give her a questioning smile, encouraging her to continue her story.

"She said she knew my mom...or knew *of* my mom. Something along those lines. She said my mom moved away an extremely long time ago and no longer dwelled in the realm of Hiddenkel. She also said that I smelled of my mother's realm. That I had been there." She stops, a broken look in her expression. "I cannot recall any realm but this one." she says. "What can that mean?"

"It doesn't mean anything about you, if that's what you're asking."

Her shoulders give off the slightest hint of a shrug. She scans the dining hall before returning her attention to me. "Can we talk about this another time?"

Another time, in some place more private, is what I hear. "Sure."

Edea said Mo smelled of the nethers, the place where Deona's father was forced to live. A place with one way in and no way out, according to Edea. One way out, according to Deona.

I'll definitely be giving this situation deep thought, and Mo and I will talk more on the subject later. But for now, I sense she's now looking for a distraction. Something less heavy and more curious to discuss.

"Did I mention that old lady is Dohlan's mother?" I grimace. And that she altered him like some sick science experiment. The thought churns my stomach.

Her eyes pop wide as quarters. "No." I nod that it's true.

"And speaking of Dohlan, I lost his ring. I think for good this time." I chew on the edge of my lip and try to decide if the lost ring is a good thing or not.

Dohlan made it sound like it was important I keep the darn thing on. Not in a relationship meaning way, but to some other end that I have yet to pry out of him.

"Your story is better than mine." Her smile is rather wicked, as if to imply she finds humor in my messy predicament.

Dohlan, son to Jaden's clan mother...my aunt from my first lifetime, boyfriend to my sister Kaia, enemy to my brother Ry, dream incubus and lurker, constantly finding his way to me. And then he gave me the ring.

That damn ring.

As if she can hear my thoughts, her smile widens. I merely grin back, fully aware that she can't read my mind. "You know," I say. "You're interest in all storylines involving Dohlan is concerning. You wouldn't be developing an unhealthy attraction to him, would you?" Something about him makes it hard to look away, stay away.

It's in the way Edea magicked him.

"Girls have always taken an interest in him. Tell her to stay away," Kaia whispers, causing me to jerk.

Mo laughs, completely unaware of my jealous sister chatting in my ear. "He's not my type."

"And what is your type," I ask, Kaia mirroring my inquiry.

"I am not sure. I always thought I would simply know when I met him or her." She shrugs.

"I'm not convinced it really works that way." But then, it kind of did with Jaden.

Although not so much the first time around, when I was Deona and he was Jove. It took a while, not terribly long, but a while to feel the tug or tether pulling us together.

A large, grayish hand slams to the table in front of me. Pulls away, leaving a small bundle of fabric.

"Gift from Clef," Klarda says, slumping into a seat at my side. With her is Al, who claims a seat beside Mo.

I stare at the tiny swaddle of cloth and something inside of my stomach knots. Clef, with his mind reading gift, had brought me the tainted scythe. What could he have possibly brought me now?

"Aren't you going to open it?" Klarda nudges when I make no move.

Mo leans into the table and stares at the tiny bundle. "Open it, Ana. The curiosity is drowning me."

I don't want to open it here, in front of everyone, and yet...after all Mo has been through, I find it difficult to deny her. Still, it's so tiny, and few things come in packages so small.

"It didn't set off any of the magical wards," Klarda says. "So, it should be fine."

All well and good if it were infectious darkness or a curse I was leery of, but it's not. Reluctantly, I reach forward and tug at the dainty string tied around the bundle. It gives with ease, pulling free and allowing the folds of fabric to unfurrow. The corners drop flat upon the table, exposing a delicate, gold ring. Dohlan's ring.

Exactly as I feared.

I suck back a breath and bite my lip.

Once again, the piece has found me. I can't escape it.

My gaze drops to my hand and the tiniest of scars circling my ring finger. A scar left by the very ring sitting on the table before me.

Mo cracks a bark of disbelief.

One second, we are discussing its absence, and the next, it's making its magical appearance.

Al clears her throat. "Should Jaden be concerned?"

I grab the ring and shove it in my pocket. "Not in the slightest. Clef is merely returning something I thought was lost. If awake and aware, Jaden would be appreciative." Of the intention behind the act, not the return of the ring.

I push away my bowl of broth, no longer interested. The jewelry's reappearance has left a sour taste in my throat.

Breathe breathe breathe. It will be fine. Just fine.

Al sits back straight and releases a heavy breath. "If this ring is nothing of concern," she says. "Why do you look so pale?"

"Do I?" I'll need to learn to better hide my thoughts and emotions. I don't need my face acting as a roadmap to all my internal struggles. "Just worn out, I guess. Madame Marrouske and I were butting heads earlier, and the confrontation has left me in a state."

"Elaborate," Klarda blurts.

At her blunt response, I choke on a laugh.

Do I tell these three everything that was discussed? I think not. "We have a difference in opinion regarding what I should and shouldn't do. That is all." I try to smile and fail.

Al shrugs a shoulder. "She is wise with many lifetimes of experience."

"Am I not, as well?" I counter. "I may not have one long, continuous life of experiences, lessons learned, but now that I have gone through the merging, I remember all my lives. All the success and failures. All the lessons learned along the way."

"Valid point," Al concedes.

Everyone at the table is staring at me. Even beings at the next table over are gazing my direction. As if they are hanging on my every word, unwilling to miss anything said. How had I grabbed their attention in the first place? Did I make a scene? Raise my voice?

"I thought so," I say to Al, then unwind my body from the bench. "Now, if you'll excuse me, I need to visit the facilities." I circle the table and squeeze Mo's shoulder, sending her a secret message; I need a momentary escape. Alone time to absorb the circumstances surrounding the ring's appearance... among other things.

Halfway across the room, before I can slip down the hallway and out of sight, Klarda grabs my arm and swings me around to face her.

She lowers her head and speaks softly. "Pay attention to your surroundings. Most all that you see here, are not here to serve our lady. They are here for the Balance Bringer and all that she represents. Keep that in mind when next you clash with Madame Marrouske."

A slight jolt rocks through me. "Let's say I wanted to undertake a mission that Marrouske doesn't agree with. Would you follow me or stand down by her orders?"

"I am one who is here for the Balance Bringer. Not the ancient elf." Her lips twist into a crooked grin for a millisecond. Then she lifts her chin to someone across the room. Winks, rather wickedly.

I follow her gaze to find Lobrka. He stares back, flushes, then turns in a quick departure.

She snickers. "I love doing that."

I swing my gaze between her and the retreating Lobrka. "What did you just do?"

She tosses me a sinful smile. "I just reminded him that we used to...um...work out our stress together. Between the sheets, on top of the sheets, far, far away from the sheets." She doesn't appear remotely embarrassed.

I gulp, try to swallow my surprise. "But you don't anymore?"

"Nah." She shrugs. "He's in a committed relationship now."

"Oh." I want to ask with who, but his personal life is not my business, so I keep my mouth shut.

"Anyway, remember what I said." She spins and returns to Al and Mo waiting at the table.

Interesting. All of it interesting. What she said about her and Lobrka, but more so, the allegiance to the Balance Bringer. The question is...do I believe her. Madame Marrouske may have put her up to this in order to test me.

I study Klarda's return to the table. She immediately engages Al and Mo in conversation and doesn't look back. I pivot, head to the bathroom, and don't return to my companions waiting in the dining hall.

Instead, as twilight begins to fall, I make my way to the back meadow. To the place Raundel mentioned Velsa and the herd dwelled.

Lights glow and race along the tree roots webbing the ground, as if the tree of life, itself, is leading the way to the unicorns I seek. I find them lounging beyond the farthest structures within the tearman.

"Balance Bringer." Velsa walks, unwavering, toward me. Stops a foot away. *"We are pleased to see you safe and healthy."*

I step forward and rest my palms against the sides of her head, my forehead to her snout. "I feel the same about you. Belmiso got here days ago."

"Being the fastest among us, he ran ahead." She says and bobs her head ever slightly.

"I'm glad he did." Memories of his arrival in the woodlands, my brother on his back, flash across the back of my eyes. "Being here is not what I expected."

I don't know what I really did expect, but I didn't envision this—butting heads with my supposed mystic.

"Having a support group around me is comforting." Even if I've been so consumed with Jaden's condition that I've made little time for anyone or anything else. The fact that Belmiso visited me while I was recovering from Edea's magical kick-start warms my heart.

"Tell us," Velsa says, and the other horses draw close, moving into a circle around me.

Knowing in my core that I can trust the unicorns with my innermost thoughts, I open my mouth and let everything spill forth. They listen, and nod, and occasionally scuff a hoof upon the ground.

When my words run dry and my mouth aches from the unloading, Velsa presses her snout against the side of my face, warming my skin with her touch.

"Where do you place your faith?" she asks. Unsure of the meaning, I don't immediately respond. *"Does your faith lie in yourself? In others? In Gaea and the energy of all?"*

I want to be able to place my faith in all those things, but ultimately… "Gaea and the universal energy."

All the horses' heads bob.

Velsa neighs. Blinks her gaze tight on me. *"Gaea and the energy of all lives in all things. It surrounds you, flows through you.*

Listen with your heart, and you shall discover the answers you seek. Not hear them but feel them. Know the course you should take."

I swallow hard. "But the elemental energies are mad at me. They have been giving me the cold shoulder."

Timbers snorts. "*Your truth glows bright around you and it is honorable.*"

"Thank you." I touch my palm to his snout. In all the time we have spent together, I think this is the first time he has spoken to me. My smile is slight but sincere. I run my gaze over all of them, Timbers, Clemens, Belmiso, Velsa. Even Nox, Zarah's non-unicorn horse, remains with the group. "Thank you, all of you."

Belmiso steps forward and runs his long tongue along the side of my cheek. Despite being rough as sandpaper, the action tickles, and I giggle. Then drop to a mumble.

"Is there a chance that you can somehow sort this all out in my head. Lead me in the right direction?"

Belmiso nickers. Shares a glance with Velsa and the others. "*Our kind is meant to be a magical muse for all. That is our role, to watch and inspire.*"

Clemens bobs his head. "*And our inspirational presence has been strong around you.*"

Indeed. They have been with me through more than anyone or anything should have to have dealt with. I press my palm to my chest, over the warmth of my heart. "Yes. Again, thank you."

Timber neighs. "*You may not always hear or see us, but our inspirational presence always rides at your side.*"

Pressing my other hand to my heart, I close my eyes and soak in the moment. Peace of the mind, body, and soul washes over me in the presence of the unicorns. A tranquility I've felt nowhere else. Blissful and loving, an overwhelming sense of soul serenity.

"*You are Gaea's gift to the worlds,*" Velsa says, moving within reach. "*What we recommend you do now is remember all that you are, and the truth beyond that.*"

"Cryptic." I scratch my head and chew on my lower lip.

Velsa's head sways to and fro. "*Just enough to set you upon the path.*"

"*You will find the path.*"

"*We believe in you.*"

"*You are alit with pure inspiration,*" all the unicorns whisper around me.

They crowd in on me, licking me until I am smiling wide, giggling uncontrollably, and my disappearing skin marks, or tattoos, are glowing a bright iridescent blue.

When I make my way back to the sanctuary of the tree, Velsa walks at my side.

"*The answers have always been with you,*" she says. "*This time...*" As in this lifetime. "*They are written upon your skin.*"

ELEVEN

My disappearing tattoos hold answers. If only I knew how to read them.

I bolt upright in my bed, wide awake. Light shines into the room through a crack running along the outer tree wall.

What time is it? How long did I sleep? Was I already supposed to meet up with Azure for more chore duty...or elemental connection exercises?

No. He would have shoved me awake.

I remained with Velsa and the herd until it was time to crawl into bed. And, although I can't summon the memory of my dreams, I am tired and achy, as if the night was restless and wrought with physical discomfort.

I rub my eyes and blink against the grit covering my skin.

A memory of waking up in my bed back home, covered in mud and bruises slaps me in the side of the head. I pull back the sheets and stare down at my body. No mud. No bruises. But...

Dust on my hands. I have awoken with dust on my hands. Crystal dust, I think.

Brushing my palms together, I wipe the particles away. The grit on me is reminiscent of when I would work at cutting, carving, and tumbling crystals in the garage...back when my life was somewhat normal.

A soft knock raps on the door.

"Anala?" Gitta says from the other side. "Raundel asked me to retrieve you. He is waiting for you in the grand entrance."

"Raundel?" I call out, slipping free of the bed. "I thought I would be working with Azure today?" I cross the room and crack the door open just enough to see her.

Gitta shakes her head. "Raundel informed me that you are with him for the day. Dress for hard work and mobility." Her lips pull straight. "And do hurry. He gets cranky when he is left waiting."

A cranky Raundel is the last thing I want to deal with today. "Tell him I'll be quick."

Not wanting to deal with the loss of Dohlan's gold ring again, I tie it to a string and slip the string around my neck, then grab a change of clothing and dash to the bath.

Twenty minutes later, I am racing to the grand entrance, my mind overcrowded with thoughts of unexplained crystal dust, a dark, horned prince in Jaden, a frozen castle, Edea's request I free Dohlan from Dreya's clutches, my clash with Madame Marrouske, my conversation with Velsa, and what could possibly be waiting for me in Raundel's company.

When I arrive in the tree sanctuary's main entry, Raundel is not alone. Lobrka stands at his side. Both towering elves, one light and one dark, wait silently with arms folded. They stare at each other as if passing unspoken information between them.

At the sight of me, Raundel turns and walks out the front door. Lobrka motions for me to follow, falls into step at my side.

"We get to torture you for a full day, maybe longer," he says, wicked laughter in his delivery.

The many versions of me remember days like this, the two elves, many times only Raundel, working with me to hone my combat skills. Smart of Meira, Madame Marrouske, to throw physical training at me now.

She'll keep me busy, my mind and body tired, so that I won't have the time or the desire to contemplate a mission to the family home.

A frozen castle that may be significant in besting Dreya.

If only I could reconnect with my elemental sides, I wouldn't need to fall back on my fighting ability. Still, it would be best to keep myself in good form. I've missed more than a few days of regular workouts, what with all the traveling, fighting, darkness cleansing, recovery sleeping.

My body is slightly out of shape...for me, an easy slope to slide down. So much harder to climb back up to peak form once muscle and endurance is lost.

So, without argument, I allow Raundel and Lobrka to lead the way.

Klarda and Al catch us near the front entrance and ask to join, but Raundel turns them away. "Another time, perhaps," he says, likely meaning three days past never.

The physical training has always ever been just me and Raundel or me, Raundel, and Lobrka. Never another.

We tread farther and farther away from the main trunk of the sanctuary tree, weaving through the forest of air roots looking every bit like their own thick trees. Leaving all other activity surrounding the tearman to fall away in the distance, we make our way to an invisible doorway. One I recall from previous lifetimes.

"We shall train in what you might consider a pocket dimension," Lobrka says, telling me something I already know. "It is the ideal training location, for we may spend as much time as we need, without worry of time lost here."

In other words, they can torture me for hours or days, without missing much, or any, time here, where Dreya is out to get me, elementals are snubbing me, Ry and Zarah are still gone, and Jaden has yet to awaken.

The two spaces move independently of each other, time-wise. Something I determine is a good thing. I can get back in fighting form and still savor the moments with the people that matter most to me.

The air becomes dense and weighted, pushing on me like a stone sinking deep into the mud. I am reminded of the torans guarding the passageways to Hiddenkel, the weighted training endured under Ry's guidance, and the many times various versions of myself have previously come this way.

Each step is more labored than the last. I grind my teeth and slam my feet forward and down with challenged force. Bushes crowd at our sides, branches and leaves hang lower into our line of site. The discernible path vanishes. Twigs snag at my sleeves, and the atmosphere is so humid, I feel like I'm drinking the air rather than breathing.

Lobrka flashes me a grin. "Almost there, Bringer."

Almost, indeed. One memory of passing through the hidden door stands out stronger than the rest for some reason.

I grab the words spoken to me at that time and recite them. "Don't trust your eyes. They may deceive you. You must feel the truth in any given situation."

"Very good," Lobrka says.

Raundel does not respond, even though he had originally delivered my quoted speech. I highly doubt he has forgotten.

"Before now..." before a version of me that had the benefit of outerworld experiences and education. "I hadn't realized how much you sound like Yoda," I say to Raundel.

"I do not know this Yoda you speak of, but he sounds most wise," he replies without a hint of humor.

I stifle a laugh. A moment later, thick waves of heat distort the surrounding spaces. Everything loses clarity, distinction, and…as we step through the invisible door…everything falls away.

We're in the midst of vast emptiness. Silence is everywhere. The ground swallowing each footstep.

"This should be good." Crystia appears at my side, rocking back and forth on her heels while flexing her fingers together. I do my best to ignore her.

She, too, remembers this training space. My sisters, any version of me, may appear in corporeal form while here. Not only I, but everyone, can see every version of me that choses to appear. Every triune member over the millenniums. We work together in the training. The remembering and relearning. Sparring against myself. My many selves.

I never realized how incredibly strange that was until now.

Has my view been so deeply affected by where I grew up this time around?

A sandstone pillar materializes off to the side. Raundel saunters over and leans against the support. Evaluates the version of me now standing before him.

"Your strength comes from the combine," he says, meaning me, my sisters, my many lifetimes. "You must work as one. You shall practice here until you hone your muscle and mind memory to sing like nature's song."

To the other side, Lobrka walks to a large set of intricately carved wooden doors that have appeared. Sliding the set of doors to the side, he exposes a wide array of weaponry.

Ry would be drooling.

Lobrka makes his selection and returns to stand before me. "Shall we begin?"

I search my many memories for a time Raundel has chosen to sit out and I can't find one. I shoot him a questioning stare. "Aren't you going to be a part of this?"

"You will do well working on your techniques with Lobrka. He is a fine instructor," Raundel replies.

Lobrka laughs. "What he really means to say is that I am the superior fighter. Dark elves have always bested the light."

"Not so," Raundel retorts. "You would be wise to watch yourself."

Despite Raundel's even tone, this is the first sign of discord, albeit slight, I have seen between them.

Lobrka shakes his head. "Ignore him," he says to me. "The white troll has been grumpy since yesterday."

Yesterday. Since I woke up from whatever Edea did to me? Since my less than pleasant conversation with Meira? Am I the cause of his bad mood?

I grimace and decide not to press the matter. Instead, I get busy training. Awakening my mind and muscle memory, tapping into the many times I'd gone through this routine in the past. The only difference this time is an unbalanced combat talent between Kaia and Crystia. Something that didn't exist before the previous versions of Jaden and I did what we did.

A snap of a stick. A separation of a soul.

His soul.

Mine, already split, became unbalanced. Kaia not only got an unhealthy portion of the darkness, but she also received all of Crystia's combat talent.

Crystia whines and sighs and continues to try, nonetheless.

"You bring other things of great value," Lobrka tells her. "You are quick and nimble on your feet. You communicate with the other species and have a strong warrior gene. You make Anala a stronger, faster Balance Bringer."

She torques her lips up to the side. "*So, basically I'm an amp or booster.*" The disappointment in her voice is undeniable.

"You're my rock, my foundation," I say. "And that is an extremely important role. We do this thing together, okay?"

She laughs. "*Like I'd say no.*" She smiles mildly and swings her blade back and forth like a pendulum.

I try not to shake my head. She really needs to learn proper sword etiquette.

Lobrka wags a finger. "The idea that each of you is a separate individual is a flawed perception," he says. "You are all one, and you are all each other."

An idea more easily understood than genuinely practiced with success.

But we try.

We continue to practice and train as if we will some day fight as a team, but we all know, when and if the day comes, I will be the only one holding the sword.

Various incarnations of me have heard rumors of a crystal-encrusted saber belonging to the Balance Bringer, one that when lifted in battle, all Balance Bringers, present and past, will be armed to fight and the enemy will feel their blows. But such a saber has never been seen.

It is a myth. A legend.

Jaden's words whisper at my ear. *"...based on truth...our myths and fables are different than the ones you grew up with."*

If that's true, where is this mythical saber?

Lobrka works us into the ground. Prods and pushes us for endless hours. Until my palms hurt and bulge with blisters. Sweat drips from my brow like rain. Crystia is equally worn, if not more so. Kaia, on the other hand, isn't the least bit winded. She's ready for another round. I'm glad she's on my side, even if we have a few issues to work through.

Namely, Dohlan.

"Stop." Raundel waves his hand and steps between Lobrka and me. "You depend too much on what you see and hear around you. You must put more trust in what you feel and know in here." He taps his chest. "Reach out with your inner senses."

He waves Lobrka away. The dark elf wanders to the side and takes a seat on the ground, wrapping his long arms around his bent knees. Sets his keen gaze on me...on Raundel.

"This should help with your relearning." Raundel lifts his arms, and the space around us is instantly shrouded in a misty veil.

His location is no longer visible. The scene is reminiscent of one of my enigma-loop-protected dreams. When Jaden surrounded me with dream catcher webs and Dreya still managed to get at me, somewhat. A layer of white keeping her from me.

Previous incarnations suffered through similar training. But none of them experienced the white gauzing nightmares filled with attacks from Dreya.

"I can't see anything," I mumble.

"*I think that's the point.*" Crystia whispers in my ear. "*Duck!*"

I duck, drop, roll. A blade slices through the air above me.

"*On your right.*" Kaia murmurs.

I spin left. A sword scrapes across the back of my leather armor.

"You are not trying, Bringer." Raundel's voice booms from beyond the clouded wall. "Reach inward, expand outward, feel."

"Nature isn't working with me right now. I can't use it to determine anything." I reply, my voice raspy.

"You do not need nature to determine where I am. Trust your instincts. In a fight, hesitation may become your enemy." The words throw me back to fighting as King Marduk. His hesitation lost him not only the fight but his life. I will not make that same mistake.

Kaia sucks back a breath. "*My fault.*"

"No." I say and close my eyes. Staring at the white wall clouds my instinct. Maybe, if I don't look at all, I'll do better. Like when Ben Kenobi blindfolded Luke Skywalker.

"*But father...*"

"Not now." We have a skill to master, so now is not the time to divide our attention.

We work in a shroud of white for what feels like an eternity. We rest in large, luxury tents between rounds, enjoy meals that magically appear with a dining area in which to eat, and clean the dirt and sweat off in crystal clear showers set upon a circle of trees.

We push, and train. Trying again and again, improving with each new attempt. Until we're not, and we're sloppy with exhaustion. Then we rest, wash up, eat, and go again.

When Raundel determines our skills are sharp, he calls it a day on our training.

It may be a day in the world surrounding the tree sanctuary, but I'm feeling rather confident that we spent a year, possibly more, in the training time bubble.

Lobrka and I walk side by side back to the compound, but before I can escape to my room, Raundel pulls me aside.

"What were you doing last night?" he asks.

I frown. "Last night, as in the training dimension or whatever? Or the night before we went in?" Can I remember that far back? I tap my memories. After arguing with Meira and catching up with Mo, I had relaxed in the meadow with Velsa and her herd.

"Before," he says bluntly.

"I was talking with the…" I stop myself before I blurt out the word unicorn. No one else knows, nor needs to know. He tilts his head as if mentally nudging me to finish my sentence. "I was talking with the horses. Is that a crime?"

"You were talking to the horses in the dead of night?"

I'm certain he doesn't consider the hours prior to midnight as the dead of night. And I was definitely in my bed before midnight. My nose wrinkles. "What do you think I was doing?"

"If I knew, I would not have to ask." His gaze is tight, and I feel a mountain of accusations within his stare.

"I'm sorry you don't like my answer." I yank my arm free from his hold. "Now if you'll excuse me, I'm tired, sore, and in need of a bath."

I walk to the washroom with now a new concern to my list. What was I doing in the dead of night? And why don't I have any memory of it?

An image of crystal dust coating my hands flitters across my mind.

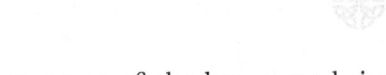

THE STING of the hot water brings a wince to my face. I slide carefully into the bath, painfully aware of every new ache and strain. I lean back and let my hair fall over the back of the tub.

I have enjoyed far too few hot baths and showers since setting foot in Hiddenkel.

Closing my eyes, and breathing in the steam, I savor the moment.

"Why did you withhold vital information about father? You should have told them."

Kaia's voice causes my muscles to tense. With a heavy sigh, I open my eyes and gaze up at her, standing at the foot of the tub.

I love my sisters. I really do. But a little privacy at a time such as this would be nice.

"I didn't withhold anything. I just chose not to mention it. Under the circumstances, the information wasn't relevant or necessary." I close my eyes and try to pretend she's not there. It doesn't work. Her presence is a soft warmth at my toes.

Something in my chest tightens, clumps like a blob of dried glue.

If anyone has been holding back information, it's her. Not telling me about her relationship with Dohlan. Her connection to Dreya. The details surrounding her death, her cottage, or all the things found there—the mother's mirror, the door to the nethers, and the memory waters in the garden.

In truth, Kaia has been quiet about a lot of things. Too many things.

Sensing her presence still firmly planted at the foot of the tub, I open my eyes and narrow my gaze. "Why didn't you ever tell me you didn't die in that field but were taken?" She jerks back. "Are you dead?"

She must be dead. After all, she's here with me, as part of me, spiritually or otherwise. Still, I can't help but wonder.

She stares back at me, not saying a word.

"*Don't even bother.*" Crystia quips.

I jump, splashing water out of the tub.

Crystia sits on the side of the tub, her attention flittering between Kaia and me.

"Are we having a party in my bath?" I make no attempt to hide the annoyance in my voice. "Because someone forgot to inform me of this fun fact." My delivery is pure sarcasm.

Crystia grimaces, her expression filled with a thousand or more apologies. Kaia merely frowns.

"Where can I find you, Kaia?" I ask. "Where should I look for your body? Is there a chance I'll find you alive?" A memory flashes at the back of my mind. There and gone. Hardly a sliver of a thought. A body trapped in crystal.

"*Leave it alone!*" Crystia's voice strains, catching me off guard.

Kaia disappears.

I blink and turn to Crystia. "What was that all about?"

"*Is your skull so thick?*" She bolts to a stand. "*Didn't I tell you to drop it?*"

In a flash, Crystia vanishes.

I finally have my bath all to myself, but I can no longer savor any serenity in the moment. I went through the binding, and since my sisters are a part of me, shouldn't I already know the answers I seek from Kaia?

Nothing about what just happened makes sense.

All enjoyment zapped from my system, I dry off, dress, and head to my room.

Find Raundel inside, waiting for me.

The emotion on his face is unreadable. He sighs, tilts his head. "You remember Izza?"

TWELVE

I zza, the young Balance Bringer trapped in a temple of trees, hunted by a monster version of Garr. A young Balance Bringer no one else seems to remember. None of my other incarnations, nor Madame Marrouske.

Just me.

And now, Raundel.

"I overheard you talking about Izza to our lady," he says. "Yesterday, in the library."

The yesterday that now feels like a million years ago, when Raundel sat at the table by the door and pretended not to be listening. "What do you know about her?"

His chest rises and shoulders stiffen. "She was the second incarnation of the Balance Bringer, but she never realized her destiny. And for whatever happened to her, our lady Meira, nor any Balance Bringer who has since come, appear able to remember her." He dips his head toward me. "Until you."

I balk. "What makes me so special?"

His face tightens with clear scrutiny. "I do not know. I was hoping you might be able to tell me."

My shoulders shrug and my head shakes. "If no one else remembers her, why do you?"

He steps back and settles against the edge of my bed. "As far as I can tell, only the Balance Bringer line, Meira, and Edea were affected."

Those involved in the origins of the Balance Bringer. I gnaw on the inside of my lip.

He stares into the space between us, his thoughts appearing miles from the room we now occupy. "I remember because I sought her out on Meira's request. But when I returned with information of what I had learned, Meira no longer remembered the request *or* the girl. But I had seen her with my own eyes. Talked to her, without revealing who I was. I even located her future consort, Dharmic."

His gaze flickers to me. "You call him Tracer. Like your Jaden, and like Jove, he too had the sight. He knew things about his future. About her, and what she would mean to the worlds, to him. I watched him from afar as he cast a crystal encrusted saber for her. Saw that it made it into her hands by way of another."

The fabled saber of the Balance Bringer. It's real. But then, what happened to it after Izza disappeared?

Raundel shakes his head. "Izza and her sisters vanished before she had the chance to properly meet her forever-bound consort. Her soulmate and twin flame."

I settle against the bed beside him. Even without Izza and her memories being a part of me, I still feel the pain of Raundel's story. It cracks a fissure through my heart.

He sighs. "He never stopped searching for her. I checked in on him a few years after Izza's disappearance only to find him a distraught mess. Driven to madness by her loss, or his gift, or nature. Possibly a combination of them. I suspect he was a more powerful seer than Jove, most definitely more powerful than your Jaden." He huffs a laugh.

My gaze narrows and my fists clench. I want to obliterate the insult that slipped from his lips. Possibly his jaw along with it. But I hold my stead. Jaden may not be the strongest seer ever, but he's my seer.

I shift in my half-sit to face Raundel. "Why do you think so?"

His lips pull to the side in a slash of a smile. "There are tells among the Fae. Some more obvious than others. This would-be consort to the Balance Bringer was a horned Fae, but I knew him not to be a king of his people. Nor did I perceive him as an exceptional hunter. He was either a shaman or magic wielder. Either of which leads me to believe he was extraordinary with the sight."

A version of Jaden with horns. Could it be the same version of him Azure and I witnessed in his room yesterday? My heart double thumps.

Izza is still trapped in the temple, and her consort is likely long since dead. "What happened to the saber?"

"Rumor has it, Izza was so touched by the gift, that she stored the saber in her heart," he says. "I'd never given the story much credence until your binding. And even then, I didn't allow the thought to bloom. Not until you mentioned the girl by name the other day."

"I don't understand." I shake my head. "What are you trying to tell me?"

"At one point, during your binding, I witnessed a flash in the Lagoon of Lucidity. For a moment...only one..." He swallows hard. "I could have sworn I saw a crystal encrusted saber clutched to your chest." I gasp. "But once the binding was done, and we were pulling you and your Tracer out of the water, there was no saber to be found."

If the saber had truly been present, maybe it was only visible during those minutes when I was with Izza, trying to help her get free.

Raundel and I talk for close to an hour about Izza, her consort Dharmic, and the fabled saber. I don't tell Raundel about having seen Jaden with horns like Dharmic, but I do mention my suspected Garr connection.

"Garr has changed much over time," he says. "The creature should have passed on long ago, and yet he still lives, looking little as he did then."

Kind of like Edea, I think.

Meira merely looks a thousand years older and Raundel appears pretty much unchanged.

"I have come to believe," he continues. "…that when Deona fought the infected troll, and Garrthmal got stuck to the creatures back, a seed of the darkness was left within him. A seed that rooted and grew, changing him over the years, into the thing he is today."

I relive that experience through Deona's memories. His theory is a reasonable explanation for what has happened to the boy that was once a good friend to the original triune.

"With the change, and time," Raundel adds. "His infatuation with you, or the original Fianna, has turned ugly and consuming."

Memories of him accosting me in the city of the treeites rush to my mind and I shiver.

When our conversation finally wraps and Raundel leaves me to sleep, I am so exhausted I do little more than face-plant to the pillow.

ON WHAT WAS day two for those living in the sanctuary, but felt like year two for me, Raundel insists on continuing my physical training. He gets more involved than he did previously, and his mood is slightly lighter, as if our conversation about Izza has cut weight from his soul.

We enjoy no more sleepovers in the training space, but rather, visit and train on a daily basis. I start each day exhausted, hints of crystal dust on my hands. And I end each day even more worn, worked to the point of breaking by Lobrka and Raundel. I see little of Mo, too tired to socialize. And I spend my time nodding off with a sleeping Jaden.

On the fourth day, I awake to find the picture of Crystia and Caesar beside my bed. I can't remember when I last had the picture in my possession, and I'm guessing it's been kept safe in Jaden's miracle bag. He's the only person I can think of to do such a thing, deliver the picture to my room, but he has yet to wake up.

On the fifth day, Gitta informs me that Madame Marrouske has decreed I return to chores that have me working with nature. I have been reaching out to the elements, intermittently throughout the days, and detected a tad less resistance. But I was too busy, too drained, and too focused elsewhere to properly work at making any real connection.

So, on this fifth day, after an hour in the early morning, sinking my fingers in the dirt, extracting weeds from the garden, I'm directed back to laundry duty. Working with the first element with which I originally made a connection…water.

I had hoped, expected actually, that after what I had gone through with Edea's magical ritual, my elemental magic would be back to full force by now. I am beyond eager to make my connections work.

So, I make my way from weed duty in the garden to the task of washing at the creek, at a brisk pace, not even bothering to first wash my hands. Baskets of laundry are waiting when I reach the water's edge.

"Took your time," Azure says, lounging in his usual place against the tree, book in hand.

The spine is upside down. Clearly, the words aren't holding his attention, and he's only pretending to be passing his time reading. His gaze flitters between the book and a large crystal resting at his side.

A crystal similar in color and shape to the one Jaden smashed in the school parking lot. The one in which I saw Ruby's reflection. I even used the stone to contact her when I feared for Jaden's life. That's probably what Azure is now doing...trying to contact Ruby...or waiting on her to contact him.

Grabbing the first item from the top of the laundry pile, I remove my boots, roll back my sleeves, and start washing.

"Someone left a picture in my room the other day," I say, attempting to pull Azure into conversation. "You wouldn't happen to know anything about that, would you?"

He abandons the book, clearly done with pretenses, and picks up the crystal, rubs his hand across the smooth surface. "Jade thought you might like to have the image." He plays with the stone like a child fascinated with a new shiny toy.

I blink. "He told you that?" I imagine Azure has made many visits to see his brother during the time Raundel and Lobrka have been subjecting me to training torture. "I had a second picture." One of Crystia and me with Ry. Both pictures came from Crystia's locker at the Cat Preservation Center.

"He did," Azure says. "And he wanted the second picture, the one with you in it, left at his bedside."

My heart squeezes, and the sudden urge to go see Jaden hits me. I want to drop the laundry right here in the stream and run to him. But I can't. I have elemental work to do. A broken connection to mend.

Azure studies the crystal's surface with a weighted gaze.

My attention shifts from his face to the crystal, then back to his contemplating expression. "That thing is a way to communicate, right?"

He nods, his hand drifting over the surface of the stone.

I dip and scrub an overly large shirt. "I saw Jaden break one of those at school once. Smashed it to the hard ground."

"Break one?" Azure's eyebrows lift, and he chuckles softly. "That explains a lot. Ruby was rather upset that he didn't communicate more after he went in search of you. She made sure to message often to complain."

I scoff a laugh. "Guess he was too busy with schoolwork to find idle conversation time."

Even without evidence, I know my words are a lie. For all I know, he didn't even bother to turn in any actual schoolwork. He could have been flunking all his classes, and I wouldn't have had a clue.

But he was keeping tabs on me and holding a darkness infected Skylar at a distance in order to protect me. In that setting of yesteryear, that's all that really mattered.

That and ultimately getting us all here.

Azure's lips press together. "He used to watch you there a lot. At this place you call school."

So he said.

Azure tilts his head toward the crystal. "I was hoping to communicate to the others, but this one doesn't seem to be working. Either that or the magic of this place is somehow interfering. I don't know which."

He tries to pull something forth within the stone, but all that appears is a faint glow before it sputters and dies.

"You miss them?" I wring excess water from the shirt I am washing.

"I want to know where they ended up and that they are all right."

My stomach churns and I avert my gaze, swallow hard. I wouldn't mind knowing about Shadow and Clef. I probably never should have asked Shadow to help me that night, but had I not, so many things would have remained unknown to me.

That was the night that Edea worked her magic on me. Whatever happened to that magical kickstart?

This is the first time in days that I haven't been too exhausted or too distracted to give the elements my proper focus and respect.

I drop into silence and work. Wash. Relish the caress of the water against my hands, the breeze kissing my cheek, the soil beneath my toes, the fire warming my heart. I wash until my hands look and feel like dried prunes, while waiting for the elements to respond...or Azure to break the silence and share more consuming thoughts. I get neither.

With each dip, rinse, and wring, I reach out to the surrounding elements with my sincere apologies.

"You want to talk about it?" I say, finally breaking the silence.

"About Jaden?" he replies quicker than I was expecting.

I heave a breath and nod, not the least bit surprised by the topic.

"I went to Madame Marrouske," he says. "I told her."

I bolt upright, allowing the item I am washing to slip from my hands, into the water. "Told her what?"

"About Jaden," he replies, shifting in his seat upon the ground. "About what we saw."

"I thought we agreed..." My throat closes. *Agreed to keep it between us until we figured out what's going on with Jaden.*

I shake my head and drop my gaze to the towel floating away from me, attempt to straighten the thoughts running rampant in my head.

A dark, horned prince version of Jaden. Dharmic, I suspect. Dwelling just beneath the skin of my Tracer.

Madame Marrouske, Meira, and I are already at odds about a few things. I fear what her course of action may be regarding Jaden now that she knows. Assuming she didn't already.

I snag the towel's edge, preventing it from drifting farther away.

"I can't stop feeling him...hearing him in here." He presses to his head. "At times, I feel like I am losing myself to Jaden," he adds. "Madame Marrouske wasn't surprised. She even said the change was a likely outcome."

Fire races through my blood and burns across my neck, my cheeks. I shake my head, unable to comprehend what Azure is saying...or unwilling to. Meira knew Azure might start feeling like this. Like he was losing himself to his brother. And she was okay with that.

My teeth clench.

"A likely outcome." He sounds miles away. "How is such a thing to be expected?"

Has Madame Marrouske...Meira...betrayed Jaden...Azure...Jove...me? She said nothing to me when I brought up the topic of Jaden the other day. Nothing.

My grip on the towel tightens. If anything other than cloth were held in my hand, it would break.

The water of the creek begins to slosh, and the wind whips around me with a ferocity. It lifts and hurls the basket of laundry into the sky...unnaturally so. Articles of clothing and cloth are tossed in all directions, tumbling through the air, dropping into the water.

Azure lurches forward, in an attempt to catch several of the scattered items. They fall around us like oversized, over-weighted snowflakes. The basket connects with a wild splash upon the creek's surface, dousing us. Catching me heavily with a sheet of water to the face.

Azure bumps into me, and water spirits race around us. Around and around, creating wide, thick waves. The force pushes us closer together. Then slams into my ankles, knocking me off my feet.

I fall into Azure.

He catches me, and together we cling to one another, slipping and sliding on an unstable surface, struggling for purchase. We abandon the task of saving the laundry in favor of saving ourselves from dropping into the creek. Articles float on the water's surface, drifting ever farther beyond our reach.

Azure loses his footing, and we tumble onto the outer bank. With a firm grip upon me, he shifts his body to cushion my fall.

I land on top of him, the palm of his hand resting on the small of my back.

I'm torn between wanting to laugh or cry.

"Are you all right?' His voice is ripe with laughter.

My gaze drops to his. To the eyes staring back at me. One blue, one green. They should both be blue. Azure for blue. Blue eyes. Jaden for green.

I'm reminded of Jove—Jaden's first incarnation, with his eyes of green, that were sometimes blue, and other times, one of each.

He studies the curve of my neck. Fondles the gold ring hanging on the string around my neck.

I suck back a breath. Is Jaden somehow inside of Azure?

His hold on me tightens, and his laughter quells. Becomes serious contemplation. His breath warms my cheek, and for a moment, I don't want to pull away. I want to know if he tastes like Jaden. Is becoming Jaden.

"Awkward," Crystia sings out behind us.

I jolt. Scramble back and away.

Azure is *not* Jaden. Just as Crystia or Kaia are not me.

The earth grumbles and shifts beneath me and Azure. Something large, coarse, and hefty explodes from the ground, driving a wedge between us, and tossing Azure into the bushes at the base of a large oak.

Collapsing into a small heap, my muscles shaking, I heave a breath to steady my emotions.

Close. Too stupidly close.

How could I even...

"You're lonely," Crystia says. *"Don't be so hard on yourself."*

Azure cusses, extricates himself from the bushes.

The ground trembles. And the large oak behind him moans, shudders, and twists, sending a shower of leaves upon us. A few stick to my now wet clothes.

"Sweet Gaea. What does this mean?" He raises his hand, something held in his palm.

"What is it?" Shelving the awkward moment to deal with later, I move closer to get a better look at the item in question.

"Ruby's ring fell from the tree." He points to the leaves sailing downward from the branches above.

Of course, it's Ruby's ring. With the big blingy red stone, who else could it possibly belong to?

I scrutinize the tree trunk and branches. "Are you sure you didn't have it on you somewhere?"

"Positive," he says matter-of-factly.

The tree twists and moans a moment more before settling back into place. The surrounding nature song continues as if nothing unusual has just occurred.

"Hold a minute." A crazy thought runs through my head. *Could it be possible? My elemental connection is sparking back to life.* I contemplate the whirling wind and sloshing water that led to the awkward moment with Azure. Followed by the exploding tree root.

I crouch down and wrap my hands directly over one of the oak's large roots where they snake along the surface. Reaching out, as I had prior to my dark infection, I half expect to slam into a wall and get pushed back...but I don't.

Instead, lady nature is waiting to show me something. Grabbing me by the metaphysical hand, she tugs me forward and we sail along root systems, over underground waterways, and around small tunnels, until we're beyond the protection of the sanctuary.

We climb the air roots of the massive banyan tree guarding the entrance and making up the expanding woodlands. We move through the tree's system until we slow at the woodland's edge. There, Ruby waits, her hands clutching, knuckles whitening.

Understanding floods through me.

The tree carried Ruby's ring from the woodland's edge to us here at the water. A message to Azure from someone who loves him. Misses him.

"Quickly," I say to Azure, my hand splayed out before him. "Give me something personal."

He hesitates, confusion clear in his features.

"It's a message to Ruby. She's waiting."

He jolts, then pulls a pendant from beneath the collar of his shirt, places it in my hand.

Careful not to scratch the stone, I set it gently on the ground, beside the nearest, large root. Thin wispy fingers sprout from the ground, wrap around the pendant, and pull it under the soil.

Staying connected with the tree, I follow the pendant's path, all the way until it is dropped into Ruby's awaiting hands.

A flicker of emotion touches her eyes, her face. It's a look I've never seen on her. I'd swear she is fighting back a tear. Despite her dislike for me and general rude behavior, the love she harbors for her fellow Augurs is undeniable.

With a deep-felt thank you to lady green, nature, I pull back, granting Ruby her private moment.

Azure stands at my back, waiting. Ruby's ring clutched tightly between his fingers. His eyes glisten with what I take as hope. And hope is what I have to give. Hope and love.

"I think the ring was a signal that you are on her mind. She appears safe and well. She's at the entrance to the woodlands, just outside the city of Palinot."

Pain flashes in his eyes for the briefest of moments. She's so close and yet so far. She can't return to the sanctuary because of me, and he won't leave because of Jaden.

"Thank you. This means a lot to me." He holds the ring to the light shining through the tree cover. The red stones glisten. "This reminds me," he says. "I have something for you."

I blink wide. He already left me a picture. My physical symbol that even in his vegetative state, Jaden is thinking about me. I can't think of anything else I could want or need from Azure, especially after the awkwardness that transpired a few minutes ago.

He pulls something small from his pocket and offers it to me. A small prophetic chocolate.

I haven't had one since the village.

After everything we've been through, are still going through, Jaden still finds ways to pass me chocolates, like notes in class. My insides burst with warmth.

Behind me, the water of the creek starts to bubble.

"Um." Azure nudges me away from the water, with a light touch of his hand to the small of my back. The water settles, though my insides do not.

The chocolate is warm, on the soft side. Likely from being kept in Azure's pocket. But I don't want the chocolate so much as I want the message.

Remembering Clef's reaction when I shared one of my chocolates, I offer this one to Azure. He accepts. Smiles to the taste. "Jaden recalls this flavor," he says.

I try to smile but don't know how I feel when it comes to Azure and Jaden becoming more and more like one person.

I shift my focus to the message awaiting on the tiny square of foil.

Life does have do-overs.

A tear forms at the corner of my eye. "How does he always know?" My question is a mere whisper.

Azure shifts closer, his motions stiff and awkward. He pulls me into a hug, pats my back. "He knows because he is your Tracer. It is his job to know these things."

I guess so. Jaden isn't the weak seer Raundel made him out to be.

Gitta bursts through the trees, her breath heavy.

Azure and I instantly pull apart and snap our attention to her. "Are you all right?" I ask.

"Fine." She leans forward, pressing her hands to her knees and takes a second to catch her breath. "Raundel told me to come find you." Her words are directed at me. "Lord Ryland and Lady Zarah have returned."

THIRTEEN

R y and Zarah have returned. No word about my mom. I need to know, and I need to see them, hug them all.

Leaving Azure and Gitta behind, I bound for the tree sanctuary, dirty and wet and uncaring. Slam through the front door into the empty grand entry.

Knowing Ry the way I do, he'll be all business first, cleanup and rest later.

I race down the hall to the left, scanning the nearby gathering rooms. Halfway down the hallway, I come upon an occupied room. Bodies all gathered around a table, appearing to study a large, rolled out map.

I skid to a stop in the doorway, and all heads snap my direction. Ry, Zarah, Mo, Raundel, Lobrka, Klarda, Al, Madame Marrouske. No Mom. But...*Bree?*

I jolt and blink, twice, rapidly.

Bree, the chick from my old high school. *What's she doing here?*

Her cheeks flush, as if she may have heard my thoughts, and she blinks wide, taking me in. What does she see when she looks at me? Can she even identify the girl she knew from school, somewhere beyond the elven ears, bright colored eyes, and golden-streaked hair?

"Ana!" Ry crosses the distance in a few long strides. Wraps his arms around me. The warmth of him near is a much-needed elixir. A part of me never wants to let him go.

I hold him close to my heart and fight the unexpected desire to fall apart in his arms. I've been holding myself strong all these days—days magically stretched into years—since he's been gone, and I hadn't realized how tired my soul was until now.

With Jaden so cut off from me, I could have really used Ry's emotional support.

He pulls back and pinches one of my ears with his fingers. Wiggles my new petite elven ears. "Now look at these, will you. We look less and less related with each passing day."

I sniffle and purse my lips against the burn in my eyes.

Ry's smile morphs into concern. "Are you all right?" He glances over me. "Have they been treating you well?" He shots a warning glance to Raundel, Lobrka, Klarda, and Marrouske…Meira.

"I'm fine," I say. "They've been fine." Mostly. "I just missed you more than I realized." I wrap my arms back around him and hug him once more.

"I missed you too," he mumbles to my crown. "Missed you tons."

Zarah encloses us both in her gloved embrace, joining the emotional reunion. "Every day, he'd be mumbling, I wonder how Ana's doing? I wonder if Ana's okay? I wonder if Ana's getting everything she needs out of that place?" she says with a humorous chime.

Mo coughs. "I think they've been working her too hard."

I glance sideways to note her scrutinizing Raundel and Lobrka.

"I'm fine. Really I am." I step back from the hug and study the map laid out on the table, then shift my gaze to the people in the room. "What did I miss?" I ask, my attention zeroing in on Bree. Her lips pull taut and her hand swings in a tight wave.

Ry's palm presses lightly to the space between my shoulder blades, guiding me closer to the gathered group. "Do you remember Bree?"

The girl from school who worked with Ry and Jaden to keep a dark infected Skylar from passing on the infection to me. That was before I knew who and what I was. What I was intended to be. I nod. Her hair used to be different. It's grown since I last saw her. It's also a softer black with light wisps of violet highlighting.

Without a local hair salon, she's going to take on a whole new look in a few weeks.

"Bree and I met a few years back, shortly after your accident…" The night Jeremy died, I fill in mentally. "We had a bit of an adventure back then, and I knew she wasn't your average, human high school student." He tosses her a smile. "She has been chosen to step into the role as your new mystic."

Bree is *the girl* Madame Marrouske kept bugging me about in all those visions during my journey here. *Where's the girl*, she kept asking me.

Bree steps forward, hand extended. "You look different than I remember," she says. "But it's really nice to finally be open and honest about all this."

"So…" I bite my bottom lip. "You knew? About Hiddenkel? About all this?" I wave my hand to include the room and the people within.

"For awhile now." Her lips twist to the side, and her gaze slips to Marrouske. Meira.

My gaze jumps to the old mystic.

First, Edea talks about running out of time and dying. Now, Meira has chosen a replacement, as if she is expecting the same. Is their expiration date rapidly approaching?

"It is true," Madame Marrouske says. "This girl shall inherit all of my skills and knowledge."

My eyes tighten. Meira is clearly keeping something quiet, despite her declaration of open communication.

"Well, then." I clasp Bree's hand and shake. "You and Ry will have to fill me in on this adventure you guys had…when we get the chance, of course."

Madame Marrouske places a soft hand upon Bree's arm. "Bree and I have a few things to attend to first, and then she is all yours."

A frown pulls at my lips. I lean close to Meira and lower my voice. "Can I talk to you for a moment?"

"Of course." She leads me to the corner of the room.

Everyone else returns to their discussion over the map, plotting where Dreya's forces were last seen, where Mom took the bulk of the immortal forces, and what areas of Palinot are in need of further assistance. Ry leads an animated discussion with Raundel, Lobrka, Kladra, and Al, while Zarah, Mo, and Bree listen in.

I turn my back on the group, so that no one may read my lips…should that be a thing in this group. "What's going on with you and aunt Edea?" I ask. "You're both acting like you're at the end of your long lives."

"Maybe it is because we are, my dear," she replies. "Our lives have been long, indeed. The goddess was kind to gift us with the longevity that she did."

A stern scowl pulls into place on my face, and Madame Marrouske…aunt Meira…smiles mildly. Then sighs. Shrugs.

"I foresee events in my future that shall limit my ability to continue forward," she says.

"Do these events have anything to do with aunt Edea?" I cock an eyebrow.

"They might." She peers past me to Raundel. A quick glance over my shoulder lets me know he isn't paying us any attention. "You heard our conversation the other night. Edea has lost her way."

They may both have. I bite the inside of my lower lip. "What are you planning to do?"

"It is yet unclear."

"But you think a replacement is necessary?" I glance briefly at Bree, who stands near Zarah and peers over the map.

She chuckles. "I'm not getting any younger."

But every previous version of me recalls working with Meira. I am the only one who has any familiarity with Bree. A tiny twinge of panic attempts to blossom in my gut. I refuse to give it fuel to grow.

A sound at the door pulls my attention.

A fully cleaned up Azure enters the room and joins the gathered group at the table. He now wears Ruby's ring on a string around his neck, much in the way I keep Dohlan's ring safe, free from getting lost once again.

Azure's presence is a reminder of another pressing question.

I swing back to Meira. "Did you do something to Jaden and Azure?"

"It is merely a little magic to heal what has been broken." Her attention flitters to Azure, then back to me.

My chest tightens. "But Azure has a life. People he loves and who love him."

"So he does. And I shall not take that from him." Her eyes darken. "Not yet."

"What does that mean?"

"When the time is right, the two men will once again be one. Whole." She sighs. "But until then, I have summoned the many incarnations of the boy to help fill the gaps in his torn soul."

"You've done what?" My voice pitches, causing me to

immediately hunch and cover my mouth. Laughter sparkles in her eyes. "What will that do to Jaden?"

"In truth?" She blinks. "Nothing has been called to him that wasn't already a part of him, in the larger scope of life. He will be who he was always meant to be but with more remembered experiences…as you yourself now possess."

I bite my lower lip. I do remember the many mes. The many memories of me. Can I deny him the same? Still, are either of us the same if our various personalities merge? I honestly have no idea. No version of me does.

I blink and swallow hard.

She pats my cheek with a wrinkled, withered hand. "All pieces of him will be whole and free to shine." She spares Azure a quick glance. "Aside for the one, of course."

"Hey," Ry calls to us. "Are you two going to stand in the corner telling secrets the whole time? Or will you be joining us before sundown?"

"One moment," Meira replies, then cups my upper arm with her palm. "I hear you made an elemental connection today."

Several, actually. I blink, taken back with surprise. "How did you know?"

She raises her hands and motions to our surroundings. "The tree is everywhere. Nothing is said or done that it does not perceive."

Noted. Do I need to worry about the tree narcing on me in the future?

I nod, my lips pull into a tight smile.

"Tomorrow, I want you to continue working on your elemental abilities. See if you can not get them up to full strength." She pats my arm and circles around me, making way for the group gathered around the table. "Bree." She motions to her with a wide arc of her arm. "Come with me."

Bree waves at me. "I look forward to a gab session later." She follows Madame Marrouske from the room.

Their departure signals the slow wind down of all tactical talk. As the conversation begins to peter, I study the map, now recognizing every labeled location, thanks to the binding with my many incarnations. I am even aware of a few placed not listed. No one discusses the lands beyond the seas to all sides, because Dreya's focus is here, in Hiddenkel.

But I realize, with a small squeeze to my chest, that my destiny is greater than her domain. The spread of darkness knows no boundaries. Honors no treaties or territories. And it is the darkness I must stop. More so than Dreya.

The group eventually breaks up and heads in different directions. Raundel, Lobrka, Kladra, Al, and Azure in one direction. And my original group in the other. Ry, Zarah, Mo, and I wander down the hallways together, weaving through the kitchen on the way to the resident wing, where all our rooms are situated.

"Why didn't Mom come back with you?" I ask, as we cover the final stretch, leading to Ry and Zarah's room.

"She wanted to come, to see you," Ry replies. "But now that she has returned to the land of her birth, she has once again resumed her role as commander of the king's forces. And as such, duty comes before all else."

"An absent king," I mumble.

He opens the door to his room and ushers us inside. "She is the queen. Thus, her decision is wise. Of course, you are the next in line and true ruler, should King Marduk be officially declared dead."

His words are weights to my gut. I don't want to rule, and I don't want my father to be dead.

I catch Ry glancing up and down the hallway as I step past him into the room. No doubt, he thinks talking within the privacy of his room will grant us a bit of secrecy. But after my recent conversation with Madame Marrouske, I wonder if a place exists within the sanctuary, much less the woodlands, where one need not worry about being overheard.

"She sends her deepest love." He closes the door. "And I know where we can find her, once we leave here."

He pulls something from the small of his back and hands it over to me. A small journal he had tucked in his pant line. A quick glance inside and I realize it's a book like the one Mom used to communicate with Dad those many years ago. There is a message from her. If I write on the page, my words will appear in her companion book.

I hug the journal to my chest and drop into the only chair in the room.

"Besides Jaden's condition, what's keeping us here?" I say. Mo and Zarah take a seat on the bed, and Ry leans against the wall, crosses his arms. Narrows a tight stare on me. I shrug, flaring my hands to the side. "Besides the binding, I don't feel like being here has been a great use of my time." I glance over each of them.

"What about the old hag's guidance?" Ry asks. "Hasn't she been helpful in that respect?"

I shrug. "Truth is, now that I remember all my lives and all my attempts to right the scales, I'm not sure she can provide me with anything I don't already know, or how to do. I mean…"

I tilt my head back and glance at the ceiling, as if I might find all the words I seek etched above my head.

"Every past version of me has fond feelings for her, but that doesn't mean she isn't stuck in her ways…which I think she is. My past selves haven't always been successful at fulfilling their destinies and I feel like, for the first time, because of my exposure to a different upbringing, I am coming at this thing from a fresh perspective. Looking at the variables and wanting to approach them all from a different angle."

Ry nods and glances as Zarah, exchanging an expression of understanding and knowing.

"I will support whatever course of action you deem appropriate," Mo says.

I smile in thanks.

Zarah's shoulders straighten. "While we were in Palinot, I visited every street, collecting history as viewed by the inhabitants. Under Ryland's direction, I paid careful attention to details that might pertain or be helpful to your cause. In so doing, I gathered lots of story bits surrounding previous Balance Bringers, the story behind the city's main statue, sightings of Kaia many years past, recent sightings of Dohlan, the behavior of Dreya's enslaved troops, and..."

She grimaces. "A lot of disappointment around Balance Bringers in the past. Failures or less than spectacular outcomes."

A heavy sigh rises and falls in my chest. "All pomp and circumstance without the substance," I grumble.

"The stories here are unlike the ones I have collected in the outer regions," she continues. "It would appear, the people living closest to the nucleus have a darker opinion, or have, at least, ditched the rose-colored glasses." She smiles. Glances at Ry. "That is an expression from your world, is it not?"

"You don't need to try and emulate outterworld talk," Ry says to her. "Just be yourself." His eyes are warm and gentle, and their simple exchange leaves me feeling like I've witnessed something best kept in private.

"Anyway." Ry tilts his head toward me. "The very vague point Zarah is trying to make, is that you are likely right. It may be time to come at this destiny of yours from a fresh perspective. So..." He glances at Zarah and Mo, then back to me. "Where do we start."

That's the question, isn't it? The question I keep asking myself.

We discuss the where and what and how for over an hour without any definitive decisions, at which point, I excuse myself to go check on Jaden. Zarah tags along.

Mo stays behind to further discuss what she learned about Opal and the Augur clan during her captivity. Turns out, the vanquished Augur clan members, Ruby, Shadow, and Clef, are currently holed up at a small Palinot inn. I don't find that the least bit surprising, given the fact Ruby was at the woodland's boarder earlier today.

Jaden's room is close…all our rooms are close in proximity to each other…so the walk is short.

"I heard there hasn't been any change," Zarah says, more as a question than a statement.

I push the door open and offer her entrance. "I wouldn't exactly say that." We step inside and let the door swing closed.

Jaden is lying flat on his back, arms straight at his side, like always. On the bedside table sits the picture of me with Crystia and Ry. Positioned just as Azure said it would be.

Zarah absorbs the scene, then looks at me questioningly, waiting for me to expand on my leading response. So I tell her.

Tell her about Ruby's curse, and how I now can't touch Jaden without physical pain. Tell her about the version of Jaden both Azure and I witnessed. And I tell her what Madame Marrouske admitted to doing, pulling Jaden's earlier incarnations into the man he is now to fill the void left by the missing soul piece that is Azure.

"I'm sorry, Ana," is all she says. What more can she say? Nothing, really.

So I stand at the foot of the bed, and stare at him. My hands clutched to the bedframe.

Zarah rests a gloved hand on top of mine and stands beside me, gazing at a sleeping man. Wishing him to wake up.

After endless minutes—ten, twenty, three…I don't know— I turn and head for the door.

I am tired of spinning my wheels here and getting nothing accomplished. Time to figure out how to change things for the better.

I open the door and...

Bree steps forward. "Ry told me I could find you here. I hope you don't mind I tracked you down." Her gaze shifts past me to Jaden, and her arm gently nudges me aside so that she may enter the room. "Is that Jaden?" she asks. "I heard he was..." Her words fade away.

"What do you want?" With a sudden urge to protect Jaden, I grab her shoulder and spin her around to face me. My execution is harsh, for which I am immediately remorseful. Still, I don't apologize.

Memories of a day back in high school flood me. Bree sitting at the desk beside me, tap, tap, tapping her foot. Prodding with comments about Jaden, Skylar, and me. My emotions had gotten the better of me and caused the electricity to burn out in a somewhat theatrical way.

Did she know then what I was? Is that why she didn't look surprised, but amused?

Her face softens, seeming to sense my emotional distress. "I'm sorry he's like this," she says. "I'm sorry you are too."

I flinch. *What is that supposed to mean?*

"Once he's better, you'll feel better," she adds, then turns to Jaden and moves to the edge of the bed. Her hand drops lightly onto the curve of his shin. A moment later, she snaps her hand back and turns to me. "I came to find you to let you know I'll be taking the oath tomorrow."

I glance at Zarah. She shrugs. "I don't know what you're talking about," I say to Bree.

"Right. Guess this is also new for you." Her lips pull into a tight line. "Before the mystic Marrouske will grant me any of her magical knowledge, I must swear an oath to you and your ever-ongoing pursuit of balance, and all that good stuff." She scratches her neck. "It's not some write-your-name-in-blood kind of oath, but a true, elemental magic binding sort of thing."

"Oh." My head jerks back. At least Meira is being

cautious and not just giving away her lifetimes of experiences on a whim. "When is this happening?"

"Tomorrow." Bree grimaces. "I know. Super soon, but she wants to get moving on the next stage. The transfer." She, being my aunt Meira, Madame Marrouske. Transferring all her knowledge and ability to one of my old classmates. I wonder if the transfer includes her memories, as well.

A frown tugs at the edges of my mouth.

"I know what you're thinking," she blurts. "This..." She waves a hand between us. "You. Me. It's weird. But..." She strikes a straight finger to the air. "It's going to be an improvement. I've been paying close attention to Marrouske ever since I first came into contact with her."

"Today?" I offer.

Bree shakes her head. "Two years ago."

I startle. How was she in contact with my mystic back then, but I wasn't?

The mystic did try to reach me through the computer, but I refused to respond, to play her game. That might have *something* to do with the why.

"She's a smart lady," Bree continues. "No doubt about that. But a stuck-in-the-old-ways kind of lady. You and me, we bring a new generations way of doing things to the table and I think we're going to blow the old limitations wide open."

Zarah gasps.

"You don't like the idea?" Bree blinks wide and stares at Zarah.

"No. I." Zarah falters. "I think it's revolutionary."

"Right on, sister." Bree extends her curled hand, awaiting on a fist bump Zarah is unfamiliar with and doesn't return. Bree's hand drops to her side.

"It's okay," I say, raising my hand in waiting. "I gotcha." Bree and I knock fists.

"Great." She smiles wide and I return the delight. Zarah joins in, as well. "Can't wait to get started." Bree slams a fist into her open palm. "Two years ago, one crazy bitch made my life hell. I'm anxious to repay the favor."

A conversation with Madame Marrouske floats to the surface of my thoughts. Revenge is not the way. I suspect, after Bree finishes the transfer, she'll feel the same way, and returning any favors will drop from her agenda.

"Dreya," she says, causing my eyes to pop wide. "She needs to go down."

FOURTEEN

B ree tangled with Dreya two years before I even knew my aunt existed. Or, at least, remembered.

Bree also tussled with my mom. *My mom.* A woman of endless secrets. More things to ask her about... should I ever see her again.

Bree had knowledge about me, even before I did. And had previously met my mom as commander of the immortal warrior force. For those reasons, she knew to seek my mom out when the time came. Their previous connection allowed Bree to hitch a ride with my mom, here to Hiddenkel. To me and the mystic.

This new information, along with the already daunting tasks and circumstances pressing on me, keeps me from a restful sleep. Bree, a girl from school, is to become my new mystic. My mom...and the family cat Oscar...are here and currently moving farther away from me.

Jaden is still sleeping...and apparently merging with his many past selves. Azure might be becoming an extension of Jaden. Edea wants me to free Dohlan from Dreya's control. A woman determined to kill me. Something unspoken is going on with my aunts Meira and Edea. The memory of Izza has been wiped from all previous versions of me, as well as my aunts. And...

I'm exhausted.

I'm sure more concerns exist. Things I am forgetting in my restless sleep state, as I toss and turn and try to find silence of the mind.

But, on the bright side, my elemental connection appears to be on the mend.

Before crawling into bed for the night, and after writing a less-than-ten-word message to my mom in the open communication journal, I spend dedicated quiet time meditating and reaching out to the forces of nature.

My coupling between Balance Bringer and the elements of Gaea is clear and present. It's a warm wind stirring my soul. A soft, cool kiss upon my skin, my mind, my heart. I know, deep within my core, that I'm one with all, and all is one with me.

And yet, once my eyes become too heavy to hold the meditative state, my mind's hold upon serenity slips and my thoughts tumble into unrest.

The world turns black, fades, and then...

I jolt awake, Dreya's angry face filling my sight.

"Get out," the ice queen screams, the chill of the surrounding frozen castle nipping at my senses.

I get out. Fall back asleep.

"*Big magic has consequences,*" Edea's voice mumbles at my ear.

My arms tighten around my pillow, scrunching it into a ball.

"*I have summoned the many incarnations of the boy to help fill the gaps in his torn soul.*" Meira whispers at my side. "*He will be who he was always meant to be.*"

Edea again, whispering ever so slightly. "*The old you was shred open to allow the new you to step through.*"

Velsa. *"Time to bloom, spread your wings and fly...remember."*

I toss to my side, kick my leg free of the covers. Once again, allow the black of sleep to envelop me, carry my concerns away.

When the veil of nothingness slips away once more, I am walking amongst the trees, the grit of crystal dust powdering my palms. My legs move me forward, refusing to give my mind an ounce of control.

A dream? An ancestral memory? Maybe I'm actually sleepwalking.

The weight of my eyelids gifts darkness and solitude once again.

My heart shudders, a fleet of butterflies engulfing the interior of my chest, and a thousand tiny bells chime a song, one I've heard before.

My eyes pull, reluctantly open.

I have crossed the sanctuary threshold, set off the perimeter alarm, and I can't stop myself. I'm not in control. A familiarity drives me forward. One I know as sister.

Dohlan steps clear of the trees.

Beholding him through Kaia's perception, he's more beautiful than I remembered. A light to brighten a darkened heart.

I wonder if that element is part of the magic Edea endowed him with. Part of the thing that makes him a magnet for Kaia. A lazy blink, followed by a semi-wicked grin marks his eagerness at our approach...mine and Kaia's.

He's clearly aware that it is Kaia, and not me, Ana, who is now in control of my physical body.

I worried, just a smidgeon, that something like this might happen, when he asked to speak with her the other day. But, despite that tiny worry, I didn't allow myself to believe Kaia would do this. Shove me in the backseat of my own life. My body.

But this is Dohlan. Her Jaden. If the roles were reversed, would I do the same?

His expression softens, promising restraint, gentleness.

"Is it done?" he asks.

"Almost," the Kaia within replies using my lips, my voice.

Is what done? I scream the question in my head, but Kaia ignores me.

"*I want to touch him, feel his face in my hands. Taste his lips on mine,*" she says to me. "*And should I do so, will he feel the same?*"

No, I think. Because, despite whatever attraction may exist here, with this sinful Fae god, I belong with Jaden. I chose him. Chose Jove, and every version thereafter.

As if responding to Kaia's longing, Dohlan pulls us into his embrace.

A tiny gasp escapes my lips...and Kaia gains more control.

Driven by her want, my hands trace the lines of his chest, familiarizing myself with every curve of him.

I need him. Need him, so badly, her words whisper within me.

"Go back to sleep, Ana." His voice is soft, his smile deepening. "Give Kaia her moment."

He leans forward and nips at my lip, and then, with a shift of his weight, sends us falling backward to the ground. His lips press to mine, tentative and gentle, yet quickly delving into deep passion. He swaths me in tangy spice and honeysuckle. Scents Kaia associates with home and belonging.

Their kiss is long and ripe with hunger, and when their lips finally separate, my body is gasping for breath.

"My love," he says, his words meant for Kaia, not me. "I have waited too long for this moment." His powerful hands glide across my body, and I shiver, thrill to his touch. My thin dressing gown does little to buffer the sensation of his skin upon mine.

His hand lingers at my breast, and his kisses tingle at the curve beneath my jaw. "Desire is too strong," he murmurs into the nape of my neck. "I need you as I have always needed you, but Kaia...this is wrong. This is your sister's body, and I don't believe she would ever..."

Want. Need. Give in.

"You only worry about my satisfaction, and I'll handle Ana." She tugs him closer and slides her hand down his backside.

No. You cannot…I protest, fight with elven ferocity for control, but the scene morphs and I suddenly find myself laid out on a blanket beneath the trees. The sun filters through the thick leaf cover above, and Jaden…

Jaden slides a finger across my cheek, sweeping a stray hair from my face.

"You push yourself, again and again," he says. "Giving so much and taking so little." His lips press to mine, and it's night and day, coming together in the perfect sunrise. Radiant color and warmth.

He pulls away, a mere inch. "You are my everything."

And you…

You are…

My hand glides the line of his back and slips into his slacks.

His purr engages, the desired result achieved. Our lips lock, my gown lifts, and his fingers slide below my beltline.

"*What the heck, Kaia?*" Crystia scolds.

You are not you, I finish my previous thought, regaining weak control of my senses with a blink. And another.

The image of Jaden's face, held in my hands fades, revealing Dohlan's sad, guilty grimace.

My strength and willpower surge to the forefront, knocking Kaia beyond the backseat. I mentally shove her in the trunk.

"Crap!" I shove Dohlan away. "Crap, crap, crap."

Scrambling across the dirt, I try to put continents worth of distance between us. I have to settle for feet. Yards.

Dohlan sits in a lazy fashion upon the ground. "Ana…"

I shake my head, fast and hard. "Don't." I slam a flat palm to the air between us. "You have no right to talk to me."

My body is fuming, my skin burning, and all I want…

All I want is to hit something. Smash it, him, Kaia, to pieces.

"Please, Ana. Let me talk to you." He reaches for me.

I turn away. I can't breathe, and my internal inferno has heated to the point of freezing.

"*Kick him where it hurts the most*," Crystia says. Kaia protests with a loud *no*.

Everyone told me not to trust Dohlan, and yet I had, so I guess I shouldn't be too terribly surprised by his betrayal. But Kaia…

Her actions were a total violation of my will, my body, and our sisterhood.

That last one just might hurt the most.

"*Sisters may clash*," Deona says softly. "*But they always forgive.*"

"Shut up," I scream and press my hands to the side of my head.

I don't…How could she…

"*Ana?*" Crystia says.

"*I'm sorry,*" Kaia placates. "*But you have to admit it wasn't all bad for you.*"

"*Oh please.*" Crystia grumbles.

Kaia continues. "*Dohlan is sexy, and desirable, and…*"

All these voices in my head, they need to stop. I scream. The power of my scream silencing the surrounding woodlands and sending an outward wave of energy across the earthen floor. Fire bursts to life, climbing the trunks of the surround trees.

Dohlan jumps to his feet and, in a flash, is at my side.

Fire and heat. Heat and fire. Elements of anger and humiliation. *I can't. I can't.*

I can't breathe.

Dohlan gasps for breath, his face turning red…like we're trapped in a bubble and someone shut off the oxygen.

The fire consuming the surrounding trees dwindles and becomes no more.

"Please. Ana." Dohlan claws at his neck, his voice raw.

My brow furrows, my anger refusing to abate, and yet, I realize I started the fire. And I cut of the supply of oxygen.

He drops to the ground at my side.

"*Please*," Kaia whispers in my mind. "*Please don't do this.*"

Who started this? It wasn't me. Not from the get-go.

I grind my teeth, then inhale deep, release the fury. *Don't give into to your emotions,* I tell myself. *Revenge is never the answer.*

I release a breath, allowing the oxygen to flow once more.

Soon, others will arrive to witness my humiliation. I recall the bell chime of the perimeter alarm. I'm surprised Marrouske's guard elves aren't already here. I bury my face in my hands. My eyes burn, but I refuse to cry.

Dohlan gasps for breath and rolls toward me, reaches out. The tips of his fingers glide across my arm, leaving goosebumps in their wake. "Ana…"

My entire body flinches away from his touch. *Violator* my thoughts scream.

Both him and Kaia.

The now familiar chorus of tiny bells chimes in a far expanding line at my back. The sound is followed by a loud thrashing that turns my head. A blur of something jumps clear and falls to the ground.

Dohlan bursts into laughter.

"*Well, that was awkward,*" Kaia says, regarding the fumble of the new arrival.

Crystia hushes her. "*Ana doesn't need to hear from either of us right now, so keep your mouth shut. You've already set off a bomb of chaos and destruction.*" They both fall silent.

Dohlan stands, pushes the tail of his shirt back into the fold of his pants, and brushes the dirt from his slacks, a mild chuckle still rolling through his chest. "You, chose that over me?" He gestures to the man slowly pushing himself up from his fallen crouch.

Jaden.

My heart squeezes to a stop, then explodes to a double beat.

Jaden is here, awake, shirtless, shoeless, and clearly weakened.

With a jolt, I scamper to his side and slip under his arm, adding my support against his shoulder and faulty stand. "What…" I stammer. "How are you here?" His breath is labored, and his brow dappled with sweat.

Electricity zaps through our connection, a plethora of painful needle shocks. My body reacts out of instinct, jerking me from Jaden's side. He collapses into a lean against the nearest burn-scorched tree.

A silent curse grumbles within me. Because of Ruby, I can't even add support to Jaden in his time of need.

"Really, Ana." Dohlan chuckles. "You could do better."

Jaden raises his gaze to meet Dohlan's, and something animalistic flashes in his eyes. Animalistic or of darker Fae.

I want to touch him, show him I am here for him, but doing so means instant, constant pain. And I don't yet know if he also feels the pain, or if it's just me. But, if I can't give him physical support, I can still stand up for him in other ways.

"You're wrong," I say to Dohlan. "Jaden just pulled himself out of a dark coma for me. That's dedication. How can I possibly do better than that?"

Dohlan lifts an eyebrow and scrutinizes Jaden. Jaden continues to hold a tight stare filled with heated emotion.

"Would you kill for her?" Dohlan asks.

A gruntle laugh rises in Jaden's throat. "If it came to it, without hesitation. I'd give my life for her. Can you say the same?"

"It would never come to that because I am strong and

smart enough to keep us both out of any such compromised position." Dohlan smirks, turns to leave.

And yet, he failed to save Kaia from such a fate.

Jaden pulls his back straight and squares his shoulders. "Did I say you could leave?" Dohlan spins back, humor delighting his facial features. The male-to-male challenge bringing a sparkle to his eye.

Jaden jabs a pointed finger at Dohlan's mocking smile. "You, sir, are to never touch her again. Not without her express permission. Not one of her sisterly incarnations but Ana's. Do you understand me?"

Dohlan pulls one of his many crooked, wicked grins casually to his lips. "She gave her permission." His gaze shifts to me. "You recall, do you not?" He eyebrows arch. "The night was cold, extremely wet, and the Palinot alcove was drenched in the dark of night." He throws me a wink.

My breath catches in my throat. My chest squeezes against the slowed beat of my heart. At the time, I was acting out of distress and stupidity. Not anymore. And a yes then does not mean a yes whenever.

Jaden lurches a step forward, a growl rising in his throat. His fingers curl, and he swings a sharp punch destined for Dohlan's jaw.

But Dohlan easily avoids the attack with a swivel.

Unable to pause his momentum, Jaden tumbles and falls, but quickly rolls onto his back and stares up at his target. Dohlan smirks.

That dark emotion flashes in Jaden's eyes again. He leaps to his feet, the vision of him flashing back and forth between the barely healed guy who pulled himself out of bed for me and the darker, horned Fae version of a past incarnation.

All humor slips from Dohlan's face, and he takes a step back, his finger wagging in a loose point to Jaden. "That's new," he says with a hint of disbelief. "What was that?"

Before I can respond, Jaden snaps forward and grabs

Dohlan by the wrist. The dark, horned version is gone, and a tired and irritated version of the Jaden I know best holds Dohlan steady.

Dohlan yanks away, attempting to extract himself from Jaden's grip, but…to my surprise…is unable. I take note of the weave of energy working in and around them and realize Jaden is utilizing some type of magic to keep Dohlan in place.

When did Jaden learn to use such magic?

Meira's words once again whisper through my thoughts. *"I have summoned the many incarnations of the boy to help fill the gaps in his torn soul"*

The statement is trailed by Raundel's thoughts regarding Jaden's earlier, horned Fae incarnation. *"He was either a shaman or magic wielder."*

Mere seconds have elapsed since that horned version from Jaden's past made itself known. Could that incarnation have awakened some knowledge within Jaden that he is now tapping into?

Dohlan narrows his gaze on Jaden. "You are under the impression that I am bad for her." He tilts his head in my direction. "But can you be so sure?" His gaze shifts between me and Jaden. "With all that I am, and all that I can be, I have a better chance of keeping her safe."

"She doesn't need someone to keep her safe," Jaden replies with a growl. "She needs a partner. Someone who listens and works with her." A muscle in his cheek twitches. "Not someone who is undermining her at every turn."

Dohlan's jaw tightens. "How long did it take you to track her here?" Dohlan barely pauses, cutting off any opportunity for Jaden to respond. "I would have been here in a flash. That is how precise my tracking of her is."

A shudder races over me.

My blood. It was one of the first things Dohlan ever said to me. *"Your blood, my dear."* He kisses my hand. *"It sang to me. Led me straight to you."*

Whatever this blood thing is between us, it's not stronger than the connection I have with Jaden. Lifetime after lifetime, we have found each other. Chosen each other. Raundel called us soul mates, twin flames.

Dohlan sniffs me out like an animal hunts its prey. Jaden and I find each other through the pulse of our thoughts, the beat of our hearts, and the magnetic pull of our energy.

"If he was at all slow to find me tonight," I say, in defense of Jaden. "It's because he was *in a coma* seconds before setting out on the search." A lopsided smile tugs at the edge of my mouth. "Coma patients deserve a little slack in immediate expectations."

Dohlan frowns at me, as if surprised I defended Jaden. But he shouldn't be. I've never been anything but honest about my feelings where both men are concerned.

Bushes rustle around us, and the security detail I had originally expected step into view. Raundel, Lobrka, and my brother Ry. Each stern male projecting a formidable stance.

"Again, Ana?" Raundel says with a cock of his head and a narrowed stare.

Lobrka crosses his arms. "Why are you outside the safety of the tearman?"

"And why..." Ry jabs a hard point to Dohlan. "Is he here?"

"Take him," Raundel says with a flick of his finger and a frown at his lips.

"What? No." Dohlan tries to pull from Jaden's grip for the second time. "It would be a mistake to take me."

At Raundel's order, and ignoring Dohlan's protest, Lobrka advances. Takes hold of Dohlan, and with Jaden's assistance, ties the golden god's hands behind his back. Jaden's movements are slow, tired.

Ry ruffles. "Why not just kill him now and be done with both him and his continued interference?"

My mouth drops open. I knew my brother hated Dohlan,

but killing…that's rather extreme in this case. Not to mention, Dohlan continues to be a friend to Ry's fiancée, Zarah.

Lobrka yanks Dohlan tight to his side and snaps his attention to Ry. "Our lady suffers you because you share blood with the Balance Bringer. Do not presume to use that small allowance to push your bloodthirsty warrior ways upon our kind."

Ry's face reddens, contorting into a mosh pit of distemper, yet he holds a steady control on his rage. Lobrka stares him down, his big black oval eyes blinking every few seconds, as if waiting for my brother to explode, and counting the time through a prerehearsed routine.

Raundel waves a hand between them. "There is no record of any young Balance Bringer showing up here with one of the Warrior race at her side. This is a unique situation. So much about this time around is unique. The sheer size of her accompanying support group only being one." He tosses me a mild smile. "It is clear to all here that the tides are changing." He shifts his gaze to Lobrka. "We must all make adjustments."

Lobrka's nose wrinkles, but his gaze shifts to me and I sense a desire in him to understand and accept. Perceive as much in the flow of his energy.

"Warrior," Raundel says, forgoing my brother's name. "Can you control your emotions and help Lobrka escort Lord Marsoun to containment?"

Ry glares at Dohlan, his eyes the color of dull gun metal. "Born and raised to be even tempered," Ry replies and joins Lobrka. The two move Dohlan forward, toward the sanctuary perimeter entrance.

Dohlan struggles, fighting the pull of Ry and Lobrka, and glances over his shoulder at me.

"Ana." A sense of desperation slips into his delivery. "Do not let them do this. I cannot protect you if you do."

I stare after him, not sure what to make of his declaration.

Ry jerks hard on Dohlan's arm. "She doesn't need you protecting her."

Azure abruptly breaks through the tree line, making a beeline for Jaden who, once more, leans against a nearby tree for support. Azure moves to his brother's side and wraps an arm around him, helping him stand.

"That's him, isn't it?" Azure asks with a jab toward Dohlan. "He is a concern. I perceive a strong connection running deep. Blood deep."

My back straightens. "Are you talking about me and Dohlan?" Dohlan always claimed a blood connection between us, but I had foolishly hoped it would go away.

Azure nods. "I detect more than just the infected," he says. "And whatever *he* is…" He motions to the departing prisoner. "He has some sort of valid claim here."

I choke on a cough.

"Listen to him," Dohlan calls over his shoulder. "Don't let them lock me up." Ry and Lobrka yank him forward, dragging him through the trees, and out of sight. None of us acknowledge his parting words.

Azure's face hardens. "Your connection runs much stronger," he says to Jaden. "Clearly the more dominant. But whatever this other thing is, it needs to be dealt with. Not ignored."

Jaden heaves a heavy breath and nods, and, with Azure's added support, starts making his way back toward the protection of the tearman, me and Raundel at their back.

Jaden barely holds his own. He's too weak and this confrontation took too much out of him. Even though I am glad he's here with me, awake and talking, he never should have gotten out of bed. Not for me. Not yet.

"I had to come," he says, responding to my unspoken thoughts. "The moment I felt what was happening, what you were feeling, nothing was going to stop me."

"I can always depend on you." I smile, the thought of Jaden's moral and emotional defense warming my soul.

Because the night is thick with darkness, and Jaden has drained all of his energy in my rescue, Azure and I see him straight back to bed. Azure heads back to his own room, leaving me to fall asleep in the chair set beside the bed.

Until...

"Get out!" An iced-over Dreya screams in my face.

With a harsh jolt, I awake in my own bed, my hands crusted with grass stains and dirt. And resting on my bedside table, a filthy blade.

FIFTEEN

T he nightmare of Dreya forgotten, I ogle my hands, the dirt, the blade. Something about the scene sparks an ancient memory. One rattling through the halls of my mind.

"What in all of Gaea?" The words tumble from my lips.

"You're welcome," Kaia says, a mere voice in my head.

I close my eyes and breathe deep. Exhale, attempting to temper my emotions in the process. The embers of anger over her earlier actions still smolder in my chest. Body snatching me. Using me to have her way with Dohlan.

I shudder. Gag on the bitter taste now permeating my tongue.

Neither of her deeds were remotely acceptable.

Clearly, she didn't learn the intended lesson—my body is off limits to the control of others. Sisters included. Because…I survey the dirt covering my hands…she's done it again.

"It's a form of an apology," she says. *"The best offering I could think of, given the circumstances."*

"A dirty knife?" I throw back the covers and drop my legs over the side of the bed. I never changed from the nightshirt I

was wearing last night when everything happened. I may have
to burn it later.

"Don't you recognize it?" Crystia chimes in.

With a heavy breath rattling through my ribs, I pick up the
knife and study the hilt, the blade.

Countless years of dirt and something other is crusted to
the surface. My thoughts tumble back to a moment lifetimes
ago. Deona and Jove making a pledge to a forever connection
under the guidance of Aunt Meira.

"But we buried this knife," I say. "Out by Raundel's place.
Near Estala and Fianna's graves." I turn the weapon in my
hands, studying every angle. Every particle trapped to its
aged finish. "How is it here now?" Obviously, Kaia body
snatched me and had me go get it, but... "What I mean to
say is, why? And how did you get it without setting off the
alarms again?"

"Who says she didn't?" Crystia replies, a hint of humor in
the response regarding the perimeter alarms.

"We didn't leave the sanctuary," Kaia says simply. *"We had the
earth bring the blade to us. She brought it deep into the safety of this
place, and you dug it up mere yards from the front door."*

"And the why?" I ask, but neither sister responds, because
they know I already hold the answer to my question. Because,
whatever outside force is afflicting Jaden, it began here, with
this blade.

"Thank you." I set the blade back on the side table. "Now
that Jaden is awake, maybe we can get some answers. Possibly,
as soon as today."

Every part of me, past, present, splintered-soul sisters,
agrees.

AFTER BREAKFAST, Mo and I head to Jaden's room, a tray of
eatables in hand. I have the dirty blade strapped to my leg,

within the confines of my boot. I'm hoping that testing the knife in his presence might provide some answers.

And, if he hasn't yet eaten, I'm going to make sure he gets something in his belly. But before we can get to our destination, Gitta leaps into our path.

"He is not there," she says. "The two brothers are with Raundel. They wait for you in the water temple." She grabs the tray of food from me and sets it on the floor, to the side of the path. "I shall show you the way."

We head outside and circle around the circumference of the tree sanctuary...the mother of all trees...the massive tree of life.

Mo leans close and lowers her voice. "Have you utilized the journal to communicate with your mother, yet?"

She was there when Ry gave me the book. She knows what it does and, in this case, its intended use. She knew I was struggling for the right words to write.

"I did." My lips pull taut. "I decided to keep it short."

She pauses, and I suspect she is weighing her desire to know against the inclination to grant me privacy on the topic. The desire to know wins. "What did you say?"

"I told her I miss her, and that I forgive her."

"For not returning with your brother to see you?" she asks.

"Nah," I say with a shake of my head. "For hiding my truth from me my whole life. And for trying to block my return to Hiddenkel."

Her mouth pops open, but her gaze returns forward, and she drops any further conversation.

I find it easy to mentally move away from the topic of my mom. The air is abuzz with activity, and many new faces are present all around.

Short, stump gnomes hustle away from the tree, all appearing to head in the same direction. I ask one where they are going, but he only gives me a disgruntled look in return.

"Grumpy as usual," Gitta says, reminding me of my first

introduction to them. Gitta had suggested that civil behavior among the gnomes was not necessarily common. "There is much activity and excitement over tonight's ceremony."

Bree's oath to me, the Balance Bringer, and the passing of Madame Marrouske's magic. I'm still a swirl of uncertainty regarding my feelings about the whole thing.

"Want to see?" Her eyes brighten, her face lifting with excitement.

"Yes," Mo blurts before I can get one word out for or against.

With a smile brightening her beautiful elven face, Gitta leads the way with Mo and me trailing behind.

The path takes us away from the main house to a clearing set amidst a collection of outer buildings. Wood and land nymphs dance and skirt and rush in preparation for later. Other species, tall, slender, beautiful, and moving with unworldly grace, are also hard at work. Beings I'm only familiar with through the memories of my previous incarnations.

Gitta spins to face us. "Because so many requested to be present, our lady decided to hold the ceremony at the center of the complex. She is hoping to boost morale by allowing them to be present." She dips her head. "But she also does not want too many unknowns lingering near the tree's core."

An over sense of protectiveness flairs within me, and I'm not so sure that even this location is set at a safe enough distance. With a sweeping gaze, I take in everything from the weed-speckled ground to the weathered buildings and the busy, preoccupied crowd, all the way up to the tree cover above.

The tree of life…this world's seed…must always be protected.

"Tonight, is a serious matter," Gitta continues. "But there will also be much merriment."

"A celebration?" Mo asks. "With drink and dance?" Gitta

responds with a nod, and Mo flashes me a wide grin. "How long has it been since you danced?"

Honestly? Not since Skylar's party…back in the world of my raising. Of course, I don't care to bring up that night, not with things being so incredibly different now. I merely give Mo a shrug as a reply.

She grabs my shoulder and shakes. "We need to get some fun in you before you shrivel up into a bitter hag."

"Ha. Ha." I roll my eyes, then motion to the clear focal point of preparation, offerings to the various elementals. "Marrouske is comfortable with this location?"

I glance back at the tree sanctuary. Everywhere within the complex, the tree is close. Too close to allow a bunch of too-happy and possibly drunk fantastical creatures to get their party on.

Gitta shrugs her ear into her shoulder. "It is not for me to say. I only follow directions." She tosses a sideways glance at the busy beings setting the ceremonial stage, then veers back to our original course. "We shouldn't delay any longer. Raundel is a punctual creature."

So, I've been told, on multiple occasions, throughout many lifetimes.

The water temple is on the other side of a nondescript entrance, down a flight of stairs formed of tree roots, and at the end of a lengthy tunnel carved into the ground, between the thick, spidery wood rootstock.

The gentle trickling of water leads the way. The deeper we move through the passage, the trickle turns to a steady flow, then a burst of nature song.

At the end of the path, a large room of earth and stone, surrounded by streams of water shrouding the walls and finding their way into generous pools of brilliant blue. And, in the farthest corner, a cascading waterfall slams into a slanted stone floor. The water swirls down a massive hole where the wall meets floor.

Surrounded by the water and the stone of this place, my skin buzzes.

Raundel stands near the entrance and tosses me a swath of fabric. "I was not expecting an extra," he says regarding Mo's presence. His appraising gaze sweeps over her.

"I am sorry." Gitta dips her head.

"Should I leave?" Mo asks, her gaze taking in the empty space. Her forehead wrinkles, as a frown plants upon her lips. Aside from our party standing at the door, no one else is visible. No one else. And yet, Gitta told us we would find Jaden and Azure here.

"This is elemental magic practice, right?" I ask, my eyes glazing over at the pristine pools awaiting. "Let her stay."

Raundel scowls, then tosses Mo a second swath of fabric and dismisses Gitta.

My gaze drops to the fabric in my hand. "What are we supposed to do with these?" I straighten and stretch the material to discover a onesie.

"Change into it." He raises an eyebrow, as if to imply the question ridiculous.

I glance over him from head to toe. "Right here? Out in the open?"

He rolls his eyes. "If you are feeling modest, you may change back there." His arm swings in a loose, directional point to a short wall of rock angling into the room.

"I am." Feeling modest. I hug the fabric to my belly and step around him.

Mo and I march across the room to the designated changing space. Leading the way, Mo slips behind the wall and yelps. I jolt forward like a zealous hero racing to the rescue, only to come face to face with Jaden and Azure.

They're wearing trunks, similar in color and fabric to my onesie. Their discarded clothing is neatly folded and set on raised stones at the back of the tight space. A cane leans against the wall, beside the clothing stack.

I blink from the cane to Jaden. He's focused solely on me, a smile warming his lips and cheeks. "Good morning," he says, his green eyes bright as a lush meadow on a sunny day.

"We are done here," Azure interrupts, pushing past me and Mo. "The space is all yours."

Mo's gaze follows him as he rounds the wall. "That was rude."

Jaden grabs the cane and presses his weight into it. "Forgive him. He didn't get enough sleep." I stare at the way Jaden clutches the cane.

"No excuse," Mo replies. "I failed to sleep as long as I may have liked, yet I am still civil."

"He could learn from you." Jaden flashes her a humored grin, then notes my gaze focused on the cane. "Temporary," he says, raising the cane off the ground. "While my body regains strength and muscle memory. I was down for a long time."

Too long. I bite my lip. More sacrifices made for me. All because he helped me in the Lagoon of Lucidity.

His gaze, pinning on me, warms. "See you in the water." His tone is a purr, a caress along the edge of my ear. Using the cane, he points toward the main space of the water temple, then leaves us in private.

When I've carefully wrapped my crystal wristbands within the folds of my discarded clothing and concealed the dirty binding blade inside one of my boots, Mo and I emerge, dressed in our onesies, ready for water work. All three men are waiting for us. All of them uniformed in matching trunks.

Raundel must not have been feeling modest as he appears to have changed in the wide-open space. His hair is tied back with a leather strap, but all his fine warrior attire is set neatly folded at the far side of the room.

He motions to the blue glimmering pool. "Time to get to work." He hands me a tumbled stone as I pass him and step into the water. His words are a buzz in my ears. He's explaining what he wants me to do, but I already know. I'm expected to water pass the stone from my hands to his, then to Jaden's, and Azure's, and Mo's. Not necessarily in that order, but he's seeking the execution, not the person to whom I send the stone.

But first...

I close my eyes and sink to the bottom of the blue pool, much like I used to do in high school gym class. With the hug of the water all around me, I remain unmoving, hearing only the muffled sounds of the surface...at first. Until the tiny water spirits break their silence and sing.

"*I am your servant.*" I send the message to all corners of the pool, and beyond. I have come to realize anything during my stay here, it is that I am here for Gaea, and not the other way around.

When I pull to a stand, rising out of the water, ready to begin Raundel's elemental practice, the water works with me, answering every one of my requests.

We start by passing the stone through the movement of the water, and quickly shift to other things, whirlpools and water cyclones. Liquid walls and trenches. Waterfalls stop and restart, dribble and crash at my requested rate.

"Wind," Raundel commands.

I shift my focus to the air in the space, the way the water-falls shift and ride the particles. "Hello, beautiful," I whisper. A gentle wind whips around me, as if in answer to my compliment. "Without you, we are nothing," I say. "I am your servant. Guide me."

The circle of wind morphs into a small, tight cyclone moving around and around me. Lifting me slightly off the pool's floor. Rising droplet of water above the sparkling pool like a shook snow globe.

"Show them what you've got," I say to the element. In response, it whips around the others in the room, lifting and tossing their hair.

"And earth," Raundel directs.

I survey the walls, floor, and ceiling. The stone, packed dirt, show of tree roots. "Without you, where would the water flow or the wind blow?" I whisper, gliding my hand over the rock wall at my side. "You are the home to which we all gather. I am your servant."

The stone beneath my touch pushes out from the wall several inches, and from a crack running the rock's side, a vine pushes free, blooms with green.

"Good," Raundel says. My back jolts straight, and a smile pops to my lips. He's complimented past versions of me, but I can't recall him doing so this lifetime.

Mo pats her chest. "Truly remarkable."

"Thanks." I smile at Mo, then spin to Raundel with humored surprise. "I've been missing a praise from grumpy uncle Raundel."

He scowls. Flicks a finger in the air. "Keep working." He turns and climbs out of the pool.

"Which part didn't you like?" I ask, tracing his movements to the shower of water in the corner. "The grumpy or the uncle." He ignores me and steps beneath the falling stream.

"You are quite the force," Azure interjects, his blue eyes an edge of dull. "But perhaps you should not irritate the ancient elf."

I scoff. "You're new here, clearly still learning the relationship dynamics. Why don't you tell him, Jaden." I spin to my tracer and stop short, all joy and humor evaporating.

Jaden's eyes are a cloudy mist, the sign of an incoming vision.

"Jaden?" I push against the water, taking a step closer, and instinctively reach out. My fingertips barely brush the skin of his arm, each tiny hair filled with collections of jolts. My hand folds in and away.

His head snaps back, his body jerks, and feet slip, dropping him beneath the water. He sinks like a weight, making no motion or effort to right himself. To pull himself back up and breathe. The pool isn't deep enough that we should have to worry about anyone drowning, and yet...

I scream his name.

He doesn't attempt to lift his mouth above the water.

Plunging in after him, I grab for his arms. Water rushes at me from the side of the pool, the liquid temperature dropping to a frigid chill.

Cold. So cold. Ice cold.

No elemental chat fills my mind, my soul, but the sensation feels like a message, one felt in my gut.

Icy water swirls around me, tightening my chest. And then, the freezing touch melts, becomes temperate again.

My hand wraps around Jaden's arm with a zap, zap, zaaaaaap, and I drag him back up. He breaks the surface with a deep drag of breath.

His eyes blink and blink, the word "key" softly slipping from his lips. He shudders fully aware and stands on his own, glancing to my troubled hold upon him. Electric pain continues to course through the connection.

The blow, no longer buffered by my concern for his life, returns to full power.

"Ouch!" I yank my hand away from Jaden's arm. If Ruby's irritating curse wasn't already painful enough, the conductivity of the water intensified the electrical shock. I stare at my hands, then at the red markings winding around my wrist. "I'm sorry," I mumble to Jaden, praying no one else will overhear.

He brushes his wet hair back from his face, shakes out the access. The clouded swirl in his eyes is gone, and his gaze has returned to normal. Mostly. Now warmed with concern, he studies my hands and the place upon his body where I touched him.

"Everything all right?" Azure pushes through the water, moving in our direction.

Jaden's green eyes narrow on me, as if he knows, knows without me telling him, what just happened. "It was nothing." He waves his brother away. "Don't worry about it."

"It did not look like nothing." Raundel sits on a flat rock at the other end of the blue pool.

His voice is sharp, as is his gaze on me and Jaden. If he heard me mention Izza to Meira during our conversation the other day, then he likely heard about Ruby's curse. The press of his forehead, the intensity of his stare suggests he may be presently putting the pieced together.

Mo stands waist deep in the water, not far from the large white elf, her mouth agape.

Moving as close as I dare to Jaden, I lean in and lower my voice. "If you are aware of Ruby's curse, I can understand why you wouldn't want to bring up the issue here." I try not to allow my gaze to drift toward Azure. It's a struggle. "But can you explain the other thing?" The meaning behind the word *key*?

He rubs at his neck, shakes his head. "I don't know." He glances down at the water. "Maybe. But not here."

Gitta pops through the main doorway. "You asked me to let you know when it is time." Her gaze slipping straight to Raundel. "It is time." With his nod of understanding, she turns and disappears down the dark, root-lined tunnel.

He uncoils himself from his seat upon the rock. "The cere-mony will be starting in an hour's time. I suggest you all get cleaned up." He drops his shorts and starts getting dressed.

I snap my attention to Jaden, turning my back on the now naked white stag elf.

The concept of modesty is somewhat lost on the older, ancient beings. So I've learned lifetime after lifetime. And yet, I never get more comfortable with the idea of them moving in my orbit nude.

"Get dressed," Jaden says to me. "We'll talk along the way."

On the way to *where*? The ceremony? Somewhere else?

I don't ask the questions. Instead, he moves away from me, wading through the water toward Azure.

IT TURNS OUT, the *where* is not the ceremony, but the place of Dohlan's containment.

Jaden and I leave Azure and Mo near the edge of the pre-ceremony celebration. Jaden moves quick enough, considering he's working with a cane. But the longer and faster we move, the more pronounced his struggle becomes.

"Why Dohlan? What did you see?" I finger the gold ring still hanging around my neck.

I should have ditched it when we returned in the wee hours of the morning, but something kept me from tossing it aside. Maybe, a slight fear it will be needed for something? What if that time were to come and I didn't have it with me?

"My vision was of him, and it was here, in this contain-ment facility." He shoves a door open and ushers me into a dark, empty chamber. "In the vision, Dohlan said something to you, and I'm getting the feeling, it's imperative we under-stand both the importance and meaning of his words."

I tug at the ring, yanking it back and forth along the string around my neck. "And you didn't want to talk in the water temple because…"

"In case she's using the water." He pushes open a second door, leading us into yet another barren hallway.

"Using the water like she did the black tar infecting the land," I say of Dreya. "Because she's part ice witch, and ice and water are of the same elemental family."

"Exactly." He pushes open the third door. In the room beyond, Klarda and Al sit, secretive conversational style in a couple of overstuffed chairs, their words soft and their fingers intertwined. At our entrance, Al leaps back and averts her gaze, as Klarda casually uncoils to her feet.

My gaze darts back and forth between them, taking in the way their fingers were linked, the new flush of Al's cheeks. When Klarda told me she worked off steam with Lobrka, I had assumed...

Klarda shrugs. "Why limit interests to one species or sexual preference," she says, interpreting my ogle. I have no response, so I return the shrug. "Now that that is settled, tell me what you are doing here?" Her muscles stiffen, her stance shifting, preparing to stop us from going any further.

Jaden nods to me. "She's here to see the prisoner."

Al spins to face us and presses her weight against the chair arm. "Him?" Her voice is filled with incredibility. "Why would you want to do that?" She studies me, then shifts her stark gray stare to Jaden. "Why would you let her? On some level, is he not something akin to your rival?"

Humor thrums in the air around Jaden and he laughs.

"Jaden has no rival," I reply. "Whatever allure Dohlan has, it isn't real. It's caused by magic." Al frowns but doesn't look convinced. "Jaden on the other hand, I..." Deona... "...fell for him..." Jove... "...simply and purely, without any magical meddling."

"Is that so?" Al folds her arms across her chest, and both she and Klarda regard me and Jaden.

"She would know," he says with a ghost of a grin. "She's the boss, with access to all her memories and thoughts, from countless lifetimes."

I toss him a weary glance. He too should have access to all that he has ever been, according to the magic Meira performed on him. Everything outside of Azure's thoughts, feelings, and experiences.

"Our lady was here earlier. She made no mention of visitors." Klarda drops her fists on her hips.

"She was here?" My eyes widen. "What did they talk

about?" About the fact that he's Edea's son? That she used him to magically attract Kaia and interfere with the Balance Bringer triune?

"None of my business." Klarda's chin rises. "Besides, she used a patch."

My nose wrinkles and I glance at Jaden. "It's like a bubble." He waves a circle in the air. "Traps time and sound. Basically, she created a private room where they could talk."

Similar to my training space. I nod. Return my attention to Klarda and, by extension, Al. "The other day, you mentioned you were here for the Balance Bringer, not Marrouske."

A deep sigh pushes at Klarda's chest. "I did." She pauses. "And I meant it."

"Then be here for me now." I relax all my muscles, showing them both that I have no intentions of fighting them. Jaden and I would much prefer their willing assistance. It sure would make everything move far smoother.

"He is dangerous," Al cautions.

Yes, but probably not to me. Mostly.

Violator, my mind screams.

"As am I." I pin them with a hard glare, then glance at Jaden and remember the darker, horned version of him holding Dohlan at bay. "We both are."

With jaw rigid and scowl tight, Klarda scrutinizes me for moments that drag out, feeling like forever minutes. "Very well," she says, breaking the tension. "But you are to remain on this side of the bars."

Of course. I wouldn't want it any other way. I flare my hands in a show of accord.

"And you are not to visit with him alone," she adds.

"I'll be with her," Jaden says.

"We all will," Al adds, and I can't help but wonder if she wants to be present to protect me, us, or him. Does she know?

Is she even aware of Dohlan's relation to her beloved Clan mother?

"Very well." Klarda leads us to another door, another room, this one lined with iron. Beyond that, yet another door. So many doors. So many opportunities to stop and contain an attempting escapee.

She opens the final door, revealing the containment, three cells, barred and stripped with iron to contain an elf or Fae. Dohlan is slumped against the wall in the middle cell.

He glances up at the sound of our entrance. At the sight of me, he jumps to a stand and bolts to the wall of bars, wrapping his hands around the confining iron.

"Ana, please. Get me out of here." He yanks on the bars. "I cannot be here. I am her key."

SIXTEEN

Her key.

Dohlan's words reverberate through my mind.

Her. As in Dreya.

It was through him that Dreya found a way into my earthly world, before I came here to Hiddenkel. And again, through him, she infiltrated my dreams.

She uses him somehow, like a key.

What would she use him for now? Could his presence here be enough for her to somehow wiggle through, overcome, or breakdown the protective barriers of the sanctuary?

I shake my head. Can't believe that would be possible. Not with the tree of life and Aunt Meira's ancient magic at work, keeping this place safe.

Still.

"We should warn Marrouske," I say.

"He could be lying," Al replies. "Think of the source."

"And who's to say our lady isn't already aware of this threat," Klarda adds, a frown permeating her strong features. "She did spend time interrogating him in a period patch."

Both Klarda and Al are positioned just beyond the door, in the space we just passed through. Jaden stands a foot inside the cell chamber. And me…I stand in front of the middle cell, three feet back from the bars. The iron bars Dohlan now clutches.

"Maybe. Maybe not." I glance at Jaden. He leans into his cane and shakes his head. A signal that he believes we have an issue of concern.

"Please believe me," Dohlan says. "Get yourself far from this place."

Not tighten your defenses, or set up a barricade, possibly an evacuation. No. He's telling me, not anyone else, just me to leave. Go now, somewhere Dreya is not.

I bite the edge of my lower lip and move closer to the bars of Dohlan's cell. Protest rises from the guarding warrior and her ward. I ignore them. Jaden says nothing to stop me, and it is his opinion, his foresight, I value most.

"What if…" I pause and press my finger to my lip, consider the idea taking form in my head. "What if we moved you outside of the protective barrier right now, would that prevent her from using you as a key?"

Dohlan's gaze fixes steadily on me. "It would depend on where she was…is…at the time I am allowed to leave." He drops his hold upon the bars.

"Oh no." Klarda moves into the room, her hands shaking as if to stop my runaway thoughts. "He is not going anywhere. Not without the expressed approval of our lady." Her jaw is set, her statement firm.

"Not even if it were in the best interest of the entire complex, you have here?" Jaden asks.

Klarda sighs, her eyes closing in the process. "I know I said I was here to support the Balance Bringer, but I do not believe you have been here long enough to understand the strength of this place. There is no outside threat we need worry about in here." She tilts her head into a new thought. "Aside from the unbalanced energies, which affect everything, the tree included."

"I hope you're right," I mumble. I don't bother to correct her that I have been here many times, many lifetimes. Many before her arrival. But something about Dreya is different... and concerning.

And judging by the expression on Dohlan's face, I'd say he doesn't necessarily agree with Klarda's assessment of the perimeter protection.

My gaze shifts away from the prisoner to Jaden, hopeful his sight will have given us something positive to hold on to, but he looks just as confused and concerned as I feel.

"If there was some major concern hurtling our way," Klarda continues. "Our lady would have caught a hint of such in her magic black mirror."

Her polished obsidian stone set on the feature table in her chambers might have had something to show, only Meira was too busy with Bree's arrival, and then the planning of the subsequent oath and knowledge transfer ceremony to notice. My lips pucker in a troubled frown.

"Whatever it is you two are thinking..." Al swings her attention from me to Jaden. "You should let it go. From all the things I have heard about this guy..." She swings her arm to indicate Dohlan. "He deserves to be exactly here. Behind iron bars."

For half a second, I consider telling her Dohlan is her beloved clan mother's son, just to see if it sways her opinion in any one direction. But it's only a consideration for a blink of an eye.

Despite all that he has done to me, or maybe because of it, it hurts to look at Dohlan. I leave the room without so much as a goodbye and no further secrets revealed.

"We need to find Madame Marrouske," I say, moving with purpose, and Jaden agrees.

Leaving Klarda and Al behind to continue guarding the

prisoner, Jaden and I head into the gathered ceremonial crowd to do just that…find my aunt Meira.

Music trills through the trees, vibrates across the ground, as pixies and devas string glowing acorn lights above. Brownies join leprechauns in beating the drums, and other items, in accompaniment of the harp and flute melody floating over the reveling crowd. Expanding outward from the ceremonial focal point, and gathering of musicians, elves and Fae and woodland creatures alike, dance, drink, and bellow with merriment.

Somewhere, deep in the ground beneath my feet, water calls to me, particles of earth carrying the message.

I scan face after face, looking for Aunt Meira, Madame Marrouske, or someone likely to be near her side. Bree, Raundel, possibly Lobrka.

A hand drops onto my shoulder, and I spin around to find Ry and Zarah, mugs of elven ale in hand. "Are you ready for whatever the old mystic throws at you tonight?" my brother asks.

I don't know. Will the ceremony continue after I tell her what Dohlan had to say? What Jaden and I fear may be coming? "You wouldn't happen to know any of the specifics, would you?"

He chortles. "You think that woman confides anything in me? Remember, I am merely being tolerated because of my relation to you." I snort, then immediately glaze.

A short hum vibrates in my chest, and my gaze wanders to the flicker and dance of light and color playing in the nearby bonfire. The flames' hypnotic affects play across the faces of my friends, family, surrounding woodland elves.

And weaves a dance…a song…in my heart.

Jaden leans in to be heard over the merriment. "You wouldn't happen to know where she is?" he asks of Marrouske.

"No. But we haven't been looking," Zarah says.

"True," Ry adds. "She's bound to make an appearance sooner rather than later. This is her party, after all."

Jaden nods, a frown of frustration dragging the curve of his mouth. "Preferably sooner."

"Why? What's up?" Ry's body straightens and his expression sobers as Zarah perks to attention.

"There you are." Emerging from the crowd, a somewhat tipsy Mo throws an arm around my shoulder. "Where have you been? Did I not tell you we needed to get some fun in you?" She glances over her shoulder. "You left me with mundane man." She points to Azure.

"I am far from mundane," he counters, stepping up to the group with a mug of ale in hand. "You merely do not interest me."

She huffs, her head bouncing forward with the sound. "Still rude." Her balance tips and I grab her, hold her upright. She laughs and I release a strained giggle.

Azure rolls his eyes. "Have any of you seen Al?"

"She's with Klarda," Jaden offers. "At the containment."

"Watching—" Azure's face pinches with stupefaction, and he doesn't finish his sentence.

Knowing Azure's intended question, Jaden affirms with a tight nod. "And Madame Marrouske…" he glances from his brother to Mo. "Have either of you seen her?"

They, too, have not seen the old mystic.

Ry pours the remaining contents of his mug on the ground. "What's going on?"

"Maybe nothing." I grimace. *Maybe everything.* "But just to be safe, I think you all should get inside the main tree sanctuary and lock the place down." Because, if Dohlan's the key, we may have just unlocked the sanctuary door for a whole lot of bad.

"But we're celebrating," Mo complains with a whine and a stomp of her foot.

Azure leans toward his brother, his gaze narrowing. "You

saw something when we were in the water temple. Am I correct?"

The light of the bonfire plays on the curves of Jaden's face, turning his solemn expression forbidding. "You're not wrong." Tension pulls taut on the muscles cording his neck.

Azure lifts his chin. "What do you need us to do?"

"Help us find Marrouske," Jaden replies.

At the same time, I say, "Get inside."

Zarah yanks one of her gloves off and grabs a nearby being. They toss her a glare and pull away. Ignoring their reaction, Zarah grabs for the next nearest individual. Her actions are clear. She's pulling history off of those around us, searching for sightings of Madame Marrouske.

"Oh." Her eyes widen. "She's over…" Her gaze shifts away from the group, her hand rising.

Ry is already surveying everything visible in the path of her turned attention, his chin jerking up in a silent directional jab to the celebrational stage arranged on the other side of the bonfire.

Raundel stands beside a makeshift stage, his arm outstretched, offering steady support to Meira and then Bree, as they climb the steps. Meira guides them to the center and addresses the gathered crowd.

"Anala Danika Raine," she calls out. "Are you ready to embrace the future?" Her voice booms unexpectedly loud for one so ancient. My heart skips a beat.

A new mystic, various versions of me whisper. *Another new thing. So many new things this lifetime.* New to us all, Deona to me, to all the versions in between. The oath and power transfer. A splintered Tracer. Dohlan. Dreya. My own sisterly imbalance.

My legs turn to rubber, and my arms, hands shake, as if on a caffeine high. My mind, jaw, tense with uncertainty.

"You've got this. You can handle anything she puts in your path." Jaden squeezes my hand. "You merely must believe in yourself." A double squeeze. He's wearing gloves to insulate our touch, and yet a faint electric jolt still reaches my skin.

"She is here." Lobrka steps to my side, grabs my wrist, and raises my hand.

"Wait," I say, my tone low. "I need to talk to her."

A crooked smile curves one edge of his lips. "Then I guess it is a good thing you will be joining her up there." He tilts his head, indicating Bree and Aunt Meira on the stage.

I pull my hand, and his hold, closer to my chest, holding my position. "Is there any other way? Can we put this thing on pause for a moment?"

"No." He tugs me forward to the sound of Mo's cheers of luck. Ry, Zarah, and Azure stare after me, clearly on edge about the concern I've introduced. And Jaden…Jaden follows me, close on Lobrka's heels.

Meira raises her hands wide. "Step forward, Anala Danika, daughter of Deona, and prepare to accept your full self."

I thought I already did that during the binding.

I glance back at Jaden, but he only shrugs in response, then hangs back to wait at the base. Lobrka leads me up the steps with a slight tug, drawing me toward center stage. When he releases me, my momentum stumbles me forward two steps, bringing me to a full stop a foot before Meira and Bree.

My old aunt harbors a sad smile, which leads me to wonder if she'd rather not transfer anything to Bree. Bree, although smiling, is doing a poor job of hide a boulder of nerves in her gut. The tension down her neck and across her shoulders is blindingly apparent.

I lean into Meira and drop my voice. "I need to talk to you."

She shifts her gaze to the gathered crowd, a forced smile tugged firmly into place. "Not now," she says between clenched teeth. "After Bree's oath is done."

"But it's important," I push.

Her nostrils flare slightly. "Nothing is more important than what we do here tonight."

I fake a smile for the sake of all the faerie and Fae folk gathered and swing my gaze past Bree, over the crowd, to Jaden. He dips his head as if to say, you've got this. But I don't. Or I definitely don't feel like I do. Meira…Marrouske… she won't listen to me. Not right now.

"On this night," Meira says, addressing the gathered group. "Beneath the light of the gallant moon, we bare witness to this young woman's…" She lifts Bree's hand into the air. "…oath to the Balance Bringer, currently known as Anala Danika Raine."

She smiles at both Bree and me. "Moving forward, you shall know this young woman by her new identity, Bree, master sage." She releases Bree's hand. "Once the oath has been made, she shall become the master sage with the allocation of all I have and all I know."

The response of onlookers, a mix of joy and shock. I seek Jaden, then my brother and friends, in the throng of bodies. Only Mo is smiling—a drunken, somewhat clueless grin. The bonfire's unruly flames sway and stab in the air between us, the pyre tugging at my attention with fevered demand.

Raundel grabs my arm, catching me off guard. I allowed the thrall of the flames to consume my attention, and I missed his approach. A huge warrior blunder. He presses my hand to Bree's in a weaved clasp, and binds of wide, leafy green snake up and around our arms, holding us firmly together.

"The words," Meira prompts, to which Bree nods.

"I pledge, with all that I am, here and beyond, my eternal loyalty, steadfast guidance, and unwavering assistance to the continued mission of the Balance Bringer, Anala Danika Raine and all those who shall come after."

The invisible markings upon my skin begin to glow and shift. Dividing, becoming more. More that move with a swirl over the leafy binding around our arms. Up and around the green the markings go. Around and onward, onto her skin, then into the flesh of her arm, vanishing from sight. Both symbols and leafy bond.

My blood begins to sting, traces of her riding the current through my veins. Her nose wrinkles, clearly experiencing something on her end, as well.

"Do you feel it too?" I ask.

"If you mean, your elemental storm tying boy scout knots throughout my system, then yes." She swallows hard. "This will take some getting used to."

Sounds like I got off easy, by comparison. Still… "Definitely," I say, not to any confining coursing through me, but to having Bree as a close confidant and magical partner in the balancing.

But for now, I need to stay on task. Keep my focus.

I lean to the side, grabbing Meira's attention. "Can we talk now? It may be important." I glance over the crowd, drinking and cheering, completely unaware that Dohlan, Dreya's key, is locked only yards away.

"Not just yet. There is more to do."

"But…" I rebut. Meira, with her expression stern, raises a finger, silencing me.

She directs Bree away from me. "Are you ready for what comes next?" she asks my old classmate.

Bree steals a glance at me, a grimace of worried anticipation. "As ready as I'll ever be," she says, returning her attention forward.

My fingers claw through my hair. What Meira is doing is important. I know it is. But…

"*Make her listen.*" Crystia's words are a scream in my head.

Kaia tsks. "*Forget about her, and just let Dohlan go.*"

"*There are too many unknown variables,*" Deona says.

I drop my head, pressing my hands to my temples with the force of a tightened vise-grip. Too many parts of me, with varied personalities and opinions. "Could you all just…" I mumble to the voices in my head. "Shut it."

Water sloshes and wind howls in my ear. I stare at the floor, not caring to watch what Meira and Bree do next.

"Ana," Jaden whispers, leaning over the edge of the stage. "Are you all right?"

I want to assure him that I am fine, but it would be a lie. With Meira refusing to listen and all the other incarnations whispering in my ear, swarming my internal thoughts, anxiety has crept in and now taps against the edges of my soul.

Come. Let me burn it all away, an alluring elemental whisper, with a crackle, crackle, crackling. The fire beckons me with its dangerous song, sparking my pores to prickle. And making me painfully aware of the filthy knife tucked into the side of my boot, scratching at my calf.

Burn, the fire murmurs. *Burn the water to gas.*

My skin is hot, sweaty, and my stomach roils. I think I may vomit.

Scorch the ground, the trees, consume all the oxygen.

I drop to my knees, and both Meira and Bree are instantly in a crouch at my side. A breath later, Jaden joins them.

Meira lays her palm to my forehead. "She's burning up."

Raundel steps forward, tall and straight, staring down at me. "Has it begun?"

I don't know what he's talking about, so I shake my head and search for answers in Jaden's eyes. Even as my blood chants *fire, fire, fire.*

"Breathe," he says, his thick-gloved hands caressing my back and gently pulling my hair away from my face. But in the face of this change, even his gloves are not enough of a buffer. Electricity strikes like lightning, fracturing through the flames consuming my body.

He snaps his touch away.

Burn, whispers through me in response.

The bonfire explodes, reaching for the tree cover. The

gathered attendees screech. Somewhere to my left, and to my right, large booms shatter the air. More howls and screams.

"Ana." Ry's voice rises over the commotion of the panicked crowd, but I can't see him, and I can't answer. My skin...my mind...is melting. Being consumed by the intensity of the sun.

"We need to cool her down." Jaden's voice sounds distant, as if he's moved several feet away.

Water. Ice. Please.

My throat is dry as sandpaper, and the intake of oxygen scratches with razor claws.

"We need to get her to the Tears of Clarity," Meira replies. "Or at the very least, the water temple."

The water temple is closer.

My body convulses. Each tremor a release of tension and energy. Followed by cracks and booms and screams. So many screams. So many booms. The sounds suggest I'm lying on the edge of a battlefield. But I'm on the stage, in the middle of the tree sanctuary.

"*Open your eyes and remember.*" Deona murmurs at my ear.

Remember Deona harnessing the power of fire. *But it was not like this. Not like this at all.*

"I am your servant." The words are hardly a sound from my lips, but it is all I have to give, at the moment. My offering to the arrival of the final element. "I am your servant," I mutter again.

"What is that?" Bree leans close, tilting her ear to my lips. "What is she saying?"

"I can't touch her," Jaden says, sounding too far away. "It will only cause her more pain." The admission is followed by a clipped explanation of Ruby's curse.

Meira grunts. "Raundel, can you pick her up? We need to move her to the water. Cool her down."

"I can help you with that."

I recognize that voice.

And I don't *want* to recognize that voice.

My chest rattles and my heart stops.

Opening my eyes to the burn, I lift my head and stare at Dreya. She's a pillar of crazy calm in a sea of chaos and destruction. Her smile, as wicked as her intentions.

Her shifty gaze sweeps over me, then wanders to Meira. "You were never going to keep me out of this dreary hole of yours forever," she says, not to me, but to my aunt. "He told me, you know, *Sol.* Told me what all of you did to him."

She points an accusatory finger between me and Meira. "Leaving him trapped in isolation for centuries...longer...can you even comprehend the sheer torture?"

Deona's shock is a tumble of stones in my chest. Sol, Jove's friend. The first to be infected by the darkness. Patient zero.

But even more interesting than the fact Dreya knew him... which I am now determined to find out how...is the emotion laced in her delivery about tortured isolation.

Always try to understand your enemy. The thought flashes through me, and I'm not sure if it's pure Ana, lessons drilled into me by Ry, or something nudged forward by a past incarnation.

At Dreya's back, ice and snow spread outward, sending the fleeing crowd skidding on the ground. Ry races up behind her, a dagger held firmly in his hand. The last time he went up against the ice queen, things didn't turn out so well for him. I won't allow any repeats while I'm still alive.

"Please," I mumble to lady green, the earthen element.

A tree root springs from the ground, catching his foot, and sending him toppling to the ground, a loud curse escaping his lips. Dreya doesn't appear to notice. The activity thrumming at her back is ripe with the arrival of her monster-morphed puppet squad. Fifteen or twenty. It's enough. The crowd that gathered for Bree's oath isn't interested in fighting. They are retreating to the trees. Or are attempting to.

Lobrka and Ry have engaged the attacking force and now

take on the majority of Dreya's soldiers. Klarda and Al, having raced from the containment, help in the struggle. And Mo…like she had that night in Palinot, has once more shifted forms. Appearing to have shaken off the alcoholic affects sufficiently enough; she now brings the battle in the form of a massive troll.

Shoving against the internal burning and desire to ignite everything into flame, I push to a shaky stand.

"What did they do to you?" I ask, not knowing who *they* are, but confident they exist.

They could be her parents, my grandparents. Possibly my father, maybe someone else. But someone clearly did something to her. Something life shattering. Personality altering.

For a moment, hesitation and anguish flash across her features. But I no sooner blink, than her face has returned to harsh stone. "If it is cooling you need, then it is cooling I shall deliver."

The temperature plummets.

Frozen leaves, like stones, drop from the surrounding trees, and ice crystals erupt across the stage. They even form on the hem of Meira's gown.

Jaden moves in front of me, as if to shield me from the cold, and Raundel yanks me backward, putting distance between me and Aunt Dreya.

With a quick glance, Meira verifies that the two men have me, before tugging Bree away. "In case I have no more tomorrows," she says by way of explanation.

Her words make me dizzy. She couldn't possibly be suggesting Dreya is more powerful than an ancient elf from the beginning of time?

Bree and Meira scurry toward the trees. Within their cover, they crouch near to the ground, and mumble a string of words between them, while pressing hands to each other's heads.

With a look of amused delight, Dreya parts her blood red

lips and laughs. "Give her everything. It will make no difference. I have seen her in action, and she will fail to hold
firm."

They continue with their spell, ignore Dreya.

"And you." She waves a hand to indicate Jaden, Raundel,
and me.

Jaden lifts his cane into the air, as if it could act as a
barrier to stop her magic or approach. She smirks, her violet
eyes hardening.

"There is nowhere you can drag her that I cannot reach
with my icy touch." The urging of the fire within me dulls, my
toes and fingers now freezing and turning to ice. "Maybe a
heart of ice will compliment your frosty feelings for your dear
aunt." Her hand twists in the air as if she's turning the dial on
her magic.

My chest grows heavy, freezes over. Ice cubes rattle in my
breath.

A group of nymphs screams. Dart past. It's a momentary
distraction, pulling at both my and Dreya's attention.

In the nymphs' wake, something dark emerges from the
throng of battling bodies. Approaches Dreya from the rear.
It's the sway and curl of a long, black jacket. The hint of sun-
kissed hair in the light of the high moon.

A hunter. Her key.

He snarls, baring his teeth. "After all our time together, I
could have sworn you are the one a heart of ice would
complement." Dohlan flashes me a quick glance, as if veri-
fying my life has not yet ended, but the full heat of his intense
stare pins on Dreya and remains there.

"Thank you for opening the door." She lays her palm to
his cheek, granting him her attention. Despite all the rage I
want to direct at Dohlan, I am thankful for the reprieve. Short
as it may be.

Fire attacks under my skin, begins to thaw the ice filling
my veins.

"Thank Ana for releasing me from my prison," he replies with a coo.

My eyes blink wide. How did I help him when I've been on the stage, burning to death?

They both turn their attention to me, and Dreya hums a purr.

"Unexpected, yet helpful." She smirks, then turns back to Dohlan. "Now go kill something over there." She throws a point over her shoulder, indicating my brother and the others. "Kill everything."

SEVENTEEN

Dohlan's body turns to stone. One trapped on an unstable, jittery surface. Jerking as if he needs to go wreak havoc as Dreya suggested, but he's fighting against the inclination.

Marrouske steps an inch into my peripheral view. "I thought we had an agreement, Lord Marsoun."

Did she and Bree finish what they needed to do? Does Aunt Meira, Madame Marrouske, have any magic left with which to fight? Or did she just give it all away.

And…

Where's Bree?

Behind us, the trees and breeze whisper for only me to hear about a new master sage in the making. About Bree.

Dohlan's jaw tightens and nostrils flare, a scowl cutting across his lips. "If you recall," he says in reply to Meira. "It was your people who brought me here." He doesn't turn to look at the mystic, but keeps his attention glued to Dreya.

"An agreement?" Dreya's brow arches. "Without consulting me?" She flashes him a you've-been-bad frown. "We will have to make adjustments to your chains."

Dohlan snarls.

I gasp. Against my internal temperature conflict, or the new knowledge of Dohlan's state, I'm not sure.

Edea's words whisper as a reminder in my thoughts. "... *free my son from Dreya's control.*"

I never wanted to follow through on a request more than right now. No one deserves to be chained. Not like that. Not to the will of another.

"Now go do as I say." Dreya waves a dismissive hand to the fighting at her back. "Kill them."

His body shudders, and with tremulous motions, he turns to leave, his legs moving like lead. But even as he is following through on Dreya's order, the strain on his face, the twitch of his lip, speak of a Fae fighting her control with every one of his breaths. His hands roll into tight fists, and he pulls to a stop. A puppy fighting against a hurricane.

His gaze finds me, sharp and intense. "The ring?"

My body jolts, my hand reflexively grabbing for the circle of gold hanging at my neck.

"Use it." His words are rough, choked in his throat.

He turns away, his gaze swings past Dreya as he resumes his walk toward the fight, toward the given command to kill. But his steps are short, clearly still fighting the order.

Dreya's face turns fury red. And if her gaze could burn, Dohlan would already be ash.

With a slight tilt of his head, he yells over his shoulder. "You have to wear it."

Dreya laughs. "His words are nothing more than his attempt to put a ring on you. He so likes to toy with the young and naïve."

I don't listen. Instead, I tug at the string holding the ring, my fingers fumbling what should be an easy task.

"Let me help you." Jaden grabs the string, turning it to find the back. The latch or tie. I can no longer remember how I put the darn thing on.

Without a word, Raundel reaches in and breaks the string, sending the ring tumbling free into my flailing hands. I attempt to line the ring up, slip it on, but I'm shaking. Jaden takes control, slipping the ring on my finger unceremoniously.

"Why am I shaking?" I keep my voice low for only him to hear. I have never been the type to shake when nervous. Not even in the face of danger.

He scrutinizes me, then yanks off his glove and places the back of his hand to my forehead. I jerk away from the immediate electric jolt.

"Extreme temperatures," he says. "First high, then low. I believe your body is struggling to absorb what happened and find a healthy balance."

Great.

"Look at this," Dreya saunters a step forward. "I allowed myself to get distracted and you started thawing out." She lifts her hand as if preparing to intensify her magic once more.

Meira rushes forward. "Leave her alone."

With an exasperated sigh, Dreya flickers her hand away from me, toward Meira, sending a spray of slush. Large chunks slam into her, knocking her to the ground. With a predatorial hiss, Raundel cuts to her side and helps her up.

I flair my hand, showing off the golden ring now adoring my finger. "Stop," I yell to Dreya, to Dohlan. To whomever will listen or be affected by whatever magic the ring possesses. "You must stop."

Dreya laughs, a deep, belly roll cackle. "You thought that ring had the power to stop me?" She snorts. "Think again, child. You do not possess the power to stop me from anything." She takes a casual step toward us.

Leaping free of the battle at her back, Lobrka drops and slides, his sword swinging for Dreya's ankles.

Knock her down; then strike her out.

Only, she spins on him at the last moment, before his blade can connect. Ice shoots from her fingertips, covering him in frost and gluing him to the ground like a distorted, elven ice sculpture.

Klarda comes racing to Lobrka's aid and Dreya sends daggers of ice flying into the warrior hobgoblin's path. Klarda deflects and deflects but receives several cuts.

Taking advantage of her temporary distraction, Jaden grabs my ringed finger with his gloved hand, and examines the piece of jewelry more closely. "This is a mate's ring," he says.

"What?" I balk. "Why didn't you tell me that before?"

"I couldn't smell the blood, as I was then," he replies. As he was before Meira's magic.

"How…" I choke on the question, not sure I want to know how the ring smells of blood.

"Don't use the power of the ring on her." He tilts his head toward Dreya. "Use it on Dohlan, to countermand her order."

My gaze shifts to Dohlan's carnage in the center of the mob. He is destroying anything he touches, while keeping his forward motion slow enough, pained enough to hold him back from my crew…my family. Blood and bodies are flying and falling.

And my family, the hold a wide berth.

Except Klarda, who is trapped against a tree.

Dreya froze Kladra's hair to the trunk, rendering the warrior incapacitated…until she finishes cutting her frozen locks away. Which she currently works at doing. Dreya, choosing to be done with Klarda, turns back to face me.

"Where were we?" she taunts.

Only, I'm looking past her, searching the chaos for Dohlan. Ry fights a couple of Dreya's grunts, while keeping Zarah close at his side. Al ghosts in and out of the fight, taking out foes. Troll form Mo clobbers and clobbers. And Azure… holds his head in his hands, his eyes squinted shut…

Azure is about to get his throat slit by Dohlan.

I clutch my ringed finger to my heart and scream Dohlan's name. "Don't hurt them," I say. "Not any of my friends or family."

He's muscles relax and he lowers his weapon, not turning to face me. A vision of destruction, he tips of his blond hair are fringed with blood, his visible skin speckled with it. He is s destroyer of lives and emotions, and yet...have I stayed his killing blows?

Azure, having realized how close to death he stood, stumbles to the ground and scrambles, slow at first, then quickly away.

Azure is safe and Dohlan is still.

I steel a steady breath, shift my gaze.

"Hurt her," I add, swinging my arm out to indicate Dreya. She professes to hold his chain, but if the mate ring on my finger is able to override her command, maybe, just maybe...

He slowly twists, glancing over his shoulder to me, a delightfully wicked grin lifting his wicked lips. And then he's a blur, flashing across the chaos, to Dreya. His hands connecting with her body, his fingers curling around her neck and tightening.

And tightening.

Her fingers clawing at his grip. Her lips parting in a silent scream.

"Come." Raundel calls from behind us. He's carrying an unconscious Bree, and Meira...Marrouske...hobble-limps at his side. "We need to get you out of here and fortify the tree." He tilts his head in the direction of the water temple.

"What about the others?" Jaden asks, while directing me to follow Raundel. I sense his desire to join the fray, make sure our friends make it out okay. Weak and in need of a cane, I can't allow him to do so.

I spin, and scream. "Mo!"

The troll's head whips in my direction and, understanding my wild arm gestures, grabs Zarah and Azure, tosses them over her shoulders, and barrels our direction. Ry follows suit. But Al, she rushes to Klarda and helps finish sawing through the strains of hair trapping the hobgoblin to the tree.

We make it as far as the nearest outbuilding when an explosion sounds, and ice shatters in all directions. Frozen spears and clumps slam into trees, walls, people. Hail and slush drip from the leaves above like salt rocks from the sky. A harsh winter white covers the ground in an endless, treacherous terrain. And Dohlan...

Dohlan falls in an unmoving, limp lump upon the ground, Dreya looming over him reeking of countless negative emotions. Fury, the strongest among them.

"You aren't going anywhere," she screams, a long pointy finger jabbed in our direction.

"Yeah? Maybe you aren't either." I don't know where my response comes from. It just pops free of my mouth. I try to be snarky and cool, and I come out sounding ridiculous. Childish. Only...

With one quick sweep, I take in the surroundings of the battle destruction...a once beautiful section of the sanctuary. The land now sad and hurting, and she is to blame.

Elementals whisper in my blood. The land would like to get its hold on her, give her a piece of understanding.

"She's all yours," I say to lady green.

Roots shoot from the soil and claw at her legs and feet. She freezes them to the point of shattering. Which she does, shatter and shatter and shatter. Yet, where one root is shattered, another one stretches free of the frozen earth.

The exertion of working with lady green weakens my limbs and births a fine sweat upon my brow. If I manage to get out of this situation alive, I may sleep several days straight. My recovery may require it.

Behind her back, Dohlan lifts his head, sways, then pushes to a stand. He appears barely able to stand.

"Cute trick," Dreya says to me, and starts stomping a

march in our direction, freezing and shattering roots along the way.

With a flip of her hand, icy ropes snap into the air, and cut straight for me. Before her fury can reach me, Jaden steps in the way—a hint of his horns beginning to show—and lifts his cane in the air. Mumbling a barely audible incantation, he thrusts it forward like a spear and lets it soar.

It hits its mark, piercing Dreya through the shoulder. Her scream chills the temperature twenty degrees. Dohlan is on her before she can retaliate, grabbing her and dragging her out of sight.

I'm still physically shaking, though not nearly as much. My system moving closer to finding a balance between the fire now living in my veins, and the cool calm of water swimming over my soul.

Dreya and Dohlan may be gone to Gaea-knows-where, but the mutated soldiers fighting Dreya's battle remain. Her absence does nothing to slow their brutal attack.

Raundel paused, unconscious Bree still in his arms, and surveys the fighting, the perimeter, the tree cover, then sends a shrill whistle to the sky. It's a message, a call and request, letting others know the worst of the dangers is gone and help is requested.

His gaze drops to me. "I do not suppose there is any chance of you using the elements to clear the enemy from our home?"

Home…because this place is so much more than a sanctuary for some.

With a deep breath, I attempt to stop the mild tremors in my arms, hands, legs.

The touch of Jaden's gloved hand presses to the curve of my waist, his arm wrapped loosely around me. "She needs to settle her system first," he says, answering for me.

He glances over me, his horns gone, lips tight, and his assessing eyes a brilliant shade of green. "This time, the elemental transition hasn't dropped her into a metamorphic sleep, so I am hopeful she'll be at full form soon."

A quicker transition because of what Dohlan did to acclimate my system more readily. Or the ritual Edea performed on me. Two things I choose not to bring up in the present company.

Meira motions Raundel to resume their exit. "We should get both of the girls clear of here, anyway. The others can handle the dregs."

Ry volunteers to lead the cleanup and kick-out mission. Klarda, Al, and Mo join him, as do a few new able bodies that slink free or drop down from the surrounding foliage. Zarah and Azure remain with us. The latter, cradling his head against the pain, no doubt caused by the many present infected. His beautiful gift, feeling the infected and who knows what else.

Zarah presses close to my side. "That was scary. Are you okay?" I nod that I will be…hopefully soon.

With Zarah and Jaden at my sides, Raundel, Meira, and Bree in the lead, and Azure bringing up a miserable rear, we make our way back to the water temple.

Meira lowers herself to a raised stone set beside one of the blue pools in the temple, while Raundel locates a dry patch on the floor. A space away from any misty overspray produced by the various waterfalls where he gently lays Bree. My old classmate and new master sage doesn't move. Not so much as a twitch or eye flutter.

I chew on my lower lip. "Is she going to be all right?" Bree looks practically dead. And outside, beside the demolished ceremonial site, we left Lobrka frozen to the ground. Will this night end with an unwanted body count?

The edge of Meira's mouth twitches. "She should be.

Eventually. I gave her a lot at once. More quickly than I had planned. But under the circumstances, I felt it was best. I did not want to take the chance of losing what I know, should things have gone worse than they did."

Her gaze shifts to Bree and her expression softens. "She reminds me a bit of myself when I was her age." Her lips pull into a soft smile. "It will take her mind and soul time to process everything, but when she does awake, she should be in good form...for the most part."

So... "You just mind melded her with lifetimes and lifetimes of..." I raise my hands at my side and shake my head. "Everything?" *Bree could have a meltdown. On a nuclear level.*

"Assuming I understand you correctly..." Her smile cracks wide. "I did."

I suck back a breath and blow it out through my nose. Stare at Bree. When I melded with my first element, water, I was out for two or three days. Surely, an unspeakable amount of memories, knowledge, magic will take longer.

"I imagine you are feeling better," Meira says to Azure, redirecting the group focus. "Now that you are here, insolated from the infected havoc outside."

"I am. Thank you." He takes a seat, rests his hands upon his knees, and closes his eyes. Jaden pats his back, as if to say, *I am here for you, brother. Whatever you need.*

"Lovely." Zarah spins in a circle, taking in everything about the chamber.

The glistening blue pools, the colorful stone, the heavy rootstock veining parts of the walls, and the countless waterfalls of different sizes and strengths.

"This place keeps throwing surprises at me," she says. "No memory I have ever collected has given me the tiniest glimpse of the tree and its many wonders."

Meira huffs a slight laugh. "We do our best to keep everything about the tree protected."

"Speaking of," I say, thinking of Dreya and all the

infected she led into the sanctuary. My heart cracks from the carnage and ruin. Broken bodies, trampled and mangled nature.

"You are not wrong," Meira replies, as if reading my mind. "Until we can verify Dreya's status and where Lord Marsoun took her, you are not safe here."

Jaden's shoulders straighten. "I impaled her."

"Indeed." Raundel steps to Meira's side. "But until we hear otherwise, she remains a threat. A good warrior never assumes a wound inflicted, no matter how dire, will be the end of conflict...or life."

"It shall not be." Aunt Meira's tone is sullen. "Not in this case." She stares at the ground, as if seeing something we cannot, then shakes her head and raises her gaze to me, to Jaden. To each of us in turn. "We could not save Sol," she says of herself, Edea, Deona, and her sisters.

With a slight shake of her head, she continues. "If Dreya is somehow a product of his, there is no telling how much darkness courses through her. But however much that may be, I suspect it is more than enough to heal her from such a wound. And likely, heal her rather quickly."

"But Dohlan..." *He'll take care of her. Keep her from doing more harm.* I was wearing the mate ring when I told him to do so.

I glance down at the circle of gold still on my finger, and immediately start twisting, pulling it free.

"He is no match for her." Hints of unease weather the lines of Meira's face.

I jerk slightly back. She sounds as if she doesn't expect Dohlan to survive his attempt at stopping Dreya...on my behalf.

"But..." My brow presses, stomach tightens. "She wouldn't kill him. She likes him. Tugs at him like a toy."

Zarah gasps. "Dreya might kill Dohlan?" No one responses.

Instead, Meira says, "And if she did?" *Kill him?* Meira's

gaze is filled with gentle understanding. "It would be a mercy. I have no doubt, he would agree."

In my head, Kaia is screaming. Screaming and pounding the inner walls of my skull.

I stumble back a step and drop to a sit. Chew on my thumb nail and stare at the ground. Jaden settles in at my side, his hand hovering over mine, as if he wants to comfort me, but doesn't, because of the pain Ruby's curse will bring.

"She'll come after me again," I say softly. I sense them all staring at me, but Meira is the only one to respond, with a soft word of affirmation. "And when she does," I continue. "I shouldn't be here. I should draw her elsewhere, away from the tree."

"Agreed." Meira pulls herself to a stand and turns toward the doorway.

The slam of the outer door, followed by a small herd of heavy footfalls, marks the approach of not one but several.

Klarda, her hair now a ragged shoulder cut, charges into the temple, Al, Ry, and Mo at her back. "A sufficient number of like-kind came to our aid," she says, while Ry and Mo move past her to the rest of us, whereas Al remains firm at the hobgoblin side. "The enemy is free of the main grounds and is currently being chased to the outer wall."

Raundel's spine straightens. "Lobrka?" Last any of us saw him, he was encased in frost.

A tight nod. "Lobrka is being thawed and attended to by the healer."

Raundel's tension appears to relax with the report, just as Klarda rambles off each status like she's reading a line item on a report. "Our sources have yet to locate the ice queen, but report that she has not crossed the outer barrier." Meaning, she's still somewhere inside the tearman. The tree sanctuary.

Meira nods, a frown of unwilling acceptance at her lips. "I was afraid of that." Her gaze sweeps from Klarda, to me, then lands on Raundel. "We must induce the healing."

Raundel's face tightens. "Are you sure that is a good idea? We do not know…Never before have we…"

Meira raises her hand, silencing any current or coming protest. "I know. But it must be done. For Glynnii's sake."

My heart squeezes. "Glynnii?" As in Deona's mother who was absorbed by the tree.

Meira huffs an almost silent chuckle, albeit humorless and curt. "We had to call this beautiful seed something." She pats a large root veining through the wall at her side. "It did not seem fitting to continuing calling her tree, and no other name was more fitting…under the circumstances."

Ry opens his mouth, but Jaden speaks before he can get a word out. "How do you intend to heal the tree?"

"Why do you even need to?" Al asks, and Klarda shakes her head, telling her to remain quiet.

"It is all right," Meira says with a dip of her head toward Al. "I doubt the shadow stag is the only one wondering."

Al flinches at the title used by Meira.

What is a shadow stag? A cross between a white stag elf, Raundel's people, and someone of Shadow's people? Or something different?

Meira glances over the people in the temple. Every one of them has their attention trained on her. She sighs through the side of her mouth.

"Tonight, Glynnii has been burned and frozen," she says. "Chopped and sliced with heavy weapons. But more significant than any of those things, she has been up close and personal with the infectious darkness." Meira turns a soft gaze to Azure. "You know what that feels like." He quietly nods.

"She is not so bad, and she will heal quickly, but…" My aunt frowns at me. "In the interim, everyone will have to leave."

I balk. "You mean now, don't you?"

"Soon."

My gaze sweeps over Jaden, then Ry. "Where to? Dreya may be close at our heels," I remind.

"Mom," Ry blurts. "By way of Palinot."

"To collect the rest of our clan?" Azure asks.

"A side benefit," Ry replies. "We stop in Palinot because its far enough to draw Dreya away, while also being close enough that she'll want to immediately follow, before we can slip from her expected grasp."

Raundel crosses his arms and sets an evaluating gaze upon my brother. "Smart, and yet dangerous."

Meira waves a get-busy hand and moves toward the projecting wall behind which Mo and I changed earlier. "If Dreya is still within the sanctuary barrier, she cannot be allowed access to the Tears of Clarity, the Lagoon of Lucidity, or the magical properties found in these few pools."

She waves to the surrounding water temple. "So, make your preparations. When the healing is induced, there is a chance Glynnii will expel everyone, almost instantaneously."

"What!" Several of us explode at once, demanding clarification.

She stops next to me and takes my hand in her frail hold. "Within one of Glynnii's many magical chambers, there is a doorway leading to nowhere."

She glances at Raundel, and they exchange silent words with the tilt and dip of their heads. "But it may lead to somewhere, for the right individual, or in response to the correct request. You may be the right person."

Her gaze darts to Raundel, then swings over the entire group before returning to me. "Raundel will show you the way."

She steps to the edge of the space where Mo and I had changed into our water onesies, then glances back at me. "Keep your team together. Your Tracer, your warrior, your master sage." Her attention slips over each of them, in turn. Jaden, Ry, Bree. Then she steps behind the wall.

For a moment, no one moves or says anything, until Mo

rushes forward and glances behind the rock wall. "She's gone."

She swings back to the group, her eyes wide.

"There's a door in the wall somewhere." Raundel offers.

"A door, leading to a passageway," Klarda clarifies, continuing the explanation. "One that eventually connects to the Lagoon of Lucidity chamber."

"Come." Raundel swoops Bree up into his arms and turns toward the back of the chamber. "We must see if the tree will allow you to use the door or not."

I jolt. "It's a question? Not a for-sure thing?" The passage might be a dead end? A waste of time?

"Do you recall ever using the door?" he counters.

I do not. I don't even recall ever *seeing* the door. Discussing the door.

Raundel pushes a shoulder against the back wall of rock and a passageway slides open.

"Why do we waste our time?" Klarda says. "The door has never opened. Not for anyone."

EIGHTEEN

"For all things, there is a first." Raundel's words ring through my thoughts as we make our way to the never-before-opened door.

If it's never been opened, how do they know it actually is a door? Maybe it just looks like a doorway.

"If we're gearing up to leave…" Ry is saying at my back. "There are a few things I wouldn't mind grabbing."

I wouldn't mind collecting Mom's journal, I think. I'd like to know if she replied to my entry.

But Klarda argues with him, telling him there's no time. "You are lucky you have all your people present and accounted for," she adds. "You must think of the situation from that perspective."

After a few curves, turns, and a whole lot of footsteps, Raundel pushes open a wooden door set into an arch of stone and tree roots. The room beyond is no bigger than my bedroom back in Faredale. Smaller than I had anticipated.

And completely empty, aside for our entrance and two other doors, set opposite one another.

One, small and humble in appearance and the other, large

and covered in a wiggly design of clustered, webbed rootstock. No visible doorknob.

Four walls, three doors.

I gesture to the latter. "I'm going to guess that's the door that has never been opened." Emanating from said door, and vibrating through the chamber, is a low, thrumming energy.

"Another first added to the list," Deona whispers from a corner of my mind.

The rest of the group funnels into the room, each with various reactions of curiosity.

Zarah spins in a slow circle. "It's amazing," she says softly, a sense of awe in her tone.

"Never before have I felt anything like this," Azure adds.

Jaden motions to me and approaches the root-covered door. "You think Ana might be able to open this? Even though no other Balance Bringer has before." His question is directed at Raundel.

"No other has tried," he replies and readjusts his hold of Bree.

Jaden's fingers skim across an invisible barrier protecting the surface, the disruption making incandescent waves. The directional ripples draw my attention to a portion of the door where the roots curl and twist, creating a design reminiscent of the torans used to mark...and protect...the doorway between this world and the world of my upbringing.

Coincidence or meaningful?

"Well," Klarda says, the last to enter the space. "Shall we get to it? If Anala turns out not to be the key, I would like to make my own exit plans before the tree makes a decision for me."

Al clears her throat. "Because we shall all be evacuated without notice, by way of tree magic?" Klarda confirms with a short nod.

"There's something...familiar." Jaden's image momentarily flashes to his previous, horned incarnation, then back.

"It's slight. Weaved masterfully throughout the other energies." He beckons me forward.

I glance at Raundel, as if I require his permission, and
instantly regret the gesture. He merely nods toward Jaden and
the door.

"Do we need to worry about any blowback?" Ry asks. "If
it doesn't work? Or even if it does?"

Klarda huffs. "Be quiet and let her try."

Slipping in at Jaden's side, I wonder if I should be worried
that his other incarnation has made so many appearances.
Not that I necessarily mind. He smiles at me, encouragingly,
so I raise my hand to the invisible field protecting the door. It's
warm to the touch. Warm and tingly.

The prickle moves from my fingertips, up my arm, and
into my whole body, then tugs at my core.

"Daughter."

The word whispers around me. Through me. The voice of
the tree. The voice of Glynnii.

My friends, and the room, thicken and blur, as if trapped
in clear Jell-O, and I inhabit the air bubble in the center.

"I am not Deona, and you are not Glynnii." My gaze
wanders to the ceiling where the core of the tree spirals
upward out of view, in shades of soft brown, dressed with
wide rings.

*"A clear truth. But you are my daughter, nonetheless, as all things are
my children."*

Because all things begin with the tree of life. My lips pucker as I
consider that concept. Then I glance from Jaden, to Mo, then
Zarah and Ry. "Are they all right?"

*"All are fine. You are in what your people call a patch. A bubble
outside of time. I would never intentionally hurt my children."*

Not even Dreya, I think.

"None," she says as if hearing my thought. *"There are no good
or bad souls. Only good or bad choices."*

After everything I've seen, this lifetime and the many

before, that is a hard concept to accept. But I'm not about to start a debate with the tree of life. Not here, in her core. And not now, when time is of the essence.

"Some make more bad choices than others," she adds.

Many, many more. My lips press tight and I nod. "If all things are your children, then why are you only talking to me right now?" I swing my arm in a wide arc, indicating my friends.

"All are my children, but only you, and what you are, were brought to fruition by harnessing my core magic." The original magic performed by Meira, Edea, and Glynnii. The magic that made Deona the first Balance Bringer.

I survey my friends once more. Take stock.

Bree is still unconscious in Raundel's hold. Mo has a large gash on her arm and an ugly bruise on her brow. Ry has a new tattoo forming at the curve of his neck, any wounds received in the recent fight likely already healed. Klarda has a small cut on her nose, another on her cheek, and several bruises are just starting to make their presence known against her gray skin. Zarah is biting a nail, Azure rubbing his temple, the slightest hint of horns show on Jaden's head, and Al…

I don't know enough about Al to properly evaluate her, but she appears to be ghosting, not fully in a physical state.

"Well then…since we're so close." I motion between me and an area of the wall thick with roots. "And we're all your children…would you help us escape this situation?"

"In what manner would you like me to help?"

My gaze circles the room, not knowing the best place to set my focus. The roots of the tree are all around me, as is the voice. My attention settles to the door of question. "This is a door, is it not?" I ask. "Can you open it?"

"It is up to you to open the door. Only you decide your future."

Not true. "I didn't decide to be the Balance Bringer, nor be hunted by Dreya."

"You may not always get to decide what is thrust upon you, but you

decide what to do with it and how to react. Thereby, deciding your future."

"Okay." I allow the word to slip from my lips with slowed reluctance. "How do I open the door?"

The air around me pulses with one heavy thrum. *"To strive for the future you most desire, you must release the multitude of unwanted emotions you carry in your heart. They weigh you down. Hold you back. Often spiral your energy in the wrong direction."*

"Easier said than done," I mumble. Not a single one of my incarnations learned to live free of *emotion*.

"Magic is created through emotion, not thought. In order to bring magic to life, you must have emotional intention."

I blink and consider the many times I've used elemental magic. I wanted to make things happen, so wouldn't that come from a place of the mind, not the heart.

"Remember clearly," she whispers.

A shiver races through me, the word *remember* triggering a memory. A memory and a dream of the unicorns. *"Time to bloom, spread your wings and fly,"* the unicorn said to me.

Remember, bloom, spread my wings, and create with emotion. Preferably, positive emotion, I presume.

But...

My mind reels from the conversation with the tree to a thought, a mind image, of the unicorns and horse grazing near the edge of the sanctuary. They need to get out, race to safety...while they still can.

Also Gitta and Lobrka, what of them? And my mom's journal? The starburst crystal carried from the other world? Ry's wanted weapons? So many things being left behind to consider.

Mentally, emotionally, I am spiraling away from the tree and the door. Away from the task set before me.

"Your worry of stuff is misplaced. You must trust in the divine. When your emotions are in tune with the universal energies, all will be provided as needs arrive."

I scoff. "When has that ever happened?"

The air squeezes out of me and the vision of the room and friends around me vanishes. No longer standing in the core of the tree, all around me spreads the meadow where I first met Velsa.

"You wanted an example of when an answer to a need was provided by the divine," the tree says.

"It was my sister Crystia that led me and my group to Velsa and her herd," I argue.

"You cannot expect the divine to simply materialize something from nothing when your need arises. The divine energies work through others. In this case, your sister, guiding you to Velsa's herd when the need was most pressing."

The words come at me from all directions, and whether what she says is true or not, I shake my head. Find the truth within them both difficult to accept and hard to dismiss.

"It is understood that this is difficult for you, having been raised with worry and stress and fear ingrained in your process. Conditioned to accept such emotions as normal, even expected. But my children lost their way long ago and the struggle to return to your truth is not without strife."

Worry, stress, fear…all things I am feeling regarding those unaccounted for in our current perilous circumstances. Velsa, the herd, Lobrka, Meira, Gitta. Even Dohlan. My heart squeezes with overwhelming love for them—each and all of them.

The vision of the meadow fades into a new scene. One I recognize as the last place I visited the herd, the far edge of the sanctuary.

"What would you say to them?" the tree asks.

"I'd tell them to go in love and race to safety." A proud smile tugs at my mouth. Not pride for my message, but for having known the unicorns in any part of my life. Always calm, beautiful, and strong in the face of discord.

A pulsing blue light races across one of the roots lining the wall. The shimmer vanishes into the earth beyond. In the visual of the herd, a root breaks free of the ground, bursts thick with leaves. The leaves dance and sing, using the language of Gaea to send my message to the herd far beyond my physical reach.

Velsa bobs her head and turns to the others. With a neigh, they all move at a gait in the direction of the barrier and exit to the woodlands beyond.

"They'll be safe. I know they will." I press my hand to my heart as a smile warms my cheeks. "Thank you."

"It was you who sent the message. Not me." The image around me begins to shift once more. *"Just as it was you and your love that helped nudge this unfolding into action."*

A moment ago, the surrounding scene gave the impression I was outside, amongst the green and banyan air roots. Now, I could be standing just inside the door of the infirmary. Gitta, with aid from the healer Airmed, is helping Lobrka stand. His hair is wet, and his dark skin now has a hint of blue. His arm is in a sling, and he limps as if walking on tiny, ice spikes. But he's alive and upright.

"Thank you," I whisper, just as the scene changes once more...to Meira.

She's someplace I've never seen. Not this life or any life prior. And yet, something about the location rings with familiarity. An ancient stone alter, encrusted with roots and vine, sits in the middle of a room heavily covered in rootstock of all sizes.

"The place of your birth," the tree says.

I realize I am gazing upon the place of Glynnii's death.

Kneeling beside the covered alter, Meira whispers an incantation.

"Is she?" I don't need to finish the question. The tree of life knows.

"She is sending me into a healing statis. Soon, the spell will be complete, and I will be cocooned."

"For how long?" I raise my hand to the image of the alter. The tree wrapped around the ancient stone.

"As long as necessary."

"But…" I swallow hard. "Is it necessary?" All these beings, that for countless years, decades, eons, have known nothing beyond living in the sanctuary. What will they do?

Meira and the ancient alter are gone, and now laid out on the screen before me is a crumpled and bloody Dohlan. Dreya marches away from him, blood dripping from her nails. And with those bloody nails, she is slicing at every tree root she passes, cutting and freezing, cutting and freezing.

I feel the pain, within my connection to the earthen elements, lady green. Dreya is attempting to freeze the tree… possibly to death.

"No." The word is a razor blade in my throat, and my love for the life of the surrounding tree explodes in depth and weight. So much so, I fear I may collapse beneath the immensity of it.

"Trust, Balance Bringer. You must learn to trust your intuition."

The patch of time surrounding me shatters, and my friends return to life and action as if nothing happened.

"Well," Klarda blurts. "Get started."

The root-covered door pops open with a clack and a small puff of dust.

Klarda gasps, and Ry whistles.

"It is done." Raundel announces the obvious, then turns to Klarda. "Take the sage, go with Deona, and keep them both safe. I shall retrieve Lobrka, and we will find you."

I want to argue with him for calling me Deona, but now is not the time. "You better hurry," I say. "Dreya is attacking and inflicting significant damage to the tree. Plus Marrouske has almost completed the spell for the healing encasement, or whatever."

Raundel hands the care of Bree to Klarda without a word,

then rushes out the door on the opposite wall. Not the one through which we entered.

Al raises her chin. "Looks like everyone but Anala missed something."

"We can talk about that later," Ry replies.

"Indeed," Azure blurts. "If the old elf is about to put into motion whatever it is she's about to do, we should get moving."

Zarah nods. "And draw Dreya away."

Jaden pulls the door to a full open. "You want to do the honors?" he asks me. His eyes sparkle with excitement and a hint of challenge. The space beyond the door is pure darkness, but I'm fully committed, and one hundred percent up to the challenge.

We need to go so that the tree may be saved. Healed.

I glance over my shoulder to the rest of the group. "I don't know how this is going to work, so stay close." Taking Jaden's gloved hand in mine, and ignoring the echo of Ruby's curse electrifying our touch, we plunge together through a curtain of magic veiling the entrance, and step into the space beyond.

The invisible markings covering my skin burst to life in a bright glow of blue. Matching marks take form in the spaces all around us. All of them...on my skin or in the surrounding space... shift, turn, and spin, like the moving of pieces on a puzzle lock box.

When they stop, and the markings fade, the darkness is no more. Thick green crowds us, swirling and pushing at our stability. A terrestrial in between. Between choices and worlds.

"How does this work?" I reach out, hoping to grasp an unseen doorknob.

"You must know," Jaden says. "Somewhere in your gut, you must have an inkling of an idea what to do."

The warmth of bodies pushes into the space behind us, their breathing, hitched with fear and anticipation, the dominant sound. A high wind slams into our backs and the door through which we just stepped slams shut.

"Do you think that was it?" Mo asks. "The healing activation, and banishment of all being that aren't the tree?"

No one answers, but I'm confident that we are all wondering if she is right. Did Velsa and the herd get out in time? What about Raundel, Lobrka, Gitta, Airmed? And if they were still on the sanctuary grounds, what became of Meira? Dohlan? Dreya?

A circular window opens at our side, and beyond, a place I vaguely recall from a few past lives.

"Mother's there," Ry calls from my back, pointing to the Garrison seen through the window.

On my other side, another circle to another space. This one focused on a castle powdered with white and dripping with ice. The place from my dreams. The place where I must go if I want to stop Dreya.

Two choices. One on either side of me.

A third option appears, directly ahead. A vision of a street somewhere in Palinot City.

"*Your heart wavers between the choices,*" the tree says. "*You must choose the one that beats the strongest.*"

One will take me toward the task of stopping Dreya, hopefully, somehow. Or at least, severing her control over Dohlan. Another will lead me to my mom...whom I miss dearly. And the final choice...

Far enough away from the tree while being close enough to draw Dreya to us.

With the healing cocoon being activated, I'm not sure the objective behind the plan still holds up, but Jaden's clan is in Palinot and, as much as Ruby annoys me, she and Azure should be together.

Save the tree. Reunite family and friends.

With one step forward the options at our sides dissipate. No chance of changing my mind, and with Jaden at my side, I lead the group through the remaining portal. We leave the green of the in between behind us, and the portal releases us with reluctant suction.

We slip through the oval opening, get tugged and pulled and tightened, much like we had when we dove into the water doorway that brought us to Hiddenkel. Only, this time, we aren't swimming, and we aren't spit out at the bottom of a lake. We stumble into a dark, muddy street somewhere in the shoreside city.

Someone witnesses our arrival and gasps, scurries away.

The rest of our party tumbles free of the portal, bumping and collapsing into one another. The portal expelled us at the base of a large tree, framed by a circular stone wall, and sitting in the middle of an intersection between three converging streets.

The ground at our feet is soft and damp inside the protected spot of land for the tree. The street beyond dark, and the nearest burning lantern flickering dim.

"Bleeding bark and bloody berries. Where did you all come from?" Shadow emerges from the nearby gloom, his eyes wide with incredulity.

NINETEEN

A smile instantly warms my lips. One goal—locate friends—has already been accomplished.

"Shadow." His name is a burst of pure enthusiasm from my lips. I climb over the short wall and dart across the open street, throw my arms around him in a healthy hug. "I feel horribly guilty." *For pulling you into my scheme and getting you kicked out of the sanctuary.*

"You should be." He pulls back and glances over me, a wide grin cutting across his face. "If you are arriving looking the way you all do, and in this manner ..."

He motions to the tree, the battle worn attire, and bodily injuries. "Clearly by the use of magic...then I obviously missed something exciting. And you know how I feel about excitement." He chuckles, then more closely surveys the group behind me.

Jaden, Azure, and Al are already at my side, shoving me to the side to collect their own greetings. Hugs and warm words are exchanged, then Shadow nods a hello to Ry, Zarah, Mo, and Klarda.

"Who's that?" He motions to Bree's limp form, now slung over Klarda's shoulders.

"The new master sage," she replies.

His eyes widen. "Seems I missed several big somethings indeed." He pauses, as if considering what to do next. "Welp."

He tilts his head in a quick gesture to the side, then turns into the motion. "We should get going before curfew enforcement finds us. Follow me. You all look as if you need a strong drink and a soft mat."

"Since when is there a curfew?" Jaden asks.

"Since Dreya's attack," Ry, Zarah, and Shadow say in unison.

Ry tosses me a sideways glance. "It's one of the things Mom initiated, in order to help locate any unwanteds lingering in the city."

A logical reason. Although, if one does not want to be found, plenty of hiding places exist in the city. I investigated a few of them the last time I was here.

A tight head shake pushes the dark, unwelcomed memory away. And I walk silently between Mo and Zarah.

Like a small band of weary soldiers returning from battle, we follow Shadow through the moonlit streets, toward the current residence of the Augur clan.

He glances over his shoulder and counts our numbers. "Where are your too-tall elves, or the high witch?"

Klarda bristles. "You will watch your tongue," she snaps.

"Relax," he placates. "It is all in good fun. They are the ones who expelled me, after all."

"With good reason," she retorts.

He tilts his head, a resigned smile tugging at the edge of his mouth. "Fair enough."

"Have things remained quiet?" Ry asks, redirecting the subject. Shadow nods. "And are you still at the same place?"

Shadow again nods. "Saw no reason to relocate. Not as long as Ruby…" His gaze shifts to Azure.

"Tell me," Azure says.

With a sigh, Shadow wraps an arm around Azure's shoulders and tugs him in a side squeeze. "She's going to be ecstatic to see you. These past few days…well, she's been more miserable to endure than usual." He turns his head toward Azure. "You know what I mean."

"I do," he replies, and both he and Jaden nod in acknowledgement. Even those of us who don't know Ruby well understand.

Azure sighs with a hint of relief and rakes his fingers through his hair. "Try not to judge her too harshly." He smiles meekly at me. "She may see relationships and strong connections, but she lacks skill when in comes to navigating her own emotions."

I bite my tongue against the snarky comment fighting to explode off my tongue.

Shadow continues. "I don't know how you managed to get her your pendant, but ever since she returned to the lodging house, with the piece around her neck, she won't stop clutching the stone and staring in the direction of the woodlands, as if she is expecting you to stroll down the street at any moment."

"Well then…" Azure entire features lift. "I look forward to surprising her."

Shadow chuckles and Jaden slaps Azure on the shoulder.

The rest of our walk is filled with mumbled updates, briefing Shadow on all the excitement he missed, and him updating our group on the activities of the three clan members. Which, for the most part, has been them talking to any local who they thought might have information…no matter how slight…on the clan mother Opal.

Within the large group and the open street, I choose not to vocalize anything I know with regards to Opal…Edea. Even though the windows of the homes and businesses we pass are closed and the lighting dim or off.

I finger the gold ring. Dohlan likely knows more, anymore. And if he isn't dead, there's a chance I *might* be able to summon him. *Maybe*. I've never had a mate ring before, in any lifetime, and so I'm not familiar with how it works and what all it can do.

At a street junction, Shadow pauses and turns to face the group. "This place lacks the finery of the last place you stayed at here in the city."

His word choice makes me grimace. The last place we stayed was hardly lavish, or anything close. Fine maybe, but not fancy.

"The kitchen is subpar," he continues. "The food barely passing for edible. And the clientele is mostly quiet or passed out drunk. But the liquor is strong, and the rooms have beds. Although, the accommodations sleep many, and there is little privacy."

"Sounds like a four-star establishment," I quip.

Ry rolls his eyes, but no one else says a word, my joke clearly lost on them.

With a blink and a blank expression, Shadow turns and leads us forward. Within a half block, the lodging comes into view. The front door bangs open, and two men stumble out, one dropping his bottle to a crash and shatter on the ground. The men laugh, then complain, stumbling away with a drunken swagger.

"I did warn you about the drunkards," Shadow says with a frown.

Before the front door can fully swing to a close, a bois-terous release of song escapes into the night air. One painfully out of tune voice singing louder than all the rest. A voice belonging to a woman.

The three Augur clan men exchange glances filled with

surprise and panic, then take off at a hard dash for the building.

"Ruby," Al says, by way of explanation.

The voice belongs to Ruby. Totally out of character from what I know of her. She has to be drunk. Like, seriously, bottom of the barrel drunk.

"You don't want to join them?" I ask.

She smirks. "They can handle it. Besides..." She eyes Klarda, then Ry. "You might need me, should you get ambushed before we make it inside.

Klarda huffs a laugh. "When it comes to a fight, I *need* no one." She shifts her gaze to Al. "Want, on the other hand, is a different story." She grins wickedly at Al. Then winks. Returns her attention to the path ahead.

Ry clears his throat. "Should I be insulted by your comment? It sounded as if you consider me a capable warrior."

Al laughs. "Only you can decide if you should be insulted or not."

"What about me?" Mo asks. "I can be formidable."

"Indeed," Al replies and turns to study Mo. "What was that monster thing you turned into?"

"A troll," I blurt. Deona fought them, both as normal and infected. Their existence in this world had been an anomaly, since she had previously relocated the species to the nethers.

Zarah sucks back a tiny breath. "There hasn't been a troll sighting in ages. Ages upon ages."

Because I banished them to the nethers.

"How did you know what one looks like?" she asks.

Mo shrugs. "I have no idea. I simply knew."

Opal's...Edea's...words to Meira jump to the front of my thoughts. "*...the girl in there....*" Referencing Mo in the next room. "*...she came from the nethers.*" The nethers, where Deona relocated the trolls, among other species. Another juicy mystery to stab my knife into, at a later time.

Ry yanks open the door and offers all the women of the group entrance before himself. Inside, Shadow and Clef are silencing the crowd, while Azure and Jaden guide Ruby down off a table. She slips and falls into Jaden's arms.

She laughs, a hard bark, then stares up at him with a frown planted firmly on her lips. "You are different." She bops him on the nose with the tip of her finger. "How are you different?"

He opens his mouth, as if intending to answer, but she squirrels out of his hold.

"Later," she says with a slur. "It is this one I want." She tumbles free of Jaden's arms and fumbles right into Azure's. "Missed you." She plants her lips on his, drags him close, and kisses him feverously.

Shadow and Clef look away, even as the rest of us stare on. The spectacle that is Ruby is a circus act I can't drag my gaze from.

When their lips finally separate, Ruby is gasping for breath.

"Are you all right?" Azure asks. "Never have I seen you this…" He stops himself before he can fill in the blank. Drunk. Intoxicated. Smashed.

"I am happy." Her voice takes flight with the expression of her emotion. "I was not feeling so great." Her shoulders and face droop. "But then, I saw mother, and I celebrated…plenty. And now, I feel…" She extricates herself from Azure's hold, and, with a childlike squeal, she raises her hands to the sky and spins in place.

The spinning stops. She grabs her stomach and lurches forward.

In an instant, the Augur men are moving and directing and grabbing. Clef fetches a pale. Shadow, a tankard of water. Azure directs her to a chair. And Jaden takes a step back, scrutinizes the scene playing out.

"Why don't you take her upstairs?" he says. "Somewhere

out of view of the other patrons. Get her hydrated, and let her sleep it off."

Acting on the suggestion, Azure lifts Ruby's arm over his shoulder and guides her to the stairs at the back of the room. "Somebody show me where I am going," he calls over his shoulder. Clef rushes to his aid.

Klarda huffs a laugh. "That was unexpected." Everything about her tone expresses her general dislike for Ruby.

Jaden and Shadow cross to our location. "She doesn't usually drink to extremes," Jaden says.

Shadow shrugs his head into his shoulders. "She has been exceptionally sad and irritated lately."

The two men exchange a calculating look, as if thoughts and words are bouncing back and forth, only understood by them.

Al crosses her arms and studies every shadow and corner of the room. Shabby wood floor, dreary stone and plaster walls, a crackling fire in the hearth. "If she saw Mother, where is she now?" she asks.

Shadow frowns, shakes his head, and surveys the room. All of us visually scour the room, but neither Opal, nor Edea are anywhere to be found.

"It is possible..." Mo swings a two-finger slash in the air. "...that she was drunk enough to have imagined the reunion."

With a general mumble of agreeance, plans are made to clean up...wounds especially...grab a swath of shuteye, and meet back in the main room at dawn, in order to take stock of our situation, our knowledge, supplies, and possible assets.

The upper level of the building is divided into six large communal sleeping spaces. Under Shadow's direction, our group appropriates two. Of which, he further insists on assigning one to the men and the other to the women. Everyone is too tired to argue.

He enlists Clef and Al's help in redirecting any one not of our group into one of the other four rooms. And once arrangements are settled, Azure leaves Ruby to her alcoholic coma, trusting Al to keep a close eye on her.

After a quick scrub of my hands and face, I settle into a cot beside Bree. She twists onto her side, and I jolt, surprised she moved at all. She folds her hands under her head and her eyes flutter open.

"Are we having a slumber party?" she asks, then drops back into a heavily sedated state.

"What is a slumber party?" Mo asks, standing at the foot of the bed.

"Ana. Oh Ana." Ruby stumbles across the room. She drops onto the side of my cot and swoops me into a strangle hold. "I am so sorry," she slurs. "I had no idea. I have been so stupid and rude and manipulated. I hate myself for playing the part she designed for me."

"Um. Okay." I wiggle out of her hold and push her back. Her eyes are bloodshot and unfocused.

Mo stature stiffens. "What is she talking about?"

"I have no idea." I glance over the room, searching out Al. Find her and Klarda wrapped in each other's arms, dead to the world. Zarah is asleep in the next cot over, tiny snores emanating from her throat. I, too, should already be dead to the world. *It's been a day.*

Ruby's head lurches forward. "Mother told me what she did. What she made me, and I am…I am…horrified."

"What did she do to you?" Mo blurts, no sympathy in her delivery. I hold my reaction steady.

Ruby sniffles and wipes at her nose. "She designed me. Dragooned me to be a wedge between you and Jaden." She gasps. "She made me this…" She frantically waves her hands up and down, indicating herself, her body. "On purpose."

She drops into my lap, her hands folded beneath her head, and begins to bawl.

Opal…Edea…messing with people's lives? As much as I should be surprised, I'm not. Not after learning what she did to her own son. She somehow altered Dohlan to attract Kaia, and now I learn she did whatever it is she did to Ruby, in an attempt to drive a wedge between me and Jaden.

All the manipulation, it makes me ill. Creates a roil in my belly.

But if Edea was willing to magically mess with her son, and tinker with Ruby's purpose…

Wonder what she did to each of the others. My heart squeezes. *I wonder if she did something to Jaden.*

Everything Edea has done has been directed at the same purpose. End the bond I made with Jove during my first lifetime.

Why?

By her reasoning, because the bond hasn't served up much success when it comes to previous Balance Bringers effectively righting the scales.

I recall my lifetimes that include wins, and I consider the many times I failed to achieve the goal.

Edea may actually have a point.

A POT OF STEAMING COFFEE…OR Hiddenkel's version of coffee…and several empty mugs are waiting on the table when I drag my too-tired body down to the main room.

As expected, Ry, Al, and Klarda are already seated at the table, sipping their morning wakeup juice and murmuring secrets. Jaden sits with them, quietly listening. I blink wide awake. He's the dark, horned incarnation from a previous life.

Does he simply decide how he wants to look and then, bam, presto?

At the sight of me, he rises and pulls a chair from the table, offering me a seat. I thank him, stare at him, accept the seat. Nibble on my lip and try to avert my gaze so as not to appear too interested, but everything about this version of him has me curious, wanting to know more. Explore more.

As I settle into my seat, all eyes turn to me. Ry leans into the table and narrows his gaze. "This is an interesting development." He tilts his head in Jaden's direction. "You failed to mention this new change."

"I am right here," Jaden says, with clear indication of annoyance, his eyes darkening like the forest at night.

"We can all see that, devil prince," Ry jabs, cracking a smile.

Jaden snarls but is quick to relax his apparent irritation. Before my Balance Bringer binding, I can't recall him ever snarling. He's definitely becoming more colorful. My hand reached to sooth, but quickly pulls back. *Ruby's curse*, I remind.

"This is a new development," I say to Ry and the others. "I'm still processing. But he's the same guy, where it counts." *That and more*, since all his incarnations are now a part of him.

Jaden's gaze softens with what I take for gratitude, and his mouth pops ever so slightly open. His lips are suddenly all I can see. All I can focus on.

He shifts his chair back, turning to address me directly, and I manage to blink myself back to attention. "Does this form displease you?" he asks, tracing a finger along the edge of my jaw. A finger with a slightly sharp nail. I try to hide my shiver and avoid staring at the tiny fraction of his chest visible, or the press of his muscles against his shirt and sleeves. I fail spectacularly.

He notices and smiles. "Does my adjusted personality upset you in some manner?"

A grimace pulls to my lips, and I shake my head. He's still the same Jaden, to a degree. I can sense that, but any new aspects are parts of him I have loved in another lifetime. In fact, various versions of me, recognize those bit and pieces new to this incarnation of him.

None of that is necessarily unwanted or unattractive. I can and will adjust, and I believe I will manage to do so with ease.

But the current predominant physical manifestation belongs to a version for which I have no accessible memory... because that was Izza's lifetime, and Izza wasn't present for the binding of sisters and Balance Bringers. So, coming face to face with him is new.

Another new thing this time around.

"It's not that anything about you is displeasing," I say, my gaze lingering a smidgeon too long on the horns protruding from his thick tangle of hair at the sides of his forehead. They are swept back with a delicate curve, as if pressed and cast by the wind, and spindled to communicate both charm and seduction.

"But..." he presses, leading me to continue my explanation. I'm still staring at his horns, my thoughts momentarily lost. And he's moving ever closer, his breath mingling with mine.

"Sorry," I say with a shake back to my senses. "It's like I said. I just need time to adjust to the change. I got used to you one way, and now you're..." I lift my hands as if to present him to himself.

The words are a half truth because, yes, I got to know him one way and now he's more. And yes, it will take a little getting used to. But...

I blink and stare. Gods and Gaea. I think I want to grab his horns and kiss him eagerly.

His lips tug upward on one side of his mouth. "I am the culmination of all versions my soul has chosen to present, lifetime after lifetime. You had no problem with the individual parts. I hope you will now not find issue with the whole, as we stand combined."

"So..." I chew on my lower lip. "All the different versions of you are in there?" I point to his chest. Want to press my palm to the sculpture of him. "And you decide which version gets to come out and play...so to speak?"

"No." His response is sharp and definitive.

"There are no versions to take turns. There is only me." He tilts his head to look down at me, his gaze filled with curiosities and wonders. "All the different incarnations, the various personalities I have lived by, merged into one. This one. The Jaden you've come to know, but with more memories, knowledge, and experience." He presses his hands to his chest.

Klarda clears her throat, drawing my attention. Klarda, Ry, and Al are all staring at Jaden and me, daggers of annoyance in their eyes.

Ry's eyes narrow. "How about you two save the foreplay for later."

"Right." I cough. "We can discuss this at another time," I say to Jaden, and return my attention to the planned discussion—taking stock of our situation, our knowledge, supplies, and possible assets.

Ry runs down the list. "No horses. Few weapons. Light on warriors. And an extraordinary group of exhausted newbies... mostly. Basically, we have a lot of gaps to fill."

I take offense at the newbie comment, after all, I've lived and remember more lives than any of them. But I choose not to bring that fact up. "Don't forget our pros," I say. "More agility, wit, and likability." I smirk.

"Not helping." Al drops the weight of her folded arms on the table.

Someone yanks the chair at my side away from the table, and Mo takes a seat, a bowl of slop in her hand. "Ana is currently providing the much-needed tension break," she says, adding to the current conversation.

She tosses me a grin and a wink, then notices me inspecting her breakfast. "Looks delicious, no?"

I cough into my fist.

"Like I told you last night..." Shadow drops into one of the other open chairs. "Barely edible."

Clef takes the seat beside Shadow, across from me. "But it gets the job done."

The rest of our group files in and fills all the empty seats at the table. Ruby and Azure appearing a bit tousled, and Ruby is clearly nursing a hangover.

"Nice of you all to finally join us." Klarda sweeps a glare of judgement over each and every one of them.

"Hey," Clef says with a scowl. "The sun has yet to peek its head into the sky. I think we are doing well enough."

Klarda glowers but doesn't pursue an argument.

"As I was saying," Ry cuts in. "We're low on just about everything. Including information." He smiles inwardly, as if a thought has just amused him. "But, if we have nothing else, at least we still have the boat stowed at the port."

The boat that brought us here from Zarah and Ry's homestead. The same homestead he blew up upon our exit, hoping, no doubt, to catch Dreya in the explosion.

We didn't.

"Information is what we need the most." He leans forward and stares down the table at me. "Do you think...Ana." He tacks on my name as if to clear any doubt as to who the question is intended for. In case the sharp, pointed stare wasn't enough. "Well...could you use your gift with the elements to locate all the missing players? Gather their location and condition?"

A curious idea. I riffle through my memories, searching for a similar action. All evidence I unearth suggests, probably. Although I would have preferred more hours of sleep, I am moderately refreshed and magically refilled.

"I'm happy to give it a try." I glance around the room. "But not here. Someplace where I'm closer to a water source and unadulterated earth."

"We'll do that then," Klarda declares before Ry can say

anything. "Eat up." She raises a chin to the people gathered around the table. "We must get a move on." Her gaze shifts to Ruby, then Zarah. "We will need a few to stay with the master sage."

When no one volunteers, Klarda and Ry choose. Zarah, Ruby, Mo, Clef, and Azure.

It's a lot of people to watch one sleeping girl. But I don't care to have an audience watch over me while I attempt communication and a subsequent search with the elements, so I make no argument.

After our bellies are full enough, the five of us: Ry, Jaden, Klarda, Al, and myself, stride up the street, toward the wood-lands, the nearest space of unadulterated earth. Klarda knows of a small well set near the city's back gate. Water. We make way for a quiet spot somewhere between the two.

The sun has barely begun to light the sky when we find our spot. I settle on the ground, legs crossed beneath me, and fingers laced through the grass. A communal well is less than three feet away. I can feel, hear, taste the water in the cavern far below.

The touch of green tickles my skin, the tang of water wets my senses, the caress of air hugs the curve of my cheeks, my neck, and the fire of the sun's heat warms my back...my crown.

I close my eyes, find a peaceful place within to dwell, to sit. Make a request of the elements and wait. I don't have to wait long. They poke at me, awaiting my request.

I'm looking for our friends, our family, our enemies. Can you help me locate them all? The ones present at the sanctuary last night, moments before Meira set the tree's healing cocoon in place?

My body thrums, fast and heavy, high in the chest. Excitement and acceptance of my query.

Wind moves the fastest, bringing me information on all the people we left back at the lodging house. Thanking the wind, I ask the elements to keep searching.

Meira, Raundel, Lobrka, Gitta, Airmed, the unicorns…Velsa's herd. I make a mental list. *Dohlan,* I add. *And Dreya.*

Roots erupt from the ground at my fingers. They wrap around me in a gentle touch and thrust images at me, as seen from the trees outside the sanctuary gate.

Gitta run-limps with Lobrka at her side. Raundel and Airmed race at their back, dragging a torn up, half-conscious Dohlan between them.

"Dohlan," Kaia yells. My body prickles with heat.

His chest is marred, sliced and diced with countless cuts. Cuts from Dreya's nails. I recall how she used them to cut at the tree. They had been covered in blood at the time. Dohlan's blood. The wounds on his chest are deep and wide and…

She tried to claw out his heart!

My hands fist in the grass, and a firestorm explodes through my system.

A foot from the sanctuary gate, Dohlan stumbles. Using the momentum of his falling form, he shoves Raundel forward, then collapses, dragging Airmed with him to the ground.

Raundel is thrust through the magical barrier.

The healing cocoon activates with a whoosh and a pop. The blast of energy throws Raundel farther forward to the ground beyond. He spins onto his back, searching for Dohlan and Airmed, but he's too late. Everything and everyone inside the sanctuary walls is trapped in a whirlwind of magic and untamed energy…and then they are gone.

Just gone.

A trail of Dohlan's blood left floating…falling from the air.

Flames erupt at my hands. Race outward across the grass.

TWENTY

T he image of Dohlan's bloody chest is trapped, like sticky paper, in my mind. I can't shake the visual or vanquish the memory. Did she do that to him because I used the mate's ring to free him from her command?

I press my eyes closed tight against the onslaught of tears.

Heat is a fury in my blood, and beyond, flames lick at my skin.

My friends are crying. Ry…Jaden…they're screaming for me. My name a plea on the wind, asking me to stop, or to open my eyes. But the image of Dohlan, it has me trapped in its snare and I can't look away. Can't find release.

"Stop her," someone yells.

"What are you doing?" another hollers.

My elemental senses detect movement through the grass and around the fire.

"She won't hurt me." The voice is soft, and kind, and belongs to Jaden.

A gentle hand wraps to the curve of my shoulder, sending harsh electrical stabs. *Ruby's curse.* When he says my name, it's a whisper freeing me from the horror, and pulling me back to the now. I blink up at him and he pulls his hand free, removing Ruby's shocking reminder.

He kneels at my side, looking every bit the Jaden I know from school, the farmer's market, my dreaming, the majority of our journey here in Hiddenkel.

"Pull back the fire," he says. "And then we can talk about it."

It, meaning that which sent my emotions into chaos.

I blink away from him to the group standing beyond my hedge of flames. The fire burns in a low reaching arc. Although, presently still, evidence upon the grass suggests I was the ignition source and the small blaze quickly traveled outward to its present location.

"I don't know how I did that." Even as I say the words, my pulse and rage are calming, and the fire follows suit. Growing smaller and smaller, until it pulls into the earth with little more than a whisp of smoke.

Ry rushes forward and presses his callus-covered hands to mine. "Are you all right? What did you see?" He leans in to scrutinize my condition.

"I saw..." I sniffle and wipe at an escaping tear. "I saw Dohlan." I shift my gaze from Ry, to Jaden, then back to Ry. Neither reveal an emotional reaction. "Dreya tore him to pieces." My voice cracks. Inside, Kaia is reeling, withering, screaming.

"Well, if that's all." Ry stands, stretching tall, and casts a frown down at me.

Jaden heaves a breath and watches me, his eyebrows pressing into the bridge of his nose. I detect sympathy in his gaze, his energy, but something else too. Jealousy. Jealousy for any bond I share with Dohlan, even if it was made not by me but one of my sisters.

"I'm sorry if he is hurt," he says, his tone soothing, clearly meant to calm. "I'm sorry if his condition pains you. But we need to know…"

"Yes." I interrupt. "I need to gather far more information than just Dohlan's fate." I suck back a centering breath, pulling it all the way to my core. "Let me just…" I wave my hands along the line of my body. I need to settle my mind. Reconnect from a place of harmony.

Jaden shifts, preparing to step back and give me space. I snatch his hand and push it to the ground beneath my own.

My gaze snaps to his. "Stay," I say. "Add your strength to mine." He accepts my request with a nod.

Working with the elements and receiving their visual messages is different than getting pulled into ancestral dream walks or nightmare induced visions initiated by Dreya's dark and tarry land infections. Yet, I am hopeful Jaden will be able to see and experience all that I do.

"Take two," I mumble, and give myself to the elements once more.

The wind whips around me, playing with my hair, and kissing at my skin. The earth rumbles beneath Jaden's and my hands, roots rising and wrapping lightly around our fingers. Water sings at our side, a few splashes rising from the well and sailing through the sky to find us. The heat of the sun, although still present, is more subtle than before, fire bowing out of my second request.

But the three connected elements are more than enough to meet my needs.

The trees and wind show us Raundel, Lobrka, Gitta, and Airmed making their way through the woodlands. With the tree of life now trapped in a dormant state, the air root tunnels that somehow sliced time and distance off their travels is not available to them. Lobrka's condition has them moving at a slow to moderate pace, and the path before them is long.

The visual from the trees and wind shift, as if a camera is

swinging to a new location. Zarah's horse wanders amongst the trees, appearing lost.

"Velsa? Belmiso?" *The unicorns?*

The elements return with nothing to share.

"Unicorns are most magical creatures," Jaden says softly for only us to hear. "All other magics protect them. They must want to be seen if they are to be seen at all."

In other words, they are choosing to hide, even from me.

As much as I try not to be hurt by that possibility, and likely reality, my chest still tightens.

I am beyond blessed to have as much contact with the unicorns as I did. Resignation sighs through me, and I turn my thoughts to my mystic, mentor, and aunt from another life.

Meira, Airmed, Dreya, and Dohlan, the remaining targets left to locate, have been scattered...or relocated...far and wide.

The wild crash and thrum of the sea against far away shores shows me Dohlan. He is laid out on a pad of crumbled stone, in a place I recognize from my earliest dreams of him. The ruins of his family home, Marsoun mansion.

"Who will care for him? Help him heal?" Kaia asks with a whimper.

I move to the next without entertaining a response.

Dreya is the next for wind and water to locate. She is standing in an opulent, ice-covered bedroom. The one from my dream. The tree sent her back to her childhood home, just has it had with Dohlan.

I wonder.

Dreya's face burns bright with fury, as she stomps down the halls and out the castle's front door. She'd been sent back hours ago. She no longer lingered in the ice palace but was making plans to come find me. And her path would take her right past the Maitias Garrison's stronghold.

Earth grabs hold of me, becomes my new guide, familiarizing me with the Garrison Stronghold. It's primarily hidden from view, mostly set underground. Mom is now there, with countless immortal warriors. A full corps, possibly a field army.

"Dreya may choose to come at us by water," Jaden whispers. "Bypassing the land and the Garrison. It's the most direct route."

My hand pressed upon his tightens. I almost welcome the new sting of our touch. It's a reminder that good and bad are often intertwined.

"Now that we know where our enemy is…" I can't finish my sentence before the shared vision rapidly changes, yanked to a new location by all three elements. Jaden and I find ourselves gazing upon Gradnar's Gourge. Deona remembers the place well.

"Is this where…" I'm about to ask about Airmed or Meira when the location changes again.

The scene of the giant troll takedown is replaced with a swamp, filled with floating lights.

I suck back a breath. "It's like movie magic."

"It's magic, all right," Jaden says. "But this is no movie."

I attempt my question a second time. "Is this where Airmed or Meira are currently?"

Our sight swings with the swift wind, drops to the water, racing over pebbles and around intruding rocks, then climbs the trees and gazes downward from the leaves. Whispering leaves. A structure, similar to a massive tree-side hive clings to the tree trunk below. Below our source of sight, but still significantly high above the ground.

A large oval opening is cut into the side of the hive, through which Airmed pokes out her head. The whisper of leaves intensifies. They are talking, sending countless messages in all directions.

"I am here, where I belong," Airmed says, be it to the leaves or to us, it is unclear. "And for now, this is where I would prefer to stay."

The whisper of the leaves mellows, turns to song, and our vision of her location pulls away. Spins to Meira...as seen from the earth at her feet, then the heated air rising around her. Pulled in on herself, and crying, Meira sits in the midst of a vast wasteland.

"Is this Meira's home?" Dohlan was sent to his family home, Dreya to the ice castle, and Airmed appeared to be home, so it stands to reason...

"The tree is now her home. Her heart," the air whispers. "But this is the place of her origin. It was once a ripe and luscious land, protected by the elven queen." Earthen elementals share visions of the land as it once was, vivid with the colors of nature, adorned by creatures, big and small, magical or not. "Time as not been kind to this land."

My heart aches for Meira. I can't imagine how I would feel if I returned to my family's Faredale house and found it burnt to ashes.

"Is it far?" Jaden asks. We know the distance Dreya and Dohlan must travel to get to us. And we can estimate the travel time of Raundel and his crew. But this place, where Meira is an unknown.

The wind lifts a small piece of fabric torn for the hem of Meira's skirt. The current carries the fragment high in the sky, sends it flying with the speed and force of a vortex. It passes over a lake as large as a small sea, skims the treetops of the forest of whispering leaves, skirts the edge of the swamp of floating lights, passes over a quilt work of waterholes, ponds, and tiny lakes, a wall of mountains at their side, dodges into the Palinot Woodlands, clears the tree of life, followed by more woodlands, the wall and gate, and then...

Something drops on top of my hand.

I open my eyes and stare down at a frayed fabric swatch.

My muscles and tendons yawn, and my head dips with newly added weight.

Far then. "Guess we won't be seeing her anytime soon." I'm torn between feeling heavy for Meira's absence and being eager to explore my freedoms without her stuck-in-the-past view pressed upon me.

Except…should Bree awake, who will help her understand and navigate whatever it is Meira did to her?

"Ana." Ry points to his nose. I wipe at mine with the edge of my finger.

Blood. A lot of blood. Thick and clear. A brilliant red.

"You did too much," he says. "I'd rather you not exert yourself like that again."

I make no promises.

My return walk to the lodge is slow and stiff, my head swimming and body acutely aware of every hour of sleep missed. Jaden walks at my side, his arm safely at his side, and wearing the face I'm most accustomed to. No horns.

"You look…familiar?" I toss him a sideways glance from beneath the fall of my hair.

His body jerks with silent laughter. "I would hope so. It would be disheartening should you be able to forget me so easily."

"Oh, don't worry," I tease. "You will never be easy to forget." *Striking eyes…swirly eyes. Kind, charming, attractive. And now, a dash of dark and horns.* I smirk.

He grins back, his eyes brightening.

"And you chose to release the horned you in favor of the Jaden I know best because…"

His brow pressed. "Because, in that moment, I thought it would help you to see a trusted face."

Familiar. Trusted. Loved.

Except, doesn't that apply to all versions of him?

"So…" I bite my lip and drag my gaze over him. "Can you change between your different incarnations at will?"

His chest heaves and his attention slips from me in favor of the path before us. I'm staring at him, Jaden. Then Jove, then another and another and another. Finally, the darker, horned Dharmic turns his earthen gaze back to me for a long, drawn-out stare and blink.

"Any of them," he says, once more appearing as my original Jaden.

"Wild," I mumble. "But you have only one personality? You're not split between them like some personality disorder, right?" He nods, his lips lifting. "So then, why the many different looks?"

Now, I can't help but wonder if I took on Kaia's appearance when she body snatched me the other night. Kaia, as Madame Marrouske spelled her to look, hair and eyes dark.

"You have always been the Balance Bringer," he replies. "But I have been many things during my many lives. Now, those many things are here…" He slams his hand to his chest. "Working together as one. I have access to the original seer ability of Jove, the woodland sorcery of Dharmic, the limited shifting ability of…"

"Hey." Shadow shoves between us, glances at us both, then trains his gaze on me. "That fire bit you did back there was impressive." He gives me a sharp nod of approval, then turns to Jaden, slaps his arm over Jaden's shoulder. "And you, brother…What the bloody bark did I just witness? How many faces you hiding in there, and how come we've never seen this before?"

By *we*, Shadow means the Augur clan. Opal's collection of kids with various magical abilities. Jaden once told me, that when they were all young, he was the only one of them who had no obvious magical talent. He could only see me, and since none of them could see what he saw, they deemed him non-magical.

Jaden chuckles and the sound lightens my heart. "You guys never did believe me when I said I fit in."

Shadow bows his head. "You're right. We weren't the most supportive family back then."

The return walk to the lodge is twelve times longer than the walk out. No doubt, a product of my ever-growing exhaustion.

Once again, Edea's words haunt me. *"Big magic has consequences."*

Reaching far and wide across all of Hiddenkel *has* to be considered big.

When we arrive at the lodge, the main room is empty, aside from a few halfway to drunk patrons. One is already passed out at his table.

"They wouldn't have left," Ry says, heading for the stairs. "They wouldn't have been so foolish."

Klarda leads the pack of us following at Ry's rear. "What if something happened?"

"Look at this space," Al says, swinging her gaze around the room. Messy, dusty, but nothing amiss. "Nothing happened. The stench likely drove them upstairs." She tilts her head toward the couple of drinking companions, seven days out since their last bath.

My feet move with the weight of cement blocks, each stair climbed, more than the usual effort.

"I'm feeling extra tired," I say, reaching the upper landing.

Jaden's smile is soft and soothing. "Then you should rest," he replies. "I have all the info right here." He taps the side of his head. "I can be your voice."

My voice at the planned strategy meeting set for an hour from now. I should be there, but his offer is tempting. Extremely so.

Big magic has consequences.

I study at him. His half-lidded eyes and weary stance with which he holds himself. What about Meira's big magic where Jaden is concerned?

We find the rest of our group gathered in the room

Shadow designated as the woman's sleeping chamber. I flip a lazy wave toward the vocal greetings and climb onto a cot.

"Just because I'm taking your advice," I mumble to Jaden. "Doesn't mean we're finished talking." About the appearance shifting, the personality merging, the knife tucked in my boot.

His grin whips into a deep frown, as he lunges for me. But the image of him is already dimming at the edges.

I pass out, and swim in utter darkness.

Awake with a start.

Azure sits on the opposite cot, staring at me. "That was the worse nosebleed I have ever seen."

Great. More blood loss. Likely because of the level of magic I used.

Blinking the sleep away, I push up onto my elbow. "Where is everyone?"

"Downstairs." He glances over the collection of cots filling the space. All are empty, aside from two. The one I'm using, and the one holding my soon-to-be new master sage. "It would seem, holding a strategy meeting around a table is easier than a setup such as this."

"They kicked everyone out," he continues, anticipating my next question. "Including the staff. Privacy is a must."

I sit up and swing my legs over the side of the cot. For a brief moment, the room spins, then stabilizes. "Why aren't you at the meeting?"

"Someone has to babysit." He smirks.

"Mo or Zarah could have stayed with me and Bree."

He shrugs. "They both wanted to be present at the meeting. Ruby, Clef, and Shadow, included." He flips a hand to the sky, barely lifting it from the surface of the cot. "I do not mind. I feel like I am there, anyway. With Jaden being present." He grins. "Plus, I got a little used to being your babysitter."

I wince at the idea of him feeling like he's in two places at once. The comment upsets me enough that I don't bother to

respond to his babysitting remark. "Do you think the magic Marrouske used to help Jaden is somehow effecting you?" …
because you are both part of the same soul.

"Maybe." He sighs and ruffles his hair. "I know what we are, Jaden and me, and I have come to terms with it."

"Have you told Ruby?" My mind flips to the drunk Ruby crawling into my cot last night, apologizing for things she'd done. Things Opal had manipulated her into doing, being.

The edge of his lips twitch. "No. We had other things to share." His eyes glaze and a smile spreads gently to his lips.

His appearance is enough to make me blush, and I suddenly feel uncomfortable in my seat. Never will come the day when I want to talk intimate relations with him. Especially if it involves Ruby. I avert my gaze and try to unstick the image of them kissing in the rain from the forefront of my brain.

"Besides," he continues, his smile fading. "She has been in an odd head space today. I figured a conversation of that depth could wait until she is in a better place." A mocked humorous smile tugs to his mouth. "It is not like I am dying any time soon."

In this war of balance, the war against Dreya, any of us could die at any time. Thankfully, based on where the elements placed Dreya, we have a few days before we need to worry about her personally.

"So…" I glance at Bree. "You, me, and a comatose girl. What shall we do?"

His back straightens. "I thought you would want to join the strategy meeting."

I do, but I also don't want to leave Azure alone and bored, left to stew in his thoughts and emotions surrounding what he is, what he is to Jaden, and what all that means for his life, before and after this point.

"Nah," I say. "They can figure out all the details. You and I can have some fun." I glance at the window pushed into on the outer, slanted wall. "What would you say to a rooftop view of the city?"

"I would say I am intrigued."

"Let's go, then." I cross the room and push open the window. The slope of the roof borders on extreme, but manageable.

We climb outside and take up positions on either side of the opening. Locations chosen so that we'll easily be made aware should anyone enter the room at our back. And, with a quick turn of the head, we should be able to easily identify that who.

We sit on the roof, staring toward the harbor. The sun glistens off the water in a dance of light and shadow. Activity within the city below has begun to awaken, with the clang of bells, the clomp of horse hooves, the chatter and shouts of citizens.

"I have been many places," Azure says. "I have been to lands beyond the Go-deo Sea."

The Go-deo Sea surrounds all of Hiddenkel. I know this because most of my previous incarnations are aware.

"None have felt as…" He pauses, as if searching for the right word, or emotion to describe. "Disconnected," he adds. "From their true selves. The people down there."

He motions to the streets yet to fill with the day's activity. "They go about their day to day out of a sense of routine. They are not happy. They do not follow their passions. They simply survive. And surviving is not living." A heavy sigh moves through his chest.

I stare at him, seeing him in a different light than previously. Azure sees to the core of things, I realize. He saw my infection and the bond between Dohlan and Kaia. Does he see what is missing in people as well? Their happiness consumed by a life they move through without purpose or passion?

And to have traveled beyond the sea…

Jaden and Azure are rather young, all things considered, for Azure to be so well traveled.

"Mother loaned me out to many," he says. "Ruby told me her new thoughts on Mother, but I have trouble..." His words fade and he swallows hard.

Hard to think anything less than kindly of someone you love, someone who raised you, and should have had your best interests at heart. But Opal...Mother...Edea...is clearly complicated.

To spare Azure any further hurt, I keep my thoughts silent, and extend an empathetic hand. He accepts, and we sit on the roof together, hand in hand, watching the city bloom into action. Counting the bodies as people make way for the lodge in search of their morning fuel.

Which is clearly not the food.

The noise from the first floor is equivalent to an out of tune and out of practice party band. The sound vibrates through the building's supports, clear up to our place on the roof.

"Nice place your friends picked," I say.

Azure snorts. "Few eyes pay attention in a joint like this."

Fair point. I nod.

Then catch sight of movement near Bree's cot.

In a flash, I am spinning and slipping through the open window. A heavily cloaked man is bent over Bree, appearing to...

"Are you smelling her?" I ask, revulsion tainting my words.

The man stands, throwing back the hood of his cloak. "Hello, Fianna," Garr says.

TWENTY-ONE

After all these lifetimes, Garr is still obsessed with Fianna. Like a needle trapped in the groove of a scratched record. But his fixation on Deona's long dead sister is not my current concern. I narrow my gaze tight on him, and his closeness to Bree.

"Why are you here?" I skip over why are you still obsessed? And what have you done to yourself that you are still here, alive, and so physically different?

His gaze swivels from me to Bree's sleeping form laid out before him. He jabs a thumb in her direction. "Why does she smell like that elf, Meira?"

Masking my surprise of his question, I curl my hands into fists. "None of your business. Get away from her."

"Or what? You will kill me?" He flairs his hands out at his side in a show of dramatics. "I invite you to try."

"What happened to you, Garr?" The question comes from Deona. "We used to be friends." *You used to be nice.*

"You happened, Deona." His nostrils flare. "You happened to me."

Azure slips through the window at my back. "Is everything all right?"

"Garr was just leaving," I reply, not chancing a glance in Azure's direction.

Garr's brow rises. His back straightens and he folds his hands into the front of his cloak. "Did I interrupt something? I must say, I am not surprised to see the two of you together and I was hoping I would run into you again, Jove. Or whatever it is you are calling yourself these days. Jaden, is it?"

Visions of Jaden's odd behavior when we first met Garr flash through my thoughts. Garr's control and the dagger in my boot.

"Oh, he's not..." I start to tell Garr the man at my back isn't Jaden, but Azure pushes in front of me, fumbling my words.

He stands as a protective barrier between me and the goat man. "What is it you hope to accomplish by coming here and harassing Ana?"

Garr grins as if the opening he's been waiting for just appeared. "This." He snarls.

Then lurches, pulling something free from the interior of his cloak. His arms jerk forward, releasing items from both hands. A glint, flash, and Azure jolts back, slamming into me, and collapsing.

Oh my "Gaea," I scream. "What have you done." My chest caves in on my heart and I can't breathe. The room is suddenly too tight. Too lacking of oxygen.

No no no. This can't be happening.

"Ana," Azure wheezes and slips to the ground, two throwing stars imbedded in his chest. "Tell Ruby..." His breathing is shallow, his words struggling to be heard.

"Hold on." I slide to the ground with him, cradling his head in my hands. "She'll want to hear what you have to say from your own lips."

He laughs. It turns into a cough, a cough of blood, and then cut short by a wince of clear, extreme pain.

I brush my hand along the side of his face. *It's like looking at Jaden. It could have been Jaden.*

Still. Having. Trouble. Breathing.

"I have wanted to do that for so long." Garr shakes his head and sniffs the air, as if savoring the scent of Azure's blood. "You have no idea."

Thunder rolls through the outer corridor, and before I can catch my breath, Ry is bursting through the doorway, followed by Klarda, Al, and Jaden. Garr turns to meet them, as if he'd been expecting them all along.

"You," Ry seethes.

Garr bows, clearly taking satisfaction in what he's done. But the moment his gaze lands on Jaden, his entire body stiffens.

"But I…" He glances back to me, cradling Azure. "I killed you," he says, turning back to Jaden. Garr's shoulders droop and head bows. "How could I confuse…"

"What did you do?" Jaden sidesteps to see around the large man standing between us.

Before he can comprehend what he's seeing, or form any kind of response, Clef, Shadow, and Ruby explode into the room, smacking Jaden in the shoulder and knocking him off balance.

"Take him," Ry orders of the group.

Ruby's gaze finds me and Azure, and her mouth drops open. Horror instantly pulls at all her features, and she clutches at her gut, screams. The screaming and howls don't stop. She starts to crumble, and Clef is there to catch her, swallow her into his embrace and hold her against the pain.

In that nanosecond, everything bursts into action. Ry and Klarda jolt forward, their arms outstretch, reaching for Garr. But he ducks and blocks. Al and Shadow vanish into smoke and dust, mass around the fleeing Garr, and reappear, their arms and hands around Garr's neck in a strangle hold.

But, despite the situation, Garr doesn't have the look of a defeated man. He stares at Jaden and I can't help but fixate on the memory of our arrival at the city of Treeites. Garr somehow had power of Jaden's actions. And now…

Jaden's focus blurs. Then he jerks into action, dashing forward. He grabs Shadow and tosses him into a nearby cot.

"What are you doing?" Al and Ry yell in unison.

For a flash, struggle is evident in Jaden's features, as if he's trying to fight whatever is happening to him internally. His hand clenches and unclenches. His horns appear and vanish. And then he's a cyclone of wreckage, knocking my people down and free of Garr.

A path for the door now clear, Garr sprints for the exit. Beyond the threshold, Zarah waits in the corridor, her ungloved hands raised and waiting.

I can't let him get to her, even if her chronicling ability may come in extra handy with regards to Garr. At present, he's too dangerous.

"Ana." The calling of my name is low and splintered with pain.

I drop my gaze to Azure. His breath is labored, his pulse slow, and his energy fading. "I know," I say. "I will sever Garr's control and protect Jaden."

But first…

Remember. Spread your wings and rise above. The message floats through me as a reminder of who I really am, and who I am meant to be.

Determination fills my core with an inferno hotter than the fires of Guardoone, and I pin my attention on Garr, his hand already reaching for the door casing.

Despite Zarah's small frame and expression of sheer panic, she stands solid and unmoving.

"No," I mumble. The message to Garr and no one else.

I reach forward, as if I may be able to stop him at the door, from my place across the room. Elements, hearing my request, respond. New life springs forth from the old, dry wood of the floor and doorframe. Vines weave a net across the entrance, sealing the opening.

They wrap around Garr, trapping him in place. He releases a roar of fury.

"We had him," Zarah says from the other side of the vine entrapped Garr. "Massive Mo was waiting off to the side, ready to grab him."

Jaden, still fighting our friends, our family, struggles to get to Garr, as if intending to release him. But no one in our party relents. While Jaden doesn't hold back his attacks, not a soul in the group wants to hurt him in return. Still, they are many against one. They punch and slam, and finally drag Jaden to the ground, pin him.

"What's wrong with him?" Shadow asks.

"Garr," I reply, matter-a-factly. "And I might have the answer." I pull the wrapped blade from Deona and Jove's original binding from my boot. Garr's eyes blink wide.

My heart, more than my mind, respond with the answer. Flames erupt from my palm and race up the length of the knife, my fire searing and severing any magic held to the weapon.

Something inside of me shatters. Flies apart in a million or more pieces. I fight against the scream rising through me. But Jaden doesn't. He bellows loud enough to shake the walls.

With a tiny gasp, I realize it is Meira's casting that held the various versions of me and Jaden together throughout our many lifetimes. With the magic gone, for the first time, since our first lives, we can make the choice of our own accord. Stay together or walk away.

I drop the blade at my side, not wanting anything more to do with it.

Jaden's struggle ceases and everyone holding him down

reluctantly backs away, ready to pounce at the slightest change.

His eyes widen and head turns toward me. "What did you do?" Fear and panic ring in his delivery.

"I released you," I say, my heart squeezing with the message. "From Garr, and from me."

I'mdyingI'mdyingI'mdying.

My heart, my vision of the future shredded to pieces.

Garr laughs and snickers, glee sparkling bright in his eyes. "I win after all."

"Shut up," I snap and press my fist to my heart. Try not to cave in on myself.

The others are moving away from Jaden and converging on Garr, discussing what to do with him. Kill him. Keep him as a prisoner. Take him to my mom at the Garrison.

Clef releases Ruby and she dashes to Azure's side. Within a moment, Jaden is kneeling at her side, a tear making tracks down his cheek. He makes no move to wide it away. Resting one hand upon his brother's chest, he tugs Ruby into his embrace with the other, allowing her to release all her emotions into the plane of his chest.

Clef and Shadow hover silently at their backs. And holding true to her role as a superior warrior, Al stands with Ry and Klarda discussing Garr's fate...but her attention often veers over her shoulder to Azure.

"Heal him," Ruby pleads. "That's what you do." Her frantic stare swings back and forth between me and Jaden.

"I am a healer of the elements, not of beings." I frown, wishing the truth were different.

She snaps a wild gaze to Jaden and he shakes his head.

"I have only ever been able to heal the Balance Bringer. That is my gift," he says, an attempt to sooth in his tone. Yet, even as he says the word, I note the doubt flicker in his features.

That *was* his gift. Was, until I severed the tie, destroyed the magic. The magic Meira used to bond his gift to me. "That was before," I whisper.

His horns flash, there and gone. "I never asked to be released," he replies with a growl.

Careful not to jostle Azure, I lift my hand to Jaden's cheek. "We don't need a magical bond to define our relationship."

His features soften and his gaze drops to Azure, cradled in my lap.

"I shall try," he says, and lays his palms upon Azure's chest.

Jaden's energy roars to life. It's warm and musical, dancing all around us, focusing on Azure. Azure moans, spits blood.

"Let me go." He moans.

"No. Never." Ruby takes his hand in her own and trains all her focus, her love magic on him. It tingles in the air between us, strong and forceful, unhindered by the tears flowing freely down her face.

"It will never work," Garr says, from his vine entrapment in the doorway.

Everyone's attention snaps to him.

"The blades," he says. The blades of the throwing stars. "Each was dipped in poison."

"No, no, no." Ruby shakes her head and reaches for one of the throwing stars embedded in Azure's chest.

"Don't," Jaden and I both yell.

She freezes. "But the poison. We need to get it out."

"The damage is already done," I say. "And if you touch either weapon with your bare skin, you risk poisoning yourself."

"But..." Her breath comes fast and hard. "We need to do something." She wipes at her nose using the back of her hand. Her eyes are a harsh red and brimming with tears.

I seem to recall, learning in either health or science, that the human body is roughly sixty percent water. I wonder if it is the same for Fae and other creatures? It couldn't hurt to explore with an elemental test.

Closing my eyes and focusing all my energy on my hands, I call to the water within Azure's body. Little...so little...responds.

Garr snorts. "The poison was chosen to combat your elemental magic. No matter what you do, you will not save him. The poison has likely already reached his heart."

"It will be all right." Azure's voice is the whisper of an injured mouse, barely audible. He tries to smile at Ruby, and she tries to smile back, but he is unable to hold the expression and her face is shrouded in ugly tears. He raises his hand to her face, cups her cheek. "I'm thankful...we. Had. This last night...together."

My heart cleaves in two.

None of this is all right. Not at all.

Ry punches Garr in the face. I'm guessing a release of frustration on Ry's part, but it shuts Garr up. For now.

"Let's move him to a bed," Clef suggests.

The members of the Augur clan, minus Ruby, transfer Azure from the floor to a cot. Where they stand vigil around their fallen brother. Jaden attempts, again and again, to heal Azure, but no healing occurs.

Jaden sheds few tears, but the agony is harshly written in every line upon his face.

I take up a seat on Bree's cot and watch from afar. I cared for Azure, but they loved him more. Knew him better. They were family, and they deserve this time with him far more than I do.

I drop my face in my hands. *Poor Azure. Poor, poor Azure.*

It could have been Jaden.

"Ana." Ry drops a hand on my shoulder. Clearing my face of any emotion, I turn my gaze to meet his. "How are you feeling?" He points to his nose, referencing my earlier nosebleed. I ignore the question, so he moves on. "I hate to be insensitive, given the circumstances, but do you think you could help us get Garr free from your trap and maybe open the door?" His lips pull into an uncommitted grimace. "Zarah is stuck on the other side."

And Mo, I mentally add. *Zarah and Mo.*

WITH A GRIMACE, I finish twining the vines around Garr, securing his arms and legs.

Mo points to his face. "You should do something about his mouth, too. So that we need not listen to his blabber."

Garr chuckles. "A little kiss," he says to me, then sweeps his gaze past Mo and Zarah. "And this entire situation will be a whole lot sweeter."

Klarda smacks him across the face. "Quiet." The command is harsh and threatens punishment if ignored.

A long, wide leaf sprouts from one of the vines and slaps across his lips. He mutters a complaint into the cover. Klarda grins and gives me a nod of approval.

I help her hold Garr's ties and direct him down the stairs to the main room below, where Ry waits. He jogged downstairs to chat with the establishment's owners while Klarda and I prepped Garr for movement.

Ry turns at our approach. "I've made arrangements that should work for now. Temporarily. But we'll obviously have to make other preparations." He waves us toward the back room.

Behind him, the staff avoids eye contact, while clanging and banging items around, rougher than necessary.

"They're less than pleased with the arrangement," Ry explains, and pushes open a door to the back. Ushers us through.

Klarda huffs and tosses the staff a glare. "They will remain quiet?"

"Yes," he replies.

We move Garr through the back room and down a narrow set of stairs to a dank cellar. With the reawakening of the vines, we secure him in the far corner of the dark space.

"What if I need to…you know…relieve myself?" Garr asks, his words a mumble against the leaf covering his mouth.

Ry smirks. "Figure it out." He turns and walks away. The rest of us follow, leaving Garr alone in the cellar to brew in his failure.

Zarah pushed in between Ry and me. "If you let me touch him, I may be able to pull useful information from him. Things that can help you."

As much as I detest the idea of Zarah touching Garr, the idea is interesting. All his history, with Deona and since, is likely to answer *a lot* of questions. But he's infected and I can't forget that. Can't let myself forget that, for the safety of my friend and future sister-in-law…or whatever they call it here.

"Too dangerous," Ry says, and I agree.

"Zarah." I touch a soothing hand on her arm. "If he has the infection coursing through him, there's no telling if that would transfer to you through your chronicling gift." I shiver at the thought.

"Understood." She nods, releasing a shiver of her own.

Klarda grunts. "We could try punching answers out of him."

"That could be fun," Mo adds.

We return to the bedroom, our moods instantly plummeting.

In the time it took us to secure Garr downstairs, Azure has passed away.

Ruby sobs into Jaden's embrace, and the other three Augur clan members stand solemnly, with heads bowed, mourning the loss of their friend and fellow family member.

I sit on the side of Bree's cot, refusing to intrude on their private moment.

Ry takes a seat on the cot beside me. "Zarah and I are

going to pay the Immortal forces a visit in order to secure Azure a proper burial, and possibly transport to Garrison."

"A service would be nice," I say, with a bow of my head.

"A service and a bigger boat for travel," Mo adds.

Zarah lightly clutches Mo's arm. "Boat or other form of luxury transport." She gives us a weak smile, then turns and leaves the room with Ry. "Azure's family deserves comfort in this time of sorrow."

It feels like only minutes, and yet days since I sat on the roof with Azure, watching over the city. I can still summon the warmth of his touch against my palm. And now, I shall never feel him, argue with him, laugh with him, ever again. The thought is foreign, and a void in my soul.

I started the morning with visions of Dohlan's chest carved to bits, and now Azure is dead. All before lunchtime. Ry says this is war, and I know losses are to be expected, but I'm not a fan. I drop my face in my hands and allow the weight of the day to absorb into my muscles and emotions.

"Ana." Jaden takes a seat beside me, and I raise my head slowly to meet his grief-stricken face. His eyes are dark, rimmed with crimson, and tear tracks stream down his face. The sight crushes my heart. Even in his sorrow, he scrutinizes my condition.

Ruby now cries in a huddle with Clef and Shadow, while Al meticulousness attends to the cleaning of Azure's chest.

I open my arms wide, an offering to him to use me, find any comfort he can in me and my embrace. He accepts, crumbling into my hold. His shoulders shake, and he presses his face to my belly as he releases the onslaught of emotion.

I hold him endlessly, until he is ready for whatever comes next. All the while, electric pain seers through me, but only me. Jaden's lack of reaction suggests that whatever Ruby did, it's directly solely at me.

"I don't...I can't..." His words are strangled, drowning in agony.

"I know, Jaden," I say, fighting the flow of tears.

I rub his back. Run my fingers through his hair. Hold him close to my heart. He was there for me when I lost my sister. I want to be able to provide the same for him, in the loss of his own sibling.

"I'm so, so sorry. I wish…" *That I'd seen the attack coming. Been fast enough to save Azure. Been able to do something, anything.*

"We all wish things could have turned out differently," he says, shifting his head so that his ear is pressed to my belly. "But please don't think any of this is your fault."

"I was here." My voice spikes, both with the guilt and the pain of Ruby's electric shock coursing through me. "I should have been able to see the attack coming and stop it." I suck back a deep breath, then let it go. "He was your brother. I should have been able to do more for him…for you." I choke on the words and crack a sob.

His words fall away, and he shakes in my hold for unending minutes.

Jolt. Zap. Züing. Electricity coursing through me every second we are connected.

My eye twitches, but I don't let go. Won't let go.

He jerks back, pulling himself completely free of my hold, and stares at me. Glances over me as if he has just realized the curse I've been suffering.

"Please don't," he says. "Don't blame and don't deflect. Neither is what I need right now." His red-rimmed gaze bores into mine. A tear streaks down his cheek.

My breath is long and deep. "Whatever you need. Say it and it is yours."

His frown deepens. "What we had a moment ago, that is all I need."

"Then why stop." I open my arms for him once more, beckoning him forward.

"But Ruby's…"

I wave any talk of Ruby or the curse away. "Forget about

that right now. Let me be what you need." No pain that the curse inflicts can compare to the mental and emotional ache pulsating through my entire system. No doubt, a fraction of what Jaden is experiencing. When he doesn't move, I whisper. "Please."

He falls back into my arms, and we hold one another, crying until the tears run out, and all that is left is throbbing, and aching, and exhaustion. And a strong powerful sting ruling over my body.

"Doesn't that hurt?" Ruby asks, her voice rough and husky.

A breath drags through his chest. "In so many ways."

Jaden and I pull apart and turn to meet her gaze, messy and red and wet with tears and snot.

"I'm sorry," I say to her. "I tried…"

She spins away and composes herself before looking back. "I know. What happened here today wasn't *directly* your fault." She sighs. Drops her gaze. "And you tried. I know you did. And what I did…" she reaches for me and rests her hand over my arm. "Was deplorable." A warming tingle encircles my wrist. It circles and retracts. "I shall never again allow myself to be manipulated in such a manner."

She pulls her hand away and studies her palm. A matting of red ink is sinking into her skin. "I recant my curse, and I hope that someday…" she glances between me and Jaden. "Someday you will both forgive me."

Jaden grabs her hand in both of his. "Already done."

She sniffles against the tears. They both do. Then she pats his shoulder. "Thank you. You've always been the forgiving type." She wipes the tears from her face and pulls her stature straight. Looks to me. "So, where is he?"

Garr. The thing responsible for her lover's death. I blink, my head jerking back slightly with the action. "Oh…you shouldn't…"

Ry steps into the room and knocks on the doorframe, pulling our attention, my sentence forgotten.

"Look who we found." Ry steps aside, allowing Raundel, Lobrka, and Gitta to enter the room. All three of them stand tall and straight, appearing incredibly formal and terribly uncomfortable.

Raundel steps up to Jaden and Ruby. "We heard about your loss. We are deeply saddened and grant you our sympathies." Lobrka and Gitta bow their heads in accordance.

"Thank you," Jaden says, closing his eyes against the new streak of pain rippling across his features.

I rise and give them each a hug filled with every emotion currently stirring in my core. "We're all glad you made it here so quickly. And safe. It's been a day, and I expect we won't be staying long."

Lobrka raises his head. "To be expected."

Raundel lifts his chin in Bree's direction. "No change?"

"Not yet." I glance past them and past Ry to the corridor beyond. "Not to be rude, but where is Zarah?" I swing a quick gaze around the room. "And where is Ruby?"

My chest tightens and weights.

"Garr." Jaden bolts to his feet. "She went looking for Garr."

I race down to the cellar, Jaden and Ry a step behind me. Through the backroom, down the narrow stairs, and—*slam*—throw upon the door to the dark, dank room that is currently Garr's prison.

Ruby spins to face me. "Look what I found down here." She steps to the side, revealing Garr as I left him, tangled and wound in vines. And slumped against the wall, close to his side, Zarah.

"You wouldn't happen to know a Baba Yaga?" she asks, holding up her ungloved hands out before her. The exposed skin of her fingertips now darkening with infection.

TWENTY-TWO

Ry shoves Ruby out of the way and dashes to Zarah's side. "What have you done?" An edge of panic cracks his voice.

"What I felt needed to be done," she replies.

Her fingers are black, the infection having taken hold when she touched Garr in order to collect his history.

Black fingers. But just the fingers.

The day Mo and I tangled with the infected beasts in Ry's weapons locker, we had both gotten infected, but it hadn't been far enough along to fight off an elemental cleanse. Maybe the same could be said for this case.

Although, I had prayed to the water in the river, it was water from the sky that had ultimately cleansed me and Mo.

"Let's get her outside," I say, with a hard point toward the stairs.

Zarah shifts her gaze past Ry to me. "Garr has lived and seen a lot. The Baba Yaga gave him his extraordinarily long life. But he is not immortal. He can be killed."

Garr had mentioned a Baba Yaga to Deona, the day they had all set out on their journey, mission, to find the tree.

Deona hadn't given the old witch any thought past that day. Now, it would seem, she should have.

"Come on." Ry lifts Zarah to her feet and ushers her toward the stairs. "Outside we go. I'm getting you far away from him."

Ruby crosses her arms. "He is no threat. Not now." Her tone is blunt. "Whatever she did completely knocked him out."

It's true. Garr's head is bowed forward, and his body is slack, held upward by the tangle and tie of the vines.

Ruby sighs. "Of course, I still want to kill him."

"She gave him a long life," Zarah says, as Ry directs her up the stairs. "And softened his fawn features. But the exchange cost him dearly."

"Tell me," I say, falling in line behind them.

"Later," Ry demands. "You can talk about this later, after she's been healed." He marches her up the stairs.

Ruby hesitates, likely contemplating taking a moment alone with Garr or following us to see what is about to transpire. She decides to come along.

I reach out to the elements as we climb out of the cellar and navigate the main floor. By the time we hit the street, my connection with earth and air are solid. Two steps outside of the lodge and it begins to pour. Large water drops straight from heaven.

Yanking Zarah from Ry's protective hold, I drag her into the open with me, making sure every part of her gets drenched by the falling rain. I don't know if that's truly necessary, but I'm not taking any chances with my future sister-in-law.

Jaden, Raundel, and Lobrka sprint through the lodge entrance, out into the street, but Ry stops them, and shoves them along the side of the building.

Sparing them nothing more than a mere glance, I train my focus on Zarah and try to recall the words I'd used the last time…the only time…I'd done this—cleared the dark infection.

"Is this going to hurt?' she asks.

I smile, although it's weak, given the circumstances and the day. "Let's hope not."

I summon the words from my soul. Speak to the elements, above and below. "Blessed water from the sky, life blood of all the earths, I ask you grant us your healing caress and cleanse this girl's body of this dark malicious touch."

Zarah coughs. Then coughs again. Drops to her knees in a coughing fit.

I lower to the ground with her, continuing to hold her hands…and hold her body steady throughout the croaks and pants. The black of her fingers fails to thin, despite her many barked convulsions.

"Heal her, please," I mumble to the elements, yet still nothing changes.

I'd been infected, twice. And both times I overcame.

Pinning my gaze on her, I tighten my hand hold. "Give it to me," I say. "Give me your infection."

"What?" She balks. "No. No." She shakes her head. "I'm not going to do that."

"It's not a request; it's a demand."

The last time I was infected, the state of me was wicked. And the healing took a nasty toll on Jaden. But being what I am, I'm banking on my system, my core, my elemental magic and connections, having learned something…hopefully a lot. And that *something* will help me combat what currently dwells in Zarah. When Raundel first saw me in my infected state, he suggested such learning might be the case. I hope it's so.

"I wouldn't even know how to," Zarah says.

My lips pull taut. "Leave it to me."

I close my eyes and reach out with all the energetic strength I can summon. Then tap into the water in her body, the air flowing through her lungs, her blood.

Give it to me and set Zarah free.

Give. It. To me.

Something cold and clammy slithers over my soul, my skin, sinks into my blood. My body shakes, starts to jitter.

Zarah gasps and I open my eyes.

Her skin is clear, and the darkness now creeps across my hands and arms. I jerk away, severing our hold and any chance of the infection returning to her system.

"Get away," I say, a seethe of breath. *My body knows what to do. My body knows what to do.* I repeat the mantra, willing it to be so. And in that moment, I do. I know.

"Do it," I mumble to the element dwelling within me.

Fire erupts in my veins, racing through my blood, spreading out to my muscles, tendons, skin. Everything burns. Burns with the intensity of a thousand and ten suns. Burns the infection to less than dust.

I collapse in the street and a downpour slams upon me, turning the heat within me to steam. A minute later, the rain dwindles to a trickle.

Jaden, Raundel, Lobrka. They're all at my side a fraction of a second later.

"Zarah?" My inquiry is a mumbled croak.

"She's good," Ry answers from somewhere beyond the wall of males surrounding me. "You healed her."

Jaden traces the tip of his finger along my jaw. I shiver despite my exhaustion. "And you?" he asks. "Are you all right?"

"I think so." I lay my cheek against the muddy road. "Tired."

"And singed," Raundel says, dropping a cloak over me.

Ruby leans over the men surrounding me and scrutinizes my condition.

"Show off," she says, then turns and walks away.

Lobrka hisses after her, then returns his attention to me.

"We will need to find you some new clothes, lest you draw too much attention."

A snort-laugh jolts from my throat and then I fall silent.

"Come on." Jaden scoops me into his arms, being careful to keep the cloak wrapped around me. "Too much magic, and too many emotions expended today. I expect you to sleep for a month after this." He winks, then carries me into the lodge and straight to his cot.

I AWAKE to sounds in the outer hallway. The room is dark, little to no light shining in through the window. I can only assume, I slept through the rest of the day, now yesterday, not rising until the next morning. Morning, and not evening, because so many cots are occupied.

Jaden's arm drapes over me. He's pressed against my side, sound asleep. He has the face of the Jaden I know best, but the horns peek from his messy hair on either side of his head. What does it mean that the horns are present when he sleeps?

I trace the line of one horn with the tip of my finger. Jaden moans but doesn't awake. It feels as if ages have passed since I've been able to touch him, feel his skin against mine. I press deeper into his warmth and savor his breath where it brushes against my skin. I trace his horns, his jaw, his lips. His perfect, I need-them-on-me lips.

His lips part and I pull my finger away, contemplate kissing him. But he's asleep, and in a room full of other people is not the ideal place to wake him in such a manner.

Reluctantly, I shift away and carefully fold back the blanket. Beneath the shared cover, I'm still wrapped in Raundel's cloak. Naked beneath. My singed and burnt clothing…what was left of them…lay in a pile on the floor beside the cot.

Whispers, then footsteps in the outer corridor. My attention shifts to the partially open door, where a tiny light flickers, followed by the waft of a sweet-smelling tobacco.

Holding the cloak around me, I rise, take count of the sleeping bodies, then go in search of a situation update. Ry is not among the sleeping, so I expect to find him as one of the sources behind the whispers.

I tiptoe from the room and slip into the hallway.

Lobrka removes a rolled smoke from his lips and turns his tired gaze on me. "It is for the pain," he says, and tilts his head toward his bandaged arm trapped in a sling.

He's leaning against the wall, one knee lifted, and likely leaving a filthy boot print on the plaster at his back.

I move to lean against the opposite wall. "Does it hurt a lot?"

He shrugs, then glances over me. "Gitta was supposed to be retrieving new attire for you. Has she not found something yet?"

I tug the cloak tighter around me. "I don't know. I've been sleeping."

He nods. "She should have left it beside your bed for you to find upon morning."

"It's fine." I push away from the wall. "I'll go check in the other room. See if she left it for me in there."

"I shall go find her." He stands straight and flicks the smoke away. Turns toward the next sleeping chamber.

I step in front of him. "First off…" My gaze zeros in on the discarded smoke. "Pick that up."

He frowns, a most grouchy version of the expression.

"Secondly," I continue. "I said I would take care of it." I glance over him, making sure to portray judgement in my eyes. "You stay here, smoke, and feel better."

I turn into the next sleeping chamber and glance back. Lobrka is retrieving the discarded smoke from the floor. With a smile, I step into the room and gently push the door to an almost close.

Al and Ry are at the back of the room, beside a shrouded Azure. They are wrapping cloth around him. Over the top of him, and under the base of his cot.

Clearly, they are binding him so that his body won't move should…when…he be transported. Apparently, Ry plans on taking the entire bed. Not just Azure's body.

I wonder if they told Jaden they would be doing this? If they gave him the chance to be a part of preparing his brother's body for whatever is next? I recall Deona wrapping her sisters in a death shroud covered with flowers.

"Everything has changed."

My attention snaps to the comment.

Sitting up on her cot, staring at me is Bree.

"You're awake." Surprise spikes my voice.

A few of the sleeping bodies mumble, shift, or roll over. Ry and Al both turn to me, fingers to their mouths and a shush on their lips. Sorry, I mouth and lower my volume. I take a seat on the cot across from her.

"I am…awake," she replies. "It's weird." Her lips press and twist and pucker, her expression morphing with whatever emotions are swirling in her head. "I feel like me and I don't. I have all these new memories. *So* many memories, and the detail of each is incredibly vivid. Far clearer than my own from just the other day." Her head snaps up and she stares at me. "Did you know elven memories were so intense?"

I grin and recall the countless memories belonging to my other incarnations. All of them had elven or Fae blood, to some degree. Their memories aren't so different from mine, as far as clarity is concerned.

But then, I am a mix of the Hiddenkel races. I don't have any human blood, and so I don't know what it feels like to have human memories. Not really.

She nods, seeming to understand, even though I have yet to speak. "You aren't human. I forgot that for a moment.

Surprising," she says with a smirk. "Considering how not human you now look."

My new petite elven ears, my eyes and hair…I lift my arm and stare at my skin. Some of the swirls of my vanishing tattoos momentarily appear as if responding to my silent summons. She isn't wrong. I look very unhuman.

Her chin dips into her neck and continues. "But the truth is, Meira's memories and knowledge far exceed my own, and it's all in here, as if I experienced them, learned from them…" She shakes her hands at the side of her head. "It makes it hard to distinguish me from her. Do I just not exist anymore?" She blinks up at me.

I smile, and pray it conveys the warmth and under-standing I want to send her way. "You're whatever and whoever you chose to be. Don't be *her* because she asked you to take on the role. Own this new you, and use the gifts bestowed upon you, in the manner you find most suiting."

"Thanks," she quietly says, then leans forward and lowers her voice. "Because, I feel like, as wise as she was…is…at some point, she got stuck in a cycle, or routine, and she lost the ability to see beyond what she knew." She inches closer. "I think the answer to this lifetime's rumble, lies outside of the box she has been working within. Been trapped in."

My entire chest sighs. "Thank you." I grab Bree's hands and squeeze them between mine. "I think we're going to make a great team."

"I hope so." She smiles wide. "We're a couple of firsts for these people."

More firsts.

"Two outsiders taking on major roles on the inside of the largest recurring mission this world appears to have."

Indeed. I nod. "A couple of outerworlders." I pause. "Is that what you meant when you said everything is changing?"

"Oh no." She shakes her head. "I guess that's a part of it, but it's bigger than where you and I came from." Her gaze shifts to the surface of the cot at my side, then back to me. "But maybe you'd like to get dressed first?"

I glance down at Raundel's cloak wrapped around me and chuckle.

She nods to a bundle of folded clothing on the cot. "Gitta left that for you." On the cot I had previously used. Makes sense that she would leave my clothing here instead of next to Jaden's bed.

I take the clean clothing and, still a victim of modesty, change in the washroom.

Gitta is waiting for me when I emerge. "Bree wanted me to tell you that she has escorted your brother and the others downstairs. They have moved Sir Azure's body in preparation for transport."

"Why didn't they wait for me." I move past her and head toward the stairs. "I would have helped."

She dashes after me. "They had all the help they required. Lord Ryland, Warrior Alabaster, Lobrka, and your Jaden."

More than enough muscle to carry Azure. Still, I would have like to have made myself useful.

I jog down the stairs and find the main room empty. I glance in the direction of the cellar but opt for the front door of the establishment. In the street, I find them gathered around a couple of transport wagons. One resembling a cage on wheels, and clearly intended for moving Garr, and the other, covered in a simple cloth to conceal the body laid within.

I step up to the group, without saying a word, and listen in on the conversation.

Both Garr and Azure are to be transported to the dragon wall surrounding the city, and the regiment of soldiers who have remained stationed there. Azure's service will be held at sundown. And the rail for the garrison will depart three hours later. It will travel through the night, getting them to Mom's location in two days' time.

Ruby arrives, flanked by Shadow and Clef. They say their farewells to Azure while I watch Garr get chained and loaded into his wooden cell.

He snarls and glares at me. "Do not think putting me in chains and a cage means you win."

I never viewed anything with Garr as a game or contest. "I'm sorry I didn't see your pain sooner," I say.

My words catch him off guard and he flinches. The soldiers drop a cover off the sides of the cage, blocking any further reactions from my view.

With both wagons loaded, the squad of soldiers takes them ahead to the later designated meeting point, and we head back inside. Ruby asks to be left alone and follows the wagons on foot, but Shadow keeps an eye on her, using an effective camouflage ability.

"If we don't need to be there until later," I say. "Let everyone sleep. They all need their rest and a solid recharge."

"That's doable," Ry replies.

Both Lobrka and Al grumble about going back to bed and head for the stairs. Clef follows. Ry, Jaden, Bree, and I make way for one of the tables, where Zarah quietly waits.

Her eyes soften at our approach. She stands, and gives me a hug so tight, if I were human, she'd press the air straight from my lungs. "Thank you," she says. "Thank you for what you did. Healing me and taking on the burden."

"Happy to help," I say simply. A truth easily spoken. I'd help Zarah in an instant. Accepting her praise...I'm still working on that part.

Seeming to accept my response, she steps toward Jaden, and presses her gloved palm to the curve of his cheek. "How are you doing?" An extra ounce of melancholy bleeds into her features.

"As well as can be expected." His eyes glisten with unshed tears, but he manages to pull a gentle smile to his lips.

She nods and turns to Ry and me. I get the sense she

wants to ask more of Jaden, yet chooses to hold back. "What will they do with Garr?"

"They won't do anything other than hold him," Ry replies. "You needn't worry about them robbing us of potential answers with his death."

"I don't trust soldiers." She dips her head.

"I know you don't." With the curve of his finger, he lifts her gaze to meet his once more. "But you can trust these guys. I picked them myself."

Zarah glances over each of us, hesitating on Jaden and landing her gaze on me. "We need to be careful with him. That cost I mentioned…in exchange for the long life and softening of his fawn features…it was the slow loss of his compassion and empathy, while his desire became all consuming."

"Fianna?" I ask.

She hums. "Fianna, Deona. You."

Bree clears her throat. "He was always too clingy. Always."

I glance at her sideways. Note the way she recalls Meira's memory and comments on it as if it were her own.

Zarah dips her head and glances up at me through the fall of her bangs, as if she is trying to hide. "I saw in his memories what he did to your second incarnation." Izza. "His desire was beyond his control. His species has always had strong desires in that area, but he had never been so wanton. He didn't mean to…" She shakes her head. "Didn't mean to."

Poor young Izza, trapped and scared, hiding in one of Gaea's earthen temples from a monstrous Garr. Izza hadn't shown me anything beyond that moment drenched in her distress. What had Garr done?

"He killed her, didn't he?" I ask.

Jaden morphs into his darker, horned version and releases a low, predatory growl.

Zarah jolts, jerks back, her eyes growing wide. "Oh. That's new. Have I seen that before?" She swings a pointed finger at him.

"It's new," I say to Zarah and rub my hand down the length of Jaden's arm. He calms, then returns to his earlier physical form.

"Excuse me," he mumbles, tucking his chin into his neck.

"Marrouske did some magic." I say by way of explanation, with a slight wave of my hand to indicate Jaden.

"It's interesting," she replies.

Ry coughs a laugh. "If you mean interesting, as in disturbing...definitely."

"Oh, I don't know." Bree glances between me and Jaden, a touch of wickedness in her gaze. "I find it rather sexy. Wouldn't you agree, Ana?" My face warms and I suddenly find the floor interesting.

Do I find the horned version of him sexy? Or the fact that he can change back and forth? Is Bree able to see into that part of me like she did back in school when she spoke to me about Jaden back then?

I can sense Jaden's gaze on me, and I realize...I don't feel him like I used to...before I burned the magic set with the blade and severed our bond. I didn't realize I'd be cutting our internal connection.

"Anyway," Zarah says, coming to my rescue with a distraction. "I thought you'd want to know that he came across Kaia in the meadow one day. She was with Dohlan, and she didn't look like a Balance Bringer sister, with her appearance being magically masked, but he recognized something in her. Something that reminded him of Fianna."

The pulse increases.

"He didn't do anything to her," she continues. "Didn't even talk to her. But he did talk to Dreya, who also stood within the cover of the trees, watching."

"Dreya." Her name falls from my lips like a lead iron. "She's connected to the infected people of Hiddenkel, the enslavement and now mutilation of Dohlan..." Zarah gasps, clearly not unaware of what I had seen happen to him. "The murder of my father, the abduction and likely murder of my sister Kaia, the dark veins webbing through the land, the weather storm cursing my family home, and now, Garr."

I release a heavy sigh. "I don't care what Meira…" Ry and Zarah shot me a questioning look. "I mean Marrouske said, that ice witch needs to be dealt with."

"What did Madame Marrouske say?" Ry asks.

"That she wasn't my concern," I say with a hint of irritation.

Bree crosses her arms. "I beg to differ."

A smile cracks across my lips. School mate, witch, master sage, and soul sister. I kind of want to fist bump her right now.

The lodge door thrusts open with a bang and Ruby dashes in, slides to a stop. "Did you see her? Did Mother come in here?"

TWENTY-THREE

"Where did you see her?" I ask Ruby regarding her sighting of Opal...Edea.

She points toward the shoreline. "Down the street. She was watching the wagons pass."

"It would make sense," Jaden says. "That she would come to pay her respects for my brother." He sighs, a sigh filled with a hundred and ten woes.

With a sympathetic smile on my lips, I glance sideways at him. Before I severed our connection, did he sense the truth of what I know about Edea...Opal? Does he know that Dohlan is her son, or that she expects to die soon? Does he know she's the one who made *so* many things difficult between us this lifetime?

"If that were the case..." Ruby's voice rises. "Then why is she not here, with us, right now." She throws her arms wide at her side, palms up, and twists back and forth, referencing the room and the people present. "None of you have seen her in the same light as I recently have. She has manipulated all of us, from day one."

No one reacts to Ruby's words, as if they expect them to

be the ramblings of a mad woman. A woman wild with sorrow. But I know what she says is true.

Edea's agenda has been harmful to those around her, and everyone needs to know. But such a message is neither easily delivered nor accepted when it involves someone close. And on this eve of Azure's death is not the time.

I shift my attention to Shadow. "Did you see her, too?"

His shoulders rise and head shakes. "I saw something, but I don't know what. My focus was on Ruby." Worried what she might do to herself or someone else are the words I expect he thinks but doesn't say.

Ruby glances around the surrounding group. "None of you believe me, but I will prove it to you. Just you wait."

She spins and stomps toward the door. She gets as far as the next table over, then crumbles into a chair and releases a hail of tears.

Jaden's lips pull into a tight line. "I've got her," he says, the struggle with his own grief clouding his eyes.

I want to be the one who is there for Jaden in his time of loss, but I cannot relate to this specific loss in the way Ruby can. Maybe they will find solace in their shared heartbreak. I wish him luck, and then squeeze Ruby's shoulder.

"I believe you," I whisper, then head out the door.

Mo follows me into the street. Together, we search the many faces and shadows for any sign of Edea. We find none.

"I believe Ruby, too," Mo tells me. "After what that old lady did to me, stealing me away and making me sleep. I know she is capable of unkind things."

We move inside and pass the time with a card game, but our hearts and minds are not in the activity. The next few hours are slow moving misery.

When the time comes to head to the wall, Ry's soldier buddies provide transportation by way of a sixteen-person wagonette. Ry sits in the front with the driver, and the rest of us find a seat on one of the two inward facing benches in the back.

Despite the attention we draw from the citizens we pass, the ride is quiet, the mood continuing to hang over us like a storm cloud ready to erupt.

The large dragon statue that burst to life and uncoiled the last time I was in Palinot, remains stretched along the shoreline, protecting the city and its citizens from any further water invasion.

Just because Dreya left, doesn't mean she won't come back. Not as long as I am here.

"The dragon won't return to its original stature until released by the garrison," Ry explains.

Azure's funeral pyre is arranged on the back of the dragon wall, within a widened platform between the water beast's small wings. The dragon's neck stretches up and arches back, extending his head over the service location.

"Thank your people," Jaden says. "They have shown Azure a great honor."

Ry pats Jaden on the back. "I've been told that Azure did a lot for the forces and the continued war effort." Shadow and Clef mumble in accord. Azure, himself, had mentioned being outsourced to the military for many years.

Ruby wanders off, starts collecting wildflowers from a small bloom discovered on the outskirts of the wall. Before long, the rest of us join her in the collecting, Gitta proving to be the most skilled in quick, bountiful flower fetching. All that is gathered is showered over Azure's shrouded body in a show of love and respect.

In the ways of an official warrior's farewell, each attending individual is given time alone to say their goodbyes. A custom which brings many reddened eyes and tears. And when we have all had our say, we join in a song about a warrior's trip to the beyond.

They light the pyre, transforming any of Azure's lingering

energy to smoke and ash. A symbol of endings and new beginnings. The smoke rises into the darkening sky, through the gills cut in the stone dragon's over-reaching head, and out through his raised, open mouth.

Jaden and I stay at Ruby's side long after the other's have wandered away, in search of various tasks to busy their minds. I clasp his hand firmly in mine, attempting to shield him from the sorrow, but no shield is strong enough to cure the pain of such loss. Only time can make living with new missing pieces bearable.

The night sky slips into full darkness, the stars shinning bright above, accompanied by the dance of fireflies drawn to the flicker of flame. Crickets and grasshoppers celebrate a life that once was with their nature song, and Ruby adds to the chorus with her sniffles and occasional sob.

The night and setting are perfect...if there is such a thing...for sending off the soul of a loved one.

Stepping away from Jaden and Ruby, I move toward the pyre, and call upon the fire element within me. A small flame ignites in the palm of my hand. Flicks still, then vanishes, taking with it all sounds of the night or crackling fire before me.

I spin back to Jaden and Ruby. They aren't moving. A quick glance at Azure's pyre reveals the same of the fire and flame. The stars no longer twinkle, and the fireflies are frozen in the sky.

Someone has trapped me in a time bubble, a patch. The question is who. Who is capable of that level of magic?

The tree of life is cocooned and Meira is too far away to be the source. Bree is now likely capable, but she would have no reason to implement such tactics to talk to me. She need merely ask. This is too subtle to be Dreya's style, besides, she too must travel a great distance to reach me.

The only one left I can think of is...

I glance at Ruby, then Jaden. Hear his earlier words

whisper at the back of my head. *"It would make sense that she would come to pay her respects for my brother."*

I slowly spin in a circle, examining everything about my surroundings. "Show yourself," I say. "I know you're here, Aunt Edea."

She steps from the deepest of shadows cast beneath the dragon's head. She's draped in a full cloak that covers her head and hides her face from view.

She gestures to Jaden and Ruby on my right, and Azure's pyre on my left. "I wanted to see them all one last time." She folds her hands together. "You included."

The words *one last time* ring in my ear. "So, the time has come?" For you to die, or whatever it is you see coming.

"The time already came," she says. "And I am barely holding on." She throws back her hood, exposing her face. The aged, blind-eyed appearance she wore as Opal, Mother of the Augur Clan, is now partially webbed in an inky vine.

I gasp, jerking back a half step.

"I know." She pulls her hood back in place. "I have looked better. The infection fights to absorb into my skin and blood, and I have held it off for so long, but I grow weak from the fight."

She shoves back her sleeve exposing her arm covered in a cross work of black smudges and squiggles.

I raise my chin to her infect arm "You were hiding that the last time we met, weren't you?" She nods, a frown planted firmly on her face. "Does your son know?"

"He does not need to know. He is already burdened by so much." She folds her arms into her sleeves and rest them across her middle. "To late, I have seen the errors in my choices, the paths taken. Those choices have hurt him, you, and so many others for whom I care."

"Maybe you shouldn't have walked away that day." The memory of Edea walking away from Meira and Deona is as strong as memories from a day ago.

"Maybe you are right, but I cannot change the past." Her eye sparkles as if with a hidden secret meaning. "I had trouble with you being bound to that boy."

Jove. Don't worry, I'm not anymore. I grit my teeth and keep my expression even, unrevealing.

"You should not be bound to anything of this world, for you are not of this world." She bows her head. "Only, Meira could not see past the child she had come to think of as her own. She wanted to protect you…and I cannot fault her that."

Not of this world. This is the first time anyone has actually said that to me. That truth hits me in the gut and knocks the air from my lungs.

"But you, my girl," Edea continues. "You never needed protection. Not by or of either of us. You have always had the protection of the goddess and her elements. And Meira and I, we were a couple of young, foolish elves back then. So determined to save this world from its destruction."

"It's still here," I say, motioning to the spaces all around us.

"Ah, well…" She tilts her head into her shoulder, glances to Jaden and Ruby at our side. "But notice the shape of things."

Not great. But I'll figure out a way to fix that. Somehow.

"You might have righted the scales long ago, had you not been bound to fallible creatures, and weighted with an over-caring heart."

My eyes grow wide. How can she think of a caring heart as anything other than an asset?

"Deep down, I believe you have always known what you needed to do," she says. "But your heart got in the way, caring and listening to the rest of us, telling you to do this, and do that, when really you should have made your own choices."

I feel that statement. I am ready to make my own choices, but I won't ignore my heart in the process.

I cross my arms and study her. "If you love me, and

them..." I glance over at Jaden and Ruby. "...so much, why take the chance of coming here in your current state?" You could have ended up attacking us, possibly even killing us. I take a step in her direction.

Her hand flies up in a quick stop motion. "Please do not come any closer, for your own protection."

I narrow my gaze.

"I came to give you three things," she says. "A reminder, a request, and a fact to help your quest."

"Let's hear them, then." My head drops into a soft tilt.

"First, the reminder, as you already know..." She raises a single finger. "Save my son. Untether his fate from that of Dreya's."

"Wait." I shake my hand in the air. "Are you saying that if we destroy Dreya, we destroy Dohlan, too?"

I recall the look on his face after I used the mate ring and he then attempted to choke the life out of Dreya. I didn't witness how or why that ended. Only saw that he was not the winner.

"It is only a theory," she replies. "But one I would prefer not to test."

"Noted." I dip my head. "And I had not forgotten the request."

Although, saving Dohlan is a personal request, and not a big picture, save-the-worlds issue. Acknowledging the truth is painful, but a must.

"Second." She raises a second finger and holds them firmly in the air. "It is an unknown fact, that your Aunt Dreya received her water curse at the bottom of the family lake."

The lake at the frozen castle. The reason I need to go there. Find the source of the curse, end the curse, take away Dreya's water and ice power.

"I need to go to the castle," I say, and she replies with a silent nod.

"Strip the water curse from her, and she will be empowered with the darkness, but her abilities should be significantly less." She grimaces. "Or so I hope."

Okay. Bottom of the lake, I tell myself. I'm going to the bottom of a frozen lake.

"And the request?" I ask.

Edea lowers her head and falls silent for a beat. I count the crack, crack, crackle of the fire.

"I want you to kill me," she says.

My entire body jerks, a gasp strangling the flow of my breath.

"I." I shake my head. "I can't do that."

"But I can." Ruby steps forward, her eyes dark and intense.

I realize with a start, that Edea ended our suspended time talk a moment before she made her request. When I once more heard the crackle of the pyre. She knew I'd say no, and I'm fairly certain she was banking on Ruby's lack of hesitation.

Is that why she told Ruby the truth the other day? To build a strong enough anger in the Augur clan member, that she would willingly try to end the clan mother?

"No Ruby." I throw my arm out as a barrier and step in front of her. "There has to be another way."

"But she's asked for this?" Ruby argues.

"Listen to Ana." Jaden steps forward and takes hold of Ruby's arm, as if preparing to hold her back. "The light does not choose to solve issues through the loss of life."

Opal releases a dismissive laugh, snapping all our attention to her. "Balance favors neither the light nor the dark," she says. "Its only concern is for the equilibrium."

In other words, she is saying that, as the Balance Bringer, I am neither an agent of good nor bad, but a servant meant to realize a desired end. Still…to take her life to prevent further spread of the darkness…

My chest tightens. Presses my ribs into the tender of my heart.

"I could heal you," I say. "I have had success in the past."

"I saw." She smiles. "And you think you can do the same for me? Maybe move on to Dreya and heal her too?"

Wouldn't that be the point of my own infection? Learning to heal?

Edea huffs a tiny laugh. "Listen to what's inside of you. Do you feel this is something you can, or even should do?"

Can I? I don't know. Should I? Probably not.

I bow my head and shake ever slightly. Words for any response are lost in my throat. Neither Jaden nor Ruby step in to fill the void of silence.

"As I expected," Edea says after a long, drawn-out moment. "And that is all right. I stopped anticipating the discovery of a save. I got this gift from Dreya." The gift of a dark infection. "When I fought her for my son's release. Within the gift, I can taste a sliver of Sol's essence remaining."

"Which son?" Ruby asks, her question lost beneath Jaden's voice of concern.

"Are you telling us that Sol has been trapped in the dark all this time?"

Edea ignores them both and stares at me. "I never regretted my actions, fighting for him, even if it shall end in this manner."

I swallow against the lump stuck in my throat. I can think of no larger sacrifice, so willingly given, and for results that were unrealized. That is why she has asked them of me. *"Free my son."*

Another way must exist for Edea. A way other than death.

"I have a thought," Crystia says. I'm taken aback. My sisters haven't spoken in some time. *"What if we trap her in the crystals, like Kaia?"*

Kaia's grumble rumbles through my soul, her emotions hardening my muscles, pulling my tendons tight as strung bowstrings.

What? Fire explodes through the flow of my blood, and I remember a dream. A dream with a person trapped inside of a car-sized crystal. What crystals?

"*The crystals have done nothing to save me, nor suspend me,*" Kaia says, her whisper filled with a collection of emotions. Most notably, frustration at my now knowing, and guilt for having tried to keep the secret in the first place. "*They have, in fact,*" she continues. "*...slowly drained me, while denying me death. Death would have been preferable.*"

Kaia and all her secrets. My boiling blood erupts with a flash of flame in the palm of my hand. As if following through on my original intention, before Edea showed up with her many distractions, I send the element to Azure's pyre with an added thrust of my emotion.

The fire billows with the boom of cracking thunder, ignites in brilliant golden light. What's left of Azure vanishes.

I gasp. Ruby yelps.

And Jaden falls to his knees with a wail.

Ruby and I rush to his side, just as people come running from every direction. Our friends, family, a multitude of soldiers.

Opal...Edea...makes no attempt to run.

Jaden clutches his heart and rocks back and forth on his knees. In this moment, his features remind me less of himself, than they do of Azure. And for an instant, I sense Jove take control, then release.

Soldiers surround Edea, their weapons held at the ready. "What shall we do with this one?" One hollers.

Clef calls out. "She is our clan mother."

Ry stands in the space between me and Opal, and glances to me for direction. Captures my call with a single expression.

"Hold her for now," Ry replies. "Somewhere secure. This one is well versed in the use of magic." Al steps to his side and whispers words that appear to be arguments, but I don't have time for her disconcert.

Jaden is in need, and I must determine why and for what.

"May I?" Zarah pushes through the crowd of people gathered around us.

She pulls off a glove and raises her hand, signaling her intention. Jaden grants her permission with a simple nod. With a slight touch of her fingertips to his temple, the transfer of information begins. An endless swirling line of symbols moving over her fingers and hand, up her arm and fading into the ether.

Or, as I recall, into the time cauldron or some such thing. A container filled with countless accounts spanning all through history.

Jaden's features relax and his breath steadies. A moment later, his eyes pop open and he raises his head.

"Oh." She yanks her hand away.

"I'm fine." He stands. "I'll be fine."

Zarah smiles at him, warmth exuding in her gaze. "I'd say you are."

Ruby grunts. "Will someone please tell the rest of us what is going on?"

"I am complete," Jaden says simply.

And I know he means that the part of the splintered soul that was Azure has returned to complete Jaden. In light of his completeness, a hint of remorse continues swims in his eyes.

I blink. Blink to the burnt-out pyre. Blink back to Jaden. No part of his mind, body, or soul remains fractured. All pieces of his him are now one. The magic infection Garr set into place is gone. And the magical bond between us, forced or willingly accepted, as been removed. He is now free to do…to be whatever he chooses.

Which, at present, is standing with the other Augur clan members and overseeing Opal's confinement. I stand beside her, ready to intervene should she at any point put up a fight.

She leans into my side, whispers at my ear. "All these people here would lay down their lives for you. None more so than my faithful little clan." We both glance toward the Augur clan members trailing our prisoner procession to the rail car where she is to be held. "They may not show it in their actions or words, but each one of them would fight to the death to protect you and your mission."

With a shudder, I return my attention forward. "At what point did you decide it was all right to manipulate the lives of others?"

"The day you were accidently created in the form of a newborn babe," she says. "When I held you in my arms, I knew right then that there was nothing I would not do for you. From that day until my death."

"Touching." I march with her and the soldiers all the way to the cell awaiting her on the rail.

Since the rail is due to soon leave for the garrison, I leave her in a cell with few creature comforts and make my way through the cars, heading for the back where I can watch the view of Palinot grow smaller and smaller as we travel.

Ry and the other soldiers are gathered in the two cars closest to the prison car. They have a map rolled out on one of the tables and so I pause briefly and take a quick study. Nothing much has changed since my last incarnation. Places and location names appear relatively the same, although, someone added Dohlan's family home in black ink.

To get to the Marsoun estate would require traveling past the Fae family castle estate. And to get to the castle means going beyond the garrison to which we now travel.

"Dreya received her water curse at the bottom of the family lake."

What are the odds, Mom will be on board with the idea of an immediate mission to the frozen castle? And if she isn't…it will be next to impossible slipping out of a fortress packed with warriors answering to my mom.

Or would they answer to me?

Either way, I don't have time to find out.

Ry gives me a smile and slight chin raise. A silent hey, I see you. I reply in the same fashion, then head farther back in the line of rail cars. I pass Gitta on the way to the transitional door. No doubt, she's present in an observer capacity. Likely sent by Raundel to keep him apprised of anything of interest.

Miserable job. Poor girl. I smile and move to the next car.

Ruby, Clef, Shadow, Al and Klarda are gathered in the third to last car. Shadow and Clef encourage me to join them, but I keep moving with the excuse I'm looking for my O.G.... original group.

I find them, plus Raundel and Lobrka, in the next car, the second to last car. As it turns out, the last car doesn't offer much space at all, is barebones, and missing the comfort we all enjoy—padded chairs and sofas. Jaden is presently stretched out on one of the sofas, snoring softly.

I stare at him for several long, drawn-out minutes, my attention glued to his face. Then my gaze wanders to his lips, and finally his horns. His horns...*oh Gaea help me*...I want to fondle his horns.

My skin flushes and I bite my lower lip.

"He's been through a lot," Zarah says, as if I need an explanation.

"I know. He deserves the rest." I peel my gaze away and drop into a seat beside Bree and Mo.

Bree shifts to look at me. "You used your elemental fire on Azure, didn't you?"

"Yep." I nod, twist my lips together.

"According to Meira," she says, then noting Mo and Zarah's confusion adds. "Madame Marrouske. The Balance Bringer's fire is stronger than the Fires of Guardoone."

Somehow, I already knew this.

"Wowa," Mo's eyes grow wide. "Does that mean you can create similar weapons?"

"Why would she want to?" Zarah counters. "She has the favor of the elementals."

Raundel clears his throat. Both him and Lobrka lounge in

oversized chairs at the front of the car, their legs outstretched. "The gifts of the Balance Bringer are not to be used for something as trifle as weapons forging."

He glances at Lobrka, and they exchange a look as if to say, *children.*

Both elves return to their reading.

No one says anything for several minutes. If I had to venture a guess, I'd say Mo and Zarah were intimidated into silence by the overbearing buffoons. My silence is due to an overactive mind. I'm thinking about our situation, considering all the known pieces, and planning my next move. Bree watches me intently, as if waiting for my disclosure.

The train lurches forward and slowly tugs into motion.

"I'll be back," I say. "I've never been on a train before." No lie. "And I'd like to watch the scene move past from the back."

Excusing myself, I head to the farthest spot of the last car —a small, outdoor platform. I lean into the railing and feel the rhythm of the rail's motions vibrate through my body. It's getting faster with each passing moment.

Bree, having followed, leans into the rail at my side. "What are you doing?" A leading question, the answer to which I get the feeling she already suspects.

A quick glance into the car at our back tells me she came alone. "Watching the city one last time."

"What are you really doing?"

I'm going to the bottom of a frozen lake.

Just a little faster I will the train. *A little faster, a little faster.*

The train chugs and chugs, thrums, thrums. And, there, reaches the optimum velocity.

"I'm going home," I say to Bree. "You're either keeping your mouth shut or coming with me."

I move to the step at the side of the platform. A step open to a rushing landscape.

I steel my breath and jump from the train.

TWENTY-FOUR

My feet hit the ground with a solid thud. Momentum shoves me forward into a tumble. One I embrace and leap free from, back to my feet. I spin around and watch the rail take my friends and family out of sight.

This is a temporary separation, I tell myself. And one that is necessary for everyone's betterment. I will see them all again.

"That. Was. Painful." Bree shoves and kicks at the tangle of twigs and branches clinging to her. Tiny berries cling in her hair and stain her clothing. "Remind me to never do that again."

"You didn't have to come," I quip and offer her my hand, pull her to a stand.

"And leave you alone to face whatever foolery you intend?" She smirks. "Not likely. But you know..." She glances to the departing rail. It's little more than a dark box vanishing over the curve of the hillside. "It won't take them long to realize you're missing."

I nod. "That's why I waited until the rail was moving at a good clip. In order for action to happen on their end, word will need to spread to the top." In this case, Ry, as he's the highest commanding officer in my absence, and the only one who can stop the rail. "They'll need to slow, then back track, which should prove to be time consuming. Never-theless…"

"We need to get moving," she says, completing my sentence.

I swing a finger in her direction. "Bingo."

We move out at a jog, making our way back to the outskirts of Palinot City. Avoiding the wall and any of the soldiers stationed there, we slow our pace and stay to the shadows as we traverse the sleepy streets. Even if we were regular citizens, we're out past the imposed curfew, and *that* will draw attention.

The large statue head of the dragon mother used to cover and protect the area I currently seek—the harbor where we'll find the boat. But now that the dragon has uncoiled, lifted its head to the sky, our intended destination includes a trace of guess and estimation work.

We follow curves and turns until I spot what I am looking for; the stairs leading all the way down to the harbor. We descend at a measured pace.

"What exactly is the plan here?" Bree whispers, her gaze in constant motion, searching for trouble.

Up ahead, boats dotting the waterline have come into view. Somewhere amongst them is the boat that brought me to Palinot.

"Zarah and Ry have a boat tied up in the harbor." I smooth the hair across the top of my head and make a mental note of every visible boat that might be Zarah's. "We're going to take that boat to the port nearest the Royal Fae Estate." The place where my dad and aunt Dreya grew up.

Her brows arch. "We'll have to travel right past the garri-son. Risky."

"I didn't say this was going to be easy." In truth, I don't expect any part of my plan to be easy. "But it will help if we can slip through that watery pass before the officials"—my mom—"have been made aware of the situation."

In the distance, the high-pitched whistle of the rail slices through the silent night. Both our heads spin toward the direction of the sound. "Come on." I jerk my head in the direction of the harbor, and we shift from a quick walk to a run.

Zarah and Ry's long boat is in the last row of tethered water vehicles. I unmoor the lines holding the boat's side and Bree handles the front of the vessel. Once done, we shove the boat away from the dock. Without the motor running, a gain in momentum, and steering capability, we simply float in place.

Bree grimaces. "You know how to operate this thing?"

"Sort of," I say. "I kind of watched Ry." I scan the deck, then the command set above the cabin. "We need to burn wood in there." I point to a small drop down on the front deck.

"You have no idea, do you?" Bree's frown deepens, and she scratches her temple as if trying to summon the information from somewhere within herself.

I should know. With all my remembered lifetimes, I would have thought at least one version of me had operated a boat such as this one, but no. No memories of this complicated long boat exist in my head.

"I do." The boat bobs, a new weight having dropped onto the bow.

Bree and I jerk, spin around, come face to face with Mo.

She grins at us. "Where are we going?"

My chest squeezes. "You shouldn't be here. It's dangerous."

She plops her fists on her hips and gives us both a lazy frown. "If I should not be here, then neither of you should be here either." Her gaze drops to the stock of wood in the drop down set between us. "Besides, it would appear you need me. That is..." She glances over her shoulder to the city. "If you want to get this boat moving out of the harbor any time soon."

I grit my teeth and stare at her. She doesn't say anything. Neither does Bree. They are both waiting patiently for my decision.

Bring Mo, and we get the boat clipping along to our destination. Maybe Mo gets hurt when we get where we're going. Maybe she doesn't.

Don't bring Mo, she remains safe in the city...until Dreya shows up. And Bree and me, we fumble around with the boat, maybe get it working, but if we do, precious time is lost.

"The cat has got to already be out of the bag," Bree prompts. "Our absence..." She swings a lazy hand between me and her. "Might not have set off warning bells right away. After all, Balance Bringer, Master Sage. We have things to discuss, right?" I shrug. "But now her..." She motions to Mo.

"Oh." Mo waves her hands. "I covered for you."

"How so?" I cross my arms. I want Mo both to come and not come, and I'm frustrated with myself for entertaining the idea of carrying her into danger. I haven't forgotten Meira's warning about going after Dreya. The possible costs. But then, hasn't everything about my mission here in Hiddenkel been dangerous?

Mo's smile stretches, pulling the curve of her lips from ear to ear. "I shifted into your likeness." She motions to me, and I gasp. I'd been aware she could change her features into another humanoid type. After all, she became a guy at the Treeite city. But to copy the face of someone others were familiar with. The possibilities are suddenly crowding my mind.

"You can do that?" I ask, finding her admission hard to swallow.

"Sure." She blinks wide, and suddenly I am gazing on my own face. My hand flies to my lips. "I can do others, too."

With a shift and a blur, I am staring at Ry, then Jaden. It's their faces, but on a smaller, deformed body.

"Disturbing," I mumble.

"Yeah." She tugs at her attire. "I need looser clothing to imitate the males properly."

"So, you made them believe you were me?" I push. "And then what?"

Her smile returns. "It was obvious to me, that whatever you were up to, you would require time." Her gaze sweeps between me and Bree. "Why else would the two of you leave without saying anything to anyone? And jump off a rail." Her voice hitches.

She immediately covers her lips and hunches, glances around. No one beyond us appears to react, so we are safe for the time being.

Mo continues, her voice barely louder than a whisper. "I may have suggested to Zarah that Ry was missing her, and the rhythm of the rail would make for some interesting alone time."

"Gross." I grimace, not wanting to think of my brother in that way.

"What?" Mo's expression is drenched in confusion. "They are sexual creatures. And a rather sexual couple. Have you not noticed?"

The sexual exploits of my siblings, Ry or Kaia, are not my favorite topics. Mo likely can't understand because she doesn't have any known siblings.

"Can we just move on," I say. "Please."

"Okay." She nods, her face blinking to the seriousness of the task. "Jaden was still asleep, so I simply told Raundel and Lobrka that I was going to spend some alone time with Bree, exploring our new mystical connection, and that we preferred not to be disturbed."

"Not bad," I admit. "And Raundel bought the lie?" If Mo was able to sell herself as me to an older-than-dirt elf who has known me through a multitude of lifetimes, that is saying something incredible about her ability.

She shrugs. "Seemed to. I was wearing your face, and he did not study me too closely." Her smile brightens once more. "So, can I come?"

I glance to the city at her back. The low glow of the street-lamps, and the quiet, uncrowded walkways. I would prefer to get moving while the world still sleeps.

"Fine," I say through clenched teeth. "You can come."

"Great." Mo's demeanor beams. "Leave the boat to me."

Bree leans in at my ear and whispers. "It may come in useful, having a shifter at her level of ability."

As much as I hate to admit it, I agree.

Bree and I stand back and watch Mo as she piles wood into a burner and ignites the flame. She pumps and primes, pulls a lever or two, and nudges the steering wheel. In a matter of minutes, we are gliding out of the harbor, out into the open water.

The anticipated trip will be longer than a day, but I work with the water to speed us along our way. Mo and I stay awake, several hours into the middle of the night. Me moving the boat swiftly through the water, gaining us greater distance and Mo operating the boat. Bree takes the opportunity to sleep. Something we all do in shifts…after Mo shows Bree and me how to work the controls.

The following day brings limited sight of the shore, leaving little distraction to pull me from thoughts of Garr's attack, Azure's death, Jaden's reaction to me severing our connection, Dohlan's torn open chest, Edea's infesting facial rash of dark-ness, and Ry's undoubtably infuriated reaction to my unan-nounced exit.

Inside, Kaia is crying for Dohlan and Crystia is attempting to calm her, while reassuring me Ry won't be *too* mad. I'm not so sure.

"Do you ever think about Skylar?" Bree asks, clearly

noting something in my expression and sensing the need for a mental diversion.

Odd question, bringing up my high school nemesis, but I go with it. "I used to, but I haven't thought about her in quiet a while. Guess my mind got a bit crowded." What with all the Dreya dodging, infection healing, secret uncovering, old and new relationship building and dismantling.

"Well," she continues. "The day after your sister's..." She pauses and grits her teeth. "You know..."

My sister's funeral service, I mentally add with a nod. The day I somehow managed to look into her thoughts.

"I ran into her at your house."

Why in all of great Gaea would Skylar be at my house?

"Weird, right?" Bree says, playing off my clear surprise.

Skylar being at my house isn't the only thing that is weird. *Why were you there?* I think.

"I was only there," she says, as if in answer to my unspoken thought. "Because..." She slams her palm to her chest. "Master Sage." A winning smile pops to her lips.

I stare at her, eyes wide. How long had she known about her part in all of this? Two years? I was the only one kept in the dark.

"Anyway, she was pretty upset," Bree says, continuing her story of Skylar. "Babbling on about an emotional wound involving Jeremy and you, and how she needed to see you."

Jeremy, my date, who had lost his life to the tree after the school dance. A first in many events that would eventually lead me here to Hiddenkel.

"I told Skylar that you wouldn't be back, but there was a good chance I'd be seeing you soon." She tilts her head. "Hopefully soon. Anyway..."

I blink and stare and blink. I have so many questions, and I suspect that history she and Ry hinted to having will answer a lot of them, if not all.

Bree grins like the Cheshire cat. "She asked me to give you

a message." She pauses, either for affect or to gather her thoughts. "She told me that something strange happened between the two of you in the church parking lot after the service."

I nod, recalling the spilled water bottle and the touch that accidentally extracted the truth behind her dislike for me... her jealousy and secret affection for Jeremy.

"She said that whatever happened, it was eye opening and healing. And after a night of processing, she felt better than she had in years." Bree raises her brow. "So, she wanted to thank you."

My posture stiffens. "Well..." I don't know what to say. "Surprising."

"Isn't it though?" Bree says. "I think you healed some emotional wound she'd been feeding for years." She sighs. "So anyway, messaged delivered, but I think the real point I wanted to make, sharing this information with you, is that...if you could do that for Skylar, Dreya should be easy peasy."

I explode into laughter and Bree giggles with me. But we both know Dreya is on a whole new level, partially because I suspect she isn't fully right in the head.

"She really could be quite the bitch, couldn't she?" I ruminate regarding Skylar, thinking the shared tale is much more about giving closure to Skylar's story. She and I are truly done, and she is healed.

"Most definitely."

"So, tell me," I press. "What brought you to my house that day, and what's the history between you and my brother Ry?"

"First off..." She raises a finger. "I didn't know Ry was your brother until recently."

Bree delves into her story about meeting Ry during a convenience store robbery and joining her brother's coven in a ceremony that resulted in her not only meeting Meira but being chosen as Meira's eventual replacement.

Whatever is going on with Meira, that she feels she won't

be around much longer, she's known about it for awhile now. At least two years.

Bree also met my mom during that adventure. She had shown up in her capacity as commander of the immortal warriors. And because of the meeting, my mom recognized Bree when she showed up at the house that day. For that reason, aware firsthand of Bree's connection to Hiddenkel, Mom brought Bree along when they left that world to come here.

Bree giggles. "I thought about dragging Skylar along just to see her expression when she stepped into a new world."

I fake a laugh with no clear emotion in the action. It's my job…and in my heart…to rise above petty emotions such as revenge. Meira told me that and now I feel it.

Bree's expression drops, as if she realizes or feels it too.

By the time her story comes to a close, Mo is sitting at the table with us, listening intently to every spoken word. And my mind is reeling over how much everyone in my life has hidden from me.

"We've hidden much, too," many of my previous incarnations whisper.

I need yet another diversion. "Anyone hungry?"

Ration supplies left in the galley are sparce. And without a single perishable to be found, our meals consist of water and crackers. We pass our time with information share and planning.

The plan, get to the bottom of the lake at the ice castle, and figure out how to end Dreya's water curse, thus relieving her of any water and ice magic.

I'll go in the water; Bree and Mo will stand as lookouts. Since I saw Dreya storming out of the ice fortress, she shouldn't be there to hinder us, but other things could lie in wait. I'd ask the elements to scout ahead, but I can't risk passing out with another nasty nosebleed.

Beneath the setting sun, Bree and I stand on the bow and

stare as the garrison comes into view. Where once there had
been a land bridge, cutting off the smaller sea we now sail,
from the larger surrounding ocean, there is now a land
peninsula upon which the garrison's mighty fortress has been
built. Through Deona's memories, I recall the bridge's
destruction.

From this vantage point, forces may sail inland, or sea
bound with equal ease. They have the eastern and northern
lands at their back and need only skip over the water pass to
access the western and southern territories.

Bree sighs. "The con has likely long since been exposed."

My lips pull taut. "Let's hope word hasn't yet reached
those highest in command." I raise my chin to infer those
currently within the walls of the garrison.

"You mean your mom," she says, rather bluntly.

Mo blinks rapidly. "I forgot your mom was the commander." She shakes her head. "How could I forget that. Okay..."
She raises a pointed finger. "This is what we are going
to do..."

As we approach the garrison, Bree and I take cover in the
cabin, making sure to stay clear of any windows not draped
over. Mo changes into a loose, worn overcoat and then shifts
into an unfamiliar face. That of an elderly man, hunched with
age and ill health.

"The soldiers will see me," she says. "And think me
nothing more than a lonely traveler traversing the pass, likely
making the long trip to Season's Cape.

"Beyond the southern tip, where the Time Keep is located," I say. The place where Zarah would be employed...or
enslaved...had she not run away.

Mo's plan is rather brilliant, given the local elderly are
known to sometimes make the trip to the Keep, in order to

have their life memories collected, and presented to their family upon their passing.

"Smart," I add.

By the time we reach the passage, everyone is in place. Bree and I are hidden below deck, and Mo is above, playing the part of an elderly man making his way to the Time Keep.

I chance a peek.

Several warriors line the highest wall of the fortress and eye the vessel with intense scrutiny. Thankfully, we manage to pass without incident. Into the open waters we sail, the small port village we seek, ahead and to the west.

My turn to rest, I take a quick nap before we reach shore.

I've barely fallen asleep when Mo is shaking me awake. "Bree." It's all she says to me.

I leap from my bed, the same one I used on our previous voyage, and go in search of Bree. Find her on the deck, clutching the side rail, staring out at the water. In the far distance, a massive volcano skirts the skyline.

"*The Fires of Guardoone,*" one of my incarnations whispers regarding the volcano.

Stepping beside Bree, I lay my hand upon hers. "Are you all right?"

"No." She shakes her head. "I've been here before. During my initial test with Meira."

"You're not talking about Hiddenkel in general, are you?" I ask. "You mean specifically here, on the water?" My gaze drifts to the volcano, a most unforgettable point of reference.

"On a ship, in this general area." She turns her gaze away from the landscape to me. "It was a military vessel, and your mom was there. Dreya attacked from the water...or as the water. A massive water-carved version of her. She was incredibly powerful."

"As are we," I say, clutching her hand tighter.

She nods. "Meira is strong. And so now am I. But..." She lowers her head. "This memory, or event, I had come to believe, hope maybe, that it was an illusion created for the purpose of my *then* evaluation."

"Now that I have all the memories…" She splays her hands at the side of her head. "I understand it was a projection of things to come. A possibility foreseen."

"A future event?" I clarify. "Involving Dreya and her water magic?"

"Yes. Exactly." She nods. "And it was intense."

"Not the past, but the future?" She again nods. "Well." I clap my arm around her shoulder. "Given our current destination and mission, we'll just have to make sure we succeed and thereby change that possible future." I swivel to face her. "What do you say?"

"I say it's a deal," Mo cuts in.

Bree smiles. "Agreed." She raises her fist. "To changing the future."

I bump my fist to hers and Mo follows suit.

"To changing the future," we all chime in unison.

By the time we reach the port village and moor the boat, we are pumped for success and starving. So starving, in fact, we head straight for the first eatery we can find and order enough food to feed twice as many people.

I give Mo and Bree my meat products, and they share their fruits and vegetables with me. I can't eat half of the portions provided before my belly is tight and achy.

I push my plate aside and pat my sides. "I should have known better," I mumble. About eating so much at once.

"You should have known better about several things." I jolt and spin to the voice, come face to face with Gitta. "You have a lot of people upset with you."

TWENTY-FIVE

Gitta stands beside our table, as if appearing straight from dust…or smoke.

"Hey…Gitta," I say. "You're. Here."

"Where else would I be?" she asks. "Raundel sent me to find you and find you I did."

"How did you get here so quickly?" Mo asks.

Gitta swings a casual glance to her. "I hazed."

Hazed, as in misted…or ghosted?

I recall my first encounter with Gitta, before I knew who she was. She had appeared as a distortion in the air, wisping around me like the wind. A talent rather similar to what I understand Al's ability to be. The one that gained her the nickname white ghost.

"So, what now?" I prop my elbow on the table and rest my head against two spread fingers. "Are you going to try to take us back to Raundel?"

"Maybe." She crosses her arms and stands tall, her shoulders and neck stiff. "You have *a lot* of people mad at you. Not just Raundel." A tiny vee presses into the bridge of her nose.

"Lord Ryland is livid, your tracer riled, and Lobrka suggests you need a whack or two to the bum."

Of all things, a spanking? I shake my head at Lobrka's suggestion. I expected my brother to be mad, and Jaden...

"Is Jaden still my tracer if I unbound him from me?" I ask. The pull to him changed the moment I severed our magical link. I know he felt it, too, and now I can't help but wonder how his emotions regarding us have altered.

Not that it should matter, I tell myself. *My ultimate goal has remained unchanged. Bring the balance, external relationships notwithstanding.*

"Ana," Bree snaps. "Focus. We currently have other concerns. Worry about Jaden later."

She's right, of course. I was just thinking the same. "Sorry," I mumble, understanding that I need to check my concern regarding anyone's emotions. Not when greater issues are unfolding around us. Issues I am meant to somehow fix.

I need to get to the castle. Answers await at the bottom of the lake.

"How did you know where to find us?" Bree asks of Gitta.

Gitta cocks her head and frowns. "It is no secret where Anala wants to go," she replies and turns her gaze to me. "You made a fuss about it with our lady."

When Raundel was in the room. "Raundel told you to look for me along the path to the castle, didn't he?"

"He did. And he was right to do so, because..." She flips a hand toward our group as if to present us to some unseen onlooker. "Here you are." Her arm goes limp, then pulls back around her waist. "But why are you here?" she asks. "That is what I fail to comprehend. Why do you want to go to the castle covered in ice? Alone, without backup? And why should I not immediately return you to Raundel's custody?"

I double blink. Not that I think Gitta could successfully get us all back to Raundel, but...did she just suggest I give her a reason to allow us to continue on our way?

"Let me ask you this," I say. "Do you serve Raundel or the Balance Bringer?"

The question is sparked by an earlier conversation with Klarda, regarding me and Marrouske. I know where Klarda stands on the topic. Now, in the face of Gitta's threat, I must burrow down to her core loyalty.

She jerks back, albeit so slight it's almost unnoticeable. "Well..." All stubborn certainty washes from her features. "The Balance Bringer, of course."

"Then why don't you take a seat and join us." I pat the table, then shove a chair out with the push of my foot. Gitta accepts the invitation and settles in.

"What is it we are discussing?" she asks, folding her hand on the table.

"We are about to tell you why we need to go to the ice castle," Mo replies.

"And why it shouldn't be delayed," Bree adds.

Gitta glances around the table, taking measure of each of us.

"We're going to take away Dreya's water and ice magic," I say. "And the sooner, the better."

Her lips press into a pucker. "Are you suggesting that it wouldn't be wise to wait until we can take the seasoned warriors?"

All the warriors that would come into the situation are far too protective of me. Possibly hindering what I may have to do.

Plus, more people who might get hurt.

Meira's unforgotten words ring in my ears. *"Going after Dreya is a foolish move and could end up getting people you care about hurt...or worse."*

The fewer the better.

"Yes," I reply to Gitta. "Their presence would only complicate matters."

She scrutinizes me for a moment, then relaxes her features. "Very well."

"So…" Bree leads. "You won't tell Raundel?"

Gitta shakes her head.

Mo leans into the table. "Then, what will you do? Pretend to keep looking? Or go back to him with a lie?"

"Oh." Gitta shakes her head, her mouth curving into a perfect O. "I cannot lie. Especially to Raundel. No…" She smiles at me. "I feel like it is my duty to accompany you on this mission."

From two, to three, now four. Too many chances for someone other than myself to get hurt. I am not loving these odds. Yet, I can't turn her away. Not under the circumstances, with Raundel waiting on her return and report.

"Fine," I say through gritted teeth, for the second time in too few days. "You may come, but you are to run at any sign of danger."

Gitta scoffs, but agrees, and arrangements are made to head out at first light. Gitta so kindly books us all rooms at the nearest inn, where we sleep well with our beds soft and our bellies full.

MORNING COMES TOO SOON, and we are cutting a path out of the village and toward the castle.

"Can you save us time and haze us there?" Mo asks of Gitta.

Gitta feigns surprise at the question, which I take to mean, on some level, Gitta had been expecting us to ask.

"As much as I appreciate your confidence in my skills," she replies with a smile glued in place. "There are too many of you, and the distance is exhausting. I do not have enough energy or patience for such a task."

And only last night she had threatened to do exactly that, haze us all back to Raundel's custody. Sly little elf.

"You could have just said no," Bree replies. "You didn't need to get snippy about it."

Gitta makes a face at Bree, then Mo, and quickens her pace.

"Save your energy," I call after her. "It's a long walk." She slows and I catch up, walk at her side. "Do you get asked that a lot? To help people with what they think is a quick time and distance save?"

She frowns and nods. "It can be rather annoying."

I understand, I convey with a nod. "The next time we ask a question or make a request that you feel is out of line, just say so. We won't hold it against you for drawing a line or speaking your truth."

She smiles. "You are not stuffy as I expected the Balance Bringer to be."

Um. Thanks?

Only able to move as quick as our slowest member, Bree's human rate, travel to the castle is a solid day's walk—at a decent clip. Few wagons pass our way who are willing to offer us a ride.

The castle sits on a hill, raised above the neighboring land. The location both an ideal vantage point to view the bordering lands and possible incoming invaders and also serve as reminder to the royal family's subjects. Covered in ice and snow, it glistens like glass in the sunlight.

The closer we get in our approach, the more the landscape changes and the ice-sculped palace shifts from magical to ominous. The surrounding terrain morphs from shades of willow, gold, and beige, to tones of umber, ash, and ebony.

Until the slush and snow settle over everything, blanketing the land in various stained hues of white. The others shiver and rub their arms and hands for warmth, but I am unaffected by the cold. An aspect, I assume, of my water elemental connection. Or possibly fire.

Inside the estate's outer most gate, a thick webbing of inky dark veins slicing through the frozen lawns, gardens, and pathways, shattering the winter wonderland vision.

Taking the main stone walk toward the palace's grand entrance, I'm careful to step over and around every line of infectious black. At the very least, a touch will drag me into a Dreya-induced vision hell. At its worst, I could end up infected…again.

"Don't touch the black lines," I remind the others.

Gitta's tiny voice sounds at my back. "Oops."

We all spin to face her. "Did you touch it?" I ask, my gaze raking over every visible inch of her, searching for signs…any signs…of the darkness digging its poisoning barbs into her being.

She glances down at her feet. She's not standing on any dark lines, although she is positioned dangerously close to one. "I am unsure. What should I do?"

A heavy breath rises and falls in my chest. "We keep moving," I say. "But we also keep a tight watch on you." I shift my gaze between Mo and Bree. "We all do." They nod.

Arranging our order, we continue forward with Gitta between us. Each of us ready to take action at the first sign of darkness seeping through her or from her.

"If we touch any of the dark veins," I say over my shoulder to the group. "Then we may alert Dreya where to find us. Each inky, sticky line is in some way an extension of her." Her far-reaching monitoring system.

"Plus," Mo adds. "It feels awful." No doubt, she's recalling the infection we both suffered that day at Ry's storage locker.

"But you saw Dreya leave here, right?" Bree asks, her gaze darting from window to window of the long building stretched before us.

"I did." I saw her leaving a frozen fortress. My attention

shifts to the spires and peaks beyond the front façade of the building, attempting to pinpoint the location from my vision. "Still, we can never be too careful."

The grand front doors are five times taller than me. As I approach, I wonder how many times my father walked through this resplendent entrance. Before I am able to reach the door, push the latch, the door opens, its motion slowed against the friction of the snow-covered floor.

I pull my hand into my chest and hesitate. Study the space beyond the entry.

"I think it is all right," Gitta says. "The door simply recognizes your royal blood."

Interesting.

We move into the colossal entryway. Double doors large enough for Goliath at our back, curved stairs on either side, leading to an upper landing overlook, and passage to the rooms beyond that three RV's could drive through...side by side.

"How does it feel to be home?" Mo asks, her wild-eyed stare taking in every frost-covered detail in sight. Everything from the double staircase, the chandelier dripped with icicles, the royal crest cut in the floor and blurred beneath a layer of ice and snow.

"This is not my home." My chest burns with the statement. "It never was and never will be."

I turn in a slow circle, taking in the energy vibrating through everything around us. Too much anger and sadness continue to dwell in this place. I might much prefer to burn it to the ground than ever take up residence here.

My gaze drifts to the upper landing. Somewhere up there is the bedroom where I envisioned a young, angry Dreya yelling at me to get out.

Save that for later, I tell myself. For now, we stick to the plan.

Get to the lake. Answers...and hopefully solutions...await at the bottom.

The front door closes with a loud bang, and the entry hall sinks into a carousel of shadows.

My body instinctively drops into a defensive stance, knees bent, arms and hands at the ready.

Maybe a slight diversion before the main event...the lake.

"On your guard," I say.

The advice is unnecessary. Everyone is already prepared.

The shadows dancing on walls, shift and stretch, reach across the floor, outstretched for our feet. Memories tug at me of a night at the school's swimming pool, or the ghostly mining town in Faredale. Some time has passed since I've had to tangle with a single tenebrousian, much less several.

I have been victorious against them twice. Once when I sucked the creature into a water vortex, and the other time when accessing something inside of me that destroyed the creature with light. All the other times, I ran away.

Assessing the situation, I take in every shift of light and every flicker of darkness.

Bree's hands are moving, her lips mumbling, summoning the magic of ancient elves. "We've got this," she says. "You get where you need to go." Her magic pulses like a bass drum in the circular space.

"Not leaving you," I reply, and summon a little magic of my own. The strength of wind to my fingertips. I let it loose against the shadows, tearing at their shapes, shredding them like tattered fabric.

I call over the roar of my wind. "If any of these things get away, they'll likely run straight to Dreya." And then she will know, without a doubt, where to find us...me.

A tenebrousian lashes at Gitta, another at Mo.

Gitta hazes, vanishing and reappearing on the upper landing.

And Mo shifts, becomes a shadowy monster of her own.

Not a tenebrousian, but a creature able to move in the same manner and, with a slash of its elongated shadow claws, do damage to Dreya's dark minions.

Bree's elven magic pulses an increasing beat. On the ceiling above, her energy begins to swirl, faster and faster, creating, opening a vortex. A vacuum pulling at the shadows. At me. At all of us.

Several tenebrousian, unable to hold their position upon the surrounding walls, are yanked through the air, up past the second floor, and into the awaiting void on the ceiling several stories above.

Bree calls out to me over the roar in the room. "I need you to do something for me. When you're doing what you need to do…" Attempting to nullify Dreya's curse. "If you are able, discover all that you can about what gift she may have obtained from Sol."

Because Sol received the original, or a significant portion of the original darkness are the unspoken words I hear in her request. Darkness that likely wasn't properly dealt with from the start. Something we'll need to try and correct.

I grant Bree a two-finger salute, letting her know her request has been noted, but before I will allow myself to leave my friends and move toward the lake, I need to make sure they are safe. The threat neutralized.

"Anala," Gitta calls down to me. "Get going. We've got this." Her attention snaps back to the remaining tenebrousian holding their places. "Come and get me," she yells, and races down the upper hallway, out of view.

"No," I scream. Not yet. Not until I know they will be all right.

"*Emotions,*" something inside of me reminds. "*Do not let them cloud your judgement.*"

"Go," Bree screams at me and hurls a wave of energy at me. It smacks into me full force, knocks me off my feet, and sends me sliding across the slippery floor, through the passage leading to the wide hallway beyond.

"Not cool," I mumble, pulling myself back to my feet.

No sooner am I standing than Mo's shadowy monster form grabs the front of my jacket and thrusts forward through the following room. We crash through the outer glass doors.

"Lake," she seethes, then drops me in the courtyard and disappears into the frozen palace.

The doors between us close. Freeze shut.

Staring at the barrier standing between me and my friends, I wrestle with the emotions churning in my gut. I can't believe they tossed me out like that.

"Because you have a job to do," Deona reasons. *"They know it. You know it. Now get to it."*

My chest is tight with the emotions tied to their sacrifices.

"Don't waste these moments," I whisper to myself, then turn and head for the lake I know to be roughly a football fields distance from the back gardens' outer wall.

Through the gardens, over the wall, and across the rolling fields, to one frozen lake. A memory hits me like one of my own. A young version of my father, holding hands with a wee Dreya, teaching her to ice skate on this frozen lake.

"Aunt Dreya received her water curse at the bottom of the family lake."

Right here. When she fell through the ice.

The lake is smaller now, an attempting filling having taken place in the years since.

I stare at the thick, rough cover of ice. Bending my knees, I lay my hand upon the surface, probe the water molecules beyond. Beyond a foot of ice, water awaits.

I glance back at the garden wall of the frozen palace. See no hints as to the current state of my friends. But...

My attention swings back to the lake at my feet.

For them, and for everyone, this must be done.

I straighten, standing tall. Breathe and calm my nerve, cool my systems, my emotions, and jump.

The wind caresses me as I rise. It holds me tight and tells me everything will be all right.

I pray that is so.

I come back down, boots slamming to the frozen ground. Fire explodes through my feet and the ice, opening a perfect me-sized port. My body plunges into the glacial waters below.

TWENTY-SIX

Aware of the chill, yet not feeling the bite as I might once have, my body drops through the water like an arrow shot into the sky, cutting through resistance with swift ease.

Many ages have passed since this lake saw life outside of what has always remained, and the water elementals are thrilled with my arrival. Excited for the company. They swim with me on the downward dive.

I plummet straight to the lake floor and take a seat as I used to do at the bottom of my high school pool. The sounds of the water are a sweet chorus at my ear, and the sights, a liquid beauty only known beneath the waves. I have no need to breath the oxygen from above. My body absorbs all that I need directly from the water against my skin.

The lake floor glows with mystical energy beyond that of the norm. One location, in particular, burns brightest with transfiguration verve.

Willing the water for assistance, the liquid lifts my form and relocates me to the place of highest energy residuum. There, I allow my thoughts to project my desire.

The elements...the Ondine...respond, sharing a memory of Dreya.

Small, blue, and chilled to the bone, she sinks from a hole in the ice above to the bottom of the lake. She shivers and quakes against the cold, the pressure of the water, and the lack of oxygen.

In answer to her need, an air pocket forms around her, granting her ease of breath. And with the formation of the lifesaving bubble, the old man of the sea appears, Proteus.

"What were you doing here, old man?" Deona whispers of the old god. *"At the bottom of a lake, no less."*

Despite little Dreya's arguments that she does not belong in the water or with him, the water god Proteus suggests her presence at the bottom of the lake is an offering to him from the moon and sun above.

"Please, Proteus. Please, let me go," young Dreya pleads, offering him many wonderous things, offerings and companionship. The devotion of a powerful Fae queen, something she is destined to become.

He agrees, but his parting words are not to be taken lightly.

"The days are long, and the nights are cold," he says. "...but I am not lacking in sympathy or compassion. I shall return you to the surface, all your faculties unharmed, and with a wonderous magical addition. But every seventh daybreak you shall visit my pond and shall do so without splintering the rhythm.

"Consider your new addition a gift of my affection, one to be handled with deep consideration. My gift is a tool, one to drench your reign in unparalleled commonwealth and unity. But to break our bond and miss a date may infuse you with the opposite of the well-meant intentions.

"Heed my words, young Fae, and stay true to our accord, or a gift may as easily become misfortune."

Or a curse, I muse, then turn away from the memory and scan the lake floor. An ancient water god lives at the bottom of a small lake...highly doubtful. Access to other waterways must exist somewhere nearby. *"Where did you go, Proteus?"*

Allowing my senses to register the flux and flow of energy

upon the lake floor, a strong path takes shape, showing the flow of movement. Energies coming and going, visiting and returning to another location.

Even without the ability to trace the energy stream the Ondine, anxious to please, gather in the direction I must now go. An underwater doorway, dim except for a sliver of brilliant blue light.

Pushing off the lake floor, I whiz through the watery door to whatever lies beyond.

Warmer water. That's what awaits me on the other side of the lake floor portal. Water expands for as far as the eye can see in most all directions, except for directly in front of me. There, a small island rises above the surface. And on its shore, a sunbathing seal.

Only…

His energy, his glow, suggests the relaxing mammal is far more than any average seal.

I gather all the information every one of my past incarnations holds regarding the old man water god Proteus and then allow the water elementals to glide me to shore.

Proteus, considered old and possibly among some of the first gods, is a shapeshifter. He could be posing as a man…or a seal.

I narrow my gaze on the shoreline sunbather.

"*He will not want to stay and hear you out,*" Deona warns.

"*He will try to escape,*" Crystia adds.

Then I'll have to find a way to make him stay and listen to me. Make him see things my way and help us.

I step from the water, silent as the gentlest of breezes, careful not to alert the old god to my arrival. He's laid out with eyes closed, fins relaxed, and his belly exposed to the sky.

"Water, wind, and earth," I say, softly for only the elements to hear. "Be my ally in convincing Proteus to work with us." He'll try to get away and we can't let him. Not until after he hears what we have to say.

Creeping quietly across the sand, I reach for the seal's closest fin.

His eyes pop wide. He barks and disappears.

Turns into a fox, prepares to run.

But, knowing what I do of Proteus, I had anticipated a shifter change. My hand clamps down tight around his tail, halting his escape.

"Hear me out," I say.

He snaps his sharp teeth at my hold, but earth deflects, spraying sand in the little fox's face.

Proteus shifts again, this time into a burning log.

And again, I am ready.

Water and ice rush to my aid, dousing all of his flames.

"Many years ago, you granted magic to a young Fae," I say. "Magic that turned into a curse."

Proteus the log shifts into Proteus the shark, his tail thrusting back and forth, attempting to break my hold. His mighty bite spinning and reaching for me.

The wind lifts him and slams him to the ground, stalling his fight.

Then suddenly, the shark is no more, and an old man sits in the sand before me, my grip held tight around his ankle.

"I recognize what you are," he says. "Daughter of Gaea. Release me and I shall tell you what you want to know about your present or future."

"Favors for myself is not why I am here," I say.

"Then tell me," he prompts. "What is it you seek from me."

I loosen my hold upon his ankle, but only slightly. "I am here because of Dreya."

"Aw." His brows arch and eyes twinkle. "The young Fae princess who failed to uphold her end of our agreement."

"I need you to take it back," I blurt. "Remove it. Undo it. Whatever."

His head jerks back into the fold of his neck. "I beg your pardon. You want me to do what?"

"Take it back," I repeat.

He shakes his leg and my clutch around his ankle tightens once more. "I do not offer take backs. A gift given is forever."

I arch an eyebrow. "Even if that gift will destroy all that you hold dear?" I counter.

His lips pull into a straight line. "My waters are vast and my rivers and streams plentiful. How can a single gift given to a young Fae threaten such greatness?"

Visions of the oceans and rivers in the world of my youth flash to mind. Once clear and healthy, now polluted almost beyond repair, all because of selfish and close-minded people refusing to do what must be done to ensure a better world for everyone. Selfish and close-minded like Proteus.

What is happening in the world of my youth is a direct effect of what is happening here in Hiddenkel—the imbalance, Dreya's infectious reach.

I bet if we look deep enough beneath the rivers, lake, and oceans…

Whirling away from the plea I am making to Proteus, my thoughts dive deep into the water, the elementals traveling with me, constantly swirling at my side. Together, we plunge through the water and skim the floor until what we seek comes into view.

Black inky veins. Even here, running along the seabed.

With a snap, I am whole, standing in front of the old god. "Your water world is under attack. Have you not seen the cracks running along every single one of your waterways? The second gift…or curse…granted to Dreya by the darkness."

"My waterways have survived many an eon," he says. "They shall survive many, many more." His gaze drops to my hand upon his ankle. "Release me and I shall tell you what you want about your life. I shall not lie."

My jaw tightens. "What I want is for you to remove what-ever it was that you did to Dreya."

"This request is no good." He flicks his hand. "Make another."

"I don't want another. I want this one." My hands clench, and he flinches under the strength of my grip. "I want you to look into the future with the prophetic talent of yours and see the toll the worlds will pay for your gift to a young Fae."

He jabs a point to the air. "To the later. Accepted." He claps his hands together.

Wind and water spring to life around me, swirling with ever increasing velocity. I am sucked into a highspeed vortex. Thrust away from Proteus. Away from the island and the surrounding sea. Hauled back through the freezing lake and then tossed up and out onto the snow-covered palace grounds.

A scream bursts from my lungs. A scream of anger and frustration. A scream of a thousand and ten irritations. "If the worlds be damned," I yell. "Then so be you, Proteus." My fist slams into the packed snow. I didn't even get to ask him about Sol and the darkness. Hardly got to question him about anything at all.

Release the rage, I tell myself and take a deep, centering breath. *If I must rise above revenge, then so too must I not allow myself to be ruled by my negative emotions.*

A loud boom and crash rumbles through the frosty air, and smoke rises from the left side of the ice-encrusted castle.

My name whispers in my head like a call for help. The voice, belonging to Bree.

Without thought or hesitation, I take off at a flat run. Over the garden wall, through the shattered glass doors, into the hall running the length of the main wing, and toward the source of the roar. At the end of the hall, I dash through a pair of open doors and skid to a stop.

Once a resplendent throne room, oval in shape with surrounding high-set, stained glass windows, two throne chairs oozing with grandeur, and walls finished in gold, now it is the location of a massive hole in the ground.

The floor collapsed into a colossal underground chamber. Chunks of the throne-room floor are scattered among massive crystal pillars. Pillars so ginormous they could rival, possibly dwarf, the columns of the Parthenon, Greek temple to the goddess Athena.

Crystals wider than a car, much less a being of my size.

A memory of a body encased in crystal flashes to the forefront of my mind. A memory not belonging to me but to another. A dream walk experienced in what now feels like a different lifetime. Before Hiddenkel, and before the burden of my destiny.

I stare down at the crisscross of clear stone pillars. *Is this the place in my dream? Is there a body trapped somewhere inside one of these transpicuous stones?*

Only the space directly below is somewhat visible, the rest being clouded with shadows, or completely covered in a blanket of darkness.

"Ana," Bree's hoarse voice calls from the broken debris cluttering the chamber floor. Clearly injured and battered from the collapsing of the throne room floor, she lays among the mess, barely moving.

"I'm coming." I quickly scan for a sturdy place to land.

"No. Don't."

Her warning is too late. My body is already in motion, leaping from the castle interior to the hole in the ground.

My landing is solid and mere feet from Bree's location. But the energy drain is instantaneous.

I drop to one knee and press a hand to the ground, to hold me steady. *What in Gaea's name...*

The air is thick and oxygen thin.

And my lifeforce...

It feels as if it is being pulled, sucked, dragged into the surrounding stones.

"You need to get out," Bree calls to me, her voice scratchy.

I drag a breath and call to the elements for assistance.

"Not without you." I push myself forward in her direction.

Show me, I request of the earth and air, looking for answers regarding the nature of my location. The energy drain with which I am struggling.

Elemental reactions roll out from me in a wave, rippling in all directions, acknowledging what is and what there is to know. Crystals as old as time, spanning almost the entire expanse of the palace foundation. The royal estate built here in order to harness the energy...the power...of the mighty stones.

But something more waits to be discovered. Something hidden in the chamber shadows.

I heave myself to Bree's side. "Where are you hurt?" I ask.

"Not sure," she replies. "I hurt in so many places."

"Mo and Gitta?" I ask.

She shakes her head. "I don't know. They weren't with me when the floor caved in."

Okay. I nod. "I'm going to get you out of here." I glance to the hold above and take measure of my waning strength. "Somehow."

She shakes her head. "Can't you feel it?" Her gaze narrows. "You need to leave me and go."

"Not without you," I remind. But she's not wrong, we need to hurry, while a spattering of my energy and strength still answers my call.

She coughs, presses her hand to her chest. "But you do feel it?"

"If you mean, the strength of my physical self being syphoned, then yes." I glance around at the surroundings crystals. Clearly, they are the source of my energy depletion.

"This place," she says. "Its lifeforce has been twisted against its nature, in order to serve her." She reaches her hand for mine. "Let me borrow and show you."

Borrow energy, magic. Combine what dwells within both of us.

I grab her hand. Light blooms in the chamber. Dimly glows at the base of each crystal, exposing dark fissures and a grayish tint, rising from the base of each stone, fading into the otherwise clear structures.

"See," Bree mutters, pushing her thoughts into mine.

The direction of my attention is spun around the crystalline structures, moving deep and wide. Not seeing with my eyes, but with my mind, images of columns and pillars race past, slowing only once an obscured stone comes into view.

A body in the crystal…just as seen in my dream walk.

A brown-haired girl, features soft and relaxed, appearing to only be sleeping.

Kaia. I gasp.

She's been here, beneath the castle, all this time. She didn't want me to know because…

I can't be here. My power is…abating.

The vision jerks and spins back into action. Moves with intense speed between the gigantic stones. Pauses once more. Another trapped body. A woman in royal robes with a crown upon her head.

My eyes widen, even as the vision swings back into action. Takes me to another. This one, a crowned male, also dressed like a royal.

Dreya's parents? I muse. *My grandparents?*

Three bodies. Three points of power, amplified by the crystals within which they are trapped.

Is Dreya increasing her own abilities and strength by stealing from her magical Fae family?

It's not just the secret of the lake that drew me here. It's this. This misuse of Gaea's natural resources and the theft of powerful magic.

The vision swirls, still not done sharing the secrets of the chamber. Dodging through the dark, rising pillars to every side, the scene rushes to a fourth point in Dreya's power grid.

Marduk Maddox Raine, king of the Fae, brother of Dreya, and my father.

"Dad," the word escapes my lips as barely a whisper and I stumble back, butt to the ground.

He's still garbed in his bloody armor from my vision of his death day.

But...if he is now here, did he actually die? Or merely come close?

"They are not dead," Bree says. "But nor are they alive. Do not be fooled into believing you can save them."

"But..." I mutter.

"Ana." Warning courses through her voice. "You do not want to end up like them, another battery fueling that bitch's wickedness."

No. I definitely do not want to become an asset in Dreya's path of destruction.

She pushes up on her elbows and groans, then takes a deep breath before continuing. "You feel the crystals draining you because they have somehow been tuned to target your family bloodline. Stay down here and you risk the chance of becoming like them, drained and forever trapped in a crystal."

"Then let's get out of here." I grab her arm and drag her to stand. She sways and I brace my arm around her, holding her steady. Quickly scan every crystal and collection of broken stone that might provide a solid climb to the surface.

We take several steps, and a black mist materializes around us. In a blink, Gitta stands in front of us. Grins, a disturbing, skin-crawling pull to her lips. Her eyes are darker, skin paler, and when she smiles, her gums appear grey.

"Crap," Bree utters.

Gitta shoves Bree in the chest, knocking her off balance. She tumbles back, dragging me in a twist as I attempt to hold on, hold her upright.

Gitta grabs my lapels and tugs me close, ripping my hold

free of Bree. "I think you should stay here," she says. "I am told the crystals are cozy."

I frown but refuse to let my reaction be ruled by emotion. "So...you did step on the inky vein, then?" I glance over her infect state and start calculating all the ways to restrain her... once my energy is restored.

"I have been freed," she replies.

"Unlikely," I retort. "I'd say your new condition is a sign of the chains now strapped around your soul."

Her response is a wicked twist between a laugh and a snarl.

"Shall we get you locked in?" She motions to an extra wide crystal a few feet away.

"I'd rather not." I yank at her hold, but my strength is lacking.

Meira's warning races sharply through my senses. *"Going after Dreya is a foolish move and could end up getting people you care about hurt...or worse."*

I chose to come anyway and now Bree is injured, Gitta is infected, and I'm...I'm...

There's got to be a way out of this situation. After all, I'm more than Fae, or elven, or immortal warrior. I'm a creation of the goddess and Gaea. I am...

A shadowy monster drops from somewhere above and lands beside us, lunges at Gitta. She hazes, the magic encompassing all of us—Gitta, me, and the shadowy monster...Mo. We materialize in an unfamiliar palace room.

Slipping from Gitta's hold, I drop to the floor, still weak from the crystal energy drain. I lean against the wall at my side and pray.

Please, Gaea. Restore my strength.

Mo shifts from the shadowy monster, into the form of hobgoblin similar to Klarda and takes a swing at Gitta.

Gitta hazes an inch over and tosses me a quick glance, as if confirming I haven't gone anywhere.

"Impressive," she says to Mo. "But I have trained with and against Klarda. I know how to handle the form you have chosen."

"This is not the only form I can summon," Mo replies. "I can keep shifting so you will never know what to expect."

I think of Proteus and his constant shapeshifting. It didn't stop me from besting him...even if I didn't get what I wanted. Dreya's water curse remains intact. But at least we have exposed another threat in need of solving.

"And I can haze as many or more times as you shift," Gitta replies, then startles, stares past us.

A white mist takes shape, swirling on the other side of the room. And from the vapor, Al steps clear. The white ghost and warrior.

TWENTY-SEVEN

A l has Ry and Jaden clutched at her sides. As if the connection was necessary in order for her to ghost them with her from place to place. The guys look positively nauseous. She releases them and they drop to the floor, heave and wretch.

Al pins her attention on Gitta. "You are sloppy and leave an easy-to-follow trail."

Gitta growls. Al huffs a laugh, then snaps her gaze to me.

"The troops are currently making their way here, but..." She glances down and smirks at the two men shaking off their discomfort. "I brought these two ahead early. On their insistence, of course."

Jaden stumbles a step my direction, recovers his balance, and takes a moment steadying himself before continuing forward. "You good?" he asks of me, while making his way around the room.

"Tired." I press my hands to the floor and thrust my energy down, reaching through the floor, to the ground below. Only, the ground below is the crystal chamber—an environment that is hostel to me.

From Jaden's expression, my exhaustion shows.

Something in Ry's throat rumbles, and he pushes off the ground into a runner's stance, his gaze darting between me and Gitta.

Out in the hallway, a sound clangs, like an item being knocked from its perch and bouncing to the floor. Ry's attention snaps to the open door.

Mo's gaze drifts toward the sound as well, then swings over Ry, Jaden, and Al and settles on me. "There are still a few of those shadow minions left to deal with," she says.

"Tenebrousian?" Ry pulls his lightning wands free from his harness, his sharp gaze bouncing between the door and Gitta.

"I love a good challenge," Al quips.

The hint of a tenebrousian appears in the open doorway. It slips forward, toward the room, and, during the momentary distraction, Gitta sprints into action, lunging for me.

Bolting, unsteadily, to my feet, I throw my arms out. But Ry and Al dart forward, meeting her attack, and cutting her off before she can reach me.

Gitta hazes, avoiding Ry's swing, and reappears directly in Al's awaiting grip.

"I will protect your precious sister," Al says between clenched teeth. "Use those wands in the manner for which they were intended." She tilts her head toward the two that have now entered the space. They are being tackled by Mo in her shadowy monster form.

Ry spins with wands already in motion, hitting the nearest shadow with an explosion of light.

Hit, illumination. Hit, illumination.

One of the tenebrousians explodes in a room-brightening display of light. Without a flash of hesitation, Ry goes after the second one, and Mo attacks the third.

In front of me, Al and Gitta haze and ghost, vanishing and reappearing all over the room. I need to help them, all of them, which means I need to replenish my well of strength and energy.

Jaden suddenly fills my view, his forehead pressing to mine, as if he needed this moment to breath me in, confirm I'm not dead. As if on instinct, my palm presses to his chest, seeking the perfect rhythm of his heart. His hand wraps around mine.

"What's going on?" He pulls back and his dark, intense gaze scrutinizes every inch of me. "What has you looking so drained?"

"Crystal cavern," I say. "Beneath the palace. It's been warped to drain my bloodline."

His gaze narrows and head tilts. "Dreya?"

I don't know. I shake my head. "Has to be." I stare into his eyes. Consider the horned version of him I've seen a lot of lately. A horned forest Fae. Raundel had called him a magic wielder. I could use a magic wielder right about now. "Can you help me?"

He leans closer once more, and his breath washes over me. "Tell me what you need me to do."

Lacing my fingers with his, I again rest my forehead against his. "Lend me your strength." Strength of energy. Strength of magic.

"What is mine is yours." His head shifts, bringing his lips closer to mine. "Take what you need and do some good."

"Thank you." The words have barely left my lips before my senses are funneling his strength into my own reserves.

The flow of Jaden's energy is a glowing ball of golden warmth, expanding from his heart to encompass both of us in an endless tiddle wave of earth-rooted mana. And with the mana, a rejuvenated connection with lady green.

The elements sing for me. Call me to them.

The buzz, a spark. An ignition.

Searing blue flames at the center of my heart rekindle and intensify. Devour the surrounding cold and dark, restore my strength, and brighten my soul.

Gratitude pours into me like a tipped pitcher with an endless supply. Gratitude for my friends who continue to fight with me...for me...no matter the odds. Gratitude for Jaden and his unselfish giving of his soul energy. And gratitude for Gaea and her endless gifts. Gifts that make the worlds beautiful and worth living. Gifts that help me find and maintain my internal balance.

The overflow of gratitude manifests its own energy. A power capable of rivaling any. So vast, the power cannot be contained within my physical body. It explodes in a blast of fervent light.

The slush, ice, and snow encasing the room turn to vapor. And the tenebrousians burst into nothingness. Their attacks no more, their existence ceasing to be.

The one other time I utilized this ability to remove the tenebrousian threat, it practically took everything I had. Even now, as strong as I have become—Balance Bringer bound and elementally connected—the drag on my system is a mountain of weight upon me.

Not missing a beat, Ry and Mo shift their focus to fight with Gitta.

I want to tell them to go help Bree, but my strength is once again waning, my expenditure having been mighty.

And yet, more remains to be done.

I suck back a ragged breath and narrow my gaze on the jumpy haze of an elf.

"You can do this," Jaden says, though he too appears tired, my borrowing of his strength clearly taxing him.

Still, his energy continues to flow through me freely.

I need to finish this for both of our sakes. So that we can take a breather.

He squeezes my hand, and an extra burst of strength surges over my muscles and through my mind, drops like Niagara Falls into my heart. Miracle Grow to my internal garden.

My elemental connections explode, a lusty tree blooming from my soul and greedily reaching in all directions.

At my touch, dormant grasses and long-dead flowers. Status is inconsequential, life can blossom again. But I seek something burlier, harder to break.

I find that which I seek against a wall in the back garden— a tree still holding firmly to life, despite the constant winter climate. Plus, a little something else I may revisit, should the need arise.

The tree roots answer my request, slicing through the ground, and through the palace structure, twisting up the walls, and climbing to our room on the second level. They erupt from the floor at Gitta's feet. Wrap around her ankles, holding her in place, then twine up and around her body, trapping her like a mummy.

Her form flickers, starts to haze.

Wind crashes into the room and hugs Gitta, cutting her off from every thread of energy moving in and around Gaea. She is imprisoned in place.

Gitta's form solidifies, her face pressed into a clear snarl.

"That should hold her until I can cleanse her." I slide down the wall to a seat on the floor.

Jaden drops at my side, appearing equally exhausted. "You're in no shape."

Don't I know it. I pat his hand. He laces our fingers, holding me against slipping away.

Al pokes a finger at the roots wrapped around Gitta. "Give her time and she will haze out of this trap."

Only if my strength drops to zero. "No, she won't." I lean my head against the wall and count my breaths. In and out. In and out.

They are all staring at me, Al, Mo, Ry, as if waiting on my order, or…or in shock by the magic I wielded moments ago.

Ry hunches at my side, his hand on my arm. "Are you all right?" I nod. His face reddens, fury shoving any signs of concern out of the way. "What you did was reckless, and you are never to do anything remotely similar again."

I smile and pat the side of his face. "I didn't die. You don't need to be so worried."

"But you could have," he retorts, and a muscle at the edge of his eye twitches.

"Could have. Should have." I shrug, then drop my features into pure seriousness. "I am here, in the world, for a purpose. You have to let me act on that purpose."

He jerks a fraction back.

I haven't forgotten that day, in his car back in Faredale, when I discovered I can pull military rank over him. I may not have used my rank until now...don't particularly want to use it now...but I will if I must. And now, with the inflection in my voice, he knows how far I will go for my commitment to this mission.

Mo steps forward. "The curse?" she asks about my trip to the bottom of the lake. She is the only other one present, and in their right mind, who is aware of my original objective in coming here.

I shake my head, not wishing to elaborate further.

I'll need to find another way to deal with Dreya, since Proteus is less than amicable. But...my mind flashes to the crystal chamber beneath the palace...at least our trip here wasn't a total bust. Now we know and need to figure out what to do about it.

Ry and Mo are staring at me, but Al's gaze scours the room. "Where is the master sage? I thought she came with you?"

"She did." I try to push to my feet. My muscles ache and shake.

Ry places his hand on my shoulder and shoves me back to the ground. "You're not ready, and trying to jump into action now will only result in getting yourself or others hurt."

One quick glance at Jaden confirms he feels the same.

He is also fighting to keep his eyes open. My borrow depleted his well more than I realized.

I grab Ry's hand and pin my gaze tight on him, silently communicating the seriousness of my forthcoming request. "Bree is hurt, and I need you to help her. Where she is I cannot go, but it shouldn't be an issue for you." Hopefully.

He tilts his head.

"I'll explain later." I glance to Mo, then Al, finally swinging back to Ry. "The floor in the throne room collapsed. You'll find her there, in an underground cavern filled with crystals."

"On it." He shifts to leave, but I hold tight to his hand and yank him back. "Stay on mission. Just get Bree out of there and nothing else."

Don't look closely at the crystals. Don't get distracted by Kaia.

His back straightens. "What aren't you telling me?"

"Just do it," I reply. "We can talk about everything else later." Once Bree, and everyone else is safe, and far from here.

"Fine," he says between clenched teeth. "Mo, you're with me and Al…" His gaze shifts between them. "You stay here with Ana and Jaden." His gaze drops to Jaden, who appears partially unconscious.

Ry's face twitches, hinting that he might want to ask something, such as what did you do to the poor guy? But he chooses to keep his questions to himself. So, I tell him where to find the throne room, and he and Mo take off on their rescue mission.

Al glances over me, then kneels beside Jaden and brushes a hair from the side of his face. "He has been changing a bit."

My gaze drops over him and the various energies of his many incarnations are evident in his aura. As he put it, he is becoming whole. So…changing, maybe. Growing into his true self, definitely.

She pulls her finger back to her chest and sighs. "He continues to be devastatingly devoted to you."

"That was before I released him from the magical bond that held him to me," I say. "He's now free to make his own choices without the overbearing urge to protect me."

She huffs, a tiny sound of contemplation. "When was that?"

"I don't know." I shake my head and try to track the time. So much has happened recently, it's becoming a jumble in my head. "A few days ago."

After Garr's attack and shortly before Azure died.

"Well…" she rises to her feet and gazes down at him with a thoughtful expression. "Despite whatever it was you did, he still insisted on being here, for you, and doing whatever it was that left him in this way."

It is true, he has continued to displayed his support of me since the change. Could the drive that was once a need on his part have become pure desire or a deep-seated want? I don't feel much different after destroying the magic that bound him to me. But that's me, the focus of Meira's magic.

"What about Klarda?" I say, turning the attention away from me. "You two seem to have become rather close."

She huffs and smiles, nods slightly. "She is an admirable woman and warrior, and she is likely irritated with me for having come here." Her eyes narrow and brighten. "She is definitely irritated with you." She shakes a point at me.

Of course, she is. Why would she be left out, and I've upset everyone else by going off plan…or, their plan.

"Hopefully, she will be forgiving." Al taps the edge of her foot against Jaden's leg, jarring it slightly. He groans.

"Is he going to be all right?" she asks.

I roll my head to the side and smile at him. "He should be fine. He's just exhausted and needs to rest…replenish."

Al hums.

"When this deed is done," I continue. "I'm going to sleep for a week. Maybe more."

Al releases a sharp, one-note chuckle.

A palace-shattering rumble vibrates through the floor and walls. And something in the energy drag beneath the ground shifts.

"What was that?" Al spins, surveying the room, the open doorway.

My heart leaps into my throat, my intuition spiking and tensing my muscles.

"Ry, I think." I bite my lower lip and reach for the earthen elements. They can move through the energy-draining cavern in ways I cannot.

They are quick to confirm my suspicions. Ry defied my request, deliberately or not, it doesn't matter. He not only found Kaia's body entombed in the clear stone, but he is now attempting to break her free.

Is that a good thing? Maybe. I don't know. If removing Kaia from the equation weakens Dreya, even a tiny bit, then Ry's actions are more than acceptable.

He takes a running start, leaps, and slams his feet into the side of Kaia's containment crystal. The castle shakes.

Jaden's eyes pop open, but he doesn't move or speak, merely listens. His expression worn yet intense.

Gitta starts to snarl and growl, fight against the binds.

"Stop struggling," I say to her. "You'll hurt yourself, and I'd like to bring you back from this infectious state physically intact."

My words only appear to provoke a deeper clash against her restraints.

I sigh, feeling the fatigue clear to my soul. "Sorry it has to be this way," I say and reach out to Gaea.

Once more connecting with lady green and the earthen elements of the courtyard garden, I pull the vines of the slumber dragon straight to Gitta.

Deona, Kaia, and most all of my previous incarnations are familiar with the slumber dragon, a plant most commonly found in the Swamp of Floating Lights. Much like the poisonous squirting cucumbers shoots its seeds, the slumber dragon plant spews a sleep inducer.

Under the current circumstances, a rather ideal solution to Gitta's fight.

"Rest," I say to Gitta, as the slumber dragon flower blooms before her and spews its agent in her face. She coughs, shakes, and...falls asleep.

"Is that..." Al points to the flower scaling Gitta's form.

"Slumber dragon," I finish.

Another rumble rocks the castle foundation, and chunks of the ceiling shower upon us. I yank my feet into my chest, narrowly avoiding a large plate of plaster. A wave of shifting energy rolls through me. The results of whatever Ry is doing to Kaia's containment crystal.

"I will tell him to stop." Al ghosts away before I can say a word.

Jaden squeezes my hand. His eyes are a swirling cloud of premonition. "Out front," he says.

As if his words were a spoken activation, tiny frost eddies take form across the floor in a chaotic pattern. The room I cleared with my light and warmth, begins to ice over once more.

My muscles tense and heart freezes.

Please, Gaea. No. Don't let it be. Don't let it be.

I move to the window as quickly as my achy muscles and depleted energy will allow. The view provided is that of the snow-covered front gardens and the long stone walk.

A heavily cloaked figure approaches, their cloak blending with the shades of the surrounding landscape. Dragged in their wake, by a long, thick chain clamped to a wide collar is a man. Hunched and staggering, he leaves droplets of red on the white ground.

Dreya didn't make haste straight for me back in Palinot. Instead, she went to retrieve Dohlan from his family home first. Now she pulls him on a leash like a beaten puppy.

Inside of me, Kaia releases a dagger-piercing scream.

Fire erupts in my chest and bursts free. Surges over the castle grounds in a flicker of time. Every icy reminder of Dreya dissolves into sky-rising gas. The window through which I watch is frost free, the room normal and ice clean, and the front gardens, covered in the brown of dead and dormant grass.

Dreya's forward pacing hesitates.

I suspect she already knew I was here, but my actions...or reactions...have now removed all doubt.

"She is killing you."

Jaden's words jerk my muscles and I spin to face him. His eyes are still clouded with the sight.

I turn back to the window.

Dohlan is on his knees in the middle of the front walk, his chain sprawled out before him. And Dreya...

Dreya is gone.

TWENTY-EIGHT

"Killing me how?" I ask the question without turning my gaze from the window or the view beyond. My insides are numb. Numb and frozen.

I failed to convince Proteus to remove Dreya's curse, thus relieving her of her water-based magic. We discovered a crystal-powered cavern that has my royal family entombed and is doing a number on my strength. I am weak, my master sage is hurt, my group is divided, and now Dreya is here.

And Dohlan, still mangled and chained. The part of me that is my sister Kaia wants nothing more than to go to him.

Not now. I cannot allow it.

Dreya is priority one, and she is no longer on the front walk. That means, she must already be inside the palace.

"Killing me how?" I repeat and turn toward Jaden. He hasn't moved from his place on the floor, where he had sat beside me and granted me use of his strength. "You know what, never mind," I say and cross the room. "We need to warn the others about Dreya." If it isn't already too late. I pray it isn't too late.

Jaden doesn't move. His eyes are still trapped in a swirling prophetic state.

"We need to go," I say, my tone low but fierce. He doesn't respond, so...I slap him. His skin a warm sting against my palm.

He blinks, eyes dark. With a growl, he jerks his head to meet my gaze, his horns coming within an inch of piercing the wall.

"Dreya is here," I say through clenched teeth, my gaze darting back and forth between him and the open door. "We need to get to the others."

He leaps to his feet with a tight nod. Then tilts his head indicating I should lead the way.

I turn to go, then gasp and stumble to a stop.

The elementals are screeching. In my ear, my head, and through all the electrical connections in my body. Their message is a visual that they slam into me and wrap around me, playing as if I am fully present and observing the events unfolding.

My point of view, one of the massive crystal pillars in the cavern below the palace. Like other members of my family, I could be a body trapped in the stone, watching everything taking place in the spaces beyond.

A creature, I assume to be Mo, lifts Bree into its long gangly arms. Mo's chosen form is stronger than it appears, and she hoists Bree off the ground with what appears to be minimal effort.

Dreya sweeps past them without so much of a glance.

Their eyes are wide, faces ashen at Dreya's appearance, but they don't follow her. The creature Mo leaps free of the cavern with Bree in her hold.

The elementals' visual swings to a new location, moving quickly, with hardly a pause when passing Al's location. Al is studying the crystal containing my father, likely the Fae king she remembers. She slams the base with her sword. Gouges in the stone suggest she has done so several times before.

The scene continues to change, moving the view past pillar after column, until the one housing Kaia's body appears. An impact point of crushed and splintered crystal mars the space near Kaia's thighs.

Ry dashes onto the scene from a place farther back. He runs, leaps, and slams his feet full force into the stone. More cracks spiderweb across the surface, but the prism has yet to give.

He takes another run.

Dreya slips free of the shadows and intercepts him mid-leap with a hard backhand, knocking him sideways. He slams into a nearby crystal and drops to the ground. Rises with cuts and bruises already vanishing from his skin.

"I guess I shouldn't be surprised to see your ugly face here." He lifts his twin swords from their sheaths at his back.

She huffs. "You should be dead. I pierced you with the Fires of Guardoone."

"So, you did." He steps back and presents his healthy state. "You made a valiant effort, but I managed to heal quite nicely. Might have even gotten an upgrade," he says, referencing Zarah's theory that my blood may have gifted him a little something extra.

"Well then." She smirks. "Let's see if this time we can make your death stick."

With a swirl of her arm, a dagger of ice flies from her fingertips. Ry dodges, swings his sword in a downward arc, and shatters her blade. She tries again to the same ends.

The entire cavern rumbles and Dreya's head snaps in Al's direction. Leaving Ry without further challenge, she rushes toward Al and the crystal housing my father, King Marduk. Ry pursues. A sizable crack now runs up the surface of my dad's crystal prison.

The shared view from the elementals follows, the visual

morphing with the cut and reflection of the stones. I look down from the ceiling at the new scene—Al, Ry, and Dreya in a deathly dance of clashing weapons, both metal and ice. Dreya using every form of water to her advantage. Al utilizing the gift of her ghosting, and Ry his speed, plus the memories and knowledge of his ancestral warrior bloodline.

"Leave them be. It is me you want."

The voice is mine, yet how can it be? I'm viewing from a far, in a room somewhere on the second floor.

Dreya's gaze snaps in the direction of my voice, and I step out from behind a massive crystal column, move into clear view.

It's me. Only, I know it can't be, because…I'm not there. The girl who looks like me, who now taunts Dreya, has to be Mo.

Holy god and Gaea! What is she thinking? She'll get herself killed.

I snap free from the elementals' shared vision and return to the room with Jaden.

"We have to go, now." I grab his hand and yank him into a run.

Two long hallways, one flight of stairs between them, and we are racing through the double doors of the throne room. Bree sits on the opposite side of the room, in one of the smoked-crystal throne chairs, the room-sized hole in the floor between us.

I had previously failed to note both the exquisite quality and stone masonry of the royal seats…until now, when set against Bree's pale skin.

Her eyes are closed, and her hands clutch and caress the chair arms.

Jaden leans in at my side. "Tell her to get out of the chair." Something in his eyes remind me of both Jaden and Jove at the same time, even though Dharmic's horns are set firmly upon his head. Seers and magic wielders combined into one.

"Is there something wrong with the chairs?" I ask.

His gaze tightens not on Bree but the chair within which she sits.

I'll admit, the energy running through the two focal pieces is unlike anything I have yet witnessed. Still…

"You handle Bree." I raise my chin in her direction, then drop my gaze to the floor of the crystal cavern at our feet. "I have a more pressing witch to deal with.".

Jaden growls between clenched teeth. "I do not care for you going up against the Fae princess in this manner. Nor do I like the idea of you being anywhere near this crystal drain."

My head jerks back and I study him for half a second. "Do you have a better idea?"

"I do not." he drops his head, as if humbled by his response.

"Well then…" I lightly slap his arm. "You can dislike what I must do all you want, but I'm going to do what I'm going to do. My actions are mine to decide."

"You have made that abundantly clear." His gaze tightens and facial muscles tense for a breath of a moment, then he relaxes, as if into acceptance. "I would wish to remove your freedoms." His gaze shifts to Bree in the chair. "I shall handle your sage, and you…" His eyes burn with the fires of a thousand unspoken words. "You stay alive."

He turns and heads directly for the throne.

Bree's eyes fly open, and her gaze finds me, her hand raising in a small wave.

"Ana," she says. "This chair. It's full of…"

Jaden grabs her arm and yanks her free of the seat.

Now or never, I think, and step up to the edge of the crater. Scream. "Dreya. You've got the wrong person."

I can hardly blink before Dreya appears in the space below, Mo's version of me clutched in her grasp. Mo pulls and claws at the strangle hold upon her neck, but Dreya's strength clearly outmatches her own.

"What is this witchery," Dreya seethes, raising Mo until her feet dangle off the ground.

Mo gags and chokes.

"No." I reach a hand forward, but do not move from my spot.

Moving closer, into the cavern amongst the massive crystals, will help no one. The stones will deplete my energy, making me even less helpful to Mo than I already am.

Ice and frost crystalize on Mo's face. Snake down her chest and arms.

"Who are you?" Dreya says to Mo. "To have done such a fine job at tricking me?"

Al and Ry appears out of the dark chamber at Dreya's back. They rush at her, weapons ready and prepared to attack. They make it within a few feet of my aunt's back, then a moving storm of ice slams up before them and pushes them back with a thrust.

"I am busy," she yells to them and presses her available hand to Mo's chest.

Mo's mouth drops open and her eyes turn a dull blue, then her illusion fades, and it is Mo trapped in Dreya's clutches. Not some version of me.

"Ahh." Dreya's eyebrows arch, a hint of surprise in her expression. "Your mother is quite evident in your features." Dreya's surprise slips away and is replaced with irritation. "You are missing one important quality, though." Her lips pull into a sideways grin. "A frozen heart." Her voice is low, and dull, and filled with malice.

"Stop," I scream, and dip into the well of my energy reserves. The level is low and the radiated field emanating from the forest of crystals interferes.

I reach, reach, reach for the earth at her feet. Smaller rocks shift and jitter. A few rise and begin to swirl, as if caught up in a cyclone.

Mo makes a garbled choking sound and falls silent. Dreya

drops her on the ground, and Mo falls like a brick—solid and unmoving.

No. No, no, no, no.

My insides are screaming, and my eyes are burning.

Ice explodes from the floor at Dreya's feet, taking the shape of stairs leading to the demolished throne room. To me.

Dreya begins to slowly climb. "A few throwing stones will serve no purpose against me."

"No," I reply, and scrape at the bottom of my energy well. "But maybe…"

Al ghosts onto the stairs, blocking Dreya's path. With a finger flick, a collection of icicle spears drives at Al. She dodges and ghosts, gets hit in the shoulder.

She howls, is thrown across the room, and pinned to the wall, an ice pike pierced through her.

Her physical form ghosts in and out in place, appearing unable to shift away for the projectile cutting through her body.

Ry takes a running leap in my direction. A water sprout bursts from the side wall, turning to ice mid flow. A combination of water and ice collide with my brother, send him reeling beyond my peripheral view.

A bang and crash, and he is screeching.

I start to turn, follow Ry's trajectory, only Jaden appears at my side, grabbing my hand and tugging me his direction.

"Don't look," he says with a slight shake of his head. "Focus here." He motions between himself and Bree at his side. "Borrow from us."

His words are a clear request or command to pull from their strength in the battle against Dreya.

"How bad is it?" I ask of Ry, fear of knowing creeping like vines across my heart.

"Later." Jaden's gaze is compassionate, yet insistent, reminding me to stay on task.

Tears well at the corner of my eyes. First Mo, then Al,

now Ry. At least I can hear Al's struggles and Ry's screams. I know they are still alive...for now. But Mo... Is she breathing? Was Meira right? Did I follow a foolish plan and get my friends maimed, or worse?

"Focus." Bree grabs my other hand, pulling at my attention.

Dreya takes another step closer. "It shall not matter how many you bring against me. I am stronger than all of you combined."

"Arrogance will be your downfall." I grip Jaden and Bree's hands tight and give their internal energy a tiny poke. Both respond with a surge, from them to me. "Be with us, Gaea," I say softly. "Be our guide, shield, and spear."

Kaia's essence sparks. "Destroy her," she says of Dreya.

But Crystia is quick to make her presence known. "Rise above petty emotions," she reminds. Emotions such as revenge.

What I do now is not about revenge, but about removing that which constantly strives to skew the scales of balance. And Dreya, she is thrusting a world of weight toward the dark.

I breathe in and pull. Pull strength from my companions, verve from the earth and air, resolve from my soul. My inner core being reaches down and down and down, past the Fae makings of the palace, through the soil, all the way to the crystallized bases of the massive stone forest beneath our feet.

My focus, the primary four from which Dreya must be drawing extra power in some form or another.

Dreya shows her teeth and, lifting her hands, pulls water from the ground and sends it hurtling toward us.

Jaden tilts his horns forward, and both him and Bree raise a hand to the coming deluge. As I have pulled from them, they now tap into me, setting an invisible barrier in front of us. The water slams into the magic, washing in all directions.

"Keep your focus," Jaden says and squeezes my hand.

I do. I hold my concentration solely upon the crystal bases, intensifying the pressure of the surrounding soil upon them. Rising the temperature of the land and air around them. Pressure and heat, two things to break a stone. Tiny fissures splinter across the encased bodies of my family.

Dreya hollers and my gaze snaps to her. Then past her to Mo's frozen and unmoving body. I release all my emotion in a matching howl. Try not to think about Ry's cries or Al's noisy struggles.

Once again, I am plagued by Meira's words of warning. *"Going after Dreya…could end up getting people you care about hurt…or worse."*

My howl drops to a low growl, then a soft gnar at the back of my throat.

Meira wasn't wrong. My friends and family are paying the price for my excursion to the ice castle. But had I not come, we may have never discovered the forest of crystals being perverted by Dreya and used to fuel her dark agenda.

So, the question is, "Is the price worth it?" I mumble under my breath.

"It's up to you," Bree replies. "Make the outcome worth the price."

The fire in my core intensifies and grapples outward. My reach is followed by the crack and snap of nearby rocks. One, two, ten.

Dreya's eyes darken and her hair flashes fire bright. "This is my domain." The tail of her last word twists and rises into another scream. One clearly charged with her internal whirlwind of negative emotions.

The frost on the walls magnifies, and monstrous icicles drop from the ceiling. The temperature drops. My breath expels in a puff of white, and both Jaden and Bree begin to shiver.

I meet Dreya's screaming frost attack with a battle cry of my own. My elemental connection leaps into a frenzy and charge. Our magics slam into one another in a fury of ice, water, and frost, cyclones, quaking earth, and fire.

My energy strains, my muscles aching. I grit my teeth, concentrate, and drop to my knees. Push my strength to hold, rally above that of Dreya's. Her power pounds down on me. Comes at me from all sides.

I clench my holds with Jaden and Bree, weave our energies, amplifying our combined strength, and shove back against Dreya's press.

Water boils and evaporates, hard soil turns to mud, ice melts, and rock and stone pop, explode in pieces. My world narrows in on only Dreya and her repeated attacks. Her aura of ice framed by my wildfire flames.

Beads of sweat bloom across my skin. Begin to drip from my hair. And I breathe...breathe against the growing fever and coming burnout.

"Hold on," Jaden urges, to which Bree adds, "Justify the price."

A roar rolls through my chest and explodes in a bellow. I hunch forward and pull for the dredges of strength at the bottom of my well. Push my energy to meet Dreya's as if the worlds depend upon my action. And they do. All the worlds depend deeply on Dreya's defeat.

Love, desire, need fuel my efforts in a final thrust, sending every last ounce of my energy forth.

Firestorm whips through the cavern at Dreya's back, eviscerating her shield of ice. Devouring all signs of frost, until all that is left is spark and flame, heat...and an all-consuming swelter, searing me from the inside.

The crystals holding my family entombed, crack and crumble—unseen but felt. They release a dribbling refill to my reserves. A drop of water to a parched soul.

The roar of the fire within the cavern marries with the thunder of water, and I brace myself for another wave of attacks from Dreya. Digging in my heels and clenching my teeth.

A tidal wave careens through the underground, tunnel forest of crystals. Water thrusts through the gaping hole in the floor, erasing the flames, and washing away my sights on Dreya. Of everyone. Nothing but waves and white foam.

Enveloped by the water's power, I'm swept off my feet and sent crashing against the throne room walls.

TWENTY-NINE

The clash and smash of the water's force powers through the throne room, tossing everyone against the walls and floor like rocks trapped in a shaking bottle. Jaden, Bree, Ry, they are all washed away from me in the fray. Just as Dreya is lost in the flood.

My shoulder slams into the side of the throne. The corner of the chair digging into my shoulder blade. Before the flow of the water can drag me away, I twist and grab at the chair arm, hold firm.

At the touch of the stone, a new-to-me energy tingles beneath my fingertips.

This is what held Bree's curiosity and had Jaden troubled?

The ferocity of the water recedes through the gaping hole in the floor, like the rolling back of the tide. My finger hold is too slight, and the current's might too fierce. My grip is broken and my body tumbles with the moving water, through the hole, into the crystal cavern.

My body is tossed and rolled in the swell. I reach out with my elemental connection for stability, but my reserves are gone and my soul exhausted. In the midst of liquid mayhem, a hand grabs hold of me.

Jaden? My thoughts reach out, and then realize a moment later that our connection is broken. Our feelings are no longer connected.

But Jaden isn't the one who holds to me tight. Ry is. He has a leg wrapped around something sturdy, preventing him from getting dragged out with the water's ebb. He stops me from doing the same.

Only, the water around me shifts, caresses me like a gentle palm lifting me out of the wetness and setting me back on my feet on the throne room floor.

As quickly as the water crashed into the room, swept everything into chaos, it withdraws six to ten times faster. Mo still lies on the cavern floor, slightly displaced, but everyone else has been rearranged within the throne room.

Jaden and Bree are several feet away. Al is slouched in a corner, the ice spike that pinned her to the wall now melted. Ry sits on the ground beside the broken post he'd used to steady himself against the current. He massages his right leg and knee. And a dripping wet Dreya stands across the room, glaring.

Directly in front of me, Proteus rises from the receding water like the god that he is.

Dreya hollers across the gap in the floor. "What are you doing here, old man?"

"Child of Gaea," he says, ignoring her and speaking to me. "I took your suggestion and looked upon the future of our world." He glances over his shoulder to Dreya, then back to me. "I have decided to agree to your original request."

My mouth drops open, a tiny breath escapes, and my heart double beats. "Thank you." I pray the surprise isn't evident in my response.

He glances over me with a lazy eye and an expression I

take for a mixture of boredom and irritation. His scrutiny lasts mere moments, before he turns to face Dreya.

She raises an eyebrow. "You and I have no business, old man. Leave this place at once."

Ignoring her dismissal, he lifts his chin and folds his hands together. "Princess Dreya Etheonia Raine, Fae child who fell into my domain…"

She lets loose a howl, and raises her hands to the ceiling, releasing a swirling rainstorm. It whips at my hair and clothing, but it's not so fierce as to unhinge my stance.

Proteus is undaunted by Dreya's wind rage. "I withdraw…"

A sheet of frost and ice pikes flies directly at him…and me, mere feet beyond. He sidesteps the assault with deft speed, leaving the path to me wide open. Still too drained to call the elemental magics too me, I throw up my arms in a physical shield.

I am half Fae, half immortal warrior, and a whole lot of something goddess given. I have faith I'll survive and heal.

Ry leaps in front of me, taking the full brunt of her ice strike. Plates and pikes of frost slam into him, instantly transforming parts of his body to ice. He drops like a weight to the ground.

I'm screaming, but I can't hear my voice through the roaring in my head.

Why? Why Ry? I could have handled it.

My heart squeezes to a stop, and I stare at my brother encrusted with ice.

"It's okay," he says with struggle.

He can heal, I remind myself. *He will heal.* He's an immortal warrior.

Dreya releases a strangled cry and, with the wave of her hand, a glacial wind grabs hold of Ry and sends his body careening across the room into the wall.

Parts of him shatter like glass.

The world stops.

Nothing but a deafening shriek fills my soul.

Tiny chunks of frozen Ry are all I can see. And every part of me is screaming.

In my heart. In my head.

Out loud.

My blood is stopping and my resolve crumbling.

Jaden's arm wraps around me and waves of calm wash through my system. He doesn't numb my emotions but grants me the ability to focus and function—either despite them, or in light of them.

Ignoring their own wounds, Al and Bree rush to Ry's aid. Slipping from my calm, I want to do the same, and shift to follow that emotion. But Jaden tightens his arm around me, redirecting my focus.

"Dreya first, then Ry," he says, voice low. "Don't draw her attention to your wounded brother any more than necessary."

He's right. I know he's right. I can't look at Ry until all that I need to do is done. Because if I do, I'll crumble backward time and time again.

Dreya's attention darts back and forth between me and Proteus, as if trying to decide who makes the better target. Her face and neck are flushed, and her gaze wild.

Proteus' voice rises above the roar in my head. "I take back the gift once given."

"You cannot do such a thing," she counters.

His shoulders and chest rise and fall. "Child, it is already done."

"What?" Her teeth are clenched and eyes wide. She lifts her splayed hands up and stares at them. Jerks them up and out, as if trying to ignite a magical reaction, but none comes.

"Water and ice were a gift," he says. "One you misused. The element shall no longer respond to your command."

She hollers.

"And for your misuse…"

Her lips pull into something between a snarl and a frown. "Don't try to pretty up the situation, old man," she says. "Your gift was a curse. One *I* managed to turn into a gift."

He shakes his head as an exasperated sigh escapes his lips.

Whisps of inky darkness spring into creepy action around Dreya, crawling and withering all around her feet and legs. A gift given by, or taken from Sol.

She may no longer have her water magic, but she still has the darkness. *Is* the darkness.

I push to a stand, and preparing for her next attack, scrape the walls of my power reserve. I haven't had enough time to replenish, and next to nothing is present.

Proteus takes a step toward Dreya. "The damage you have caused rests upon my shoulders, for it is I who granted you the ability to inflict such chaos."

"Do not flatter yourself or your power," she replies and shoots me a glare. One that promises death.

Proteus raises his hands with fingers wiggling. The motion pulls forth a wicked water funnel into the center of the room. "For your countless wrong doings, I sentence you to a millennium in solitude, so that you may reflect on that which you have done."

Dreya thrusts her hands forward, as if to freeze the growing waterspout, but no frost or ice leaps from her fingers. She screams, shakes her fists, then swings. Strikes with shards of black smoke. They are swept into the spin, darkening the water, yet have no effect on its force or spin. The funnel shifts and advances in her direction.

"This changes nothing," she yells.

Her wisps of darkness engulf her and, with the speed of a Fae, she vanishes from the room.

She is gone. The immediate danger, averted. Relief washes through my heart and chest.

We did it...or Proteus did. We stripped Dreya's water and ice ability away from her.

And then I remember.

"Ry," I scream and scramble across the distance between us. He's unconscious but breathing.

His left side has been frozen; cracked, broken, and shattered. A deep fracture cuts into his ribs, a spiderweb of fissures lace his arm, a couple of his fingers are missing...*missing*...and his left leg— it's been smashed into countless pieces, still frozen and scattered.

"Oh my Gaea! Ry." I press my hands to the side of his head and touch my forehead to his. "He will heal. He can come back from this. Right?" I sweep my gaze over Bree, Al, and Jaden.

"Ana." Jaden rests his hand on my shoulder blade. I jerk away.

"Don't try to placate me," I snap. "Give it to me straight."

Al and Jaden exchange a look that sinks my gut past the floor.

"Many of his injuries will heal," Jaden says. "But missing limbs..." He shakes his head. "They don't regrow."

No-no-no-no-no. I drop my face against Ry's chest and weep.

"Such is the drawback of your fragile lives," Proteus says at my back. I don't look up. "You, child of Gaea," he continues. "Are as capable as the princess Dreya in bringing destruction upon our world. The gods will be watching."

I snap upright and stare at him.

"Choose your actions wisely." The old man of the sea disappears, and a mighty lion now stands in his place. He dips his head, as if to say goodbye, or heed my warning, then leaps into the crystal cavern, morphing into something other, and races out of sight, following the direction of the receded water.

So many things have happened today. We unearthed and damaged a crystal cavern that was amplifying Dreya's power. We discovered a throne with unusual energy in need of further investigation. And we convinced Proteus to remove Dreya's curse…her water and ice magic.

But the costs.

My heart aches at the costs.

Both Bree and Al are bleeding, not attending to their wounds. The hole in Al's shoulder and the gash on the side of Bree's head.

Gitta is infected, sleeping in a room upstairs, and I must soon find the strength to cleanse her.

Mo is…

I spin my attention in her direction. Jaden has her in his arms and is carrying her up from the cavern below.

Is she dead?

"Not yet dead," Jaden says as if he can still read my thoughts. "But barely alive."

My soul has taken over a thousand emotional stab wounds and is bleeding all over the floor.

Ry's shirt is damp with my tears and his veins glow a brilliant blue, as they had the night I managed to heal him, under Zarah's care. Now, as I watch, the wounds covering his body begin to heal—the fracture in his ribs, the fissures lacing his arm, various cuts, scrapes, and bruises.

Bree stops wrapping his hand, and Al pauses her tighten of the tourniquet on his left leg. The torn flesh closes over with fresh skin. Healed, with limbs missing.

All the oxygen is sucked out of the room, and I blink, blink wide.

Did I do this? Did I just somehow heal my brother so that his missing limbs will now be forever missing?

I drop my head in my hands and let the plethora of emotions flow.

Bree had told me to make the outcome worth the price. Had I succeeded? I don't know. My friends, my family, for Dreya's decreased power. For a better chance at balancing the worlds.

Jaden lays Mo on the ground beside Ry. Barely breathing, he'd said, but she looks like she's already dead. Ry doesn't appear much better. He'll live though. I can see that much. Not that the thought brings me much comfort. Not presently.

"Her heart is slowing," Jaden says, removing his hand from Mo's wrist.

Sliding my hands gently from Ry's cheeks, I clutch Mo's hand and press it to my lips. I place my other hand over her heart.

"This price was not yours to pay," I whisper into her skin. "Please don't leave us." I suck back a deep breath and release it. "You can't leave us, Mo. You can't."

Mo, Ry, Gitta, Al, Bree, I make a mental list and glance up at Jaden, the cut near his eye and the small chip missing from the tip of his right horn. All of them, everyone I care about was injured…or worse.

Meira's words. Her exact words. She said if I went after Dreya, I'd end up getting people I care about hurt, or worse. Our current situation falls into the realm of worse.

Was the price worth the outcome?

I struggle to answer that question.

"*And Dohlan,*" Kaia whispers. He was also hurt.

The last visual of him chained, and on his knees, bleeding in the snow, flashes across my thoughts.

He wasn't hurt because we came here. He was hurt because he attacked Dreya. Because I used the mate ring. The ring I will now carry around my neck until Dreya has been officially defeated.

Every ounce of leverage…

A clang and scuffle in the hallway beyond the throne room's double doors, snaps every gaze in that direction. A filthy hand grabs the side doorframe and Dohlan appears, as if dragging unwanted muscles forward.

The thick collar with accompanying chain remains clamped around his neck. His clothing is torn and dirty, his hair unkempt, and his shirt hangs open revealing the cuts, scars, and bruises over his heart.

Why hasn't he healed already? I know the answer as soon as I think the question. Because the heart is the source of a Fae's magic, their healing. And his heart has been damaged.

The usual sparkle in his eyes and cocky grin are absent, and in their place, a void. A pit of despair and depression.

"She wants you to know…" he says, no doubt talking about Dreya. "That she has granted you this short reprieve, so that you might tally your losses and realize how fruitless your fight is. How withered it shall become."

His gaze drops to my brother on the ground before me. His pained stare pulls countless lines to the corner of his eyes.

I stand. Take one step forward. "Dohlan." My voice is little more than a whisper.

His gaze lifts to mine, and the pain within the depths of his eyes feels bottomless. His attention shifts past to me to Jaden, lingers, then lowers.

The chain hanging from his neck jingles, then pulls taut, and Dohlan is yanked from view.

Al instantly ghosts to the hallway beyond the open doorway. She glares down the passage, before glancing back to us and shaking her head. "He's gone," she says. "There is nothing but a slight residue of dark mist."

Ry. Mo. Bree, Al. Gitta and Dohlan. They all matter to me…to us, *so* deeply. They're held firmly in my heart. And I don't know where to place my focus. I'm worried about all of them. But Ry…

Oh my Gaea. Ry.

Destiny has dealt my family far too many hard blows.

Kind Marduk…my father…steps up behind me. *"It is through the hardships that we often learn the most valuable lessons."* Still dressed in his warrior's armor, he is with me. Not physically, but spiritually.

They are all here—the four used by Dreya to amplify her strength. My father, sister, and grandparents.

"*Today*," my grandmother says. "*You have taken a significant step in the correct direction.*"

She stands at my back, tall and proud, a vision of light. Her gown of white hugs to her curves and shimmers in clear stones. Her skin is hardly brighter than the crystal within which she was previously incased, and her hair, appearing soft as silk, is swept up in two loose buns hanging low on the side of her head. Her crown, shimmering in tiny clear stones, fits close to her head.

I nod, clench my heart, and wipe a tear from my cheek. Don't respond, but stare at the distorted image of my sister through the haze of the cracked crystal containing her. Her hand is missing, as I knew it should be. But before now, I'd never given it much thought as to which hand—her mate ring hand.

"*It was the only way she could get it off of me,*" Kaia says. "*Only a mate can remove a mate ring. Unless, of course, the mate is no longer.*"

No blood pumps through a severed hand, thus imitating death, and making the ring removable.

"*I should have recognized the spark of her obsession the first time she showed interest in him,*" Kaia says of Dreya's Dohlan fixation.

My father sighs. "*What she has become is my fault.*" I turn to face him and shake my head. "*That day at the lake, had I only been able to save her sooner…*" He lowers his head.

"Her choices are her own," I reply. "And no fault of yours. Do not take that burden upon yourself."

He lifts his gaze to meet mine and smiles.

"*I knew you would make a great queen,*" my grandfather says. His hair, a weathered gray, and eyes soft with discernment, his face is one I suspect all Fae kind alike found easy to love. No crown sits on his head.

A grimace presses to my lips. "I am no queen."

My grandmother flicks her finger. "*That's where you are wrong. You are my rightful heir. Destined for the crown.*"

I close my eyes and sigh. Balance Bringer and queen. As if one world-crushing weight isn't enough.

"Ana." Jaden leans into my line of sight. "We are ready to…" He tilts his head toward Kaia and her confined crystal. He cannot see the family members standing around me. Only I do.

Al and Jaden have been busy at work, removing my family members bodies from the broken crystals. Kaia is the last one left.

"Sure." A tiny, uncommitted smile tugs at my lips but fails. "I'm going to check on Ry and Mo."

He nods. Understanding filling his gaze.

I turn. Walk away. Then pause and look back. Address my family. "Will you be staying with me?" I ask, not of Jaden but of the spirits now gathered around me.

"*We will always be with you here.*" My dad presses his hand to his heart. "*But our energy will remain within this crystal cavern, where most all of what we are has been absorbed.*"

"*I am the exception, of course,*" Kaia says. "*No bond is stronger than that of our sibling bond.*"

Or shared soul, I mentally add, and turn away, begin my climb back to the palace floor.

"*Anala, my dear,*" my grandmother calls after me. I pause mid-climb and glance back. "*You were born to be a queen. Do not fear the throne, for it is yours.*"

A throne and a responsibility I never wanted.

I join Bree in the oversized main entry, where she uses her magic to keep Ry as comfortable as possible. Not much can be done for Mo. Her frozen heart barely beats.

"And how are you doing?" Bree asks, a question with many facets.

Physically, I'm all right. Emotionally, I'm a wreck. But she knows that. Elementally… "Magically, much stronger," I say, feeling and sounding dead in my response. "With the destruction of Dreya's crystal battery, I've been able to replenish a lot of my expended reserves."

I glance across the entry to Gitta. The slumber dragon plant continues to keep her knocked out. We've been using the plant on Ry, as well…until we can get to the garrison.

I raise my chin in Gitta's direction. Hopefully, I'll soon be strong enough to try and cleanse her.

"That would make transportation a heck of a lot easier," Bree replies.

With four dead and three injured or incapacitated, our group is somewhat transportation challenged. And so, we wait, and wait, for Mom to arrive with her military forces. According to Al, it shouldn't be more than half a day before the first of them reach us.

I brush the hair from the side of Ry's face and study his calm, sleeping form. Hold back my tears. Then shift my gaze to Mo. Her skin and hair are pale gray. Dreya did more than freeze Mo's heart. I suspect she molecularly changed something in my friend.

"I think…" I chew on the inside of my lip. "I think we should hold a royal pyre for the bodies found in the crystals."

"Your family," Bree adds. "Give their souls and their magic release from the confines of this place?"

I close my eyes and grip Mo's cold hand in mine, allowing the warmth to wash from me and over her. "Yes," I reply. "My family. Their energy no longer dwells in the physical." I glance to the three covered bodies of my father and grandparents. Jaden and Al are still working on freeing Kaia. "It's time to release that part of them."

Bree nods and her attention drops to Mo at my side.

I follow Bree's gaze and squeeze Mo's hand. "But not you," I whisper to her. "It's not time for your physical energy to leave this world. You stay," I say, feeling a tingle run though me with my words. "You come back to us. To those who love you."

Her facial features are so still, so pale, she resembles a figure carved of stone.

"Don't leave us." I wipe a tear away and then shape my palm to the curve of her cheek.

For a moment, the world around me appears to still. The palace entry vanishes, and I am sitting with Mo in the midst of a vast universe. A sea of stars. Stars that charge my soul and rest over Mo. The crystals at my wrists and hanging around my neck illuminate against the surrounding dark.

And then the vision is gone, and I am back in the palace entry with Ry, Bree, Gitta, and Mo.

Mo's eyes are open, and she is staring at me.

THIRTY

Consumed by fire, and scattered by the wind, to be draped over and blended with the lands and seas of Hiddenkel. An appropriate send-off for the family of the Balance Bringer. Appropriate and hallow.

I. Am. Hallow.

Internally withdrawn from the emotional pain.

I stand between my mom and Jaden, watching the flickering flame of the pyre and feel…numb.

I can't stay in this void. Eventually, I must allow myself to feel the pain, experience it, in order to work through it, and come out the other side. But to give into the onslaught of emotions now…

I release a sigh through my nose, close my eyes, and feel the heat of the fire upon my skin.

I never expected to find Kaia or my dad alive. The tiny drop of hope I'd been given, I hadn't allowed it to blossom more than a speck. And my grandparents, they'd hardly been a consideration. But now… being faced with the undeniable truth…

It's as if Dreya's claws have dug out my heart, as she tried to do with Dohlan. I have no comparable feeling to the hallow, shredded ache from within.

So, for now, I require the void to keep me focused and functional. Until we are able to return to the garrison and take care of all the necessaries…cleansing Gitta of the infection, doing whatever we can for Ry, and get answers regarding Mo's new, curious condition.

I glance over my shoulder to her. She stands a few feet at my back, looking every bit an emotionally, mentally distant ghost. Her appearance altered, the color drained from her skin and hair.

Between Dreya's magic and my own, we did something to her. Changed her somehow. Whether her pigmentation is the only thing affected remains to be seen.

So, until these things are addressed, handled, answered… Until I have a day in a room to myself…a day to break down and a day to recover…Until then, the void serves its purpose.

Mom squeezes my shoulder, tugging me into her side. "Will you be all right if I go check on Ry?" she whispers at my ear.

Ry who, for his own good, has been kept in a deep slumber. Who arrived on mission a whole man and is now undoubtably going to struggle being able to see himself as *still* whole, given his new circumstances.

Mom's face is weary, but the hard set of her eyes suggests she came to terms with the loss of my father and sister long ago. The condition of her eldest and only son, on the other hand, is something she wasn't expecting. Despite her training and upbringing, the shock showed itself as a tight twitch of her left eye.

She arrived with reinforcements shortly before sunrise— the half a day that Al promised, give or take. Bree tapped into ancient elven magic to keep us all warm while we waited through the cold of night for help to show up at the palace doorstep.

I dip my head into Mom's shoulder and give her my blessing. She's paid her respect to those now gone, and time with my brother may prove to be a soul soothing distraction. A chance to focus on the son in need, rather than the lover and husband now lost. Mom has worn nothing but a brave face, but I have little doubt she is as wrecked as I am on the inside.

With the addition of my elemental gift, the funeral pyre burned hotter, faster, brighter, and now mere embers, is slipping into an eternal slumber.

A rainbow aura over the dwindling fire marks the release and evolution of my departed family's energy. The more that is released, the stronger Kaia's spirit grows within me—Her relief at the quittance, her pain over our father, and her agony regarding Dohlan's condition and unknown location.

I press my eyes closed tight against her desire to go. Go find Dohlan *now*.

In my mom's departure, Jaden's grip upon my hand intensifies, as if he's afraid I'll float away with the ashes on the wind, and he means to hold me here. The beat of his heart thrums against the skin of my palm, each beat seeming to say, *stay with me. Be here with me.*

I close my eyes and attempt to push all my fears and frustrations into the void now occupying a space in my chest. Crystia's death back in Faredale aside, this has been the worst week of my life…ever. Of all my lives…quite possibly.

My mind rolls over the tally once more. Ry, Mo, Bree, Al injured. Gitta infected. The deaths of Kaia, my dad and grandparents confirmed, their bodies recovered. And Azure…

He lay in my arms, slipping from life, looking as close to my Jaden as any one possibly could.

It could have been Jaden.

I had envisioned it as so back in the school pool what seems like eons ago.

The void fails to serve me and my heart sputters. All the

emotions I walled up in that moment, in the face of Azure's death, burst free.

It could have been Jaden. It could have been Jaden.

I spin to him, bury my face in his chest. "I was so scared," I admit. "When you brother died...in my arms...the thought of you...of..."

He hushes me, brushing one hand through my hair and lifting my chin with the other. A world of sympathy, sorrow, and understanding fill his returned gaze.

"I'm right here." His words, his breath, whisper over me. "I'll continue to be here for as long as you want me in your orbit."

I tip my head back to better meet his gaze, his captivating eyes—a rich jade, filled with the blooming evergreen of life. "Always and forever." My voice is hoarse from the many tears I've shed.

A gentle return smile. "Then it shall be so." His lips touch, velvety soft, against my cheek, kissing away a tear. He pulls back, regards me, then does the same for my other cheek, using his mouth to clear the visible signs of my grief.

I bite down on my lip to still my quivering. As of late, since the seventh moon after my seventeenth birthday, there has been too much. Too much pain and loss. Too much unknowing.

I need to know that he is here, healthy and alive, with me now and until the end of my days. I need to know *this* will not abandon me like so many other things.

I mold my palm to the curve of his face and brush my thumb along his cheek bone. Say softly, "You have no obligation. I severed the bond holding you to me."

"That bond was never needed to hold me at your side." He cups my face in his hands. "You are my home. The only place I have ever wanted to be."

His words are molten lava sliding through my core, warming my blood and skin from the crown of my skull, all the way down to the tips of my toes. Toes that are now curling.

His finger brushes my lips and I can barely keep from coming apart at the seams. I close my eyes and tilt my face into his touch, press into his caress. His fingers pulling and lifting, until his mouth hovers a hairline above mine.

"I'll never leave you." His breath mingles with mine, drawing me closer and closer.

"Promise?" My mouth opens, my lips wanting and fearing the connection.

"Promise."

My heart and pulse thunder, a roar of drums in my ears. And when his lips connect with mine, and we become one perfect joining, the internal and external chaos drops into a perfect stillness. Wrapping my arms around him, I tug him to me, any distance between us being too much, too far. Each sweep of his lips, his tongue, devour me, destroy me, and rebuild me whole.

His kiss, the taste of him...I want more. Need more. And I fight the whimper and moan building in my throat.

His arms meld around me and still it was not close enough. I need to feel him everywhere, know him everywhere, know that he will always be here with me.

His tongue brushes through me and my knees wobble, fingers clench at his hair.

"Okay. The boy may have some merits." Kaia's voice whispers in my head.

Startled, I jerk back and shake once roughly.

"Are you all right?" Jaden eyes blink wide as if attempted to pull awake from a dream. A dream neither of us wants to step away from. "Did I do something wrong? Something to hurt you?"

"No. Not at all." I rub my forehead. "It's Kaia. This..." I motion to the funeral pyre. "Her release, has strengthened her stubborn desires in my head." I don't want to tell him she has serious boundary issues and was critiquing the kiss.

She did me a favor, though, because as much as I need the touch, the confirmation of his presence, as much as I desire him in every possible way, now is neither the time nor the place for such a connection.

He nods, his gaze appearing to peer directly into my soul. "Have you considered merging the many versions of yourself, as has been done with me?"

I chew on the inside of my lip and try to imagine a life without Crystia quirky and positive outlook on things.

"*It would be all right,*" she whispers ever so softly.

"Maybe," I reply, and consider the differences in Jaden.

He seems to be at peace with his many incarnations merged into one and I like...more than like...the man standing before me, as much, if not more than I did before. How different would I be with Kaia's personality merged with my own? Would I become Dohlan obsessed like she is?

My grandmother's hand drops on my shoulder. "*When in doubt, turn to the throne for answers.*"

A throne cut of smoked crystal, set on top of a mammoth cavern of crystals. No doubt, drawing on their energy. Amplifying it to what end?

Snapping from my internal conflict, I return my attention to Jaden. "You were out of commission for a long time. Do you think, given the current climate, that we can afford the same for me?"

"I was deeply infected. You are not," he reminds. "Plus, you're already bound to your various incarnations, have access to all their memories. The process shouldn't take nearly as long."

"Exactly," I quip. "I have access to all of my past lives. Why would I need to take things a step farther?"

His lips tug into a lopsided frown. "You recall the memories of your previous selves like you would remember an episode from one of those television shows from the outer-world. Far different from remembering your own experiences, as would be the case should you merge all the lifetime pieces of you into your one, greater true soul-self."

He grins. "Right now, you probably feel yourself torn between the multiple personalities you have previously assumed. Does it sometimes feel a bit like a multiple person-ality disorder? Kaia did, after all, *borrow* your body for a midnight stroll to rendezvous with Dohlan."

Something I'm still simmering about. With a slight shrug, my lips pull into a grimace. Most of the various versions from my past seem to be content to take the backseat and let me make the decisions, but Kaia...she is bullheaded and persistent.

An understanding smile spreads across his lips. "That feeling would go away."

No more internal pushing. Might be worth serious consid-eration.

I breathe deep through my nose, my chest rising and falling with the release.

"What does it feel like?" I ask.

"Completely natural." He dips his head and gazes at me through the fall of his bangs.

Completely natural. The word echoes through me, and I think I feel Kaia flinch. Not from the words so much as the idea proposed by Jaden.

I shiver against the cool now slithering up my legs. With Jaden's body warmth no longer wrapped around me, and the funeral fire nothing more than smoke, I turn back toward the palace in search of the magical heat Bree has at work inside the entry. Tug Jaden to follow.

Mo stands perfectly still as I pass, her stare on me intense and filling me with guilt. Mounds upon mounds of guilt. Her gaze screams, *you did this to me. Made me whatever this is.*

I am the reason for *all* of the pain: Mo, Gitta's infection,

Ry's injuries, Dohlan's torn open chest, Bree being dragged away from her life, her family, to come to Hiddenkel, Jaden's many lifetimes shackled to me, and whatever he is now.

Make the outcome worth the cost, Bree's words whisper through my thoughts. Was it worth it? I haven't yet decided.

I move past Raundel and Lobrka standing beside the palace's main entrance. They eye me but say not a word. I keep moving, through the palace entry, past the multitude of warriors, my mom and Ry, Bree, Klarda, Gitta, and the gathered Augur clan.

"Where are you going?" Jaden asks, following a step behind.

Interweaving our fingers, I hold him at my side. "Always and forever?" I ask. "Together through it all?"

His grins, and its so beautiful it heals a tiny broken part of me. "I meant it when I said it," he replies.

He implied it, didn't actually say the words, but I won't allow myself to get hung up on semantics. I merely smile and keep walking.

I'm following a whisper in my mind, one that says the throne, with its amplified crystal energy, may hold answers for me. All the answers, or some of the answers. Right now, I'll take any answers.

We enter the throne room together and skirt the crater-sized hole in the center of the space. Several immortal warriors are working in the cavern below, making maps and measuring energy output, but the throne room above is empty…aside from us.

My grandmother's regal voice whispers over my shoulder. "*Take your seat upon the throne. There, the stone shall help you recognize your truth and the extent of your power.*"

"*Possibly, answers to help Ry,*" Kaia adds.

Stepping onto the dais and standing before the two crystal-cut throne chairs, I'm tingling with the radiating verve.

The taller of the chairs, intended for the queen—my

grandmother. For, before Dreya's fall and my father's rise to take her place, this realm of Fae has always been ruled by the female of the species.

I never wanted to rule, be a queen. But answers, solutions to help the worlds and the people I care about. That is the motivation that governs me.

I step toward the throne and Jaden grabs my hand, tugging me to a stop. "I don't know about this." He scrutinizes the crystal-cut seat before shifting his gaze back to me. "Bree was a definite no, but you..." He pauses, his attention sweeping back and forth between me and my intended seat. "I don't know about you."

"It will be fine," I murmur and slip my hand from his hold. Turn and take a seat.

Every muscle, tendon, blood vessel and vein, is immediately thrumming, zinging with life never before felt within me.

Jaden's hand drops over mine, resting upon the chair's arm. "If this thing amplifies strength, power, magic," he says. "You already abound in all these areas."

"You might be right," I reply. "But maybe this chair will unlock something within me I have yet to tap." Maybe it *does* hold the answers to my many problems. Ry, for one. Dreya, for another. I may have succeeded in reducing her magical strength, but she is still a serious threat.

"Be careful." The request is simple, and the emotion rapped within, endless. He presses a silken kiss to my forehead. "And come back to me."

Come back? I'm not going anywhere. I'm merely taking a seat in a chair.

But I'm already releasing any and all resistance to the power within the smoked crystal. Giving into the energy pulsing through the chair beneath me...the crystal cavern beyond that.

The room erupts in an elemental storm. Wind swirling in the center, over the cavern hole. Vines strangling the walls and blooming with life. Rain showering through the cracks and broken windows in the ceiling. And fire crackling inside of the crystals. The one upon which I sit, and the many of the space below.

Earth, water, wind, and fire. My elemental connections are complete, and stronger than whatever Fae or elven or immortal warrior part of me exists.

Closing my eyes, I give myself over to their power…their whimsy.

The atmosphere around me shifts. Squeezes and then expands. Heats and cools.

When I open my eyes, the throne room and Jaden are gone. I am sitting in an earthen temple, long forgotten and given to decay.

The unremembered-by-many Balance Bringer Izza stands before me, her face lit with glee. "You came back," she says. "You came back for me." She throws her arms around me and hugs me like I am her only lifeboat in an endless sea of despair.

Izza, the missing me of the past. I have found her once more. Now to change her fate, possibly her history, and start straightening the path to balance.

Ana's adventure continues in: **Uniting: The Balance Bringer**

And be sure to devour Dreya's origin story:
The Would-Be Queen

To grab your free copy of Bree's origin story, THE MYSTIC

MAKER, secure your sneak peek at future Balance Bringer stories, and ensure notification when new stories are released, sign up for Debra Kristi's newsletter.
https://www.debrakristi.com/claim-your-free-gift/

DEAR READER,

I hope you enjoyed this installment in The Balance Bringer Chronicles. Ana's story is far from done. Watch for more of her adventures to come. And if you haven't yet explored The Balance Bringer Origins stories, I invite you to do so. They really fill out the experience.

Additionally, if you have found this story to be a worthy read, please consider leaving a review. Not only do I love receiving feedback, but reviews also help other readers find what they are looking for. It's the readers and reviewers who make up the foundation of our author world, and we love you madly for all you do!

Thanks! Until next time, keep the magic real.

~ Debra Kristi

ABOUT THE AUTHOR

Debra Kristi was born and raised a Southern California girl. She still resides in the sunny state with her husband, two kids, and several crazy cats. Unlike many of the characters in the stories she writes, Debra is not immortal, and her only super-power is letting the dishes and laundry pile up. When not busy drumming away at the keyboard, spinning new tales, Debra is hanging out, creating priceless memories with her family, geeking out to science fiction and fantasy television, and tossing around movie quotes.

Find me online and connect!

Discover more about me and my books on my website: http://www.debrakristi.com/

And join me on my Facebook author page for updates, news, discussions, and more: https://www.facebook.com/DebraKristi.writer/

Follow *The Balance Bringer Chronicles* on Facebook for 'Bringer'-inspired motivational posts and fun series extras and shares: https://www.facebook.com/TheBalanceBringer/

THE BALANCE BRINGER
CHRONICLES

DEBRA KRISTI

THE BALANCE BRINGER CHRONICLES
ORIGINS

"In my humble opinion, this is one of the best, if not the best, fantasy adventure series I have read. Each book is a masterpiece in itself and captivating and addictive."

- LooseBoots, Amazon Reviewer ★★★★★

Gifted Girls

**Magic. Adventure. Family Secrets.
And Dangerous Supernaturals.**

Plus, unexpected twists that will keep you guessing
and turning the pages late into the night.

Series complete!

"Each book in this series just gets better."
-D Nerriman, *Amazon Reviewer* ★★★★★

MOORIGAD

He walked into Hell's fire for me. I would burn the world for him. I'd even give up my dragon.

In this action-packed, paranormal fantasy romance about two coming-of-age would-be lovers, Kyra and Sebastian's union and strength of character will be put to the ultimate test. The stakes? Everything and everyone that ever mattered to them.

Series complete!

"Adventure, romance, suspense, colorful and engaging characters. A very captivating [trilogy]."
- *Donna Lane, Amazon Reviewer* ★★★★★

GLOSSARY OF TERMS

- **Aubadetruss:** Wristband that harnesses the sun
- **Aura:** The invisible energy radiating from an individual
- **Balance Bringer:** Chosen individual born to the warrior and Fae races, bringing balance to the realms at the hand of a higher power
- **Bidse:** (slang) A malicious, unpleasant, selfish person, especially a woman
- **Chronicler:** Created at the beginning of time by the Elven Queen, chroniclers record the passage of time and events and deposit all historical information in the Urn of All
- **Dream Incubus:** A demon who takes on the appearance of a man in order to syphon the energy of women
- **Dream Walk:** Living an experience, past, present, or future, in a dream state
- **Empath:** An individual who feels the emotions of another soul
- **Elenari:** The first of all elven kind. The first original families of nine, later to become seven
- **Era:** A measure of time marked by a calendar of events
- **Equinox:** Time of year when day and night are of the same duration
- **Faun:** A half man, half goat lustful creature
- **Feline Preservation Center:** Home for large, endangered felines

- **Fires of Guardoone:** Eternal flame capable of killing immortals
- **Gaea:** Mother Earth, the universal mother and goddess
- **Gradnar's Honor:** Hiddenkelian warrior cry honoring the great fallen leader, Gradnar
- **Hiddenkel:** Homeland from where Anala Jannsen Raine originates
- **Lightning wand:** Weapon harnessing light used against the Tenebrousian
- **Lles dei Luz:** Hiddenkelian for 'I grant thee light'
- **Mãnah:** Hiddenkelian for 'mother'
- **Ondine**: Water spirits
- **Puteri:** Princess
- **Purusians:** A group of believers that revere the sanctity of virginity and protect their purity through separation from the majority
- **Shadowkin:** Indirect relation, associated through species
- **Tearman:** Madame Marrouske's sanctuary established around the Tree of Life
- **Tenebrousian:** Hiddenkelian name for the dark ones or shadows
- **Treeite:** A resident of Ivey City, the community built high in the trees
- **Toran:** Gateway between worlds
- **Toranik:** Stone marking a Toran defense area
- **Usoda:** One of twenty-four warrior tribes spread across the vast lands of Hiddenkel